RETURN TO
? Dumbale

W9-CKJ-024

THE TICKET OUT

for my father

Lucy Rosenthal

THE TICKET OUT

HARCOURT BRACE JOVANOVICH
PUBLISHERS

San Diego   *New York*   *London*

HBJ

Copyright © 1983 by Lucy Rosenthal

All rights reserved. No part of this publication may be reproduced or transmitted in any form or by any means, electronic or mechanical, including photocopy, recording, or any information storage and retrieval system, without permission in writing from the publisher.

Requests for permission to make copies of any part of the work should be mailed to: Permissions, Harcourt Brace Jovanovich, Publishers, 757 Third Avenue, New York, N.Y. 10017.

Acknowledgment is hereby made for permission to reprint copyright material:
"I think continually of those who were truly great" (pages 296–97) by Stephen Spender—Random House, Inc. (copyright 1934 and renewed 1962 by Stephen Spender; reprinted from *Selected Poems* by Stephen Spender) and Faber and Faber Ltd. (from *Collected Poems* by Stephen Spender)
"Outward Bound" (page 300) by Tom Paxton—CBS Songs (copyright 1965 by United Artists Music Co., Inc.; all rights assigned to CBS Songs, a Division of CBS Inc.; international copyright secured; all rights reserved)
"The Thirty Third of August" (page 361) by Mickey Newbury—Acuff-Rose Publications, Inc. (copyright 1969 by Acuff-Rose Publications, Inc.; all rights reserved)

Library of Congress Cataloging in Publication Data

Rosenthal, Lucy.
  The ticket out.

  I. Title.
PS3568.0838T5   1983   813'.54   83-8554
ISBN 0-15-190282-8

Designed by Christine Aulicino
Printed in the United States of America
First edition
B C D E

PART 1

THAT IS, I used to be the editor of a magazine, quit in anger when my boss was fired, and am now on my own. I am what you call free-lance. My friends and other survivors call me Jack. Never mind what I do; it's writing, of a sort—at one time under an assumed name for an extremely disreputable newspaper with a national circulation—and other odd jobs, including editing. I am a good editor; editing means "helping"; and after the verb "to help," the verb "to edit" is the sweetest in the tongue. I had money, some inherited, some saved after I quit my job. Part of it—once—I passed along to Jennie, who did time as my wife, and the rest I squander with my days. But I am clean and neat about it. I have looks, a body which serves me well and doesn't hurt except when I abuse it, and my clothes and I came early to an amiable understanding, which is to say I wear them well. I am neat and clean.

I see that I write in the present tense, as if we were all still alive. But it is a fact that some of us have died, and in time, when the knowledge that they are forever gone has gotten into my bloodstream, I'll tell you who they were: those who belonged to me, and died. My heart still beats. More slowly—I am older, and life has become among other things a more serious misery—but it beats.

Once, as a child, I came grinning into my mother's house in Indianapolis to tell her and my older sister, Rita, that our postman, Mr. Cromwell, had suffered a stroke. My mother—who was a great humanitarian—told me it was not seemly to smirk. My older sister, Rita—this generation's answer to Florence Nightingale, the lady with the lamp—agreed with her, and for emphasis she rapped me sharply across my hand. The lesson not to grin at death or near-death should have been well learned, but it wasn't.

Though I made an easy target in the Korean War—I am tall, I am big—I came out of that war unscathed. It would be a long time before I'd draw the lightning. I may have thought myself invulnerable. I stand head and shoulders above a crowd, must stoop in doorways, and straddle a fine line between clumsiness and grace. Often enough, I've achieved grace, but I always felt there were hazards in my size and scale, for if somewhere in this mind or body a bolt should loosen, and the structure begin to collapse, I thought I could not survive.

And so I take the long journey back. It is not an easy journey.

I remember holding a girl in my arms. I see her face as dark, though she, unlike Audrey, was not black; it is simply that her face for so long, both before and after I knew her, was hidden by a cloud in my mind's eye.

Where should I begin.

With the gentle joshing I gave to my kid brother, Dave, when he first came to New York burdened with the jam he'd gotten himself into. I must say that on his rangy young shoulders, on that day years ago, burdens sat well, and I was at first hard put to take him seriously.

Or with the money Helen Crewe, my magazine's beauty columnist and consultant, borrowed from me. Some loan. I had imagined that one day her husband, Andy, would hold out his wet hand and return the once crisp bills to me, ruined but negotiable.

Or with Audrey Mockridge's party, one of many such parties I began to go to when I lost my job and, with it—it seemed—my respectability, and moved, at first unwittingly, onto life's margin. The margin that might be another man's center but never, I thought, mine.

Or with Jennie, whom I loved.

But let's begin it with my brother, David, and take it back. Years.

I N THE FIFTIES and early sixties, I was a nine-to-five man. That all changed later, and with the change came an enormous sense of freedom, the sort, I imagine, that people experience when they first see Hell, and are happy for such great space to play in. But then, when this story started, I was twenty-eight and my life was confined within good and normal bounds.

I can see it now. There I was, my wrists shackled to my typewriter, good serviceable wrists, fine constraining shackles. Buzz-buzz-buzz went the little telephone, which like most of its species in those days was the color of baked black mud.

"Hello," I bit into it. The shackles allowed for arm motion and could be removed for emergencies, such as my human need to go to the bathroom, or lunch with an author, like the beauty Helen Crewe. "Hello," I said again.

"This is your brother, David," said David in his gritty voice. "I have *Angst*."

"I'm sorry to hear it," I said dryly. "Where are you?"

"Here in New York. In my hotel room. I'm sitting here in my shorts on the edge of a lumpy bed, and I haven't got a cent."

I swiveled around. "What's the hotel, Davey?"

"The Hotel Paris . . . I think. . . ." His voice quavered a little. He was not all that brave. He named a street on the Upper West Side. "Near the river," he added.

"What's up, kid? Are you in trouble?" I had to whisper this, practically: my shackles didn't leave much room in that office for tenderness.

"Yes."

My quick breath into the mouthpiece.

"But don't worry," he said, cutting in quickly, feeling my fear. "I think I'll live. It's only a small slug in the gut, but the doc says it's the small gut. Bring a small penknife with you to this small hotel, and we shall together carve out the bullet." He lapsed into his German accent, which he did very well. The accent game had been given added impetus when our sister, Rita, married a German psychiatrist in her twenty-ninth year. ("Barely made it, didn't you, Reet? Hope you'll be happy with the Hun," and so on. But Rita took it like a sport, or so we thought. And she seemed happy with her wise and sharply creased little doctor man.)

But it was for some reason not easy to still my anxiety even though Davey wheezed reassuringly into the phone.

"You're not really hurt?" I asked him suddenly.

"No," he said after a pause. "I mean, my body's fine. But I hurt in my mind and heart. I'm in a bit of a jam, Jack. I wish you'd come."

"Sure I'll come. Hotel Paris." I was already unshackling myself.

"Room 625," he said. "Can you make it on your lunch hour?" He was trying to suppress the note of urgency.

"I can take my lunch hour any time I fucking please," I told him. The shackles be damned.

And so, having gentled him like a mother, having told him I would come and nurse his ills, I hung up on him, and stood upright like a brother. I snatched my jacket off its black wire hanger, concealed behind my office door. The hanger rattled and alerted my secretary, who twitched her nose and swiveled her little haunch in my direction. Bambi—*he* is coming. Causing Bambi to rear on its haunches. Bambi was right.

"Marcella," I told the girl, "I'll be over at the Hotel Paris. West Side."

"What—?" she spluttered and reached for her little memo pad, without which she did not feel like a live and lovely woman. I think it may have substituted in her mind for a saucepan on the range. Marcella, Radcliffe '56.

"Care of my brother, David Church," I told her. "He seems to have just blown in from Indianapolis. So . . ." I was at the door, and I saw her blue, anxious eyes looking at me, her neck, her whole body inclined toward me; it was her job to catch my drift. I smiled. "So . . ." I repeated. "If there are any calls . . ." She nodded, and I took off.

It was High Noon, and though I was hardly Gary Cooper, I went at a slow lope for the taxi stand. I did not permit myself to think of David, for my bright young brother was my secret pride, and I would not for a moment believe he could falter. I think I felt he had become my elder on that day in our teens (he thirteen, I fifteen) when we went for a game of chance, dodging (or "daring," as I called it; the game was my idea) cars on the Indianapolis highway. It was afternoon, and one of the rules of the game was that we were not to be choosy: it didn't have to be cars, just any motorized vehicle that came along was fair game, a truck, whatever. The vehicles were like bulls, and we were the bullfighters. As they came whizzing down the highway, it was our job to outwit them.

I took a hard mechanized blow from a motorcycle. The flesh was not meant to yield so easily. I went spinning through the air; I was stunned; cut; with blood. I felt my trousers grow wet, and Dave grabbed me, dragged me to the side of the road. A noisy crowd had gathered, their sounds competing with Davey for my attention. I heard their anger. "There's a hurt boy!" someone cried. I tried to control my sobbing, heaving, dry breaths. What I really wanted to do was scream. "Cover him," someone barked. All the while, David leaned over me, his pale face visible to me like God's or my father's, even though he was frightened. "Are you okay, Jack? Okay? Okay, Jack? Okay?" Over and over again. The moisture on my trousers spread. My thighs were cold, my whole body grew cold. The driver of the motorcycle stood by the side of the highway, saying over and over again, "He got in my way, the kid got in my way. Suddenly he came, I didn't see him coming, he got in my way. The both of them, I didn't see them, the both of them, the highway ain't no place to play games. . . ." On and on, over and over. He was a college boy, the driver, but his speech, cultivated at first, became more and more ragged; he was losing his grammar at the end.

David stood over me, his shadow falling across the length of my body, making him bigger than he was, and in my mind I held on to the feel of his grip on my shoulders as he'd dragged me across the road. The memory made me glad, for if one of us could move, so could the other: one splendid motor running two cars. To discipline my breaths, which were coming like moans, I tried to mutter his name.

A stretcher came, with my parents, and I was lifted onto it. At first, I thought from the dire look in their eyes that they were going to blame David, and then, as my father leaned down over me and put a waxen hand on the side of the stretcher—my coffin, it felt like—I thought he was going to blame me. Gonna catch hell, I thought, gonna catch hell.

Dr. Frame briefly pressed a heavy hand on me. "Does it hurt?" he asked. I shook my head no. "Hurt?" he asked again, as he pressed elsewhere, always quickly, and I said, "No. No." "Hurt?" "No. *Yes.*"

Later, with my broken ribs all taped, sitting up on the examining table, I said flatly, "It wasn't Davey's fault."

"No?" said Dr. Frame. "Whose fault was it, then?"

"I don't know, sir," I said. My eyes were cast down, and I saw the dried ring of stain on my pants. I will not cry, I thought, trying to look at him with the gaze of a hero.

"Somebody's fault," the doctor mused, though it came out in a kind of growl. "Somebody's damn fool idea to charge out like you were doin' on the highway."

"We were just teasin' the cars," I explained. "Don't blame Davey."

"I had no thought of blaming Davey," said Dr. Frame.

"I'm here, Jack," David said awkwardly, leaning on the doorjamb in the half-dark. "And, look, do me a favor, quit saying it ain't my fault—they'll begin to think it is."

The logic of this was lost on me. I stared at him with utter blankness. I was hopeless, I seemed to have a fix on this, and there was nothing he could do, he must have then decided; he let it pass.

The next day, Rita brought me eats, in bed. I recovered. It wasn't serious. I loved Davey.

"You're okay, Davey," I told him, warmly unabashed. He grinned back at me. This was probably the last time we exchanged our love in words like that, like trading marbles.

The taxi swerved through the park, and turned at the cross street, then straight west to the Paris Hotel. The driver, holding the wheel, was an old Jew, for whom, I thought, we'd fought the war. I tipped him. He thanked me.

Into the lobby of the Paris Hotel I walked, and I smelled the deep green smell of chlorine issuing from a basement swimming pool. The smell of the water wafted up through the elevator shaft as we traveled, a slow and creaky ride, for the Paris had slumped since its elegant beginnings.

I knocked on Davey's door. " 'S open, come on in," came his voice, muffled and hollow.

I found David on the bed. His trousers had been carefully laid out on a chair, their owner looking alive and strong, long legs stretched halfway into the room. The blinds were drawn, his troubles wrapped in the darkness.

The ashtrays were clear. David didn't smoke. He had had a year of medical school some years back and was careful of his health.

"What is it, kid?" I asked him softly. "The way you were talking, I expected to find a woman here. Delivered of stillborn twins," I went on, set to embellish until stopped.

"Glad to see you," he mumbled. "Siddown. Somewhere in this mess." He gestured, vaguely, toward the blinds and the chair, and I walked across the room and sat. This gave me an unsatisfactory three-quarter view of him, and he knew it, but he made no effort to budge. "Oh, my God," he murmured, then put his head in his hands. As I hunched forward, it occurred to me that this was the accustomed posture of my brother-in-law, psychiatrist Carl.

"Vell?" I said.

David managed a weak smile. "I need some money," he said abruptly.

Which killed my own impulse to smile. I had always been unaccountably generous with everything but money. One has to save something, hoard some reserves; money is what I saved. But "How much, kid?" I said to my brother, whom I loved and still do, beyond all remembering.

"A couple hundred," David said. Then quickly he added, "If you can't make it, that's okay."

"Of course I can make it." Of course, of course.

"Okay, then . . ." I could hear David's deep whistle-sigh. He wanted to keep silent, I could tell, but he forced himself to ask, "Do I have to tell you what it's for?"

"If you vant to," I said, sounding unmistakably like Carl. "Maybe it would be better." He chuckled, and I slouched back in the chair, balancing my palms on my knees, but still he did not move.

"I don't much want to. . . ."

A sudden, faint shiver of alarm: was Davey in trouble with the law? "Are you runnin' from the cops?" I asked, lightly, this being after all something I could not quite imagine. A voluntary withdrawal in the nick of time from medical school (and several lies told in my behalf) constituted the extent of David's departure from the laws that govern us all. Davey was the good one. So what was he doing here, slumped before me in a shirt whose cuffs were unbuttoned, in the shorts he had slept in, his hair wild from sleep and his nervous hands?

"Not running from the cops," came the answer.

Goddamn it, I wasn't a doctor, and Davey was never supposed to suffer.

"Okay," I said, and scowled. I reached for my checkbook, and with ferocious energy wrote out the sum with the thing balanced on my knee, as my pen leaked a drop of ink on my trousers. Ripping the check—it was my last—from its stub, I watched the stain take hold, and carried my offering over to the suffering one, who was still perched on the edge of the bed. "Thanks," he murmured. "Where do you suppose I could cash it?"

"Cash you want!" I exploded, taking it back from him. "I'll cash it for you. Okay? You can wait until this afternoon, I trust?"

"Where are you going?" David asked.

"Back to my office," I said, full of respectability, in a fastidious rage over the stain on my pants. "I work for a living, you know. And there's a bank in my building," I added, as a sop to brotherly love, to reassure him.

"When will you be back?" David asked.

"About five-thirty. Can you hold out till then? Here." And I handed him a ten, from my plump little wallet. "Get something to eat," I said, grandly. He took it, and his hand trembled as he let it drop onto his pillow. "Thanks," he said. "I'll wait here for you, then."

"Okay," I said. My hand was on the door.

"Jack," he called to me. I turned. "Thanks again." And his lips drew into a tight troubled line. His eyes were bloodshot.

"Oh, God, Dave. Is it anything real?"

"I don't want you to worry," he explained. "Can't tell you what it is."

In the elevator of the Paris Hotel, I saw the stain of ink on my pants and felt the back and the sleeves of my shirt soaked.

Oh, God, I thought. I hope I didn't turn away from him. His mystery. But what else can you do with a mystery, when you go by the clock, but turn your back.

As children, back in Indiana, David and I had often gone bounding into the woods. We'd hide behind trees, climb up, slide down. Once, Davey, with a holler, retrieved me from a weak limb and forestalled my fall. And Rita, before she grew into the lugubrious dignity of adolescence, would run with us breathlessly. "Let's play mystery," she would gasp, and that became our code word for the woods. The Church kids, we three, would play mystery in the dark woods. They say when you grow up the secrets stop, and for a while that seemed to be true.

Back at my office, I fretted about whether I had been too afraid of seeing him suffer, from a cause I didn't know, to help. But I pressed into my fist the crumpled check I had taken back from Davey, tangible evidence of the love I bore him, and my mind was eased. I'll tell you what grants relief: life's exchanges, the ones that yield symmetry, clarity, and maybe art and love as well.

Marcella gave me a little shudder of welcome, glanced nervously at her watch, and automatically transferred to my hand the accumulated telephone messages. "Thank you, darlin'," I said, and started to walk away, feeling the weight of her gaze upon my back. Marcella's claim was the claim of the blind; she was always proffering a tin cup.

At my desk, I spread the messages before me. There was one from Helen Crewe. Dimly I heard Marcella blow her nose. Another's need has always brought out the best in me, and I gave the buzzer a jab. "Yes, Jack," came her Radcliffe vibrato. "Get me Helen Crewe," I told her, "and when you've got a chance, could you cash a check for my brother?" A damp pause. "I haven't got much cash on me, Jack," she said.

"I meant to go down to the bank and cash it."

"Oh, sure." Her voice brightened. "I'll get Helen for you first."

"Right." We clicked off. I sat with the telephone panel before me, white mother-of-pearl buttons set into a black box. Wires trailed off onto the floor. They lead, I thought, to the sewer, to a vast system of interconnecting pipes and tubes well below the asphalt, which drains all our voices to the sea.

"I have Helen Crewe for you," announced Marcella.

"Thank you," I said formally. Now beat it, doll. (Did Marcella suffer from the circumscribed ritual of our dialogue? Did I? Should I have cared more for Marcella? Can I bear to think about how it was for Jennie . . . ?)

"Helen, how are you?" I intoned into the mouthpiece.

"Well, it's pretty bad," I heard her sniffle, "but, then, I suppose it could be a lot worse."

"A cold, Helen?" I questioned, sympathetically. "What can I do for you?"

"Our lunch date."

"Of course, Helen," I said, making a note of it on my calendar. "Friday will be fine."

Marcella came in again, and I handed her the check. I saw her automatically turn it over to its flip side. "It's all right, honey," I told her. "He endorsed it."

"No, he didn't," she said to me, gravely.

"Oh, hell. You don't mean it."

"But I do." A little merrily now.

"Let me have it."

"What are you going to do?" she asked. "Write another check?"

"No, I don't have another one. I'm going to break the law, dear. I'm going to forge my brother's signature. If you don't want to watch, go in the other room."

"Oh, Jack . . ." She laughed.

I worked painstakingly, but the result was mediocre. I handed Marcella a sample of David's writing, to compare.

"Your handwriting is a lot like his," Marcella said, in something like awe.

"Yes. The same blood courses through our veins."

She hesitated, and I saw that her concern was genuine. Then she smiled and said diffidently, "You don't seem quite yourself. You seem . . . rattled."

Which, believe it or not, came as a surprise to me. We never know ourselves on time. I gave her a grateful smile, for she had had the kindness to know me. "Take it down now, like a good girl, to Chemical Trust."

She did; that was one crime we got away with.

I MADE MY WAY again across town, in the growing, gloomy twilight. This time I took buses, to economize.

There was Davey, waiting in his chlorine-smelling hole. I noted thankfully that no other odors had been added: no whiskey, for example. David was not a drinking man.

"You look better," I said, without looking at him. I was on edge.

"I'm okay," he said.

Perhaps it was true; or perhaps he was trying to reassure me.

"Have you got the money?" he asked. I wanted to be reassured, but he could not hide the anxiety in his voice.

"Yes, I've got it," I said, trying to swallow a rush of anger. Why was I angry at Davey's hurt? I must stop twitching about money. There are so many more important things—like cruelty, even my own. "Davey—? Now I don't suppose you could reward me for my pains by telling me what this is all about. Or if there's anything I can do. Besides this." I flipped the bills on the night table. We grinned faintly at each other, traded knowing looks, our pledge. He took the money. It didn't hurt.

"Jesus, Jack." Sweat was standing out on his brow. "I'll be grateful for this all my life. Honest to Christ." He started shoving the loose bills in his pocket.

"Put them into your wallet, you idiot," I said to him sharply. "Do I have to teach you everything?" He flushed, not because of my harshness—we had both learned a little at someone's knee and had come a way since—but because he knew I knew he was confused.

"Sorry," he mumbled, and pulled out his wallet like a good boy.

Make order of your life, my sons, Father had always said.

"Well?" I took a deep breath, and started over. "What's it all about?"

He spoke so low it was a strain to hear him, and I had to resist the unbrotherly impulse to shake him until his bones rattled. "Let's eat first. Okay? I'm hungry, Jack."

I got him into his jacket and topcoat, saw his tie was straight, and took him to a chop house. I ordered him a steak. I made him take a drink. He felt better.

Fifteenth refrain: "What do you need the money for, kid?"

He smiled a little. "Okay, brother, you asked for it. But you won't like it. And you know why you won't like it?"

"Why?"

"Because you're an artist, Jack. You've got this sense of form, of what ought to be, and . . ." He stopped there, the words locked.

"And what?"

"Butchery offends you." He broke off. "I'm about to disappoint you, Jack." A pause, and then he said, "I'm the butcher, Jack. You know? Why else would I have gone to medical school?"

I smiled. "Because Dr. Frame urged you to. Besides, you nearly flunked out."

"That's a comfort," he said.

"It was meant to be."

"I need to pay for an abortion," he said. He waited to see if I would wince, which I didn't. But the silence grew like an unnatural thing. Remember: abortion was illegal then.

Finally I said, "Look, Dave, you couldn't imagine this would come as a total surprise to me. I mean, an abortion is not a thing you consider bizarre in this day and age. . . ."

"It's bizarre to me," said David.

"Who is she?"

"The girl is in New York. She got on a Greyhound when she was sure, and—"

"And what?"

"When she was sure she was pregnant." He looked down at his lap, at the floor. "When she was sure I'd let her down."

"Who is she?" I asked again. He told me. With difficulty, he said her name. Betty Gobisch.

"She's only a junior at State. Now I've ruined her life."

Gently, I suggested that this didn't need to be so great or irremediable a trouble. He didn't say anything, and then he looked at me and scowled.

"Did you let her down?" I couldn't help asking.

"We can't get married, it's impossible. Good God, Jack, she's only twenty. Christ!" His explanation rattled on.

"Well, do you want to marry her?"

"You just don't think of marriage at a time like this." He let me absorb this, as well as I could. Then he went on: "She thinks I betrayed her."

"Why?"

"Because of the big bad bed," he said. "She's a moralist."

"Oh." What else could I say?

"I tell you, she doesn't want to see me. Only wants money for the butcher. The two hundred bucks. You know?"

The butcher, it turned out, was someone Davey had tracked down through one of his medical-student friends. "He's okay." He looked at me. "I'm pretty sure of that, Jack."

"Are you bringing her the money tonight?"

"Yes, I am." Davey's glance kept ricocheting off some point in the middle distance. I pulled him and it back. "But she doesn't want to see me. I'm supposed to get it to her through her girlfriend. Her girlfriend Virginia. Has a place on Riverside Drive. That's where Betty is staying."

"Here, drink this," I said, shoving his cup of coffee at him. "We're going to see Betty, you and I."

Yes, I told him, that was what we were going to do.

En route, David said they all used to call her Sweet Betsy from Pike. After the song.

BUT WHEN BETTY EMERGED from the inner recesses of Virginia's railroad flat, she didn't look so sweet. She cut a different kind of figure, grown-up and oddly touching. She was a curious mixture: assertive, yet withdrawn into a kind of complacency. She was done up in a shirt and jeans, her eyes were swollen, and her banked anger impressive.

"For God's sake, Virginia," she said, "for form's sake, I guess, can't you keep them out?"

"They're already in," said Virginia, helplessly.

Ignoring me, Betty looked directly across to my unhappy brother. "Have you got the money?" she said.

"Yes. Here it is." He handed it over. "I had to hold up a liquor store to get it." Davey the tough guy.

Betty's lip trembled.

"Look, Virginia," I said. "Why don't you go in the other room, so we can talk to Betty."

Virginia stood sullenly, protectively, waiting for Betty's cue.

"It's okay, Virginia. Please. Thanks."

As soon as the three of us were alone, Betty turned to me and said, "What do you want? I haven't got all night. Not like I used to."

Before I could compose an intelligent reply, she tossed me another of her curt little glances and said, "You, I suppose, are the banker."

It took me a second to figure out what she meant; then I nodded. "Betty, I thought we might talk about this situation you're in." An uninviting silence greeted this feeble beginning, but I lumbered on. "I mean about the baby, Betty. You know, abortion isn't the only solution."

"Don't tell me it's murder to kill this unborn child. I just don't want this pitch."

"This what?" I asked, feeling like an old man. But, as David told me later, she was a self-made girl, intimidated by David's accounts of our family. (He said, proudly, "Her parents didn't even want her to go to college, so she works part-time as a cook at the student union and she has a scholarship and a student loan." And so on. That part of it got boring.)

"This pitch about how abortion is a sin and a crime. I can't bear it." Again, her mouth trembled.

"Honey, I don't think it's a sin, but it is a crime, and besides . . ." I trailed off. She looked forlorn.

Suddenly, shockingly, her fist crashed down on the piano keyboard.

"Tell her you love her," I instructed David.

"I love you," said David.

She turned her back to us, rested her elbows on the piano, her face sunk into her hands.

I pushed him.

He went to her. "Bet," he said, "I love you. I do."

I gave her a kiss, brotherly, on the cheek. "A sweet girl, that's what you are," I told her. I was feeling very strong and worldly and compassionate toward these children just discovering sex and then blundering into prospective parenthood, which I personally wasn't mature enough to consider yet.

She married him; I paid for the wedding. The Gobisches came and cried throughout.

Ｈ‍ELEN CREWE WAS another matter. I decided to keep my Friday lunch date with her, even though the intervening events left me somewhat unstrung, not to mention out of pocket, and made me twenty minutes late. I entered the Italian Pavilion, my heart pounding a little from haste, and found Helen at a corner table.

Her immaculate appearance always slightly shocked me. I thought of Helen, in some secret way, as a disorderly person, so that her immaculate dress and her perfect cosmetic mask always put me off. I greeted her with apologies and felt full of flaws.

"Oh, it's all right, Jack," she said, in her deep, measured voice, looking at her watch. Her speech was elocutionary. "Though I was getting a bit edgy—I have an appointment at two." She allowed a moment for this to sink in, then rushed on to reassure me. "But I can be late. It's with the hair-dresser."

When in doubt, flatter. "Your hair is too lovely as it is. Forget the hairdresser."

"Why, thank you, Jack." She seemed honestly pleased, and her smile lingered a little longer than I would have predicted.

"What's up? You seem a little fussed. That's Andy's word," she added, with the indulgent smile she always wore when his name came up. Andy was a tubby and rather enigmatic little man. Why did he marry Helen, or she him? They seemed happy. How did they manage that?

"My kid brother got married yesterday." I left out a few details.

"How divine," she exclaimed, in a social and amiable way. "Was your whole family gathered round?"

"No. They couldn't all get in. So it was just me. I represented the family," I told her grandly.

"Your family is from—Des Moines, isn't it?"

"Indianapolis."

"Funny. We're both Midwesterners. I'm from little old Chicago."

"Chicago? Not really? I didn't know that, Helen." We had roots in common, a motherland.

"Yes. True. You wouldn't think it of me, would you? So many things you wouldn't think of me." She grinned coquettishly, and I grinned back and met her glance, but decided fast not to pursue this track of the conversation.

I became professional; the editor. We ordered; I asked her about her galleys, and she showed me what she wanted to have changed. I disputed that, and yielded this, and then she yielded something she had not wanted to yield, and I, in fairness, surrendered a minor point to her. We ate. We each had a stinger, which made her oddly, unwarrantedly flushed, and she leaned forward, apparently on the brink of a confidence, when the waiter brought the check. That seemed to daunt her. I did not really want the confidence, but I knew I shouldn't be rude or hurt her, so as I handed over my American Express card, I smiled at her encouragingly. But she said nothing. In the short silence, she drew out her compact, opened it, and with a very pale shade of powder whitened the flush of her cheeks.

"It's been a lovely lunch," she said, as she dropped the compact back into her cavernous purse and drew on her gloves.

I smiled and stood. But still she sat. I pulled the table out for her. "Jack," she said.

"Yes? What's the matter, honey?" I said gently. "You a little tight?"

"Of course not," she said.

We paused. We were at the checkroom. "Nothing serious, I hope?"

"Oh, no. Not serious. It's . . . about Andy." I looked at her. "His business isn't doing very well. Too long a story to go into now," she said, rescuing herself. "But sometime?"

"Of course, Helen. I don't know what I can do to help, but I'll be glad to listen."

We were at the corner. I shook her hand, and she returned the pressure, but not ardently, just neutrally; she was a woman I knew in the neutral zone, in the totally acceptable, stable world of everyday social and professional interchange.

"Don't let the hairdresser destroy you," I called after her.

MARCELLA WAS MISSING when I got back to the office. She was resting in the lounge, laid low by cramps.

"She can go home if she wants to," I said to Floss, Marcella's pretty and aggressive rival in the steno pool.

Floss hung around and took some of the dictation Marcella should have done—more efficiently than Marcella, actually. When we had finished, she lingered in her chair.

"You heard the latest?"

"No, what's the latest?"

"The heat's on Barney." Barney was a man dear to my heart, Barney was my boss, Barney was my friend from the day I arrived in New York at age twenty-one, hayseedy as they come. Since Myra's death, Myra was his lovely wife, Barney's drinking had gotten out of line. In fact, he'd taken to dialing the Save-a-Life League from the office.

"I think he's going to get canned," Floss said.

"No."

"He goofed on costs. I don't know all the details. He drinks too much. You know that, Jack," she said.

"I like him." There was a warning in my voice.

"I know you do. That's why I told you." She stood up.

When Floss was gone, I hesitated a moment, then dialed Barney.

"You know what those bastards are trying to do to me, Jack?" Barney shouted the minute he heard my voice.

"That's what I wanted to talk to you about," I said.

"Jesus, Jack, I can't talk now. . . ."

"I know," I said. "Come up to my place tonight?"

"You are a prince, Jack," Barney said.

My palms were damp. I owed him the world. I rested my head in my hands. Perhaps I prayed, the way we do: God, don't rock my boat.

H<small>E ARRIVED PROMPTLY</small> at seven, and full of cheer. "I am starving," he told me.

"You been drinking?"

"No, Jack. I thought you would take care of me in that regard."

"I will. Don't worry," I said, kneeling clumsily before the broiler. "You'll get your meal too."

I looked up at Barney; he hovered awkwardly in the doorway of my small kitchen.

"Sit down," I told him and followed him into the living room. When I was a boy, I lived like a boy, until I became a man. When I was a man, I was a bachelor for a time, and so I lived like a bachelor. I cannot describe my apartment for you now, except to say that it was comfortingly dark and convenient, filled with some of the books, furnishings, and objects for which I cared very much. It had a desk and type-writer, from which small offerings were frequently produced, and from which it was promised that bigger things would come someday. There were chairs in which to lounge and loaf, my record player, my bed, which I had bribed to silence. Oh, the secrets it would tell if it could: that my mouth opened in my sleep, that my beard relentlessly grew, that my pajama buttons would leave a mark on my chest as I slept, that my breath would change during the night, that sometimes I would dream.

"Jack," said Barney, looking around and sipping on the drink I had poured for him, "don't you get lonesome as hell sometimes?"

"No," I said. I went back to the kitchen and started to peel potatoes as if my life depended on it. You make love from time to time, you don't get lonesome. The women want something more, and as I grew older I tried to take that into account.

"You ought to get married," Barney said. He had followed me into the kitchen and held out his glass. "Give me another drink, Jack." His voice was sad. At least no one I have loved has ever died, I thought to myself—except my father, but that was a long time ago—and I cut my thumb.

"Dinner should be ready in an hour," I said, steering us both back into the living room and comfortable chairs. "Now, let's talk. Let's have it."

And Barney, my friend, told me the whole story, a long and sorrowful and predictable one, which he punctuated by cursing out the volunteers at the Save-a-Life League. We talked through dinner; my steak was ignored, but not my wine. Barney was exercising his indulgences like a condemned man. Since I, of course, still had everything to lose, I ate and drank with appetite and moderation.

"I can't even curse any more," he said at last, apologetically, putting his head in his hands. "I sure fouled things up, didn't I, Jack?" I couldn't speak, because it was true. Then, "I've been drinking too much. Otherwise I don't know how I'd let such a thing get by me. An expensive mistake. Costly, and by God, they'll have this head for it."

There was an appalling silence. Like a death. I looked into Barney's seamed, living face and wondered what I could say. "You don't really see any way out, do you, Jack?"

"Sure there's a way out," I said quietly, stalling. "You've been with them twenty-five years. They owe you something. I'll talk to them. If they fire you, I'll quit," I blurted out.

"You would do that for me?"

"Yes." Was I now stuck with it? The possibility both worried and cheered me. I'd never risked anything, or much of anything, before, and I owed Barney a lot. This was the kind of thing friends did, wasn't it?

"Jack," he said abruptly, "you'd better take me home. Before I get ill, over your fine bachelor sofa." He patted its arm. I helped him to his feet.

He seemed so old, defeated, in spite of my gallant offer. In the cab I said to him, "You're still getting over Myra. That's what it is. If she were here, this wouldn't have happened." If this reassured him, he gave no sign of it, so I kept on going. "It's Myra, you know that, Barney. Go easy on yourself, give yourself time."

He slumped against the window. "Don't kid yourself," he muttered. "It's not Myra. It's never just one thing. No . . ."

In front of his house, we argued. He did not want me to see him upstairs. "I am burdening you," he hollered into the deserted midnight streets. "I don't want my troubles eating up your insides."

"For God's sake, Barney, does the whole block have to know? Let's get upstairs before you puke."

"Don't talk about it," Barney warned me. But the very suggestion seemed to have weakened his defenses enough so he allowed me to slip an arm about his shoulders and help him into the lobby, into the dim self-service elevator and into his apartment. It was large and airy, and I knew that in the daytime it was filled with light.

"Lately shared with Myra," he said to me, winking, as I took in the painful disorder. He looked chalky. There were traces of Myra: her plants, thriving and green, were lined up as always along the window sill. Barney was keeping them alive; they had grown, and their leaves were tangled. Myra's books and magazines rested on the coffee table; her subscriptions to *Better Homes and Gardens* and *The Nation* had clearly not yet expired, and the unread issues were piling up. And Barney had eaten his morning eggs from a dish I'd given them, the sight of which gave me a sharp pang.

"Hard, ain't it?" Barney murmured. "But it isn't only Myra. I drink too much. That's the simple fucking truth. Get me to bed, Jack."

THE PRESSURES ON BARNEY grew subtly, like symptoms in an illness one tries to ignore. I went to plead for him, as I had promised. But face to face with them, I could not muster any eloquence. All I could think about was the ungainly shadow I cast across the pale executive carpet; my palms were sweaty and my voice cracked. God knows what I said: I pleaded for Barney, but instead I myself was offered a small increase in salary, which I accepted in total moral confusion. Meanwhile, Barney kept on drinking, and in more and more corridors his way was barred.

To celebrate my raise and to fend off a sense of chaos, I left the office with Marcella for the first time. I took her arm. We walked out into a cold wintry twilight, and I felt her shiver. The tremor passed along my limbs. "Marcella, let's have dinner," I said, and she beamed with pleasure. "Even the slush glistens," she said breathlessly, as we dashed across the street, hand in hand, dodging taxis.

In the Alpine Restaurant we were both submerged in the comfortable smell of game and dumplings. "Order something you don't usually have," I said, leaning closer. "Venison or rabbit." She gave me a questioning look, so I decided for her. Rabbit. I felt like a wolf.

On the threshold to my apartment, she hung back. I went in ahead of her and flicked on a few lamp switches. The light drew her in, and I felt better.

Her flesh had a papery quality in the light.

"How about some coffee?"

"Shall I fix it?" she asked.

"No, sit over there and relax," I said, waving her toward a stool. She perched, crossed her fine, slender legs.

But I'd be damned if I'd let this moment blossom into rapture.

There she was, in my kitchen. I gazed at her sweet, rounded face for a moment, and my heart thudded. I felt an unwonted chill of guilt—some random foreknowledge—and turned away. When I looked again, she was still there. A curve of breast was visible at the parting of her blouse, the flesh reassuringly mobile and alive, the fine leg extended. I reached down and grasped her ankle.

"Coffee's perking," she remarked.

Delicately, I sliced lemon rind into the espresso.

"Coffee's ready," I said.

She smiled. We sank onto the couch, and for openers took sips from the small cups; then, cautiously, she put hers down. I downed mine in a gulp, catching some dregs in my throat, but it didn't matter.

I reached out for her, had my arms nicely around her.

"You're one of the people in my constellation, Jack."

My grip became fierce around her. She had soft, responsive lips.

"Look," I said, "let's go into the bedroom."

"Why?"

"Whatever happens, we'll have more room." I picked her up and carried her. Of course, I know now that to sweep a girl up in your arms and carry her enfolded into the room of your choice is not an intimate thing to do.

She lay on the bed, and I took off her clothes with a practiced respect. I flung my own on the floor. I turned out the bed lamp and lit a couple of candles. Voilà: Halloween.

I reached for her, she drew me down with a wide, lovely smile, and we began.

And then suddenly, shockingly, it was no good. She would not move at all.

"Jesus, Marcella," I said. "This isn't your first time, is it?"

"No," she said.

"Then what's the matter?" I went on, sweating and gasping, while she cringed. "Am I hurting you?"

"No."

She might have been lying. I couldn't tell. I went on, watching her anxiously, while my own rapture, entirely localized, gathered rapidly despite her. In a moment, I would begin to frame those involuntary syllables of love, her name, and other words.

"Sure I'm not hurting you?"

"No." She hesitated. "It's just—you're—heavy," she explained apologetically.

Clearly I could not comfort her heart, nor she mine. I was steam-rollered now by the single, imposing need to carry through the fun.

Once it was over, I moved away from her, removed my weight.

I kissed her cheek. She nodded, made a kissing sound in acknowledgment.

"Will you stay all night, Marcella?"

"Oh no," she said promptly. She turned face down toward the pillow, on which was embroidered the legend HERS. Her small shoulders jerked back. "I've had that for a long time," I explained. It was true. I had filched it from my sister's house in Indianapolis.

Then I let her do what she wanted to do, which was to get swiftly dressed.

She sat on the edge of the bed, once again in her skirt and blouse, and with her comb and other props worked over her face and hair. Stretched out full-length, still naked, I watched her.

"Marcella," I said, clearing my throat, "there's no reason why we can't continue to work together. But I think you should give some thought to other possibilities. . . ."

I trailed off. "What does that mean?" she said finally. "That I'm fired?"

"No, not at all. All I meant is that there isn't much challenge for you in the job. You're awfully bright, Radcliffe and all."

She looked grim. "Please, Jack, I don't want to talk shop."

I shut my eyes. "Okay, okay, Marcella," I said. "I want to go on working with you."

"Won't you quit when Barney goes?" she asked.

"Not necessarily," I said perversely. My resolve to leave with Barney had not been shaken, but her assumptions about my life and career bothered me distinctly. "As a matter of fact," I said, "they've given me a raise."

"It's like a bribe," she said. "They want you to lay off about Barney. I suppose you didn't have to take it, but that would have been silly. You can't say no to money."

No, I thought. Only to love, or to a strong human need. Her words, totally lacking in personal complaint, hung oppressively above me, and to obliterate them I swung out of bed and, with an air of great competence and decision, put on my pants.

Then, fully dressed, I faced her. "Marcella," I said, "don't be ashamed."

"I'm trying not to be."

I felt fatigued. I thought of sleep with drunken yearning. "Let me put you in a cab," I offered.

"No. Oh, no," she said.

Now that I was on my feet, I felt like a broken old man.

"I would feel better if you took me home," she said.

Home meant Brooklyn.

We went on a treasure hunt for our shoes. First we found one, then another, then a large one belonging to me, a small one belonging to her, and so on.

She preceded me down the stairs, her heels clattering; the sound made her self-conscious.

On the sidewalk, I stumbled over a crack. Wildly, I hailed a cab.

My arm was around her, my hand absently underneath her coat, my fingertips feeling the silk of her blouse, the wool of her skirt. My hands moved, feeling textiles.

"You see, I'm so afraid I won't get married," she said. "If you've been hurt once, something is frozen inside you. It's like I'm paralyzed. I mean I'm terribly glad it happened."

"Are you?" I gripped her hand, suddenly gratified.

"Yes. I mean I'll always have that. But I've never loved since then. Never."

Oh. Something in the past she was talking about. I released her hand and leaned forward. "Driver, you can turn right on the next—"

"He married someone else. He said it was because I was Protestant. Have you ever been in love, Jack?"

The cab jolted and turned a corner.

"No," I said truthfully. It was a truth I rarely faced. I had said to Davey once that no man is real until his heart has been cracked wide open. He said I was right, and neither of us had ever mentioned it again.

"Mister, I can't do it," the taxi driver suddenly protested. There was a snowbank in front of Marcella's house, and he could not make the turn. He went on to complain that he had a wife and children, one of whom had been taken to the hospital Christmas Eve, and was still there with an undiagnosed ailment. Another was home with a broken leg. Besides, a year ago he had been robbed.

"You're a lucky man," I said. "If you'll just let us out here, that'll be fine."

As we negotiated the snowbank in front of her house, she fell. She sat like a child, gasping. I wanted to die. The time, friends, was a quarter to two in the morning. The employer began to tug at the secretary. I got her to her feet. I steadied her and brushed the snow from her coat. Sometimes that much is given to us when God is good. Sleep now seemed distinctly minor-league; big Jack wanted the undiscovered country.

At the door, formally, she told me good night. I kissed her forehead.

Our miserable cab driver returned; he had been driving in a circle. Hoarsely, he shouted to me that I would never get another cab this time 'a night. Snow.

Lord, he needs me more than she does.

O N THE DAY I tried again to intercede for Barney, he was fired.

"I'll be back later," I said to Marcella.

It was midmorning. I strolled out into the corridor and took the elevator up to the nineteenth floor.

"Come in, Jack," said the president. The smell of his cigar filled the spacious office. "You're a valuable man to us. We don't want to let you go under any circumstances."

"I'm talking about Barney."

"Very sad. Very sad indeed," he mused. "But, Jack, you know as well as I do that his work has not been up there."

The bright morning sun streamed in through the window. Magnificent vistas presented themselves. Didn't someone once say: "And to see, you have only to look. I beseech thee to look." You could see the glorious expanse of the city.

Rooftops gleamed against the sky. Birds in passage paused to bless us as they hurried south, the little stragglers. Giant flying machines went grandly by. I let my gaze wander past all that glass, all that transparency. I thought of my brother, and his Betty. I let my mind go; it would be so easy to let go, even to die. Except for the birds there was no life outside that window, so I came back. Here was life, in this enclosed and furnished office. I forced the words from my throat: "Give him a break, for God's sake. Give Barney a break."

I sat there, in that office, where the furnishings interrupted the light.

"Jack, I wish it could be different. But it can't," he said vaguely. "I can't even promise you I'll think about it. Because I won't." There was a pause. He added, "It has nothing to do with you."

He was wrong. It had everything to do with me.

He nodded. Why? Had I tipped him off to my intention? His chin sank into his chest. In another moment, he would unload some words of dismissal. I stood up.

And so Barney got the ax that afternoon. I felt as if I had precipitated it. I went around to see him.

Barney was a mess. He was rummaging through the vast accumulation from his files. It sat like a heap of seaweed on his desk.

"Where's your secretary?" I asked. "A man needs a secretary at a time like this."

"Lissie? I sent the poor little bitch home. Couldn't stand to see her face twisted with sympathy. Give me a face with some knowledge of evil."

"Poor Lissie," I said gently. "No knowledge of evil."

"None," said Barney. "I couldn't stand it, Jack." He looked at me meaningfully.

"I'm not sorry for you," I lied. "Can I give you a hand with that stuff?"

"No, you can't. You look too knowing. Go away."

I didn't go away. I sat down in the chair on the other side of his desk and remembered the time, years ago, when

I met him: he had given me a curled and fatherly smile, and hired me. Now he was leaving me. They were making him leave me. I cleared my throat.

"Barney, I tried. I talked to them this morning."

"I know you did." Barney swallowed. "Don't be a damn fool. Shut up about me. Cut your losses."

Then I revved myself up and said it. "I'm quitting, Barney. I won't stay here without you."

Barney shrugged. "You have a future in this dump. You've got a present. Don't jeopardize it, Jack."

"When you leave, I quit," I said firmly.

"Your devotion is touching," said Barney, "but it doesn't interest me now."

"I don't care whether it interests you," I said, watching Barney fire at his wastebasket and miss.

"Tough, then." He hurled again and made it.

"Barney," I said, "if you didn't see the handwriting on the wall, it's because it was illegible."

"Get out, Jack," said Barney. It wasn't friendly. Pain turns to hatred. I had seen his face.

I GAVE THEM two weeks' notice, but they urged me to stay on for a month. I agreed.

I had done a good thing, taken a stand on a principle for Barney, whom I loved.

And it weakened me.

I went about winding things up with a curious misplaced energy. And all the while I did this, I was shoring myself up against a sense of loss. I wasn't ill, but I was beginning to feel increasingly feverish. I was going to be wildly, implausibly free.

On the days when I allowed myself to pause, I'd remember that I had been unable to reach Barney on the telephone. I'd remember his face when he left. Barney had left me with a hurt. Well, it was his hurt, wasn't it? I would pause and hope that Barney's refusal of me would pass, like a head-ache, that he would let me help him.

Yet at the same time I was savoring my release-to-come and its anticipated fruits. My decision was made, and I was free, or would be soon. I had earned something for my six years of obedience; something was owed the part of myself that had been buried.

It wasn't just Barney. It was this six-year-old life I had led. And liked. My work had given me reassurance—the dull-ness of it, the stabilizing routines, the power. It had taught me that I would survive, that I was attached to an organism that wound up and wound down and wound up again, inex-orably. Your own moods had nothing to do with it; you crossed the threshold of the office and something else took over, and you knew you would live forever, and be normal.

It was true: something in me did not want to be edged away from the center just then.

THE DAY AFTER I left, I met Helen at the zoo. Odd to be out on a weekday morning.

I made my way slowly, like a convalescent, through my familiar streets, which were lit strangely by the sun. It was cold but the sun shone, and its brightness held me fast, beat down through my clothes and bones. I walked the few blocks from my East Side bachelor apartment toward the Sixty-fourth Street zoo.

Helen looked concerned when she caught sight of me. Her face grew soft, her eyes pools of solicitude, her half-open mouth a little hungry. Gently, she steered me into the cafeteria.

"Goodness, Jack, isn't your coat warm enough?" She peered at me.

"I think so," I reassured her. "I'm just a little dislocated this morning. First day off the job, and I slept late."

"Why are you squinting like that?" she asked.

"Sun."

"I still can't get over your quitting. What am I going to do without you?"

"There are other editors," I said.

"None like you."

"You'll be okay." I smiled at her. On an impulse I reached across the table for her hand.

"Thank you, Jack. May I get to the point?" she asked directly.

"Sure," I said, but something in me did not want her to get so directly to the point. "Want to get out of here first?" I asked. "Walk a bit?"

She picked up her gloves. "Of course," she said. "Good idea, to get some air."

I took her stiff, reluctant arm, and we walked down the cafeteria steps, past the seals flopping in the chilly air. All around me children were mewing, and I was warmed. I thought of my brother. I pressed closer to Helen.

"It's hard to talk this way," she complained.

"Then let's sit," I suggested.

"Andy is broke, Jack. Flat broke. And you know how low his morale is anyway; I think it's because he's so little—and sterile, to boot. It's just rotten for him, and rotten for me too."

"Let me get this straight," I said. "Has the business actually gone bankrupt?"

"Getting there fast," she said. "He needs money to bail himself out. His partner is impossible."

I nodded and kept nodding, then I tuned in again to hear her say: "So it would be just a few hundred dollars. That's all."

"Of course," I said blankly, and smiled at her.

She breathed a deep sigh of relief.

"Thanks, Jack. You're good to do this. It's rotten to ask you for a favor, especially at this time, but . . ." The "but" was ominous. I snapped to.

"Wait a minute, Helen? Are you talking about a loan?" My blood suddenly ran icy.

"Of course. I wouldn't ask you on any other basis."

"From me?"

She nodded.

"Well, it is a rotten time to ask me for money," I exploded. "I'm just out of a job."

Now it was her turn to look blank as she extended a delicate and unexpectedly warm hand to touch me. "Were we at cross-purposes? Didn't I make myself clear?" I knew I had to act fast.

"Now hold it. Let me get it straight," I said to her, wondering where the hell my head had been. I reviewed my bank balance—the savings account, the checking. Could I make it? I supposed so. She had caught me unawares. I cursed myself first, then her, for her damned inconsiderate, outrageous, and ill-timed request. If I refused, what excuse could I give her? I had no dependents at all.

What choice did I have? I was so uncomfortable, my prospects were vague, the sun blinded me. I figured the numbers, the dollars and cents.

"I suppose so, Helen. But it might have to be short-term. Any time I need it back, I might have to ask for it. On very, very short notice," I repeated carefully.

Now that I was no longer an editor, I was everyone's husband or broker.

We stood. I turned my collar up. "You're not angry, are you, Jack?" she asked, her lips chapped, a drop of saliva crystallized like snow at the corner of her mouth.

"Good God, no," I said. "I'm a free agent, Helen, and I don't do what I don't want to do."

The wind whipped through us, and we walked fast down the block, still huddled together uncomfortably. Debtor and creditor.

I WENT HOME and slept for the rest of the afternoon. I dreamed fitfully. I wanted a job. There was no job. I wanted money. There was less of it. I wanted a woman. Helen. She took something. She turned into a baby and clung to me, and took something.

I got up from the bed. My place and I were strangers to each other. I wandered into my kitchen and inspected my cupboard. My cleaning lady had left a can of flammable cleanser near the stove. The cap was missing. I hunted for the cap until my fear ran out. I did not find the cap, and I put my mind to other things.

What I needed was a warm shower and maybe some food. If I ate, my headache and lethargy would go.

Late that night, I woke up wanting to make love, but I was alone. I took it like a man, turned on my stomach, blew out the candle, and slept. I dreamed of jobs, of the exchange of my services for money that would come in at regular intervals. It was an optimistic dream.

I AWOKE the following morning, brisk and hopeful. I was in command; I felt well. I disposed of several telephone calls from panicked secretaries in the place of my previous employment, and finally placed a call to Floss myself to straighten matters out.

"I told them to call you, Jack," she said apologetically. "I take full responsibility. They're new, and they were in such a funk. Nobody seems to know where anything is."

I laughed and told her where everything was, and then, mindlessly, hoping to amuse her, I got personal.

"Don't be so risqué," she said primly. Then: "Uh, we miss you, Jack. I guess that's all."

"I miss you too, honey. Don't hesitate to call if you need anything more."

"I won't," she said. She sounded friendly but already remote. " 'Bye, now."

" 'Bye." I hung up and stared at the replaced receiver for a few moments. Well, all was as it should be. Then I went around my apartment whistling "Bye, Bye, Blackbird" while I dressed, breakfasted, and went through motions of washing a dish. I stopped whistling long enough to call a couple of friends at magazines and (in case worse came to worst) ad agencies around town. I told them my story, which it turned out they already knew. It was gratifying to hear them, so hearty and present. That day I lunched with one—Nelson, whom I knew from my old newspaper days—and for the next week I had lunch in relays.

Nelson put me on to several possibilities, and so did the others. In those days, I was impressive. Even my old magazine suffered a small seizure of nostalgia and regret, and put out a palsied feeler to get me back. This bolstered me; I had been rocky on my feet.

"You can afford to wait," Nelson said to me. We were in his office, being interrupted by calls. "You're in demand." ("Ever so," Jennie was to say, wryly, much later, when I sheepishly told her about it.)

Throughout the second week, I was dazed, happy, and arrogant. My watch busted and went to the jeweler's.

I looked at my calendar, and saw my friend Audrey's party coming closer. I figured by then I'd be employed big. We'd celebrate me big.

But no. Two major magazines folded, without warning. A couple of hundred men, some with families (aging mothers, dying brothers), were out of work. The New York editorial job market was flooded, and whatever space I thought I had seen open before me vanished, or was usurped. "The picture's changed," Nelson groaned to me over the phone. He was concerned for himself as well as for me, I could tell, and I said I'd buy him lunch. Over lunch, he pulled himself together, told me to hang on and not clutch, and he'd still see what he could do. I was decent and civilized. But something hateful in me (now I judged it, but usually I smiled at it, was benevolent toward it, and that way kept it at bay) wanted the favor more passionately now. He sensed this, and it made him queasy, and less willing to give.

"This mess shouldn't really affect you," Nelson said coldly, sensing my need. I offered him a cigar someone had given me the day I left my job, stolen, I suspected, from the office brass's secret supply. I didn't smoke them. He took it. "Something will turn up for you," he said.

Something didn't, not for me, then, and not for those others who had families. Eventually, most of these upstanding men were absorbed, one way or another, back into gainful employment, with God knows what consequences to the host organism. Job markets and cities, like bodies, can assimilate only so much of what is alien; then they produce antibodies.

I was not reabsorbed. My own luck had curiously changed. It was no one's fault; it was luck. It was as if the antibodies in the city had been produced specifically to resist me.

In February my money began to run short. I said to a friend at one of the penultimate lunches, "I'll break through this." The friend suggested I try television. He called it "electronic journalism" and laughed when I scowled. But some of my comrades-in-dire-straits had found refuge with the networks. And so I tried. They were cordial and their offices were civilized. But the experience was ended for me by the man who took one look at me and said, "You're too big."

"I don't want a job on-screen," I snapped.

"That's not what I meant," he said coldly.

I didn't ask him what he meant. I assumed that I was too big for their screens, and that the same measurements were held to apply off-screen too.

MORNING CAME. Take a job, any job.

So I took the job on the scandal sheet.

I did it free-lance. *Earful* was a grotesque sheet, full of freak come-on exposé and violence, what they call "chop-chop" stories. To my surprise, sex was not the first concern; it was disfigurement and violence, the underside of sex, when you take the body apart and put it to the uses of pain. Parents beating children within an inch of their lives; a little kid falling down a well, after grandpa filches her crutch; baby getting scalded; puppy bearing a terrible scar.

My job was to interview the survivors and to dig out the salient background for the chop-chop stories. The chop-chop stories pained and affronted me, but I got good at it.

Then, at Audrey's party, I met Jennie.

AUDREY MIGHT NOT have seemed black, or Negro, as we said in those days. She had a coppery tone of skin, as if she'd spent long languid hours at the beach, but she did not otherwise look like a beach girl. She was too merry, too unselfconscious for that. At least, that's the way she was in the early days, before she became a social worker. I shouldered through the crowd to greet her. She was standing next to a tall, handsome man, pinned in a corner of the room. I pressed forward, smiling.

Audrey swung around and grabbed my elbow: "Do you know Jennie Owen?"

"I don't think we've ever met." I held out my hand.

"Jack is a magazine editor," Audrey said.

"I free-lance now," I said.

Jennie gave me a little smile.

"Maybe Jack could do something for you," Audrey said.

Jennie's dark eyes looked skeptical.

"Depends what you want," I said with sudden thickness, now that I was more or less alone with her.

"I'm looking for another job," Jennie said. "I'm a secretary now. Do you know Audrey?"

"Yes," I said. "I know Audrey." And there was Audrey, right where I'd seen her last. She hadn't vanished at all. This girl, this Jennie, had merely intervened between us. The tall, handsome man was still there next to Audrey, but he had shifted position. I eyed him with passionate distaste. It was as passionate as I'd felt in a while.

"Are you going to be sick?" Audrey inquired. She had, it seemed, been eying me with equal sharpness.

"I hope not," I answered her truthfully. Then, to Jennie I said, "I don't know whether I can help you or not. I do chop-chop stories for a magazine."

"Do you teach at Columbia too?" she said and looked straight into my eyes.

In a rush of syllables, I said, "I'm going to be sick. I ought to be in the bathroom, but I don't want to leave you."

Audrey loomed back into view. "You look pale," she told me. "Lila, take him to the bathroom." Which Lila did.

I shook Lila at the doorjamb and locked myself in for what was probably forever. I'll never get out of here, I thought mournfully. "Oh . . ." I said aloud, elbows braced on the rim. Jesus Christ, I thought, like a small boy. The doorknob rattled. Someone was trying to get in. The rattling became insistent. "I'm all right, I'll be out in a minute," I said weakly. "Please let me in." Was it Lila? "I can't," I muttered. Then a strong male voice interposed. "This is an emergency." But I just hung on, weakly. Her moan reached me again, and I straightened up. "All right," I called. I doused my head under the cold water tap in the basin. Dripping wet, I fumbled in the medicine cabinet and located some Pepsodent. The tube had seen better days, but I managed to squeeze from it its last, onto my forefinger and over my teeth. Now they were pounding on the door. As I unlocked it and staggered out into the open, my comrade-in-arms and her escort lurched past me like winged horses into the recesses of the chamber.

Is there not one kind stranger in this crowd, I thought to myself. Then, like an answer to a prayer, an older man put his hand on my shoulder and said, "Better get some air." I clawed my way toward a window.

Soon after, Audrey joined me. "Feeling better?" she asked.

"Yes, thanks." I turned to her, and my head cleared. There was repose in her brown eyes, her brown mouth, from which I took some obscure comfort. She asked me if I wanted to lie down. "Hell, no," I said, and leaned far out. She pulled me back, tugging on my belt. She pulled my face down to look at me.

"You alive?" she asked. She studied me, almost clinically, then said quietly, "Yes, you are."

I was actually feeling a bit better. Audrey began to scold

me. "I never never knew you not to hold your liquor. What's the matter with you anyway, Jack?"

"I miss my old job," I confessed. I miss routine, I miss Barney, I miss myself.

"Meet Jennie," Audrey said.

"I have, I have met her," I said. And I looked at Jennie again.

I had never seen anyone so small.

She was so small she could be crushed. I would see to it that she was not.

I leaned close.

"You look as if you're about to fall," Jennie commented. Which frightened me.

"What kind of work are you looking for?" I asked. She nodded uncertainly and put her finger over her lips. I braced my fist against the wall for support.

"I'm a secretary," she confessed once more. "I work for a clothing manufacturer. That's who I'm here with." She looked around furtively. "But I was an English major"—now she was for some reason even more apologetic—"and I thought maybe I ought to use my head. I mean my brains. Get a better job."

"You're probably a damn good secretary. Which is to say, you register no intimate, no personal emotion. You're impassive."

"Oh, no," she blurted out. "In fact, I sometimes think God must love my problems, he made so many of them."

This was fascinating. "What are they?" I asked.

"Oh," she said with a little shrug, which made me notice her graceful neck, "I'm brunette when I want to be blonde, I have brown eyes when I'd like to have green."

The last secretary I'd gone to bed with was my own.

"Look," I said, "can I take you home?"

"I'm not ready to leave just yet," Jennie said to me frantically, looking in the direction of her boss.

I thought of my brother, of Barney, of Marcella, of Helen.

"I think I'd better check in with the man who brought me. I don't want to lose my job."

She looked as if she believed that everyone would fail her in the end.

S HE HADN'T LOST her job. In fact, her relationship with her boss was now on a more professional and more stable basis. I invited her to accompany me upstate on an assignment. This sounded glamorous to her and was inexpensive for me.

So on our second date, if you can call the party our first, I took her to Elmira. In the distance, as we drove, the scrubby, denuded hills looked alive, like the unquivering haunch or rounded back of a great animal. "It looks like a woman," she said shortly, and fell silent. It did indeed. It reminded me of my sister Rita, and I set my teeth grimly and drove.

"What's your assignment today?" she asked, to break the silence.

"A child drowned. Fell down a well. I have to interview her grandfather."

"It's sad, isn't it?" Jennie said, her hand on mine.

"Of course it's sad. But I'm not approaching it that way. I can't. If it's too much for you—"

"Do you want me to come along?"

I could not let her do it, but the offer meant a lot. "No," I assured her. "Why don't we find a nice coffee shop and you can wait for me. I won't be long."

"Okay," she said.

Another small silence, this time more peaceful. "I hope I don't remind you of anyone."

"Like who?"

"Oh, someone you might have disliked."

My hands relaxed on the steering wheel, and I risked putting an arm around her. "I love you," I said, moving my arm back to the steering wheel as I said it. "And I don't know why. I've never loved anyone before."

Just then I found us a coffee shop. I looked at her face. Brown eyes, brown lovely hair.

"Come," I said. "Let's see what it's like. If it's not nice, I'm not leaving you here."

"I'll be fine, Jack."

We were inside the coffee shop, a simple, antiseptic, harmless diner. Mixed clientele and a competent waitress.

I gave her a five-dollar bill. "Don't be silly," she said.

"This whole thing is silly. Order what you like; I hope to be back in about an hour."

I picked her out a booth whose window overlooked the gray landscape of early spring. I squeezed her shoulder and left.

THE OLD MAN CRIED as I took notes. He showed me a photograph of Elfrida.

"Can I have that photograph?" I asked. "I'll get it back to you."

"I don't want to let go of it. I don't know why your paper told you she was going after a doll. My Elfrida would only have gone after her puppy," he explained.

"Of course," I said, standing up.

Suddenly I didn't think I could bear it any longer. I stiffened, tried to grow numb, to ward off an overwhelming shame.

In the car I thought of Helen. I thought of that day I tried to collect the money she owed me.

SHE WAS IN BED, wearing a frayed quilted bedjacket over her nightgown, tangled in bedsheets. The room was dark. I honestly wanted to open the window. Her hair was down, her face bare of makeup. Her features now were like little wounds, and the expression curiously sensual. As she shifted in her great bed, her bedjacket shifted with her, and I caught a glimpse of her delicately boned shoulder. I looked away.

"You really sick?" I asked her shortly.

"Sick at heart, Jack."

"What's the trouble, Helen?" I asked. "Anything specific?"

"It's Andy. He's so heartsick too. He doesn't come home."

"Give him a home to come home to. This place doesn't have it, Helen."

"You're so right, Jack."

I was suddenly frightened. I did not want to leave without my money. I got up and walked over to her bed. She buried her head deeper in the pillows. I hesitated. The nape of the neck and the thin, slightly frayed nightgown straps seemed like an invitation. I moved away from the bed and eased into a large chair by the window. It engulfed me, nicely, it gave me a good glimpse of the heavy coating of dust on each slat of the venetian blinds. I looked at Helen again. She looked back at me. "Jack?" she said, "please make love to me."

She grew white as I approached the bed, and I could see that a part of her didn't really want me.

Then I lay there, feeling a chill settle over my shoulders. I was wet all over, bathed in sweat from head to foot, like a drowning man.

LEGALLY, the child is Andy's.

I did not believe a son of mine would ever be called Morrie, but then of course I had nothing to do with naming him. I have seen him only a few times. My son, to whom I am only marginally related. He makes Helen and Andy happy. He resembles Andy. Is that possible? I see nothing of myself in Morrie. Maybe when he grows up he'll be my height.

I SAW JENNIE through the window of the diner, looking serene. She stood up instantly as I entered.

We drove back to the city in silence. Finally, she said, "Was the grandfather very upset?"

"Yes, he was," I acknowledged.

"My father died about a year ago," she said.

"Jennie," I said, "the kid's grandfather was grateful to me, and there I was exploiting what he felt and letting him talk so that I could write a story for that godawful rag I'm working for. He thought I was feeling something, and I wasn't feeling anything at all."

Tears spilled down her cheeks. "I loved my father very much," she said with special emphasis, as though I had denied it.

Don't come to me with this, it's not my fault, I was about to say, then took a breath, had a moment's grace. She was asking me to share what she felt. I could have touched her, given her shoulder a sympathetic squeeze, but that wouldn't have done at all. She wanted words. She had now an inquisitive, expectant look that demanded words. Any words, except that they had to be right.

"You miss him still?" I tried, beginning to face into it and enter her mind, as I would enter a writer's prose.

"Yes. Sometimes," she said. "In fact, this whole trip has made me miss my father." I stroked her hair softly, briefly.

An idea was beginiing to form in me. A treat for our next date. Barney.

"Why don't we have dinner with my friend Barney one evening?"

"I could make a little dinner party at my place," she said.

"Can you cook?" I asked.

"Yes. They say if you can read you can cook," she said, and leaned against my shoulder.

We drove into the city in the bleak violet light of evening.

"My place or yours?" I asked.

"Mine," she said simply.

She had a small apartment in a brownstone. Following Jennie, I climbed her stairs for the first time. I looked at her small body, her slender ankles ascending before me.

At the door, she hesitated. She took off her coat. "I haven't played my stereo since it was fixed." This was nervous prattle. I leaned over to kiss her, cupped her face in my two hands. This would stop her, and it would begin something else in sweet silence. Such a sweet kiss, yielding, not urgent, probably not even passionate.

I closed my eyes against the lights and blotted everything out but her. There was only her soft flesh and the fabric. She had begun to tremble and, obedient to this, I probed with a deeper aggression.

"Jack!" she gasped. "Please go. I can't do it. I can't even cook," she said.

I kissed her forehead, leaving her to go to bed and me to go to bed, each one of us, until some unspecified time, alone. How old was she? I wondered. Probably twenty-three or twenty-four. Twenty-six? In any event, I thought, hailing a cab and climbing into it, whatever it was, at twenty-eight I must be to her an older man.

THE WATERS OF THE LAKE glistened in the afternoon sunlight. Gray. When we finished rowing, I thought, looking at the girl across from me whose head was bent so that I couldn't see her eyes, I will take her and sit her down on the grass, lean her up against a tree, and I will kiss her. It will be like speech. "Jennie," I said, "do you like rowing?"

"It's fun. It reminds me of *Little Women*."

"I am aware," I said, "of the book. Though I can't say I ever read it. My favorite was *Eight Cousins*."

"You don't mean it," she said, disconcerted to be teased.

"No, I don't."

"*Little Women* is my favorite book," she said seriously.

"Most little girls like it. It was my sister's favorite. Is it still yours?" I asked, worried.

"Yes. It holds up well. The sentimental parts you just skip and the other parts—the point of view—is very adult." She spoke with such conviction that I decided to stop teasing her on the spot.

"Why does it remind you of *Little Women*?"

"Amy and Laurie rowed on the lake in Switzerland," she murmured, as if I knew all about these characters, as if they were real. (Later, I copped a copy of the book from the library and read it cover to cover. So, when Amy and Laurie rowed on the lake, Amy and Laurie became engaged. And Amy had a sister that died. An older sister.)

I lay down in the grass, the hem of her skirt was wet, and I kissed her mouth.

"You have sweet teeth," I whispered to her. What could one do with a child-woman, except be patient and enjoy her, and, I thought grandly, bring her up.

"Nobody ever said that to me. About my teeth."

I kissed her hard. She bit me.

AT THE ZOO, we stood before the monkey house. It was red brick, small, and inviting. The one place where smell never bothered me.

"Oh look," she said, pointing to some miniature monkeys that look more like birds, swooping around and lighting on the bars in the cage nearest at hand. "Aren't they darling?" I squinted at the identifying sign: Capuchin monkeys, named after a medieval order of monks. "Look," she breathed.

"They're pretty terrific," I said. They were just like Jennie. I looked at her, at them, back at her and at them again. Wise little monkeys they were, with the adult faces that babies sometimes have. Their tails were like an extra limb on their graceful, darting bodies. Free, even in their cages. I stole a glance at Jennie. My heart melted, as I looked from the monkeys to the girl. I could live with her, I thought. Wouldn't mind her morning breath, the sounds of her body, or that she might in unguarded moments scratch or yawn. I didn't want to think about the rest. I wanted to undress her.

The spider monkeys were next, and were more like me. For them, climbing along the bars of their cages was clearly an effort.

"Their tails look silly," Jennie ventured.

I felt offended. Then I recovered. She had not meant to be careless with me. "Oh, I don't think so," I said, sniffing the pungent animal air. "But if you prefer them without tails, let's get going."

Jennie touched my arm. Lovely fingers, five on each hand.

"Let's go home."

"Home?"

"I could make us some supper," I said, after a pause.

My grip on her hand tightened, and the pressure was gently returned.

"You don't have to do that," she said.

Do what? Then I remembered we'd been talking about supper.

"Why not? It won't seem strange to you. Audrey's cat is there."

"She is?" Jennie seemed amazed.

"Yes. I'm boarding her for Audrey," I said, pleased at this piece of luck. Pusserette's presence definitely added to my credibility.

I LAY AT LAST with Jennie in my arms. In that time of her love for me she had not learned to synchronize her desire with affection. I knew later that desire immobilized her, but now I was inattentive as she lay on my bed tense, arms stubbornly at her sides, then flung amicably around my neck.

The cat moaned pitifully, prowling the darkened rooms and sniffing around the edges of the bed.

As passions, banked or flaring, got underway, it appeared to be work for her. I had a good time. Briefly, I thought of remarking to her that the Puritan Work Ethic seemed to have attached itself to the wrong target, but thought better of it. And it was nice, her struggle. How different from Marcella. Marcella had been a stick. Nice too that I hadn't had to woo and seduce her from the moment we crossed the threshold of my apartment only an hour or so before; I hadn't had to think. We'd read poetry, eaten a little. She liked Stephen Spender, "The Truly Great." I'd read aloud to her: "The desires falling across their bodies like blossoms."

We walked to the bedroom, hand in hand. I didn't touch her. She asked me to close my eyes for some seconds while she undressed.

Then as I leaned over her, my body within her, I was assulted by an innocence I thought I had outgrown. Later I would discover her, turn on the light—she'd been trembling before I'd turned off the overhead lamp above the bed. Now, in the primitive dark, I throbbed with incautious, uncaring pleasure in the body of the woman I loved. Her natural rhythmic breathing turned into gasps, her legs were accommodatingly drawn up, all her moves, her heavings, were tuned to my own. I never thought to question. "Darling," I breathed. Fuck, I thought, as I came. I said it aloud, then lay against her, my mouth open against her cheek, then against the pillow.

"Why did you stop?" she whispered.

I didn't think I could get it going again. I moved to kiss her on the lips. "Didn't you come?" I asked. She turned her head away with a ladylike containment. I would get this together later. Now I just wanted to find her mouth again and taste it and still it. When I was done with that, unable apparently to curb my own infelicitous human speech, I asked her again: "Did you come?" She gasped. Ah, the question excited her. "Did you?" I said, thrusting between her legs, moving to claw at her breasts. She was silent. "Did you?" I was growing hard again, and no longer cared if she did or

not, though in the time that followed, I regularly and mo-
notonously asked. And she never told. Later I cared. And she
never said the words that would give my heart ease. I hurt.
But the melding of our bodies apparently had broken a verbal or emotional trust. She moved again, under me. And my
coming was less full, but sweet.

"Oh, darling, will you sleep here?" I asked.

"Stay the night?"

"Yes. Yes. I'll give you my pajama top. Or you can sleep
in nothing."

I reached for the overhead light, to look at her. Her hair
was awry, her cheek an angry red where my beard had
abraded it, her legs spread. I leaned down and kissed her
there. "Don't do that," she whispered. "Did you come?" I
asked. "I want to make you come."

She grasped my head gently, not with passion, I thought,
but to remove my mouth from what she now seemed to consider a wound.

"Did I hurt you?" I asked. "Why didn't you come? What
can I do?"

"Shhh," she said. She broke from my embrace and
leaned down to stroke the cat, stretched on the blue-green
throw rug beside the bed.

This gave me a view of her uncontained breasts that was
irresistible, and I moved to fondle them. "Why is the cat
meowing?" she asked as my hand enclosed her.

"Tell me what you like," I implored her. What she would
have liked, I know now, was patience, which I was utterly
unable to give, though I thought in that moment that I would
have given her anything. What I did not know was that I was
in the mental grip of her body, and any gift that did not
involve my possession of, my immersion in, her body would
have been incomprehensible to me. I perceived her faint
struggle to extricate herself from my grip as her participa-
tion in the friction of sex. She pulled back, I leaned forward.
Ah, my God.

"Give me your pajama top," she finally said.

"You'll stay the night?" I asked, hardly daring to believe it. She would lie beside me all night.

"Yes," she said. She was in love with me and would endure. Her body's ordeal was just begun. All she knew of desire was its ache. In our later quiet moments, she loved my words as my hands moved along her body. "I want to feel your hair," I said to her once, as she lay docile, and I felt it. Fine. "Darling," I said.

The moments collect, and this is what I remember about Jennie. I remember her hands. "My hands," she said suddenly when we were deep in our love, "they've grown old." She looked at them like a bewildered child, and I took them and kissed them. "It's nice to have grown-up hands," I told her. "I love you," she said. "I am with you always," I said. "Always," I said. "Even unto the end of the world," quoting Matthew.

On this first morning, she lay in my blue cotton pajama top. She had used my toothbrush. She seemed happy. I'd fallen asleep holding her. In the morning there were dark circles under her eyes; she hadn't slept.

"The cat's meowing probably kept you awake."

"No."

"Then what?" I stroked her hair.

"I'm used to sleeping alone," she said.

"Don't be pathetic," I said, frightened.

"I'm not being pathetic. It's just a fact."

"Well, it's temporary," I said.

She looked very pleased.

"Tell me," I said over the breakfast I had prepared, "why last night? Why were you so easy?"

Stung, she said, "I'm not!"

I felt the lash of my own words. She clutched at her neck, at the collar of my pajama top. Then she fled into the bedroom to scramble for her clothes. I scrambled after her.

"Jennie," I said, "don't do this. It's such a cliché."

"What's wrong with you? First I'm easy, then I'm a cliché." She stood there in her panties, hiding her breasts. My pajama top had been flung on the bed.

"I wish God would cut out my tongue," I said, wanting to hold her, but I'd forfeited the right. "Come back into the kitchen, Jennie, please," I said. "You don't even have to get dressed. Just please come back. It means everything to me." I was frightened. "You mean everything to me."

"I do?" she whispered. Vows.

"Yeah," I said. Why was it so hard to get my breath? What the hell was the matter with my pounding heart? God. I didn't even believe in God. "Please come back, Jennie. I'll wait."

I turned and went into the kitchen. Marcella had been right. I wasn't a gentleman. When Jennie stalked out, as she would, I'd just go to bed and stay there.

She padded in, barefoot. Unable to meet her eyes, I looked at her feet. "Sit. Sit down," I said, getting up to pull out her chair. I kissed the top of her head, as she sat down.

"Don't cry," I pleaded.

She shook her head. "I won't," she said.

Carefully, I said, "I was puzzled—flattered, really—because it was only our third date. And you're so lovely."

"I'm not easy, Jack."

"Why, then, Jennie? Why me?" I looked at her, thinking I'd been brave to open my mouth at all.

"I just felt," she said—her voice was muffled—"that you really cared for me."

I no longer wanted to crawl alone to my bed. "You're right. I do care for you." Her whole body relaxed, and her face softened.

I reached across the table for her hand, raised it to my lips. My body was always truthful with Jennie. It meant everything it did. It couldn't lie to her. She rested her head now in my cupped hand.

"I felt protected by you," she said.

The cat sprang onto her lap, and she cradled it. Maybe she wanted a baby, I thought.

"While we're on the subject of protection," I said, trying to keep it light, "did you use a diaphragm or anything last night?"

"That's not romantic," she said, putting down the cat.

"I'm asking for both our sakes. Sorry I'm not more of a word man in the mornings. After making love."

"I'm careful. I have protection," she whispered, glad to hear the word love.

S HARDS OF COURTSHIP. We went to Indianapolis together to see Davey. We had coordinated vacations, mine taken on my own money and time (I was still free-lancing), hers secured from the menswear manufacturer.

The plane touched down, and there was family. Squinting, I could make out Davey at the end of the ramp, looking somewhat more robust, heavier, than when I had seen him last. At his wedding. We shook hands. He was not my height, but I felt smaller beside him. I quickly introduced him to Jennie, and before I could think of some small talk to get us over the awkwardness, he leaned over and gave her a kiss on the cheek.

"Betty's waiting in the car with Libba," he said.

"Libba?"

"She's named for Betty—Elizabeth—and that's what we call her. Actually, that's what I call her. I talk baby-talk to her. She'll probably never learn to talk," Davey said cheerfully. He steered us through baggage claim, and then to the car.

"I hate baggage claim," Jennie said. "I'm always afraid the bag will be broken or lost."

"I don't think girls from New Jersey have enough experience to expatiate on the hazards of baggage claim," I told her.

"Don't insult me in front of your family," she snapped.

A car, with a matronly Betty at the wheel, rolled into view. Beside her was my brother, holding on his lap a small squirming creature attired in pink. I was stunned by the resemblance. Davey passed this baby to Betty, who took her expertly, then extricated himself from the car and crossed to the curb to collect our bags. He came around to the front.

"Betty does a restaurant review tonight," he said, "so Rita and Carl are having the two of you and Mother for dinner. We'll pick you up there around nine."

"A restaurant review?" I echoed stupidly.

"Betty does a column for a local weekly," Davey said with pride.

"How nice," said Jennie.

"Davey," I said, hesitating before the car door, "let me get this straight. Mother and Carl and Rita tonight?"

"Yes. Okay?"

Not okay. Why couldn't they at least have taken us to the restaurant with them? Davey anticipated my question: "The family just insisted. It's for Mother, really. We'll make it up to you tomorrow night. Betty's got a feast planned. It'll be just the four of us."

I could have killed him.

"Hi!" said Betty, twisting around, and when she did so, I couldn't help recognizing the plucky, appealing girl I had helped out some months before.

"You must be Jennie," she said cheerfully to the waif who was crawling into the front seat beside her. "Would you mind holding the baby?" Jennie took the child.

"Your family is nice," Jennie said warmly.

Davey said, "Hand her back to Jack, would you, Jennie? He hasn't seen her yet." Davey could always put things to rights.

"Your niece," Davey said lightly as Jennie handed me the bundle. Next thing, she was in my arms.

I looked at the child's face. She had crinkly intelligent soft brown eyes, which focused. "Libba," I said. Saying those two syllables was unbelievably sweet. No one else in the world had ever been called Libba.

Davey looked at his daughter and then at me, in gratitude.

Shards.

Eventually we were deposited at Rita's. Since the last time I had seen my sister, she had turned into a perfect doctor's wife. Carl looked as sinister as ever, though his manner was amiable.

"Hello, Mrs. Owen," he greeted Jennie.

"Miss," she corrected him, deeply embarrassed.

"Oh," he said, laughing, "I have meant to pay you a compliment. You look married."

A frown creased Jennie's delicate forehead.

"No, Carl," I said heartily, "she's going to make her way in the world without my assistance." Since this eased no one's discomfort any, I figured I'd better explain: "That's a line from my favorite Bogart movie, *Treasure of Sierra Madre*. It gets said by John Huston to a bum." Carl grimaced, but Jennie's expression relaxed ever so slightly.

"Have a canapé," said Carl, looking around for the platter. "Mandy," he yelled to his six-year-old, who had been left in charge of domestic matters while Rita drove over to another suburb to fetch my mother.

Mandy made her way through a clutter of fancy furniture that had seen better days, carrying the platter.

"Your Uncle Jack," said her father jovially, "and your uncle's friend, Miss Owen."

"Oh, please call me Jennie."

"Hello, Miss Owen," said Mandy, not very quick on the take. Her father's daughter.

But when Rita returned with my mother, I reassessed resemblances and decided the genetic distribution in the case of poor Mandy was fifty-fifty. I felt no tenderness for Mandy, not even a hint of what I had felt for little Libba.

My mother came toward me. For as long as I'd known her she'd been an old lady, with arms not enfolding but outstretched. "This is Jennie, Mother."

My mother stared into Jennie's face, inclining her body toward her for the briefest of moments, then extended a rigid hand for Jennie to shake. "I'm glad to meet you, Mrs. Church," Jennie sighed.

Jennie's introduction to Rita had been the hardest of all. Rita exuded ice, even when she was trying to be warm and hospitable. Something in her marriage had chilled her. When she occasionally reverted to her old self, one could sense a vulnerability: ice melts and vanishes, and if Rita thawed she would disappear. But she had adapted her coldness to the necessary social forms, which meant she had become authoritarian.

"Dinner is done," she said. "We'll serve wine with dinner." Carl produced a single bottle of chianti.

"Jennie," said Rita, "why don't you sit next to my mother, on Carl's right. Mother, sit next to Mandy. Jack, you'll be at my right or left. Now which is it?" she puzzled, going into that trivial deep funk, trying to figure her left from her right.

"Why didn't you make place cards?" I asked. "I always do."

A corner of Jennie's mouth twitched into a mischievous smile. She had loosened up considerably once Betty and Davey had gotten us to their house, shown us to our separate but equal (and nearly adjoining) rooms, and jollied us up with some Scotch and frolicking on the floor with the baby and their menagerie of pets.

"Place cards?" said my mother.

"They do that in New York," Rita said, finally indicating my chair. "Don't tilt back in it, Jack. This furniture is delicate."

I settled my large frame on the straight-backed chair she had assigned to me. Next, I'd be told its convex wooden ribs were good for my spine. I looked wistfully across the table at Jennie, far far away. She was watching Carl with hypnotized fascination while he struggled with the cork on the chianti bottle—I could see that she was awed by this dinner-table formation. Surely a banquet was in the works, she must be thinking. Privately, I had concluded spaghetti, mostly because of the chianti: the smells wafting from the kitchen were impossible to identify. Rita rose as Carl poured. She returned bearing a casserole and glared at Mandy, who had apparently missed her cue to offer to help.

"That looks delicious," breathed Jennie.

"Nothing," said Rita. "I just whipped it up."

Servings were apportioned and I tasted it. Tuna casserole.

"Very tasty," I said, determined to be a good boy.

"Nice, dear," said my mother.

"Mandy," Rita said, "take your elbow off the table."

"Why is it bad to put your elbows on the table?" Mandy asked assertively. Jennie hastily removed her own elbow from the table.

"How's the practice going, Carl?" I asked him.

"Well," he said, delighted to have been asked, "I put in many hours at the hospital, supervising psychiatrists in residency. And I have a nice little private practice now. I see patients in the cellar."

"The cellar?"

"We built an office in the basement," Rita explained, "so that the patients can have complete privacy. I do the laundry when Carl's at the hospital so I don't run into the patients with a wash load, coming and going."

"What sort of cases do you get?"

"Functioning psychotics. People who have neurotic difficulty in their daily lives . . ."

"What sort of difficulty?" asked Jennie.

"Sexual. Impotence," he went on, looking sheepishly at our mother.

MY MOTHER WAS from land-locked Iowa. Old, I've said, since the beginning of time. She made beds, kept house, and cooked. Always tired, always pitiable because tired, always old. She had little to say, and when she resorted to words, it was about the Amana settlements of Iowa, and how they manufactured refrigerators. My father would begin to look glazed, as if he wondered what he'd married. Probably he wondered where he had misplaced his pipe cleaners.

My father died when I was eighteen. My mother mourned him, though it was hard to tell, since she'd been in mourning all her life. His death produced in all of us not a change but an augmentation. In my case, perhaps, of guilt and the need for physical and geographical distance. In Rita's case, of defiance. In Davey, of a natural balance. We mourned my father, all three of us. He was playful, kind, humorful, remote, shy, stubborn. He was from Kentucky. "I'm going home," he would say, for no reason at all. "I'm going home," he would say with loving mischief. And so he went home, to Kentucky, in his thoughts, I'm sure, as he died.

As children, Davey and I would hear them argue—heated whispers in their bedroom, where we never imagined them in bed. Shivering with fear, our necks stiff from intense eavesdropping, we would strain to hear what they were saying or doing. These exchanges, we discovered, were about money. We could never hear enough to be certain, but we surmised that my father was arguing with all the force of his estimable nature that our allowances be increased, while my mother argued against, with equal fervor. It didn't occur to me until much later that they probably had larger financial problems to fight out than our pocket money, but I'm sure we were right about who argued on the side of generosity and who had opposed. Funny that I should, as an adult, have my mother's stinginess, but then perhaps I am like my father too. I give, don't I? Ask Helen. Or better still, ask Barney. I always secretly believed that Rita extorted small sums additional to her allowance from my father, using feminine wiles she had not learned from my mother. Rita seemed to know something about sex, though neither Davey nor I had the courage to ask her whether our parents did it.

I LOOKED AT RITA and had to admire her. She had survived. A doctor for a husband, a feisty if to me unpleasant six-year-old daughter, an ability to produce full-course dinners with a minimum of labor. All of this represented some cushion against life.

I wanted to go home, I thought, wondering where I had heard that before, then remembering.

I suddenly felt protective about Jennie. But she looked at ease, as I caught her eye across the table. Who could tell what she was feeling?

"What do you do?" Carl asked Jennie.

"I'm a secretary."

"Oh," said my mother, in a glum concern. "What sort of firm?"

"I work for a menswear manufacturer," Jennie said bleakly.

"Did you go to college?" my mother asked.

"Yes. In the East."

"I've never been East," said my mother. "I'm afraid to fly. And Jack gets back here so seldom."

"Tell us about the Amanas and their refrigerators," I put in mischievously.

"So interesting," my mother went on, "these strange people. They wear black you know."

She is crazy, I thought, just as my sister returned with the dessert. We all sat around gloomily.

Jennie began to look around the room with a genuine anxiety. "You want the bathroom?" Mandy inquired matter-of-factly.

"Yes," whispered Jennie.

"Charming girl," said Carl in Jennie's absence. Everyone had finished eating.

"She's not a girl," my mother corrected Carl. "How old is she, Jack? Thirty?"

"She was twenty-four last week, Mother," I sighed wearily.

"Really," said my mother, her blandness covering either malice or surprise or both. "I find it so hard to guess ages correctly nowadays."

I resisted commenting on her suitability to guess another woman's age by appearance. She went right on: "I thought she was nearer to Rita's age."

The toilet was flushed and the doorbell rang. It was Davey and Betty. I was never more glad to see anyone in my life.

"I would think," whined my mother when David, Betty, and Jennie had settled themselves awkwardly around the table, "that you'd have brought Libba. I so seldom get to see her."

"We have to go now," I said, rising.

"WE THOUGHT IT MIGHT be best to get it over with immediately," Davey said to me in the car.

"How's Mom's health?" I asked.

"Not so good," said Davey soberly. "Diabetes. But Dr. Frame is keeping an eye on her."

He wasn't reproachful, but my heart sank nevertheless. I remembered Dr. Frame's hands pressing against my rib cage, after our derring-do on the highway those long years ago.

"Are his hands still steady?"

"Yes," said Davey.

We pulled into the driveway. We bounded up the front steps, leaving Davey to wait for the baby-sitter. Apparently Sadie lived on Gitche Gumee Boulevard, originally inhabited by the Indians and now being taken over by the Jews. I could have lived just as long and contented a life without being in possession of this information.

Jennie sat down beside me. I thought of the sleeping arrangements and was too embarrassed to look at her. My stranger. Unrelated by blood or marriage. She squeezed my hand.

Davey returned as Jennie and I were into our second drinks. He talked with great excitement about his work as a chemist.

"Davey, are their suitcases upstairs?" Betty asked suddenly.

"Yes," said Davey. "I think I'll turn in myself, show you the way."

Davey said good night, gave me a long appraising look, then a sudden, startling, rough embrace.

As illicit lovers, Jennie and I were wildly inept. We each shut our separate doors, and I fell into uneasy sleep to the sound of Betty's two-fingered typing.

IN THE MORNING, there was a timid rap at my door. I opened it, and there Jennie stood, in stocking feet, dressed except for her shoes, looking tired and frightened. "What's the matter?" I asked.

"Would you please come into my room?"

"Sure," I said, reaching for my bathrobe. "What time is it?"

"Eight," she said with a touch of impatience.

"It's always eight," I said, still in a daze of sleep, and I followed Jennie into her room.

"What's up?" I said, yawning, certain that, whatever it was, I could fix it.

"Look," she said, pointing to the heel on the only pair of shoes she had brought with her. I looked. A piece of fine taupe leather appeared to have been scuffed.

"How did you do that?" I asked.

"It must have gotten scraped when I was getting in and out of the car," she said miserably.

"So what? Maybe it can be covered with a crayon or something," I said. I thought of the assortment of soft pencils back at my faraway office.

"Where will I get a crayon?" she asked.

I decided to face into her trouble. "Why are you in such a panic? I'm sure once the shoe is on it hardly shows."

"Your sister-in-law, everybody, looks so bandbox and perfect," she complained.

"Don't take them so seriously, Jen. They're just a bunch of country mice."

She clung to me and I held on.

"I'll meet you downstairs," I said, finally.

THE NEXT THING that went wrong was that Davey wasn't there. He had gone to work. I resented his desertion. After all, he was my host and my brother. Then I racked my brains trying to remember what baby present I had sent for Libba and had a panicky moment of forgetfulness in which I thought that I might not have sent one at all. Did I or didn't I? My mind went blank.

Then Jennie began to choke, and Betty was slapping her on the back.

"What is it, darling?"

"My throat hurts," she said apologetically.

Betty's eyes grew wide. "My God," she said, "I hope it isn't catching."

"You'd better see the doctor," I said. "Dr. Frame will take a throat culture, and penicillin will knock it out."

"Maybe we could stop at the shoemaker's before the doctor?"

"You've got your priorities in order, and that's good."

*

DR. FRAME'S OFFICE was not nearly as shabby as I had re-membered it. He had a partner now, a younger man, and an efficient nurse.

"We want to see Dr. Frame," I said firmly. "He's my old family doctor."

"Okay," shrugged the nurse and led Jennie toward a pale green door.

I closed my eyes and turned off my mind.

Before long, Jennie and Dr. Frame walked into the wait-ing room. He was grizzled now, and fatherly, beside her. "She's fine," he boomed. "Throat infection. Get this filled." He thrust the prescription in my hand. I looked at it. Unin-telligible as usual.

"How are you, Jack?" He poked me gently in my ribs.

"I'm fine. Is she really okay?"

"Sure. She should stay in bed and take the penicillin, and she'll be okay in a couple of days. Strep throat. You used to get them, didn't you?"

"Yes." I smiled. How decent of him to remember that, in addition to my ribs.

"Now," he went on, "she's a little contagious, and while I'm sure Libba's okay, it'd be better if she wasn't around a small baby. Can you go to a hotel, or Rita's?"

"We'll go home," I said, nearly sinking to my knees with gratitude.

IN THE LIVING ROOM, a baby-sitter, an elderly woman, was poking at Libba in an effort to amuse her. I seized Jennie by the elbow and hurried her away from the baby into the kitchen. Betty was putting ingredients through a couple of simultaneous and sequential rituals. An imposing array of cutlery was laid out on the kitchen table, waiting to be polished to a blinding gleam. Betty kept referring to a cookbook and muttering.

We stood in awe of her performance until Jennie said, "Are you testing recipes for your column?" I winced.

"No," Betty replied. "This is for us, for tonight. We'll have Lobster Bordelaise. Do you like that?"

"I don't know what it is," Jennie said.

"Really? Well, then," said Betty, collecting herself, "it

may turn out to be even more of a treat than I'd planned."

I was blunt. "We won't be here for dinner."

Betty swiveled around, hands on hips.

"Jennie's sick," I reminded her. "Probably strep. We'll be catching the four o'clock plane out of here."

Betty began to cry. "I'm so disappointed," she said, trying to recover. "I wanted it to be so special." Was she, after all, just a kid? Playing house?

"So are we," I said, looking with some sympathy at the embryonic meal scattered all over. "Look, Betty, I'll take Jen up to bed, then phone the airport."

"You phone the airport, Jack. I'll go up with Jennie. Then I'll call Davey."

As they ascended the stairs, Betty moaned: "Oh, in-laws. You just don't know."

All arrangements made, I fell into a chair, exhausted. I shivered with emotion, undefined and undifferentiated.

Betty came down to heat up some soup for Jennie. I followed her into the kitchen.

"I feel rotten about this, Betty."

She was a grown-up again. "Things happen," she assured me. "We'll just all do it another time."

Sometimes Betty could be sweet. I closed my eyes and tried to think what was missing in her. And, these days, in Davey. A sense of humor, that was it. Did being married do that to you? Or being a parent? Davey had always been a fun guy. A good mimic. Whatever it was, it wasn't going to happen to me. I would joke even standing in front of an open grave.

Betty spun around to face me. "Jack, I've never thanked you properly for helping us out the way you did."

"No need to."

"It was so right for me to marry Davey. Marry into this family."

I was glad she thought so, though I had no idea what she meant. For me, the family began and ended with Davey.

"I was in love with someone else, you know."

"I didn't know." And wasn't sure I wanted to.

"Yes. There was someone else. But Davey loves me more than that other man did. And Davey's so completely dependable."

"I'm glad we have you in the family. I'm glad for Davey." I had no idea whether it was true. She poured the soup into a bowl.

"I'll take it up to her," I said. Betty handed me a tray.

"Would you like some?" And so a bowl was poured for me too. I mounted the stairs, tray in hand, penicillin in pocket, to dine privately with my darling.

She was lying on top of the chenille spread, her shoes off.

"Sit up," I said, "I got eats. Shouldn't you be in some flannel nightie, with a woolen scarf wrapped around your neck?"

"I'm too tired to laugh," she said, her mouth twitching in a little smile.

We sipped our soup like two children. I looked at my watch. "Time for another pill." Obediently she took it, washing it down with Campbell's chicken noodle soup.

"Lucky we get the good stuff, don't have to stay around for the Lobster Bordelaise."

Jennie put her hand over mine. There was a gentle knock at the door. Davey looked in. "If I'd known, we could have spent last night together," he said.

"Yeah, the restaurant could have delivered to Rita's. Though I wouldn't have missed that tuna casserole for anything."

Davey didn't laugh. His silence confirmed my theory that he'd become humorless.

"Got any good pictures of Libba?" I said.

"In Betty's study," Davey said. "I'll get them."

"No, let's let Jen rest." I patted her on the head. "Naptime," I said firmly.

In Betty's study, appointed with an electric typewriter, he began to fish through drawers for photo albums. He found

Libba's, and that special tenderness that had always been part of Davey overtook his features. We opened to the first page: an obscurely visible Libba in her mother's arms. Then Libba in the blindly loving embrace of her father. I began to choke up. I too was a father. "Jack," Davey said gently, taking the album from me, replacing it on the desk, "she's a good girl."

"She's too little to be anything else so far."

"I mean Jennie, you jackass."

"Are you sure? You've hardly had a chance to get to know her."

"I'm sure. A lot of girls have fallen for you, but this one is special."

"What do you mean?"

"She knows you, somehow. You're safe with her. Other girls you'll push around. Or they you. Same thing anyway," he mused.

"Are you telling me to marry her?"

"I don't think I have to tell you that. You wouldn't have brought her here if you weren't thinking about it."

"I told you to marry Betty," I said. "Now you're repaying me."

"You can look at it that way if you like." He was holding something back.

"But is it okay with you?" I asked. A silence. I had risked something.

Very softly, he said, "It's okay." His eyes went straight for the picture of Libba.

"If Jen and I should marry and anything happens to me," I said on sudden impulse, "will you look after her?"

"Goes without saying," Davey said.

"One has to be prepared for all eventualities."

"No, one doesn't. You're just scared because she got sick. Marry her and live happily ever after. Marry her," he repeated, this time with a strange urgency.

"I recognize an order when I hear one. Do you trust me to be good to her?"

"I trust you to be good by your lights," Davey said carefully.

"Spell that out."

"Marry her," Davey repeated. "You like her. And you don't like most people."

"Yes, I do." I was stung. "I like you," I protested.

What did it mean to like somebody, anyway? I liked some people. Or, if that was not precisely the case, I tried not to show it. That was a way of liking, wasn't it? I liked Jennie. I loved her.

"I want to see Libba."

Davey's face relaxed with pleasure. "She's in her crib." I followed him, the way he'd followed me when we were kids. We entered her shaded room. She was in her crib, asleep.

"Can I pick her up?" I asked.

"She'll wake up," said Davey. Was that so horrible? But the answer, before I could utter the question, was: "Betty says they should be allowed to sleep unless it's absolutely necessary to wake them. You'll see her again," Davey promised.

"I hope so."

"Of course. Betty and Libba and I will be at your wedding."

He was putting pieces of me together. It would all come together. My wedding. My niece. My brother. And Betty, without whom there would be no Libba.

I found Betty in Jennie's room, packing her things. Jennie gave me a wan smile, which verged on desperation. She wanted Betty out of her things. "I'll help Jen," I said. "Why don't you all wait for us downstairs."

"God," Jennie said when they were gone.

"Did she pry?"

"No. She only folded five pairs of panties, two bras, my hankie, and three half-slips. I mean four. She's efficient."

"Isn't she just?" We laughed, conspirators again, and then I went to cram my stuff, helter-skelter, into my own piece of luggage.

AT THE AIRPORT Davey had parked, and Jennie and I had checked in; now we stood, the three of us, close together for a few brief moments. I was alone with the two people I loved most in the world. According to Davey, perhaps the only two grown-up people I liked.

Our flight was announced. "I'd better go," said Davey. "We'll see you soon." He kissed Jennie on the cheek. He pressed my hand with warmth and strength. My brother.

"Drive carefully," I muttered.

"Sure," he said.

For some seconds I stood and watched his retreating back. Retreating and returning—to something I didn't understand. Abandoning me to hurry back to it. I pulled myself together. I had to be strong for Jennie.

Aboard the plane, we were assigned seats in a row of three abreast. A pasty young woman with a movie magazine sat by the window. I sat in the aisle—long legs and all that—and tried to see to it that Jennie was comfortable. I felt somehow I was failing her.

During takeoff, she fell asleep. I loosened her safety belt and drew her head onto my shoulder. There she stayed, stirring and shifting. As the altitude clogged our ears, I decided to wake her. Our neighbor, I observed, was immersed in the saga of a star who had found the sustaining faith. I shook Jennie. She was feverish.

"What?" she murmured, struggling awake. "What did you say?"

"I didn't say anything. I'm going to say it now. Let's get married."

"Oh. Yes." She said yes. In a fever. After which we were both silent, until we began our descent.

The stewardess passed by with mints and gum. I took gum, Jennie mints. Then she pressed her hands over her ears. We seemed to be lurching toward the ground. "Gum might have been better for your ears," I shouted, offering her mine.

She shook her head no. "Why?" I persisted. She turned away from me and put the mint in her mouth. "Swallow your mint and take my gum, Jen."

"No," she said firmly.

"Why?"

"I don't like the way I look chewing gum."

"Do you mind if I chew?" I asked pleasantly.

"Do what you want."

We were officially engaged, almost, and having our first quarrel. I put my hand over hers. "Swallow," I said. "Yawn." She ignored me. I'd never seen such stubborn passivity.

And so we touched down. The creep by the window stood up instantly and made motions to get past us, though the seat-belt sign had not yet gone out and a voice on the loud-speaker was instructing us to stay put. I gestured to her to sit down. Resentfully, she did. Jennie stared fixedly ahead.

Finally, Jennie and I loosened our seat belts and stood up. We crowded into the aisle together, and I put an arm around Jen. No response. I took the gum from my mouth, placed it unwrapped in an ashtray. Jennie appeared to sneer. If this went on much longer, I would become suicidal. Was this what it was like to get engaged?

Like a zombie she preceded me down the aisle and into the terminal, leading me toward baggage claim. There she stood, a wild look in her eye, no doubt once again crazed with fear that her luggage was lost. I stuffed my clenched fists into my pockets. "I'll put you in a cab," I said, "and then I'll go to my place."

She said nothing.

I saw my suitcase and grabbed for it. Now we had to stand around, cooling our heels, waiting for hers. Why wouldn't she even fight?

"Jack," she said, turning to me weakly, "I'm sick."

"Of course you are," I snarled. "You are also the biggest nuisance I've ever come across." Her face grew stiff, pale. I gasped with pain, and my eyes filled with tears.

"Darling," Jennie said.

"I'm no good," I said. "You deserve better."

"Maybe I do," she said, "but I don't think so. Just don't be mean to me."

"Why didn't you take the gum?"

Her eyes brimmed. "I never chew gum. I was thinking about our getting married, and I didn't want to chew gum."

She reached up and kissed me. Stubborn but dear. Not a mean bone in her body. "Let's find your suitcase," I said, fulfilling her most intimate wish.

We found a cab and went to her place.

W<small>HEN YOU'RE WELL</small>, first thing," I said, "I'll buy you a ring."

"No. No need to."

"Gold-diggers are made, not born. We're going to do this right. Start being greedy. Right now. Practice." She hugged me for that. She liked my way with words. Now, if she would only let me know if she liked my body. Well, you can't ask for everything immediately. And, in a way, as I watched her undress and her delicate flesh was unself-consciously revealed to me, I thought, who could ask for anything more?

"Let me check the fridge."

"There's nothing in it," she said sadly.

"Okay," I said, as if it didn't matter. "I'll get some food, and we'll get you well again in no time. Take your penicillin now," I said, offering it to her. "It should be taken on an empty stomach." She giggled as she swallowed. I held the glass in my hand, to her lips. It was fun. It would be fun to take care of her for a lifetime.

I left her lying comfortably in bed, content, an engaged lady. All taken care of but telling people and the ring. And plans for the actual wedding. I didn't want to think beyond that. Like, where we would live. Her place or mine?

When I returned with a sack of groceries, I saw that she had unpacked my suitcase and hung my things in her closet. She was terribly proud and pleased. So was I.

I sat down on the edge of the bed. We were once again afraid of each other, and I didn't know how that had happened.

Well, what do we do now? Play backgammon? I loathed TV, and besides, her set was broken. The image would only stay in focus if you stood before it, directly in front of it. If you moved away or took a comfortable nearby seat, the picture at once became grotesquely distorted. Mechanically, I walked into the kitchen. I set about washing the dishes, wondering if she'd fallen asleep, if we would get to kiss each other good night. Now that she'd gotten my proposal, she'd be careless with me. Was that true? Her secrets. I dried the dishes and put them away. I could read a book before I fell asleep. She had a well-stocked bookcase, in contrast to her kitchen. Poems of Stephen Spender. I moved my lips. "Born of the sun, they travelled a short while toward the sun . . . And left the vivid air signed with their honour." Now, why did I think of those lines? Was it something Davey had said? About my not liking most people? Jen and I had read them together. Loved them. Good thing I was tired, and tired enough to know it. I walked into the living room, and there was Jennie in her nightgown, sheets in hand.

"The sofa's not long enough for you. I'll sleep here," she concluded.

"That's crazy," I said.

"You'll sleep in my bed," she went on.

"Jennie, it isn't good strategy to be craven or self-sacrificing with men."

"I trust you," she said.

So I bore the weight of her trust.

"How'd you get to be so trusting?" I murmured.

"I don't like confessions," she said. "What difference does it make?" She was quite tense.

"I'll tell you about me."

"I don't want to know. I mean I don't want to bargain."

"Am I your second man?"

"Jack, please don't do this to me."

"Just tell me. It'll be good for you."

Her recital didn't take long. I was her fourth. The two middle ones I would hear about some other time, if ever. They were merely efforts to heal the hurt of the first.

So far, I was not jealous of him. I congratulated myself on having so adult a reaction.

Her account of what had happened between them was taking on vivid color in my own imagining. She denied that the physical pain had daunted her. She had been too swept up in the ritual character of this experience which her lover had not shared, not as a significant ritual. What hurt then?

In the morning, she had reached for him. He'd said, "Cool it."

"Did you see him again?"

"For six months or so. Once every couple of weeks."

"Did you sleep with him?"

"Can we stop talking about it?"

"Why are you asking me? Why don't you just stop?"

"You won't let me."

That was true. Caught out, I decided offense was the best defense. So I went on. "Why didn't you refuse him?"

"I wanted an affair."

"Did you want to marry him?"

"I thought so."

"Who broke it off?"

She wasn't going to tell me that. Nor would she tell me his name, or what he did, or where he lived.

"Besides, I don't even know where he lives now," she said finally.

"How old were you?"

"I don't want to talk about it anymore."

"Will you tell me sometime?"

She remained silent. All at once I felt it would not be a good idea to pursue this. I wanted her only to feel secure in her desire. For me. I had always wanted that and only that.

I looked at my watch. It was midnight.

"Okay. I'll sleep on the sofa."

We looked at each other. We were dueling. I didn't know if it was dangerous or not.

On DAY TWO of our engagement, plus possibly twenty minutes, I arrived groggily, in my pajamas, at the breakfast table, all set with cornflakes and a container of milk; Jen was pouring it into a pitcher. Aesthetic, not practical. A drop of milk, like a tear, spilled slowly over the lip of the pitcher; she didn't notice.

"In the old days betrothed people didn't even know each other," I said, stifling a happy yawn. "Look at us. We should be ashamed of ourselves."

She presented me with a bowl of cornflakes.

"May I have a spoon and a napkin, please?"

Immediately, she supplied me with both. After coffee I would check out her health more carefully. Maybe she should stay in bed. While on the subject of bed, I thought to ask: "Would you have liked your first lover to have been me?"

She slumped in her chair. She must have been asking herself what she had done to deserve this continuing interrogation. I didn't know whether I was coming or going in her affections, and hung my head in shame.

"Why are you torturing us both like this?" she asked.

"I feel fine. I thought we were both fine. I don't mean to hurt you," I told her honestly.

"You don't know what you feel. And I don't know what you feel either."

"Do you still love me?"

A silence, while she considered what to do with her power. Apparently, she decided, as was her nature, not to abuse it. "Yes."

"I suppose you didn't love me while I was interviewing you last night."

"Interviewing," she sniffed. A preposterous euphemism.

"I'll quit it," I declared.

"Please do, darling."

I remained pleased with my new-found maturity and good sense for about the time it took to wash down one more spoonful of cornflakes. Then I said, "Look, I won't get into it again, but why is it such a sore subject? You've got me now, I love you, this is in your past. What's his name anyway?"

"Ezra," she said, "but I don't want to be pestered with any more questions." It might have been as close to anger as I'd ever seen her. I don't think she knew what it was; I think she may have felt the past was not dead for her. Maybe it was up to me to help her bury it. And what I was doing was exhuming it.

Taking a cue from me—she accommodated to my subtler cues with entire grace—she gave me my coffee. She drank some weak tea.

"I can't believe we're home. And nobody knows. We could have an idyl, just the two of us," I ventured.

"Yes."

"What do you feel up to, darling?"

"Nothing."

In a moment, she was reclining on the sofa, with a thermometer in her mouth. "Don't talk," I instructed, while she wriggled, adjusting her nightgown, shifting so as not to encounter the ribbing of the cushions under her spine.

Her fever was down.

We sat side by side on the sofa, in our nightclothes, the morning sun streaming in through her windows—her place was light, mine was dim, day or night—holding hands. Slyly, I attempted to take her pulse without her noticing. She was mine. I was like a child with a toy. I wanted to experiment, to play. When I began to move my lips, counting pulse beats, the toy caught on and pulled its wrist away. That's what was the matter with me. I hadn't played enough games as a child. Harmless games. The ones I played entailed dodging motorcycles not disguised as bulls. Got into trouble. The games I'd play with Jennie wouldn't hurt either of us. At length, she said, "I'm going to shower and get dressed."

"Of course," I said expansively.

"Maybe," she said, surveying me, "you'll have to go back to work once we're married. I don't know that I'll like having you in my hair all day."

To me, the prospect she seemed to be discarding sounded idyllic. "You work. That'll give you enough privacy. By the end of the day you'll come running home to me."

"I thought maybe I'd quit my job when we got married, and learn to cook."

"Many women combine the two," I said.

"Can we settle this some other time?" she asked, shifting around in her bare feet.

"Absolutely. You're the one who brought it up. I'm a flexible, reasonable man."

She blew me an ambivalent kiss, on her way to the shower. I luxuriated on her sofa. Soon I would be her protector, legally, and she would become domestic out of gratitude. I wasn't sure, given her nature, just how the miracle would come about, but found it miracle enough to be in love, in love with a girl, like Jen, as fine as she, and assumed the rest would follow according to God's great, if not always apprehensible, plan. She emerged from the shower in white terry cloth.

"Come here," I said, holding out inviting arms.

"We'll waste the day."

"So what?" I hadn't been so happy since I'd had to stay home from kindergarten during a measles epidemic. Free. I had an uneasy memory of feeling this free once before, more recently, and learning afterward that I'd been swindled.

"Do you want to go back to bed?" I whispered.

"Later," she said. Then she whispered something I couldn't hear.

"What? Tell me. Honestly, I didn't hear you."

Very shyly: "I want to make a ceremony of it."

I released her, held her at arm's length. Her eyes were large, her expression somehow subtly changed. The emotion reflected in her eyes might have been in that moment something unassimilable. Suddenly I decided we each needed to be alone.

"I'll go home now," I announced with dispatch. "I'll let you rest, I'll pull myself together. Then we'll check in with each other, midafternoon or so."

"Sure." But she wasn't sure. After I'd showered and dressed and gathered back my things from her closet into my suitcase, she trailed me to the door.

"Don't look so desolate," I said, worried.

"I'm not desolate."

She reached for me, and I held her. I kissed her, stumbled down the stairs, and I was gone. I came back in the afternoon, of course, just as I'd said I would, but later—much later. She told me that she'd cried. With the closing of the door, she repaired to the sofa, sank into its tangled sheets, flung herself upon the cushions and, pressing her face against them, sobbed as she had not done since—Ezra.

WHEN I GOT HOME, the phone was ringing. It was Davey.

"How is she?" Davey asked.

"She's home. I think she's going to take it easy today."

After a pause Davey said, "I thought you'd be with her."

I told him, with some irritation, that I had been, virtually nonstop. "Besides," I said testily, sensing reproach, "I had to come home to do the work of the world."

"What's the matter with you?" Davey asked. "Didn't you have a good flight home?"

"Exhausting. I came home to rest for a couple of hours."

"What's wrong?" Davey asked.

"I'm going to marry her. Thanks for putting me up to it."

"She said yes, huh?"

"Yes. On the plane."

"You having second thoughts?"

"No. I'm not having any thoughts at all." That was true enough.

"What's eating you?"

"Say, would you mind holding on a minute while I close my door, drop my suitcase, and get out of my jacket?"

I did what I said I'd do—didn't I always?—and stopped also to splash cold water over my face. Just like Audrey's party, the night I'd met Jennie, after I'd thrown up. The memory took its place neatly alongside my other non-thoughts.

I returned to the phone, and sat down before I picked up. I slouched and stretched my legs, just letting the receiver dangle. Then, in panic, I said to Davey, "You still there?"

"Of course," said Davey. I heard a voice in the background saying, "It's long distance."

"I thought you were at the lab," I said penitently.

"No, I'm home."

"Could I speak to Libba?" I asked.

Davey laughed. "All she does is gurgle and coo."

I listened raptly to her little baby breaths and whimpers. Maybe Jennie and I would have one of our own, just like Libba. If it weren't a replica, I'd place it out for adoption. But chances were it would be. Jennie and Libba had so much in common. Davey got back on. "Look, can I tell Betty your news?"

"Wait. Am I doing the right thing? I think she's too good for me."

"That's a normal way to feel."

"You sound like Carl. Who knows what's normal?"

"What is it, Jack?"

"I'm dazed," I said, finally coming to grips with it. My brother would understand. "I can't do anything right, I can't do anything wrong. Someone loves me. I feel as if I'd taken a wrong combination of drugs."

"Have you taken anything?" the chemist asked swiftly.

"No. Don't be so damned literal."

"I wish I were there," Davey said.

"So do I. You're not going to tell Betty any of this, are you?"

"No. Now listen to me. Calm down. Drink some camomile tea."

"Am I going to be all right?" My collapse had taken me past tight-lipped and proud adolescence into early childhood. Davey's voice, filtered over the long-distance phone, was my mother's skirts. The ones that had never been there to cling to. I didn't care. Not with Davey. I wasn't proud. "Dave—will I be all right?"

"You are all right. Take some deep breaths." I remembered those, the standard family instructions for emotional crises. They worked, particularly if one trusted the giver.

"I'm trying. I need a drink."

"Not in the morning, you don't. It's a big thing, getting married," Davey said. "You have to get used to the idea. So does she. But you're good for her."

"How do you know?"

"She trusts you. Let me put Betty on."

So. No time to give me a choice in the matter. But there was none. I knew that.

"Jack," she said, "I'm thrilled. I like her so much."

"She likes you too."

"Oh, I wish you were still here. We could go out and celebrate. Shall I ring your mother? And Rita?"

"Please don't tell them right away." I knew I shouldn't be saying this to Betty, but she was there.

Davey came back to the phone. "How're you doing?" he asked. Before I could reply, I heard Betty's voice in the background, too close to the phone. "This call is going to cost a fortune."

Addressing myself to Davey, I said, "I think I'm okay. Your wife is right. Next time, call collect. Especially if there's any chance I'm having a nervous breakdown. Repairing me eats up time and money."

"We'll talk later," Davey said. "From the lab."

I put the receiver down. I didn't want to hear him say good-bye.

Jennie's line was busy. Telling all her girlfriends and her mother. Now I was really hooked. Tomorrow we'd better shop for a ring. Maybe her boss would know of a place where you could get one wholesale. I put on my old corduroy pants and a nice wool sweater.

I dialed again. Jennie's line was still busy. Well, the simplest thing would be to go there. She wouldn't mind. She'd be happy to see me. I shouldn't have left her alone. We could have spent the morning making love, or just lying in each other's arms.

I walked in a slow and measured stride toward her place. I bore the heat of the sun. The nearly ceremonial pleasure of it. Diffused through my limbs. I touched the stoop on a brownstone. A proud, ancient grain. Proud rock. And so I came to another brownstone, Jennie's, fronted by iron grillwork that I had never really noticed before. I had twenty-twenty vision now, after all these myopic years. I studied the grillwork, stroked the metal. I pressed the buzzer. I waited for longer than was comfortable, and she buzzed back. I went upstairs and, seeing the door ajar, let myself in.

AT TWILIGHT, in a darkened room, she told me softly, "Time to go home."

I leaned down and kissed her. I gripped her shoulder.

"I'll call you tomorrow," I said.

So I went to my place, slept alone, rent by nightmares. Nightmares that I was betraying Jennie. Strange, large women peopled my dreams, and I lusted after them, tried to subdue, bring them to their knees, with my whip. They eluded me and scorned me. Then, just as one was about to succumb, I awoke with a chill, slept, and woke again. And so on, through the long night. In the morning, at last, the dreams shaken, I vowed that I would not honor Jen's requests to sleep alone. We belonged together; at night too, at night especially, whether she knew it or not, liked it or not. I gulped horrid-tasting morning coffee. Why had she wanted me to go "home"? Home was the two of us together. At night. Wasn't she, then, betraying me? Probably not. She loved me. She was overloaded and wanted her privacy, she had said. Wanted to think her own thoughts, she'd said. It was not unreasonable; I had to allow it. But I was sure her private thoughts had traveled in the night air through the city streets, filtered into my dreams, and became the stuff of my nightmares. I called her. A sweet, sleepy voice answered the phone.

"Hi," she slurred. "What time is it?"

I looked at my watch. "Seven-thirty."

"Why're you calling so early?" All befogged, and still loving.

"I miss you," I said, steadied by the sound of her voice, my panic receding. "Why don't you come over here? We'll draw up the lists and make all those phone calls."

"Soon," she said, exasperated. Apparently she trusted me enough to be ill-tempered in the morning.

The downstairs doorbell buzzed. Joyously I buzzed back, and waited at the door. Upstairs bell rang, and I flung open the door. There stood a pimply young man from Western Union.

"Sign here," he said, shoving the telegram at me along with the piece of paper for my signature. I scrawled it and closed the door. I'd better sit down for this, whatever it was. I opened it:

WE SEND YOU OUR BEST WISHES FOR YOUR HAPPINESS.
SIGNED MOTHER, RITA, CARL, AMANDA.

I felt a chill of guilt. I should have phoned them. I'd meant to. Just forgot. Betty and Davey must have told them. Oh, Christ. I reached for the phone, held the receiver for a moment, then decided to call Mother first, the criteria being simply seniority and diabetes.

"Hello?"

"Mother, it's me."

"What's wrong?"

"Nothing. I'm sorry to wake you. I forgot about the time difference."

"Oh. Well, what is it?"

"I'm so touched by your telegram. I was going to call you, but things have been hectic here."

"All right," she said, adding tonelessly, "congratulations."

"I'm glad you're happy for me," I said, taking the bull by the horns.

"Carl and Rita and I thought about it and decided it was the best thing to do, under the circumstances."

"What was?"

"The telegram."

"Jennie and I want you at the wedding. You really made a hit with her."

"Yes," said my mother. "She doesn't have much to say for herself, but I suppose you do most of the talking."

"Do you like her?" I was reduced to begging.

"I hardly know her. You both were here and gone in a flash."

Outside my apartment, in the corridor, doors were slamming; people were leaving for work. I heard scratching sounds on my door. Jennie must have been standing there for some minutes and was trying to signal me.

"I think Jennie's here, Mom. Do you want to talk to her?"

"Another time," she said.

I sprinted to the door and opened it, losing one slipper in the process.

"My mother's cold and rural. Is your mother cold and urban? Which kind of mother would you prefer?" I asked.

PART 2

PART 2

THE LAW: There were two wedding ceremonies. The first took place in a judge's chambers with Barney and Audrey as witnesses. I kissed my bride—the kiss landed not on her lips but on her cheek. After some congratulations were exchanged in this utterly colorless, comfortably bland setting, we declined Barney's and Audrey's suggestions that we all have a drink. Jennie, quite simply, wanted nothing more than to go to her own apartment and prepare for the ceremony that, for her, would matter. Ceremony two. That was the one our friends and families would attend, which was why I looked forward to it merely as a retread, as a piece of grotesquerie. All that mattered to me, as Jennie and I now legally wed went our separate ways, was that tomorrow's rite would be witnessed by Davey and Libba. Betty would be there too.

Not Rita and Carl and Mandy and Mother. Mother's diabetes, you know.

When I got home, my irritation with my absent bride suddenly flared. What had thrown me was her seeming recoil from me, her apparent anger during the ceremony. Probably it had only been terror.

I telephoned her. Nine rings. I counted them. Mid-ninth ring, she answered. "What do you want?" she inquired.

"How do you feel?" I asked.

"Fine."

Obviously, she was not prepared to acknowledge that any important event in our lives had just taken place.

"What were you doing before you answered the phone?"

"I don't see that it's any of your business. I answered the phone as quickly as I usually do." And she broke into sobs. "I'm not sure—" She stammered.

"You're not sure of what?"

"Not sure I can do it," she faltered.

"Well," I said, "we can have today's civil ceremony annulled, go through with the religious-though-secular-as-possible non-denominational one tomorrow, and then, after a brief interval, have that one annulled too." I wasn't quite sure of how one went about getting annulments—did you need one for each ceremony?

"I don't want anything annulled," she sniffled. "I love you," she said. "It's just that I have no one to talk to."

WE HAD FOUND a small Unitarian chapel with a minister who agreed to perform the ceremony with little unction. His name was Turbot. I didn't know whether to call him "Reverend" or "Mister." For the occasion, Jennie had bought herself a lovely powder-blue dress. Let's see, for the society columns, the dress had an abridged scoop neckline, long sleeves, and a hem that fell just below what she considered to be her bony knees. "Everybody's knees are bony," I had assured her. But these days she was not at all receptive to any comments, whether reassuring, flattering, or neutral. I was apparently supposed to keep silent, to be the mirror that did not talk back. Well, the hell with all that. The dress was becoming. The shoes on her feet were a subtle beige. Her face was lit with happiness. Her rebellious hair was held in place by two delicate tortoise-shell combs and a garland of flowers. I had changed socks and, of course, underwear. Otherwise, I looked ashen.

The assembly of well-wishers was a mixed one. A few stray buddies from my bachelor days on the magazine, a few innocuous girlfriends of Jennie's. Surprising how few friends we both had. Someone, not her boss, who looked suspicously like an old beau, with a calf-like look of longing. From Jennie's side of the family: there was her regal mother, Belle, all buttoned up to mid-neck, Belle's fiancé, Rich, who was steadying Jennie's arm in preparation for the short walk down the aisle, and Laraine, her sister, with a boyfriend who claimed to be a character actor. My family, Davey and Libba, with Betty holding the infant. They took their places, and in the brief interval of hushed whispers and other modes of unease, Betty handed Libba over to Davey, who cradled her in his lap. At the time I thought that was a very thoughtful touch on Betty's part; I would have arranged the scene exactly that way myself.

Jennie had just consented to love, honor, and obey me when a wail echoed through the chapel and stopped the members of the wedding party dead in their tracks. Davey, child in lap, swiftly rose and left the chapel for an anteroom. My heart sank. Jennie's vows had been spoken in a whisper that projected, however tremulous. My vows at that moment of Davey's departure with Libba were nearly locked in my throat. The Reverend fixed me with a baleful stare, and I choked them forth, promising to cherish with a faint heart. Barney swayed in the non-breeze. But, my vows uttered, he was able to hand me the wedding band. I slipped it on Jennie's finger. She became radiant. Where was my brother? I wanted him back before this ceremony ended. But it was about to end. Turbot was intoning, and we were declared man and wife. Jen beamed at me, and we kissed.

Audible gasps of relief all around. Jennie and I, hands clasped, made our way back down the aisle into the ante-room, where we stood briefly with the wedding guests. I was numb with what I thought was resentment of Jennie's need for ritual, which I now knew I experienced as cliché. As my father would have done. Another thing about my father: he was not pious, about anything. My mother was, about every-thing, and now about her diabetes. It was her new religion. I did some rapid translation: I did not believe in God. I wanted my mother. Christ.

I craned my neck to greet these people. Audrey was dressed in a dark mauve that could double for funerals. "Come," I said. "Let's go downstairs for the reception." Belle stretched her neck upwards to kiss me; I leaned down to make it possible. My new mother-in-law's lips were aston-ishingly sensual. They lingered and made sucking sounds. I drew away.

Audrey looked at me quizzically. "You want a kiss from me too?"

"Downstairs, at the reception," I snapped.

"This isn't very well organized," Audrey said. "You all should have gone downstairs immediately and formed a re-ceiving line."

"It's lousily organized," I said. "My mother-in-law didn't lift a finger."

"And your mother's not even here," Audrey observed.

"That's right. Jennie and I are virtually orphans."

"Don't have a baby right away," said Audrey.

I shoved my hands into my pockets and tried not to look as confused as I felt.

Downstairs, Belle and Davey headed our way. I braced myself, wondering which one would arrive first, and prayed that if it were Belle I would be able to summon control over my mood. Fortunately, it was Davey.

"Don't go," I pleaded automatically.

"I'll be back in New York, maybe on business, soon," he said.

"We'll put you up," said Jennie. We had settled on my apartment as our joint home, and we decided we were going to be hospitable. "You'll be our first guest."

He bent to kiss her. "I'm so glad for Jack."

We went over to say good-bye to Betty, holding Libba who was struggling and squalling in her mother's arms.

"So we'll see you soon," I said to Betty.

"No," said Betty. "It's really too much to travel with Libba, Jack. It's exhausting for her and for me, you know." I knew. "So unless you get west, this is good-bye for a while. Till Libba's older." Libba began to whimper, and inwardly I whimpered too.

"Let's get going as soon as we can," I said to Jennie, choked with something oddly like grief at my brother's leaving. "Bride and groom are allowed to vanish into thin air, before the party's over. You haven't arranged for anything like rice, have you?"

"Oh, no," said Jennie in horror.

And so, to an absence of fanfare and rice, we left the wedding that Jen had wanted. To Penn Station for our Metroliner reserved seats. To Washington, for our honeymoon.

W<small>E ARRIVED AT</small> the Dupont Plaza Hotel seconds before room service shut down for the night. There was a small refrigerator with an ice tray in the room, and a large double bed. Musty but cozy, somehow. I decided I was going to like it. The train ride had been dull. Jen slept on my shoulder most of the way down, moaning from time to time in a way that sent shivers down my spine. I sat rigid, so as not to awaken this fitful and dream-ridden dozing. I loved her, I knew, but this lap of the journey into marital bitters and bliss was a bore. She remained groggy in the taxi, which took us to the hotel and again leaned her head on my shoulder. Obviously my shoulder was not a comforting pillow, and if she didn't break this habit of leaning her pretty head on it, she'd have a permanent stiff neck. And I was sick and

tired of all ailments, mine, hers, my mother's, and all patients' in all hospitals everywhere. In the room, she sat on
the bed looking terminally exhausted while I tipped the bell-
boy and made an urgent request for a bottle of champagne
and a bucket of ice. I didn't want to fool with the ice tray—
God knew how stale those cubes might be—and a bucket,
which, though it later turned out to be waterproof card-
board, seemed more festive.

While we waited for the champagne, we engaged in a
discussion of the chicken sandwiches that had been dinner
on the train. "The mayonnaise was funny," Jennie said.

"What do you mean, funny? It was just a normal flat-
tasting soggy piece of meat between two soggy pieces of
Wonder Bread."

"I know. I'm not talking about the sandwich itself, I'm
talking about the mayonnaise."

"Was something wrong with it?" I asked.

"Oh, no. It just overwhelmed the taste of everything
else."

"If it did that for you, then you were lucky," I said.
"Worst sandwich I ever ate. Anything else on your mind?
How did you like the grape juice?"

"It was okay," she said, answering me as if I really
wanted to know.

"Would you like to get into your nightie?" I inquired.
She was silent. "What's the matter? Isn't this all romantic
enough for you?"

"I think I'll unpack," she said.

"Go ahead."

"What's the matter with you?" she asked. There were
dark circles under her eyes.

"I just got married," I replied. "It will pass."

"You don't have to be so sarcastic," she said.

"I'm sorry. It's a defense, as Audrey would say. If I
dropped it, I'd be—"

"What?"

"Defenseless against you."

"I'm not against you. This isn't war." She stood there, looking ready to do battle.

"It feels like it," I said.

"What can I do?" she implored. "What should I do?"

"Unpack, and try to bear with me," I said.

"You look so unhappy," she said in despair.

"I'll be okay."

"I'll take a shower," she said.

"What an interesting idea."

She gave me a look of a trapped but fiercely angry animal, collected some things from her suitcase, and ventured into the bathroom, slamming the door.

I stared vacantly at the burners and the mini-oven that adjoined the refrigerator. I crossed the room, turned on each of the burners to make sure there was no gas leak, then turned them off. "What's cookin', good-lookin'," I hummed tunelessly.

I heard the sound of the shower pelting her body and the tub's floor. I needed to piss but felt that going into the bathroom would constitute a gross violation of privacy, hers and mine, and set a possibly dangerous precedent. But the need grew urgent, so I crossed the room, flung open the bathroom door, and stood at the toilet. I caught a glimpse of her through the shower curtain, looking soapy and, at the sight and sound of me, shocked. "Sorry," I said. "I couldn't wait."

"Okay," she said, modestly draping a washcloth over some valued part of her body.

"Sorry," I repeated when I was finished. "I'll wait out in the room."

"Okay," she said, "just please close the door."

I lay across the bed. I wanted to be clean too. But I wanted to lie in a bath, I wanted my back rubbed, my shoulders on which her unexpectedly heavy head had lain soaped, the back of my neck massaged. Then as I lay there came a knock at the door. It was room service with the champagne and the paper bucket. I tipped him and asked him if the radio worked. He turned it on, and some harmless music wafted into the room, opening it up a bit, giving it density and dimension. He smiled at me, as if he knew it was my wedding night. A tall Negro, with great grace and native courtesy. It had contagion. I felt faint stirrings of my gallantry returning. "Would you like me to uncork the bottle, sir?" he said to me. I nodded. "Please." He did it with skill. "Shall I pour?" he asked.

"No," I said. "I'll wait for my wife."

I thanked him more feelingly than I had thanked Davey or Betty, shadowy now, set against his courtly reality. Declining the additional tip I tried to press into his hand, he bowed out of the room.

The shower had been silent for some time. Jennie emerged, wearing a white terry-cloth bathrobe. I looked at her.

"Darling," I said, "sit down." She looked at me warily. I sat her down. My touch seemed to take the edge off her suspicion.

"Champagne?" she whispered to me.

"Yes. Can you take it on a nearly empty stomach?"

"It's not empty," she said. "I distinctly recall eating a chicken sandwich three hours ago."

I sat beside her and we clinked glasses, and sipped. "You smell sweet," I said to her, burying my lips in her hair.

"Don't," she sighed. "I seem to have an infection."

"Does it hurt?"

"I don't want to talk about it," she said.

I kissed her neck. "It'll get better, won't it?"

"Of course it will," she said. "I'm so glad we didn't quarrel on the train."

"What made you think we would?"

"We quarreled on the plane coming back from Indianapolis. When you proposed."

"Nothing to come between us this time. Is that why you slept so soundly? To ward off any annoying thing I might do?"

"I don't know why I slept. I didn't mean to abandon you like that."

"Our first separation. At least I had your head on my shoulder, so I had something tangible to cling to. More than a memory."

I poured us each a glass. "Will we kill the bottle?" she asked.

"That doesn't sound like you. Where'd you hear that?"

"Someone said it at the reception."

"You a little drunk?"

"A little," she said contentedly.

"Good."

"Don't take advantage." She smiled.

"I know the medical profession has forbidden sexual intercourse during our honeymoon. But I can . . ."

"What?" she breathed as I reached inside the terry cloth and clasped her breast. I opened her robe and brushed her nipple with my lips.

"That's all," I said, watching her grow apprehensive and excited at the same time, "for now."

I removed my hand. She refastened her robe.

"I feel so mellow," she said.

"Me too." I took her glass from her hand and refilled it. "Does Audrey know about your infection?"

"No."

"You lying?"

"No. I don't want anybody to know."

I stroked the terry cloth again, until I felt her thighs tremble.

"I feel so awful that we can't."

"This is nice too. Drink some more. It's really getting you relaxed."

Obediently, happily, she sipped. Utter trust was stealing

into this dim, strange hotel room, utter trust, one for the other, was flooding us again.

Jennie became tearful, and I took the glass away.

"It's the champagne. You're not really sad."

We set aside our glasses. I yawned.

"You know something?" I said.

"What?" she slurred kittenishly.

"We're sleepy as hell. If we don't get to sleep now, we'll have hangovers tomorrow and won't be able to stroll and look at the cherry blossoms."

"The cherry blossoms are gone. They went two weeks ago. That's what the taxi driver said."

"There must be other nice things to see. The Lincoln Memorial at night."

"We could go to the White House," she said, "and maybe see the Kennedys."

"Not if we don't get some sleep." I got to my feet, pulled her to hers, and drew back the bed covers.

Undressed, I lay beside her. I switched off the radio and the bed-table lamps. She kissed my shoulder. "You taste salty," she said.

"Don't taste too much of me. You'll get thirsty and there's no more champagne."

"There's water," she said.

We nestled in the strange, clean bed. We kissed. We slept. Wedding night, two.

HONEYMOON, DAY ONE, MORNING. I awakened to find myself in a cavern of unfamiliar proportions. My nostrils took in the faint smell of gas. I looked at my watch; ten, it said. Ten what? Day or night? Didn't I have an interview assignment at ten? No, it was something else. It had to do with my personal life. What was it? My personal life stirred beside me. I lay quietly for a moment, trying to take it all in. She had no clothes on, which was nice, but there was some interposition in force. What was it? I struggled to remember, and then remembered who she was. Jennie, who had a transitory infection. So much for lust. Thank God I was understanding and mature. I shifted position to get a better look at her. She was sleeping more soundly than I had ever seen her sleep before. Probably because she had fallen asleep dead drunk. How unwomanly, even if I had had a hand in pouring the booze into her myself, glass by refilled glass. I began to resent this naked presence beside me in a stuporous sleep. Her hair looked hopelessly knotted and snarled. She was facing away from me, in this nearly-repellent slumber, so I propped myself up on one elbow to inspect her further. Half-open mouth. Breath tinged by liquor. Trying to be charitable, I reminded myself that my own breath probably smelled too. She looked miniature and incapable and withdrawn into God only knew what kinds of unfriendly and fantastical dreams. Was she dreaming of rape? Why was her body arranged in this self-defensive position? With a chill of fear, I realized I was locked into something with this person for the rest of my life. A lifetime commitment, and life is long. If Jennie were not sleeping beside me in what I now knew to be a honeymoon hotel room, and if my brother had not returned to Indianapolis, I could pick up the phone and ask him to tell me if he'd felt the same way the morning after he'd plighted his troth. I got out of bed, not giving a damn whether she woke up or not, and staggered barefoot toward the bathroom. Inside, I looked in the mirror and liked what I saw. Much too good for the undersized and oblivious person sleeping in that comfy bed I was paying for. Lucky, she was, that I had pledged to take responsibility for her. She didn't even know her own limits, know when she'd had too much to drink. I left the bathroom to deposit the empty champagne bottle in the wastebasket, and to pour the melted icewater into the sink. I hesitated with the champagne bottle briefly, wondering if I wouldn't regret this, if we wouldn't want to keep it as a souvenir, then decided if she wanted to retrieve it from the wastebasket she could do that herself if she ever got around to waking up. I was not being particularly gingerly or quiet in any of these maneuvers, but she slept on. I returned to the bathroom, splashed water over my face, and stepped into the shower. With distaste, I noticed stray hairs, Jennie's unmistakably—I'd know them anywhere. The water pounded me full force; I needed this cleansing. When I emerged, washed in the blood of the lamb, a diminutive and not inimical figure was standing at the bathroom's threshold, wearing a familiar white terry-cloth robe. "Hi," she said, eying me as if she too was wondering what she was doing in a strange city, in a strange hotel room, with this stranger.

Neglecting the amenities, I inquired, "Have you got a hangover?"

"I don't know."

"What do you mean, you don't know?"

"I don't think I've ever had one before, so I don't know what it feels like."

"Headache?" I said, toweling myself vigorously.

"Yes, I guess," she said vaguely.

"Feel like throwing up?"

"No." She scowled.

"I guess that wasn't a very charming question," I conceded.

"No, it wasn't."

We stood there, she in her terry cloth, I in my towel, not knowing quite what to say to each other. We had to get used to being married. What was the trouble? The trouble was that she was underfoot, and though it wasn't her fault, I was having trouble getting used to the idea that this was a lifetime proposition. I wondered which one of us would die first, and which of the two alternatives I preferred.

"Why are you staring at me?" she asked.

"I'm not staring at you. You happen to be standing directly in front of me. Do you intend to stay there, or have you got any other plans?"

She sighed. "I honestly wish you were less of a grouch."

"Well, you won't reform me, so don't try. Many have tried, and all have failed, including my mother."

"I'm going to take a shower," she said, brushing past me into the bathroom. Her next remark I found inexcusably rude. "You left hairs on the sink."

"I think those are yours. They are long and kinky. I have a crew cut, as you know." I was delighted with this excursion into forensic medicine.

"I cleaned the sink last night," she said, "so those hairs are yours." To my ears she sounded viperous.

"Look at the tub, my dear, and examine the hairs you left there. They haven't budged since your most recent shower, and I had the water turned on full force."

"I know. It woke me up."

"My point is, nothing could dislodge them. Not even my shower, which, may I say, I am glad woke you up. I didn't think anything would. Or could."

"You might have tried a kiss," she said.

"One doesn't request those things," I lectured. "They are given freely or not at all."

"I don't know how I'm going to remember all these rules," she said.

"Use your mind. The trouble with you is that you are intellectually lazy."

She looked astonished. I think she thought she had been removed in her sleep to another planet. Whereas I felt, in my sleep, that I had been sentenced to life without parole. For the crime of consorting with women. I now knew that all her life, without actually saying so, my mother had been warning me against this and about this. Now another woman, Jennie, to whom I was also irrevocably bound, was muttering something.

"I know I'm not domestic," she was protesting, "but I don't think I'm intellectually lazy. I don't know what you mean. Honestly, Jack, I'm going to try my best."

"Promises," I said. "Go take your shower."

"I don't think it's wrong of me to ask you why you didn't kiss me awake."

What a big baby. But my temper was subsiding, and I felt myself beginning to relent.

"It's hard to awaken a sleeping beauty," I said kindly, "when she snores."

"I wasn't snoring," she said, horrified.

"That's something you couldn't possibly know. Just take my word for it."

She was mortified. I dropped my towel on the bathroom floor—thus establishing myself in front of an important eyewitness as possessing equal credentials as a slob—and went to kiss her. She returned the kiss eagerly, and the next thing I knew, my hands were groping inside the terry cloth. She panted and I pressed my hard-on against her, with full premeditation and force.

"What are we going to do?" she gasped.

I took responsibility for being four years her senior, an older man. "You go take your shower," I said, "and I'll go jerk off."

"I could jerk you off," she said shyly.

"Darling," I said, kissing her again. "Later. We're going to have a very ingenious and wonderful honeymoon." I gave her a little push toward the tub.

"Are you really going to?"

"I'll tell you later. Leave the bathroom door open."

She dropped the terry cloth on the floor, let me gaze at her naked, and went into the shower. I went directly to the bed, and with the most recent vision of Jennie imprinted in my brain, brought myself off with a quick and thudding, if lonely, sweetness.

As I lay there, the pulses of my body subsiding (erratically—I wondered if I would one day have a heart attack), I collected myself and thought next of Jennie. Moving from pulse to impulse, I rose, no longer erect but not uninterested either, and went into the bathroom. I stepped into the shower, and she gasped with surprise.

"Soap me there," she urged, intelligently sensing that I had not just dropped in to pass the time of day.

"Soap's an irritant," I gasped back, taking it out of her hand, and putting it on its little ledge. "How's my hand? Huh? Like that?" I steadied her. There was no rubber mat, and she was threatening to slip. "Lean against me," I said. I didn't have to tell her to part her legs. I kissed each nipple. "Close?" I asked.

She nodded yes. We went on like that for a while, she clutching at me, pressing my hand as it pressed against her, trying to wrap her legs around my thigh, but she was losing it. "I can't make it," she sighed in her subsiding heat.

"You're probably trying too hard."

"I don't want to be lazy."

We both laughed. "Just relax."

"But," she said, "I get all tense and turned on, and I can't relax. It's a contradiction in terms."

"Don't use polysyllabic words when you're sharing a kinky erotic moment with your husband in the shower. Try not to think."

"I don't want to be intellectually lazy."

I kissed her wet face. "Did you have any spasms? Did you get excited?" My questions were certainly exciting me.

"Oh, yes." What a great answer. Then I looked at her and took in her disappointment, her unmistakable posture of frustration.

"Does it feel awful now?"

"Not really," she said gamely.

I had an idea, which I would wait to spring on her. "Finish your shower and come back to bed."

"But we can't."

"We can too. I've thought of a way. A surprise. Hurry."

I went back to the bed, half wet, hoping the DO NOT DIS-TURB sign was still hanging securely outside the door, and lay there, feeling loving, feeling generous, hoping my scheme would work. Where had my earlier morning anger gone? Not to worry. Consistency was the hobgoblin of small minds, as

114

my grade school primer had brought to my attention once long ago. A lesson many times disregarded but always eventually remembered. I wondered if we were wasting time. The day would be almost gone, and we might consume it all lolling around in bed. Well, that's what honeymoons were for. It would be nice if, on our honeymoon at least, I could know for sure that Jennie could come. For starters, she came naked out of the bathroom, dampish, and dragging a sopping towel behind her, which I told her to leave on the floor. She climbed in beside me. "What a mess," she said, surveying the room. "We'll have to leave the maid an extra tip."

"Extra? For only three days? Cleaning up is their job," I groused.

This exchange was not precisely conducive to passion, so we dropped it with considerably more decisiveness than she had dropped the wet towel on the floor.

"What's your surprise?" she asked eagerly.

I hesitated. How was I going to put this? I realized I was in an area of ignorance and would have to play it blind. I didn't know how I could know her so well and not know the answer to the question I was about to put to her, let alone know how to put it.

I cleared my throat, wondering if my own unmistakably reviving lust was going to muck up my plan for her. "Jennie," I whispered, "do you, uh, masturbate?"

She shuddered. Knowing how much she disliked interrogation, I followed up the question with a gentle pass. "Yes," she whispered.

"I think," I said, "it would be a lot of fun if you did it now, while I watched. I'll hold you if you like."

She looked interested but scared. "I don't think I can," she said.

"Why not." It was not a question. She was allergic to questions, and I was determined to give her one hell of a honeymoon, which I knew I could do if I played my cards right and didn't obtrusively snoop.

To my intense relief she answered me. "I think about

certain things when I do it, and I don't think I could think about them with you here."

"Well," I said softly, "I'm going to be around for a while from now on, so why don't you just think them, or try to, and do it."

She was silent, possibly weighing pros and cons. I decided to get aggressive. "Do you want to tell me what you think about?"

"Oh, no!"

"Everyone has sexual fantasies," I said, and instantly regretted it. I had meant to reassure, and instead I sounded clinical, like Audrey or Carl. Now she'd never reheat.

But she moved closer to me, apparently not that much turned off at all. "Do you want to try?" I asked encouragingly.

She nodded yes. My lust was equaled by my curiosity, as it usually was. I waited, transfixed with anticipation, wondering what she would do, how she would look. It occurred to me that this was a first, of sorts. Once, as an adolescent, I had spied on Rita, who had stuffed paper in her bedroom keyhole to block my view if I should try anything that insipid—or did she on that occasion say "revolting"?—again. I hadn't seen much anyway, just some efficient and indistinct writhing, and the memory of it had been subsequently so overwhelmed by her mortified fury when she discovered she'd been seen, that the whole thing deteriorated into an ugly sibling spat, leaving my curiosity unsatisfied and utterly neutralizing my accompanying lust. Rita had a way of converting her own embarrassment into a weapon. Now she used it against me. So I suffered her wrath, and she had something on me—I was an incipient degenerate, a premature peeping tom—rather than I on her. Eventually, we both forgot that anything had been going on behind that keyhole; we remembered only that I, a sick and possibly dangerous boy, had peered through it. I'd been caught out when she'd finished before I had a chance to flee—she didn't rest one second after orgasm, but leapt fully clothed from the bed, flung open the door to execute quickly some other pastime or errand, and found me there, crouched and covered with guilt and shame. We repaired to the attic to have our quarrel, and she exploited the guilt and shame with such finesse that by the time she was finished I had quite forgotten that she'd had her hand between her legs, merely that I'd tried to rape her with my eye.

But this was different. My Jennie. I brought my mind back to the present; I had not thought of that episode in years. Different. I had a right to watch Jennie. I was not spying on her, I was going to be, one way or another, the agent of her pleasure's release. I wanted this for her, for us. She was looking at me anxiously. In my reverie, I had, of course, deserted her for Rita.

"I'm here," I said. I stroked her hair.

"Are you really going to watch?"

"If you want me to. I think it'll be fun."

"What shall I do?"

"Do what you usually do, and if I get in your way, let me know."

She turned and lay on her belly. She did something with the sheet, adjusting it to her body so I was put on notice that she was not accustomed to touching herself—or to being touched—directly. She lay there quietly, a corner of the sheet tucked between her legs, her hand passively in position, but not yet applying pressure to the sheet, to herself. "I feel shy," she whispered. I touched the small of her back, pressed it, encouragingly.

"What time is it?" she murmured.

"What time were you born?" I asked.

"Midnight."

"It's midnight, July 22, 1938." Her birth date.

And then she began, slowly, acutely aware of my presence, nearly paralyzed by it, and then her rhythm caught and her breath quickened. I watched, immensely touched, my hand now resting lightly on the small of her back, applying no pressure, letting her apply her own. I scarcely dared to breathe. To do so would be intrusive. Briefly I told myself that I should mark the moment, it might be the most noble of my life, and then I forgot about myself and watched this child, no teen-ager, my trusting bride fling herself into her self-created passion, chasing her sensual peaks like a kitten going after a ball of wool. She paused to rest and looked at me anxiously. I directed her head back toward the pillow and whispered to her to go on. I kept my hand on her back and trembled myself as her thrusts quickened, and she flung herself into an orgasm that differed utterly from anything I'd ever seen her experience with me before. She was utterly silent, only the long exhalation and the remaining deep shudders of her body. Had she ever come with me? With me, she would utter little cries, she would speak my name, she would behave like an actress of some gifts temporarily down on her luck and slumming to make a buck in a dirty movie. Was it, or was it not, acting, with me? This, what she had done for herself, surely wasn't. And it was so unlike anything with me. So private, so quiet. This post-orgasmic stillness frightened me.

Was she ashamed? Afraid? I had initiated this little experiment, it had succeeeded, and now that I'd discovered radium I had no idea what to do with it. Nobility was not one of the more stable or predictable of my attributes, and I was beginning to experience some worry that I would become accusatory and lose my temper. I bit my tongue so as not to say, Listen, kid, does this happen with me? Did it ever happen with anyone else? Why can't I bring you off like that damned sheet? Why can't that energetic hand flip pancakes or peel potatoes? "Jennie, darling," I did say, "Jennie, Jennie, darling." She turned over and reached for me, and as we embraced I knew that the film of sweat that covered her body was something my impatient, potent, versatile thrusts had never drawn from her. I was jealous of her damned hand.

HONEYMOON, DAY ONE, AFTERNOON. Hand in hand we walked along Pennsylvania Avenue. Jennie was shyly hoping for a glimpse of the First Family. I was acquiescent, thinking it rather touching, and not myself crazed by any wish to go to the National Gallery or the Smithsonian. Obviously, there was nothing to see behind those graceful gates except greenery and the White House itself.

"We could have arranged for a tour," Jennie mused.

"We can do that tomorrow," I said placatingly, hoping she would forget about it. I was experiencing a sensory overload, and thought it would be prudent to keep strange sights and sounds to a minimum. It was all I could do to support the fact that the young woman beside me, holding my hand loosely but lovingly, was now my wife.

"If we stand here too long craning our necks, we'll get

arrested," I said, hoping to get her away from the White House and back to the hotel, or anywhere but here.

"I'm not craning my neck," she said.

"Yes you are," I said. "You're hoping to see Jacqueline, wheeling the baby carriage." Photographs had appeared in *Look* magazine.

"No, I'm not."

"We could have gone to Vegas and seen Eddie Fisher," I said.

She gave me a quizzical look. Possibly she wondered why I was not more tolerant and gentle.

"I'm teasing you," I explained.

"Quit it, darling. I feel too vulnerable to you."

"Aren't we going to have any fun any more?" I wheedled, secretly alarmed that in so many ways we didn't seem to know how to share pleasure.

"This is fun," she said mildly, confirming what were temporarily my worst fears. "Isn't it?" she asked me.

"Not for me," I said, bravely deciding to be truthful. "I get sort of a kick out of you rubbernecking at celebrities, but frankly I'm bored."

"It's true, we haven't seen them," she agreed, trying to hide her disappointment that the moment was unshared, that I wasn't interested in her wish to be as pretty and as apparently maternal as Jacqueline. "What would you like to do?" she asked anxiously. I had succeeded in inducing a slight guilt. "Do you want to go to the National Gallery?"

"No," I said.

"The Smithsonian?"

"Okay," I said. So we got into a taxi and went off to see Sheridan's horse, stuffed. She was enchanted. Couldn't take her eyes off the results of the taxidermist's labors.

"There's the *Spirit of Saint Louis*," I was able to say, a few minutes later. Still later, "There's *Kitty Hawk*."

Her willful insistence that we subject ourselves to the exhibits of First Ladies' inaugural gowns, worn by embalmed-looking mannequins, aroused in me a kind of vacant irritability that I tried my best to subdue. Why was I so restless and unindulgent? I decided I'd had my fill after a dutiful inspection of the frock once worn by Rachel Jackson, but Jennie dragged on, right through Bess Truman, Mamie Eisenhower and then as much as she was evidently going to see of the beautiful Jacqueline. It was a perfectly appropriate feminine curiosity, but I nursed a sullen suspicion that it boded ill, that it was wasteful and frivolous and signified a greed for possessions I would be unable to supply, and that it lacked intelligence. The latter notion seized me: Jennie might be shallow and not good enough for me. I yanked at her arm.

"Let's get out of here," I said.

She smiled up at me, oblivious to the Rorschach and IQ tests I had just secretly administered and which she had just flunked. "Okay," she said agreeably, "where do you want to go?"

"I'm hungry," I complained.

She looked at her watch. It was midafternoon, too late for lunch and too early for dinner.

"Let's find a cafeteria," she suggested reasonably. I found this rationality also offensive. Why wouldn't she quarrel with me, so that I could sting her with a few well-placed words? Instead she said merely: "What would you like to eat?"

"A hamburger," I growled.

Some time later, we sat facing each other in the booth of a clean, well-lighted eatery. I munched on something that dripped and was supposed to be medium rare, and she fastidiously sipped at some iced tea, ignoring a muffin that had also been ordered to accommodate the one dollar minimum.

"What's on your mind?" she inquired politely, after a while, apparently having decided that she had suffered my silence long enough. I was suffering too, from something I didn't understand, but I was also enjoying the power this silence gave me over her. At least I hoped it gave me that power. Did she feel bothered? I couldn't tell. That was also annoying.

"Nothing," I said, having decided on a strategy designed to help me keep my head above these turbulent emotional waters.

"Nothing?" she said teasingly. Seductively, I looked at her. She didn't seem particularly vulnerable. Matter of fact, she looked quite pleased with herself. Trusting, secure, and even fond of me.

She reached across the table and touched my hand, gave it a little tug. "Too much sex'll kill you, you know," I said.

"Who's thinking about sex? You're eating a hamburger," she said.

"You're thinking about it. You think about it day and night."

"I do not. I work during the day," she said, a low blow, since she did, and I slept nearly regularly these days till noon. "And at night I'm tired and like to read a little and go to bed."

"Good," I said. "Thank you for filling me in on your habits and preferences. I wish we knew each other better. The honeymoon is a bad place to begin."

"Jack," she said, worried now, "what's the matter? Do you think we've made a mistake?"

"No." That was true. I was glad to have her there. Who else could I needle if not her?

"What's wrong with you, then?"

"Are you going to take over the cooking when we get back home?" "Home" had to be choked out.

"I guess so," she said, looking frightened. "You'll help out a little, won't you?"

"Yes."

She sighed and looked attentively at her wedding ring. She kept her gaze fixed upon it, as if it were a surrogate for me.

"Why aren't you wearing the engagement ring too?" I asked, to remind her that the real thing was there too, and that it was me.

"I thought two rings would be ostentatious," she said

automatically, truthfully. She was incapable of serious lying.

"I feel lousy," I finally said. "I don't know what we're doing here. I toured the Smithsonian six months ago, and I don't need to see it again. Why the hell didn't we go to Europe?"

"We couldn't afford it," she said. Neither of us had ever been to Europe.

"We'll be able to go to Europe sometime," she said to me, sounding both wistful and reassuring.

"I'm sorry, darling. I'm not good enough for you. This honeymoon is a bore."

"I'm not bored," she lied.

"Aren't you? Some of the time?"

"We don't seem to have planned it," she admitted. "I feel sort of lost."

"Scared too?" I asked hopefully. I didn't want to be alone with my fear.

"Only scared that I might not make you happy."

"Are you happy?" I asked.

"I don't know," she said. Now she looked properly scared. But the look appeared a few seconds too late to reassure me. I was forging ahead, from fear to anger and beyond.

"Why didn't we come here, if we were going to, when the cherry blossoms were in bloom?" I said, polishing off the last of my hamburger. "This is ridiculous."

"We were rushed enough," she said. "It doesn't matter."

Only the first part of that two-part proposition was true. The second half was dead wrong: It did matter. I looked at the crumbs on my plate miserably. How could I make this up to her?

"Tonight," I said, "we'll rent a car and drive over to the Lincoln Memorial and see the Washington Monument's reflection in the pool. It's beautiful. Have you ever seen it?"

"As a child," she said. "My father took me."

"You want to do that, then?"

"Yes. But we'll take a taxi. We don't have to rent a car."

"I thought we should do something lavish."

123

"The champagne was lavish," she said softly.

"Want some more tonight?"

"Maybe."

I paid the check and we walked out into the sunlit street. It was warm. Her cheeks were flushed and her eyes were bright. She took my arm, as if I were someone she knew very well and felt she had reason to trust.

"I've got an idea," I said. "Let's taxi over to the Jefferson Memorial. I want to show you something."

She looked happy. We had a plan. What I wanted to show her, and did, when we got there was the engraved utterance on the monument's dome: "I swear upon the altar of God eternal hostility against any form of tyranny over the mind of man." She looked upwards, scanning the words, entranced. " 'I swear upon the altar of God . . . ' " she said. " '. . . eternal hostility,' " I said with conviction. Another set of vows. Just what we—she perhaps more than I, but I too—needed. Wherever and whenever possible: a ceremony. I liked this one. I had with her help created it. Never mind if we were at cross-purposes. Reverend Turbot, with his words like shackles, was out of sight and mind. Out of my mind anyhow. I liked it that way. Out of my mind. I took her hand. It was cool and dry, her reciprocal grip unexpectedly firm. Clutching? Affectionate? I couldn't tell. I tried not to let it worry me. And I failed.

But in the evening we looked in awe upon the figure of Lincoln, the second Father of this country. "With malice toward all and charity toward none," I quoted solemnly.

"It's the other way around," Jennie said, amused.

"My God," I said, somewhat stunned. "Do you suppose I've got dyslexia?"

"No," she said. "You just wish you had more money."

The monument to the first Father of our country, opposite, glimmered in the reflecting pool.

We took a taxi back to the hotel, and for the first time paid attention to the statue of Admiral Du Pont himself. It had been visible from our window, but we'd been drunk and too absorbed and tired to notice the night before. "He lost an entire fleet during the Civil War," I informed Jennie. She tried to look sympathetic, and failed utterly. She couldn't even manufacture interest. Further, she didn't even try to stifle her yawn.

"Don't yawn when I'm talking," I snapped.

"Don't talk when I'm yawning," she said, apparently under the impression that she was topping me. But she said it with a finality that signaled that she would not be drawn into a quarrel. Not easily. I'd have to do something really rotten to unravel the happiness we had woven for ourselves in the latter part of the afternoon, touring the shrines. Maybe I'd have to slug her. Instantly, looking at her as she preceded me toward the elevator, I wanted to kill myself. How could I possibly even think of inflicting harm upon this child-woman, entrusted to me successively by a judge and the Reverend Mr. Turbot, with the compact sealed, the final blessings conferred by the likes of no less than Thomas Jefferson, Abraham Lincoln, and the Father of our country himself: Washington. Past twilight of honeymoon, day one.

Back in the room, we noted nervously that the bed had been made and fresh towels supplied. We wondered, neither of us voicing the concern aloud but obviously both experiencing it, if our used sheets and towels had been more than routinely scrutinized before their removal. She stood there, indecisive for some moments. I observed her from a reasonable distance, feeling somewhat like a zombie myself. Two zombies. Fit for the Smithsonian. Newlyweds, and already relics. How to keep each other entertained for two more whole days. I felt thankful that she had not given up her job. I didn't know how I'd keep my sanity having her hanging around all day. Evenings I could tolerate. Especially if she'd prepare tasty casseroles in advance and serve them to me nicely, with some poise and self-assurance, at dinnertime. I presumably would be spending the afternoons either out on assignment or at the typewriter, pounding at the keys non-stop for, say, two or three hours. Maybe sometimes we'd have guests for dinner. It would be nice to be proud of a wife who could cook. Read? What in hell had I ever seen her actually read except poetry?

"Do you want to have dinner in the room or downstairs?" I asked.

"I don't know." She was staring at her suitcase.

"For God's sake, unlock it or do something," I said. "Don't just stand there."

"Please stop trying to get me to bicker," she said, and retreated into the bathroom.

I stretched out on the bed, consciously resenting for the first time that on our honeymoon we couldn't screw. Was that what was back of my irritability? My feeling of nonbelonging? Or was it something she was making me feel, either deliberately or by her very nature beyond her power to control.

She emerged from the bathroom looking embarrassed and sullen. A heavy sigh. "Maybe," she said, "when we can afford it, I'll go into therapy."

"What?"

"I thought I'd see a shrink," she offered, trying another version of the same eerie and utterly unexpected notion.

"Why?"

"What do you mean, why?"

"I mean just what I say! Are you trying to drive me crazy?" I sprang up from the bed and strode toward her. "You can't just say a thing like that and not expect me to want to know any or all of your reasons, which add up to why, that's why!"

"I think I may have problems," she said, simultaneously backing away from me and looking me in the eye.

"What are they?" I was frightened.

"I don't know. I want to go home." She began to cry.

"Jennie, Jennie, come lie down." I drew her to the bed, and we lay down together. I held her and stroked her hair.

"Maybe we should have gone to the islands," she wept.

I was silent. We had considered Puerto Rico and decided we couldn't afford it. But it might have been better than this, if this was driving her into the hands of an alienist. I said as much.

" 'Alienist' is out of the last century."

"So is that so-called science. It's mumbo-jumbo, it's my brother-in-law, it's everything I can't stand. Why are you doing this to me?"

"I have problems," she sobbed.

"So you just said," I said, trying to hide my alarm, trying to be comforting. "What is it? Something old? Something new? Something borrowed?"

She smiled in spite of herself, but her cheeks were still wet with tears. Her eyes filled, and the tears spilled over again. I wondered if these little scenes were deviously conceived schemes to get attention. But she was crying in earnest, and I knew Jennie was not a cynic. Why should she be so insecure, when she so obviously had such quality? Her insecurity bewildered me. Had I contributed to it? If so, how much? Significantly? Or had she brought it to me, and was it something with which I unwittingly toyed and inadvertently exacerbated? "What is it?" If she didn't tell me, I'd go mad, I thought.

"Probably something old," she said, continuing to whimper.

"Do I make it worse?"

"When you get mad at me or make fun of me or won't talk to me, it gets worse."

"What is it?" I demanded to know. Last night it had been the site of her infection. Tonight it had floated up into her psyche.

"I don't know what to call it," she said.

"Goddamn it, everything has a name," I said.

"Don't yell at me," she wept.

"I'm trying to help you," I said helplessly, and held her tighter.

"If I knew what it was, it wouldn't be there," she said illogically, but I was not about to quibble, this was far too important.

"If it's upset you so, why now, why don't you let me help you, why do you want to go to a shrink?"

"So she can tell me what it is."

"She? Who is she?"

"An analyst. Audrey told me about her."

I spluttered, "A woman analyst? You confided in Audrey? And you won't tell me?"

"I didn't confide in Audrey. But she knows I get upset, and she gave me this woman's name."

I paused to consider this new, unfolding calamity.

"Would you rather," she asked, "I see a man?"

"No, no," I said. "A woman's fine." As long as she's not a dyke, I thought. "What's her name?" I asked, beginning to feel real despair. I couldn't afford medical bills.

"Dr. Selfridge."

"What's her first name?"

"Helen."

Oh, God.

"Isn't this something you could just talk over with me? Or Dr. Smidler?" I begged. Smidler was her family doctor. Anything but an analyst referred by Audrey named Helen. Helen Selfridge. Selfridge, selfish. How pretentious.

"I would if I could," she said.

This was impossible. I had just found her, she had just entrusted her life and her self to me. I didn't want to lose her to people who committed people to bughouses.

"What upset you now? Was it anything I did?"

"No," she mumbled, burying her face in the crook of my arm, getting my sleeve slightly damp with her dripping eyes and nose. "It's not your fault," she said, moving away from me just a trifle, possibly sensitive to my concern about the sleeve of my second-best of only two suits.

"It's not your fault," she repeated hollowly.

"That's good to know." It was, but it was also hard to keep the edge of anger out of my voice.

"Really, it has nothing to do with you."

"Well, would you mind telling me why you came out of the bathroom on the second day of our marriage and announced that you needed professional help?"

"I didn't plan to tell you now. And I know we can't afford it now."

"Right. So why bring it up now?"

"I want to feel I can tell you everything."

That was a new one. Tell me everything. She had the most secretive soul of anyone I knew.

"You can, you know," I blundered on.

"I can't. It isn't fair to you."

"Why now? That's what I can't understand. What in the hell happened to make you come up with this now?"

The answer was a totally indistinguishable mumble.

"What?" Using a mild version of brute force I made her look at me. She was unexpectedly strong in her resistance, putting me briefly in mind of her morning's energetic—what shall I call it?—self-abuse. By this time, feeling myself terribly wounded, I'd forgotten what my most recent question had been, but her frightened eyes showed me that she hadn't. Bringing to bear an extraordinary degree of self-control, I kept my mouth shut.

"My infection," she said finally, and slumped back on the bed.

"Don't you turn away from me like that," I said, gripping her gently enough, and again making her face me. I could shuttle between the two roles, good cop and bad cop, if I had to in this first serious marital crisis. "We've been all through your infection. What more is there to say about it?"

"I still have it," she sobbed.

"I know. So what?"

"I means we can't."

"I know. I told you I didn't mind," I said, though by this

time I did. And if she was inconsiderate enough to have it, did she have to make it worse by making hysterical scenes about it? But I would keep all this to myself. "Isn't it getting better?" I asked.

"I suppose so."

"So what are you fussing about?"

She flung herself out of reach, and I went scrambling after her, taking most of the bedspread with me, and pinned her to the bed.

"Jennie," I said, "you're not being fair to me. Why are you dwelling on it like this? I told you I don't mind." I could talk myself back into believing that, if I had to. It would be better for both of us, my being senior to her, and her custodian as well, if I reverted to my original unselfishness.

We were both breathing hard.

"I think it might be psychosomatic," she finally said.

"What might be psychosomatic?" I asked, wondering which one of us was possessed of the greater idiocy.

"My infection."

"Oh, Jen, stop it," I pleaded. "Please try to put it out of your mind."

"I think my mind brought it on," she said.

Was she crazy?

"Jen," I pleaded, "I'm worried about you. You're not being rational."

"I'm not?" This worried her.

"No. You're hysterical. Please. Don't make it harder for both of us."

She looked at me with wide frightened eyes. I didn't want to reassure her any more. But her fear instructed me. "I don't mind, darling," I said over and over, in my mind's eye seeing my unwomanly cold mother, seeing the first-grade teacher who had in anger once hurled my schoolbooks across the room for some misdemeanor, seeing the reproof in the eyes of my parents as Dr. Frame taped my ribs on his examining table. "I don't mind," I said to Jennie. "I don't mind."

W<small>E DECIDED</small> to have dinner in the room. Neither of us felt in condition to expose the raw self to the hotel dining room. "Goddamned expensive," I said gallantly, scanning the room-service menu.

"What time is it?" she asked.

"Nine," I said, looking at my watch. It had been my father's watch. Why had he died so young?

"How much time do we have to order?" she asked. Her thoughts were of time, mine were of death and money.

"A half-hour. I'm going to get another bottle of champagne. Do you think you would like that?"

She nodded eagerly. "Can we afford it?" she asked.

"Of course. What do you want for dinner?"

"The fish," she said meekly, diving quite correctly for the cheapest offering on the menu. "What will you have?"

"The fish." We exchanged glances, then decided we couldn't look each other in the eye, since we understood each other in this moment far too well.

"It sounds very good," she said.

The menu bore a fancy description in French, of which she probably didn't understand a word.

"Right," I said. I dialed room service and grandly placed the order, checking with Jen about beverages only to discover that for the present she would have no tea or coffee; she was looking forward instead to champagne. Matter of fact, I was too. I needed to unwind.

"It'll be here in about twenty minutes," I said. "And they'll send the champagne up about ten. What do you want to do now? Take a shower?"

"I thought we'd just sit together and talk."

"I think you'd feel refreshed if you took a shower." I needed in the worst way to be alone.

"Maybe you're right," she said doubtfully. The decision, however ambivalently taken, propelled her into the bathroom. I was thus able to repair to the slightly mangy but large and comfortably upholstered chair by the window, sink into it, and put my aching head in my hands. Maybe I should have taken the shower. The pounding in my temples grew worse. I went to the mini-refrigerator, with teen-age gangleader's force dislodged a couple of ice cubes from their tray, wrapped them in my handkerchief, and went back to the chair to hold them against my head. A compress, it was called. I'd made a cold compress. The throbbing subsided— if no one else was going to take care of me, then here was proof that I was able to take care of myself—and I looked out of the window at Admiral Du Pont. Had the sculptor captured him before or after he'd carelessly lost his fleet? The familiar sound of Jennie's fiercely powerful shower water reached me. Maybe it wasn't good for her to subject herself to that much pounding, even if it was only by water. They used water to torture people. I'd read that somewhere. One drop at a time, drip-drop, drip-drop, or with hoses, full force, and worse. The first attacked the mind, the second the body. The ice was melting in the warm room and my hot hand. A drop of water rolled down my cheek to my collar. I decided to get into more comfortable clothes. Not pajamas—that would unsettle room service—but I'd find something. I yanked off my tie, unbuttoned my shirt, and began to feel better. I pulled from the suitcase a T-shirt that Jennie considered sexy and put it on. I decided that she should ask her boss for a raise when we got back to town, so that I could buy another suit. Two weren't enough. I'd be back at work full-time. I knew I was damned good and would be again very employable, so that it didn't seem too much to ask of Jennie at this stage that she underwrite a new pair of pants. The ones I was wearing could not be put at further risk. She might want to sit on my lap when she came, dampish from the shower, or they might get rumpled if we tussled on the bed again, whether quarreling or trying to find suitable compromise positions for making love within the limits imposed by Jennie's tedious infection. The poor thing. I must continue to try to be understanding. I got out of my trousers and put on my corduroy slacks, the ones with the ribbing of which she was so fond. They could absorb whatever moisture might ensue from whatever we did next, cry, sneeze, make some version of love, or spill dinner.

Room service knocked seconds after I'd zipped the corduroys' fly. Simultaneously, the water from the bathroom was turned off, and Jennie called out, "Jack."

The knock sounded again. Jennie called to me again. Oh, Christ, what to do. "Just a minute," I yelled in the direction of room service, and went toward the bathroom. I flung open the door and inspected the wet, tiled premises. She was huddled in the shower. "What is it?" I said. "Can it wait? Room service is here."

"I forgot to bring something in here to wear. My robe," she said. "I'm shivering."

"Okay, I'll get it for you. Stay where you are and let me let the guy in. Stay in there," I yelled to the mermaid as I slammed the bathroom door and headed for the other door, where the fish was undoubtedly cooling in a rapidly congealing sauce.

The same Negro gentleman was on duty, and with a deferential but self-respecting nod, he wheeled his cart into the room. I helped him set things up, for no reason at all volunteered, "My wife is in the shower"—he nodded understandingly—signed the check and tipped him.

"I'll bring the champagne up a little later," he assured me. I felt, for the first time that day, taken care of. Somewhere, if the presence of this man could steady me, I'd find my moorings.

"The sooner the better," I said. "Give us about a half-hour."

He nodded. "Enjoy your dinner, sir."

"Thank you. I'm sure we will." Like hell we will. He left, leaving me briefly desolate. There was something I had to do. What was it? Oh, yes, get her her robe. Fuck it. Let her get her own robe. I went back to the bathroom, opened the door, and said: "He's gone now. You can come out."

"Would you please get me a robe?"

I hesitated. If I refused, she might begin to think she had problems again and brood about going to the shrink. If I brought it to her, the worst that would happen was that I would suffer mild annoyance. Courtship was nearly over. It ended with the honeymoon, and we were in the honeymoon's dead center. It would soon be over, and she'd better get used to the idea that I was not going to wait on her.

"I'm cold," she said plaintively.

"So is dinner," I said shortly. "Where's your robe?"

"Either in the closet or my suitcase."

"White terry cloth?"

"Yes."

I went to the suitcase, found nothing, then to the closet and found it hanging there, still slightly moist from the last time she'd dried herself incompletely. I sniffed at it, apprehensively wondering if it had mildewed, but it smelled sweet, like Jennie. I brought it to her, she thanked me, and then with far too many little shrugs and scrunchings about got it on. I stood there watching, sensing that it was expected of me. "Why don't you get dressed for dinner?" I asked, when the performance was over.

"Oh, do I have to?" she said. "I feel comfortable now."

"Your comfort is the only thing that counts, but I thought the waiter might wonder when he brings the champagne."

"Wonder what?" she said, astonished. "We're married."

"Well, we don't have to look so married all the time, and I don't know why he should see you half-naked. Get dressed."

"You're jealous of the waiter?"

"I don't want him to feel teased."

"Hotel waiters are used to this," she exclaimed, this worldly person from New Jersey. "It's like postmen delivering packages early in the morning. You always open the door in your robe."

"You do?" I said. "Well, now you don't. Not any more. Get dressed. Please. I'm hungry."

"Okay," she said. She removed underwear from the suitcase, a dress from the closet—I noticed that it was the one that buttoned down the front, the little minx, talk about teasing—and returned to the bathroom. I sat down at the table the waiter had wheeled in, and began to eat. She was out two minutes later, looking flushed, pretty, and fully clothed. Also annoyed that I had not waited for her. She said as much, putting it in the form of a question so as not to arouse the fury of the animal she was married to, now salivating over his long-awaited evening meal.

"I'm starved," I told her. "And I can't sit forever waiting for you to poke around getting dressed."

"You're the one who told me to get dressed."

"I didn't tell you. It wasn't an order. It was merely a suggestion. A sensible one. Sit down and eat your fish before it tastes like chewing gum."

An unfortunate reminder of a previous contretemps. After a pause, during which she apparently made the decision to forget that part of the past, she sat down and delicately picked at the sole amandine.

"How is it?" I asked solicitously.

"Quite good," she said, nibbling baby-sized morsels, resisting, I assumed, the temptation to play with the sauce, which by this time had the consistency of clay.

"That's a pretty dress," I said, clearing my throat. It was, in fact, one of her prettiest. Lavender. She had left the three top buttons unbuttoned, obviously not out of the need for haste, because she'd carefully put on some pearl button-earrings. That took time, so she'd left herself unbuttoned for some other reason. Pretty irresponsible.

I returned to my food. I had lost all appetite for anything except peace and quiet. Probably sensing that I had withdrawn my attention from her for the moment, she removed one of the earrings, with a heavy sigh.

"They pinch," she explained, laying it on the table.

"I don't want to hear about it," I said, my mouth full.

"Maybe I'll get my ears pierced," said Jennie.

I winced. "That might hurt," I said, with some genuine concern. "And I read somewhere that it carries a danger of hepatitis." Or was I thinking of tattooing?

"How can that be?" This conversation reminded me of someone, someone I knew I didn't like, but I couldn't just then identify either the person or the reason for the dislike.

"The equipment they use to do it might not be sterile," I said. "Can we talk about something else?"

"Certainly," she said.

Mother. That's who we were sounding like. Jesus. Married less than seventy-two hours and already bored and boring.

"Button up your dress," I said.

"Why?"

"It's chilly in here. You might catch a cold."

"It's not particularly chilly," she said. But she buttoned herself up anyway.

"No coffee," she remarked at length, having inspected

the tray for some minutes before announcing this discovery. I had guessed what she was looking for but had made the decision not to help her out in the interests of helping her develop something resembling self-sufficiency. If she couldn't take care of herself, who in hell was going to take care of me?

"That's right," I said. "You specifically said you didn't want any."

"Oh." A pause. She appeared to be trying to concentrate. "I remember."

"Good. If you're thirsty, drink some water." I shoved a glass toward her. "The champagne will be up soon."

"I'll wait for the champagne," she said. Then she said, "Coffee would keep me awake anyway. It's just as well."

My mother, all over again. Is this what marriage did to women?

"Do you think," I asked not unfeelingly, "that you could shut up?"

"Why?" She seemed honestly amazed.

"Because you're getting boring, that's why. If you have nothing to say, don't say it. I'm eating my dinner, which I've waited for long enough, and I don't want to hear about your sore ear lobes."

"Sorry," she said, trying not to be overtaken by humiliation, and returning to her dinner. Evidently she gave the matter brief thought and decided to fight back. "You're not all that interesting either, you know. 'It's chilly in here,' " she mimicked me. " 'Button your dress.' Why don't you button your lip?"

I stared at her. She was savage. I felt I had been slapped.

"Jennie," I pleaded, "don't turn into a fishwife."

"Then don't turn into a bully. Neither of us has to be interesting all the time."

Bull in a china shop. Someone else, once, after sex, had made that accusation. I had been younger and had gone a long time without, and I had thrust two or three times, indifferent to the fact that I was hurting her, and after I'd come she'd remarked pleasantly, "Bull in a china shop." I'd never seen her again.

"Jack," Jennie said, drawing me back into the present which, given the set of memories I possessed, seemed infinitely inviting, "take it easy. You're so high-strung."

"And you," I said, still belligerent but getting calmer, "I suppose, are not. Talking about going into analysis and everything."

"Let's just forget it," she said.

"You're reminding me of my mother," I confessed.

"How? I don't look like her."

"She's boring."

She was hurt but determined to remain in control. "We're all boring sometimes."

"Which is why I think we should both shut up."

"Okay," she said. "A five-minute moratorium on conversation. You keep track of the time."

I looked at her with some respect, and then looked at my watch. A minute or so passed. She was working her way through dinner. The plate bearing the remains of the poor fish was moved aside, and her ice-cream sundae was unveiled. She spooned it into her mouth, gave me a brief smile, made little sucking sounds, and then delicately spooned in some more. I desperately wanted to ask her if she liked it and if I could have some, but it was against the rules. I broke them anyway. "Is it good?" I asked.

"Are the five minutes up?" she said.

"Yes."

"You're lying."

"Right. Jen, I'm sorry."

"About what?" She held a spoonful of ice cream across the table for me. I swallowed it. Awful. Far too sweet. I gave her back her spoon.

"I'm sorry I compared you to my mother."

"I'm not a boring person," she said. "Nobody has ever accused me of that."

"Are you mad at me?"

"No," she said. That seemed to take care of it. I drew a heavy sigh of relief.

"I take it you like that sundae."

"Yes," she said.

"Don't eat it all. The vanilla ice cream will coat your stomach, and I want to get you drunk."

"You do? Why?"

"I don't know. Because it's fun."

"Can I unbutton my buttons?"

"Of course. Do whatever you want. Take off that other earring, I don't want anything to hurt you."

She removed the earring but kept the buttons buttoned. She took me up on the suggestion that she forget about the rest of her ice cream in the interests of getting drunk. We sat there, smiling warily at each other.

"I should have ordered some wine with dinner," I finally said.

"Expensive," she said. Oh, God, there was no help for it. We were inexorably turning into a couple of bores. Was there no help for it? And why? Then I remembered. Boredom was a cover for rage. Was that what we felt for each other?

"I love you," she said softly.

"I love you too."

"We can feel different ways about each other at different times," she said, "but that doesn't make the love go away."

Dime-store psychology, but not unhelpful. "I guess you're right," I said half-hypocritically, taking her hand.

Saved by the knock on the door. "The champagne's here," I said, leaping to my feet. "Can I tell him we're finished with dinner?"

"Yes."

I readmitted this kind man, who smiled benevolently at Jennie. I tried to remember if he'd seen her before. She beamed at him. Her look of trust returned. If only she didn't have such a transparent face, such a transparent nature. The girl couldn't dissemble to save her life. Then I remembered how disposed to secrecy she was, how enigmatic she could

139

be, the recent scene in which she refused to divulge some nameless psychological trouble, and I wondered what I could be thinking. I was sitting with the Sphinx herself. I looked at her. She gave me a frank look of joy. We aided the waiter in small ways, getting up from our chairs so that he could roll out the dining cart and set up the champagne. Again, I let him uncork it.

I tipped him. He returned the tip. "You took care of me earlier, sir. Enjoy the evening."

"Thank you," I said. He was taking care of me.

"Good night," Jennie said. "Thank you."

"You're very welcome, ma'am," he said, taking her in with a knowing glance, one that acknowledged her rare and precious grace.

He left, leaving me stronger. With a steady hand I poured the champagne, filling Jennie's glass to the brim.

"I can't drink all that," she said a moment later. I'd gotten her on the bed—we were both sitting up at the foot of the bed—and I wanted to get her silly and giggling.

"Sure you can," I said. "Go at it."

She drank. "Nothing's happening," she reported after a moment.

"Keep drinking," I said.

"Are you sure you want me to get drunk?" she asked, appearing somewhat more than usually anxious to please.

"No," I said, not knowing what I wanted or quite what I was talking about, "I just want to get you relaxed."

She sipped at the stuff, a little too frantically. I didn't care. I drank, slowly, keeping an eye on her. I was too done in to relax her myself. Everything I said to her or felt about her was wrong, and whatever was wrong with it got transmitted. You couldn't lie to her. Not really.

"How do you feel?" I asked when she'd emptied her glass.

"Giddy," she replied, handing it to me for a refill.

I smiled my Lothario smile and obligingly refilled her glass.

"I don't understand why you want to get me drunk," she

said, drinking accommodatingly anyway. "And now I've had one and a half to your one."

"So, you can count, you sly boots," I said, fondling her.

"Don't. You'll distract me," she warned. Sexual excitement would distract her from drinking? What a peculiar inversion. One drank to get sexually excited, and once one was on that road, it was only with the greatest reluctance that one turned one's attention to something else.

"I can't imagine not wanting to get turned on," I said, stroking her over her skirt.

"You often don't want to," she reminded me, while she chug-a-lugged her champagne. "You push me away when you're tired or you think I'll be, or when we can't . . ." She faltered, continuing bravely, "Like now."

"I'll think of some surprise," I said, continuing to caress her, even though she had evidently gone safely numb and was concentrating on her champagne.

"You should drink too," she said. "To keep up with me." She had downed her second glass.

"Okay." The next drink I poured would be her third. I looked at her questioningly. She nodded okay.

"I'm dizzy," she said presently.

"Slow down a little," I said. Then I ventured: "I'm wearing your favorite corduroy pants. Don't you want to cop a feel? Of the ribbing?"

With her free hand, the one not holding the glass, she stroked my arm. She loved my arm, she had told me. She loved every part of me, she had told me. I had my doubts about that, but had in mind an experiment that might resolve them once and for all on our honeymoon. We could go back home, knowing that we had fought, sought, and won.

"My trousers, Jennie," I said, taking her hand. "Don't you want to stroke my trousers?" I put her hand on my knee, and she inched it up, somewhat absently, along my thigh. I decided she was trying to placate me; she was really more interested in the champagne. But the champagne was necessary to the experiment. What to do? The champagne inside her had to be mobilized in support of this experiment. How to coordinate it? I cupped her breast. "We can't," she said, holding out her glass.

I let go to refill it. She began to drink again, her hand at absolute rest, nearly dead weight on my thigh. I unbuttoned her three top buttons.

"Aren't you going to drink with me?" she asked.

"Sure." I picked up my half-empty glass, took a casual sip, put it down on the table, and returned to her buttons.

She obediently let me undo the next four, and then she said: "Somehow this doesn't seem very personal."

"What doesn't?"

"The champagne. Your unbuttoning me."

"It's very personal. You'll see."

"What are you going to do?" She was beginning to slur. "Beat me?"

"What in hell have you been reading? You've been under the counter in some dirty bookstore in Times Square."

"No," she said, pausing to swallow. "I read Krafft-Ebing when I was in high school."

"Really? A social-studies assignment?" I asked wryly, but secretly fascinated.

"No," she said, turning to me, giggling. "It was strictly extracurricular. If they'd known about it, I wouldn't have made the Honors Society."

"You made the Honors Society?"

"Yes. Didn't I ever tell you?" She was delighted by my obvious pride.

"No," I said tenderly, kissing her warm cheek, warm from champagne, a lousy brand but I wouldn't tell her that. "You're so modest. So lovely. Beautiful. Smart."

"Beautiful?" she breathed.

"Yes. And smart," I said, wondering why she didn't need her usual reassurance about that. I decided to ask her.

"I know I'm smart," she said confidently, still swilling the champagne.

"So what did Krafft-Ebing do for you?" I inquired.

"Turned me on," she said. Her fourth glass was nearly drained.

"Did you do anything about it?" I asked, returning to her buttons.

"Yes. Don't get fresh." She was very loosened up, looser than I'd ever seen her. This was delightful. I began to hope that I wouldn't have to guide or force anything, that she'd seize the initiative when it occurred to her.

She held out her glass. "It'll be your fifth," I said, beginning to feel a little guilty.

She seemed nonplused by my count. "So?"

"I don't want you to have a hangover. It'll spoil tomorrow." I think she decided in that moment that a hangover was far preferable to anything that had happened on this sober day.

"Let's risk it," she said. "You drink too."

"Okay," I said, pouring us each another.

"You're drinking them awfully fast," I said.

"It was your idea."

"Yeah, but you're giving it total support. Go a little easy. Just sip, don't guzzle." She flinched. I knew what it was. She didn't like the word "guzzle" any more than she liked the word, say, "turf." So I repeated: "Sip." She did.

I undid two more buttons and unhooked her brassiere. Her hand trembled, but her drinking rhythm didn't break. "Dynamite breasts," I breathed.

"This is so good," she said.

I was a little worried. She was awfully absorbent. The goddamned stuff seemed to focus her on it entirely. I hadn't meant for that to happen. "You don't want a hangover tomorrow," I said.

"I won't have one," she said.

"You ever have this much to drink?"

"Of course. We drank lots of beer at college."

"I think maybe you should stop."

"I don't understand what's the matter with you," she said, and I began inwardly to tremble. The last thing I could support was another misunderstanding, let alone quarrel. "You wanted me to get a little drunk."

"Yes," I admitted, "but I thought I'd really have to coax you. You're taking to it like—"

"A duck to water," she said, flashing me a brilliant smile. "Now don't tell me I'm boring." She slipped off the top of her dress and tossed her brassiere on the floor. Briefly, I wondered if she were schizophrenic. I'd never seen her this bold.

"Why are you staring at me like that?" she asked.

I sipped some champagne, merely to moisten my throat which had gone unexpectedly dry. "You've taken half your clothes off, and you ask me why I'm staring."

"Oh, God," she said, suddenly penitent, her confidence melting as swiftly as it had built. "You don't like me this way."

"I like you that way a lot. I just didn't know you had it in you."

"You think I'm a hussy?" she asked, hope returning.

"I don't know that I'd use that word," I said. "We'll check out Krafft-Ebing when we get home and find out just what it is you are."

"Maybe they have Krafft-Ebing in the bed-table drawer," she said, reaching, her breasts swaying as her body swayed. They looked almost too beautiful to touch. I sat quite still.

"I think they only have a Bible in that drawer," I said to her. "So don't go to a whole lot of trouble to get it open."

"No trouble," she said, producing a Bible and some hotel notepaper.

"We could read this aloud to each other," she said, "or I could write thank-you notes for the presents."

"I don't think we got enough presents," I said. It was true. It just hadn't occurred to me before.

"Most of them are at my place," she explained carefully, groping in the open drawer for a pen and coming up with a pencil. She hadn't yet given up her apartment. "They're sent to the bride a lot of the time," she informed me with some self-importance. "And we'll get more. Your friends haven't sent any."

"Yet," I said. She nodded.

"Put away the notepaper and the Bible," I said. "You're being silly."

We struggled, but it was playful, just borderline erotic. I got the stuff back into the drawer and slammed it firmly shut. "There's stuff in the Bible we could read to each other," she said. "Sexy stuff."

"With our luck we'd hit plagues, prophets, and warnings against spilling one's seed into the ground."

"Onan," she said.

"My smart. No wonder you made the Honors Society." I kissed her. She was really quite entertaining this way, and she knew it, and the pleasure she took in my own pleasure made her all the more endearing. I kissed her again, but she had in the meanwhile retrieved her glass, so I got some champagne spilled on my T-shirt.

"Oh!" she said contritely. "That's your favorite T-shirt."

"It's yours, as a matter of fact. Don't worry. I don't think champagne stains," I said. She put her hand over the stain and rested it there. I think she could feel my heartbeat.

"Do you want me to take off the rest of my clothes?" she asked.

"Okay. And how would you feel about taking off mine?"

"We can't—" she began.

"Shut up," I told her, and again said, "I have another surprise."

"Will I like it?" she asked.

"You liked the last one."

She persisted, "But will I like this one?"

"You might love it," I said. Probably it was the most ignorant thing I'd ever said.

"Well," she said, "whose clothes should I take off first?"

"Yours," I said, thinking I would have made an excellent teacher. Secondary school. Teen-agers. What in the world had ever made me want to become a magazine editor or reporter?

"I want another glass," she said.

"Okay. Take off your clothes. I'll pour."

She stood up, half undressed, and clasped her head.

"Dizzy?" I said.

"Yes."

"You feel okay?"

"I feel wonderful."

"Stand there. I'll help you out of your clothes, then you can have more champagne." I'd lost count of how many she or I had had by then. I only knew that I was relatively sober, and she was quite unfamiliarly drunk.

She was quite good about shedding her garments, with one of my steadying hands there to keep her on her feet, and the other helping her out of her dress, slip, and the rest of it. She smiled at me gratefully.

"Why don't you help me get undressed," I said casually, "and then we can just lie here and get relaxed with some more champagne."

"I feel so dizzy," she giggled. "I'm not sure I can help anybody do anything."

"Take some deep breaths, and for God's sake, don't pass out. I've got some nice plans."

We lay down, side by side, and she sort of helped me out of my clothes. I felt somewhat disappointed that she didn't show interest in the various fabrics that she normally loved to stroke, like a sensuous kitten. But maybe that was infantile sexuality. We would have to check Krafft-Ebing or—I hated to admit it—Freud to be sure, but if her lack of interest in the corduroy ribbing and the rest of it signified the beginnings of mature lust, that would be absolutely dandy. We lay in each other's arms. She didn't seem much more interested in my skin, in the subcutaneous heat it was beginning to exude, but that was okay, I thought. I'd just give her a little time. Maybe she needed to be just a touch more relaxed. I reached for her full glass. She sipped at it, showing a similar strange reluctance even to do that, which moments before had engaged and delighted her totally.

"You feel okay?"

"Sure," she said.

She put the glass down heavily. I kissed her and put my thigh between her legs. After a few moments of pressure, during which I couldn't tell whether anything at all was happening to her—I knew damn well what was happening to me, and was hoping silently that she'd take the trouble to look—she said: "Do you want me to jerk you off?" I had pressed myself against her. Damn it, why didn't she just do it, why'd she ask?

"Get on top of me," I said. She lay on top of me. That was nice. We'd do it that way sometime. She sighed. I rolled over so that we were now side by side. She looked at me, mystified. Apparently she sensed she was flunking the course. I'd let her take a makeup.

"Jennie?"

"Yes?" She was drunk, curious, frightened, and at a loss about what to do with our two bodies—hers which knew little about how to get what it wanted, and mine, clearly the more educated of the two.

I told her what I wanted.

She was outraged. "What?"

"Honey, please. Lots of girls like it. You must have read about it in Krafft-Ebing. I'm sure we've talked about it."

"What girls?" she spluttered. "I'm your wife."

"I haven't asked you to do anything immoral," I said. "It's just something I love and I've done it for you."

"That's because you wanted to," she said.

"Yes. I love doing it. You might love this. Please."

Trepidantly, she slid down the edge of the bed, then rested her head forlornly on my knees. What a martyr. What could I do to help her get her courage up? I wanted all sexual difficulties and misunderstandings and blocks solved on our honeymoon, that's what it was for. I wanted to return to

New York knowing that sexual mistrust, sexual cross-purpose lay behind her, us. I'd help her the best I could, give it my best, but she'd have to help herself too. Jack helps those who help themselves. "Help yourself to another glass of champagne," I said. This she did with no difficulty at all, and downed it promptly. "You okay?" I asked. She nodded. "Just take a deep breath. It's easy. Really. I think you might love it." I directed her head downwards. Timidly, fastidiously, she touched me with her tongue. She licked it. So shy. Apparently thinking that was all there was to it, she slid back up and, her face level with mine, said: "Okay?"

I smiled and kissed her. "Okay for starters."

"What do I do?"

"Well, I wish you'd take it in your mouth."

"No!"

I decided I'd better prepare myself to give this up. I'd married a sexual hick, I might as well resign myself to that. If she wouldn't let herself be taught, I'd find some woman who liked it and catch a little of it on the side now and then. She felt my erection go down, as I was thinking these resigned infidel thoughts, and that alarmed her. She so badly wanted to please me, to disappoint neither me nor herself. We were married, she loved me. She didn't want to deny me, I asked so little of her. It must have gone something like that, her private script. For she reached for me and let my soft prick harden in her hand—it didn't take much—her glimmerings of interest thrilled me and I hadn't had nearly as much to drink as she. "That feels so good," I gasped, trying to keep my breathing in check so that she wouldn't think she had a wild animal on her hands or in her mouth. "Jack," she whispered urgently, stroking me almost too fiercely, "what do I do if—"

"If I come?"

She nodded. I caressed her hair. I wisely decided not to refer to "other girls" and their delightful preferences, so offered her a choice. Three choices. "I think you might love it," I said; it was becoming an incantation. "But if you really don't want it, I'll pull out just before I come. I know how to, I promise you."

"Maybe I won't mind the other," she said.

"I think you might love it," I said. I honestly thought she might. "Drink a little more champagne. Spill it on me, why don't you, then taste it, and—"

"Jack," she said, "they'll throw us out of the hotel."

"Honey, it's okay, just sip some champagne and take a deep breath."

She did both of those things and then did the thing she was so afraid of. I helped her, or thought I did, by indicating that she could monitor the extent of this invasion of her lovely champagne-wet mouth by gripping me with a gentle fist. Briefly I thought I was indeed a helluva good teacher, and that she was a fine student, damn near ready for a diploma, I wasn't sure whether high school or graduate school, and then as she went at me I didn't think anything at all. "Great," I said hoarsely, nearly aching with this bliss. "Heaven," I sighed. "Uh, watch your teeth." She obeyed. She even got passably good at it. What a good teacher I was. Then, thoughtlessly, I permitted to happen the thing I'd promised her I wouldn't. I lay there gratefully, exhausted, ready to draw her to me, to clasp her in my arms. But she gave me a look of panic and fled into the bathroom. I heard water running. I should go in, I thought, maybe she's upset. I did manage to get up and stagger to the bathroom door. She'd locked it. I knocked. By way of response, water from the faucet was turned on with a mighty force. Was she sick? I remembered how sick I'd been at Audrey's party the night we met. I'd hold her head. I knocked again. "Jennie? Darling, are you all right? Let me in."

No answer.

"Are you all right?"

"Yes," came the feeble reply.

"Can I come in?"

"The door's locked."

"I know that. Unlock it, sweetheart."

"No."

"Why?"

Silence.

I pounded on the door, heedless of the neighbors on either side. She, however, was alert to the possible consequences of any late-night disturbances and inevitable ensuing complaints, and flung open the door. She was pale as death. "Shhh," she said.

I took her in my arms. "What's the matter? You been sick?"

She nodded, turned, sank to the floor, and, bracing herself, vomited again. Her arms were wrapped around the rim of the toilet bowl. I lifted the seat, held her head, told her to go ahead, be sick, I was there.

"I'm so sorry," she finally gasped.

" 'S'okay, hang on, nothing to be sorry about."

I didn't want her apologies, and I was too filled with remorse to offer mine. Poor thing. If I'd known, I'd have left her alone. What did I know, after all. Only a couple of girls had done this for me, willingly, loving it, or so I thought.

"I'm so ashamed," she said, and then was sick again. When that spasm subsided, I applied a cold wet hand towel to her face and neck. I sponged her gently.

She turned to me. "It wasn't you," she gasped. "It was the champagne."

"Maybe both," I said diagnostically, having no idea of whether I was right or not. "Maybe it's a lousy combination."

She moaned. I positioned her head. God, I thought, maybe I should call a doctor. The poor thing. When she was finished, I wet the towel again and bathed her face and neck and shoulders. "Maybe I should get into bed," she whispered, utterly done in, utterly spent. Curiously, holding her, I had felt no nausea. I just wanted her to be well, and if vomiting—vomiting her entire experience of this doomed evening—would help, then let her be sick until her offended body and spirit were purged.

At length, I helped her into bed. I put a wastebasket on the floor near the bed so she could just lean over if she had to. She fell asleep quickly. I looked at the champagne. Maybe she was right, maybe it had been the booze, not me. We—she—had killed the bottle. I was learning another side of intimacy. I gave myself no grades. I was my own quite fallible and bewildered teacher.

IN THE MORNING, she couldn't face me and was, besides, miserably hung over. She claimed she didn't want anything to eat, apologized repeatedly for her sins of the night before until I silenced her by putting my hand gently over her mouth. "Why don't you go down and get breakfast," she suggested.

"I don't want to leave you alone," I said.

"I'll be all right."

"It's just as easy for me to call room service," I said. "If you don't want anything to eat"—she shuddered—"maybe you could sip a little juice."

"No, darling," she said. "Please go down."

I got it. She didn't want the sight, sound, or smell of food anywhere around her, nor did she feel she could make herself look sufficiently respectable for the room-service waiter.

What the hell, I decided. I wouldn't be gone long. "You're sure now."

"Yes," she said. "I just want to sleep."

Honeymoon, day two, morning.

I ate a hearty and heavy-hearted breakfast, charged the bill to the room, and with considerable anxiety and remorse hurried to get back up to check up on her. She was sleeping. The room was dark, musty, non-aromatic, and she lay sprawled across the bed, a victim of both our bodies, nearly as still as a corpse. I shook her awake.

"What?" she said. "What is it?"

"I wanted to make sure you were alive."

"Don't be silly," she moaned.

"I'm not being silly. I'm worried sick. Should we call a doctor?"

"No. I think I'll just sleep it off, like they do in novels."

"Is this really your first hangover?"

She nodded. Clearly, her head ached. What I'd made her do last night was a first too, but I didn't want to get into that. I was quite prepared to make it a last. Nothing was worth this. Nothing. Again, I suggested a doctor.

"We can't call a doctor every time we take a trip," she said.

"When else did we call a doctor?"

In Indianapolis, she reminded me.

"How do you feel?"

"Awful. I'm sorry, darling. I wish I didn't feel awful, but I feel too awful to lie."

"You're a bad liar anyway," I said gently. "And I wouldn't believe anything else. You look awful."

That made her cry a little. "Should I put on some makeup?"

"Oh, God, no. Just sleep."

"What are you going to do?"

"I guess I'll take a walk. If you feel well enough to be left alone."

She did. She wanted me out of there so that she could recover in privacy. I think too that she wanted back her dignity, her pride, which had been thrown up the night before along with everything else. I didn't quite understand. What she did to me made her feel humiliated; when I did it for her, she felt worshipped. I would never understand. Never.

She slept all day. At intervals, I would return to the hotel, she would awake briefly, and I would tell her she was looking a little better. Each time she said she was feeling a little better.

Toward evening, she felt well enough to ask me what I had done with myself all day. I dutifully reported on the art galleries and other obligatory sites I had toured.

"Oh, I wish I could have gone with you to the zoo."

"We'll go in New York," I said.

I became aware, now that she was better, that my patience was beginning to wear very thin, that it was close to snapping. In fact, I was nearly falling apart, with disappointment, relief, worry, let alone anger. "Can't quarrel with that," I said shortly, addressing her regretful whimpers about missing the trip to the zoo.

"Don't pick a quarrel," she said, beginning to manifest some quite passionate anger herself. Something, it appeared, along the lines of holier than thou: Thou hast violated me. But I had thought only to please thee, and thou hast in return given me a lousy honeymoon. Twilight. Close to the finish of day two.

I summoned my remaining controls. "I think," I said carefully, "that we should try to get some food in you. I think, if you feel well enough, that we should go out so that the maid can get in here and clean up this room."

"Is it very messy?" she asked anxiously.

"Well, it's been through a lot."

"Oh, God." She buried her face in the pillow. I knew it would take little to unnerve me completely at this juncture, and I struggled for self-command. In a moment, if I were not careful, I would be just this side of homicidal.

"Jennie," I said, "the room's okay. But we've got to get it cleaned up before we turn in tonight." Which was all I wanted to do. I wanted it desperately. I didn't know, in fact, how I was going to get through the next couple of hours. I knew it was more than simple sightseeing that had exhausted me, and I prayed she'd take hold of herself too, because I suspected she was also in some state of extensive emotional disrepair, and it would take little, very little, for us to capsize. "Jennie," I began again, "the room is clean enough for the maid to clean it. I promise you. Just go in and shower and get dressed, and we'll eat a light meal." She looked queasy. "You may not know it," I went on, "but you are hungry. And you'll feel better once we eat. And we'll take a little walk. It's nice out. You'll like the air."

I never wanted to screw again. I didn't know how my wife felt about it, and it was barely possible I would change my mind, but at the time it didn't seem even remotely reasonable ever again to feel desire. I would take it minute by minute, and if Jennie would let me, hour by hour, and somehow we would get through what was left of this day. Even worse than yesterday, I noted briefly, far from ready to face fully the ominousness of it.

She sat up. Good. She was going to be cooperative, and maybe this marriage could be saved. "Do you think what I had last night might have been a virus?" she asked unexpectedly.

What was she up to? Saving face? Whose? Hers or mine? "It's possible," I said warily, "but I don't think so. I think you drank too much." I couldn't read her expression. "We both did," I added. "Go on. Shower."

"Oh, I don't think I need to shower," was her next bombshell. "I'll just splash some water over my face, brush my teeth, throw on some clothes, and—"

"Darling," I interrupted, wanting to whip her, "I think you want to shower."

"I don't, actually."

Maybe she did need a shrink. What would her treatment entail besides more money than I had? Confinement? Well, that might be necessary. AA, an alcoholic friend once told me, told you to take it one day at a time. "You need a shower," I said emphatically, then waited in terror for her to do some additional irrational flailing so that there would be no alternative but to capsize. And, maybe, capsizing would be our only hope of rescue.

"Why are you saying that? You usually get annoyed when I say I want to shower."

"Sorry to be terribly blunt," I said, still holding on desperately to the controls, "but this may be one of the few times when you need to shower, and I don't understand why you won't."

"I resent the suggestion."

"I'm sorry that you resent it. I call it as I see it." A euphemism. I wondered how the room would smell to an outsider. We'd spray the place with perfume before we left. Of that I'd make sure.

She stood there, naked, glaring at me. "I don't think I need a shower. I don't want you to start making me feel unclean."

"You've got some wires crossed. I'm not trying to make you feel unclean. You don't need purification, you need a simple bath. You were sick last night, you've been sleeping all day, it's hot and you're sweaty, so go rinse off. You'll feel better."

"I suppose you'll feel better too," she said with unmistakable and, to me, bewildering annoyance.

"I would as a matter of fact," I said.

"Okay," she said, as if she were humoring a rabid bat.

"Make it snappy," I said.

"Don't you give me orders," she said violently. "Don't you try to degrade me." She was breathing heavily. I waited for what would come next. So was she, apparently, and was having difficulty finding anything sufficiently vile. "You," she finally spat.

"Just go in there and cool off, before I shove you in there by force. Obviously, you consider me a Nazi."

She couldn't and wouldn't admit it, but the look she gave me as she slammed into the bathroom was worth a thousand words. Right again, I thought grimly. Pity this wasn't on television, and I wasn't a quiz-show contestant. Might pick up a few bucks. Cover the first fifteen minutes of her therapy with Dr. Selfish. Maybe she'd need shock treatment too. Had I done anything to deserve this much fury? Was I a Nazi? Maybe all men were. Good thing there were so many World War II movies around, the girls knew how to peg their enemy. I wanted to weep for the dissolution of my love, but knew I didn't dare. If I confronted it now, I'd be lost forever.

She came out of the shower holding a towel around her

and, with her back to me, got dressed. Efficiently too. Pro-pelled by what? Fury? I didn't think I could face into her anger.

"Don't be cross with me, darling," I said. "I know you've had a simply rotten day."

"All right," she said shortly. "Just don't do that to me again."

I wasn't sure what I wasn't supposed to do again, but let it pass.

"I promise," I said, not knowing what I was promising, just knowing that to do it blind was possibly very danger-ous.

So we went out for supper. She ate with relish, looking at me as little as possible, but appeared to be mollified. I was tabling my own objections to—never mind the euphe-mism, horror at—her behavior, but was feeling unbearably put-upon and far from mollified. Sleep would black it out. Couldn't she see the extent of my emotional pain, the pain of my loss of feeling for her? Would it return? I was sick with confusion.

"Are you okay?" she asked, after she'd packed away din-ner.

"Yes," I lied. "Just sleepy." That part was true. "Are you sleepy?" I asked hopefully, knowing she was unlikely to be, having napped away the day.

"Not quite," she said equably. "I feel much better," she notified me, not seeming to realize that I was wrecked and past caring.

"Good," I said.

"I'd like that little walk," she reported.

Oh, you would, would you? This was worse than the Army. I paid the bill, and, arm in arm, we walked the streets of the capital. "Tomorrow's Sunday," announced the high-school honors student.

"Yes," I said, hoping this was the end of that exchange.

"I'd really like to see the White House," she said long-ingly.

"The inside?"

She nodded yes.

"I don't think they have tours on Sunday," I said, having in fact no idea whether they did or not.

"Can we find out at the hotel?" she asked.

"I suppose so." Why didn't she shut up? She knew the answers to these questions about as well as I did.

"Will you ask?"

"One of us will," I said gruffly.

"Will you remind me?" she asked.

What was eating her, what did she want, proof of my love? What was this? All I knew was if I didn't get to bed soon I'd have a heart attack.

"Sleepy yet?" I asked.

"A little."

"Let's get back, then. Okay?"

"I'd like to walk some more."

"Then you'll have to go by yourself. I can't make it any more."

She turned to me, worried, and for the first time appeared to take in something of my torment. "I'm so sorry, Jack. I've given you a hard time. Let's go back and go to bed."

We walked back to the hotel. I was weighing the feasibility of taking separate rooms, or rooms with twin beds, but as we approached Dupont Circle I came to the weary conclusion that it was hopeless. We were stuck with each other for the present. I hoped I'd feel differently in the morning. Friendlier.

"I'm hitting the sack," I said promptly as we closed the door to the room behind us.

"Aren't you going to take a shower?" she asked in neutral tones.

"I took one this morning. I'm just bushed."

"All right," she said coolly.

We both surveyed the bed. It had been made up, thank God, so that I could try to pretend that it was a different bed altogether, not the one on which we had so disastrously lain, separately and together, in the past hours, among the darkest of my life. I got undressed, climbed into pajamas, then lay back upon the fresh-smelling sheets. The bed had amplitude. Only a slight shift of the covers alerted me to the presence of the featherweight body beside me, close, but not too close. I was grateful for the accident of this distance, and then I realized it was her tact. "I love you, Jack," she said softly. "I'll never forget how you took care of me last night and today."

"I love you, too," I whispered. We didn't kiss. I fell asleep. End of honeymoon, day two.

On Sunday, the third and last day of our honeymoon, Jennie awoke early and announced that she wanted to go to church. After her shower, she stood next to the bed as she was dressing—I kept my eyes closed, but she seemed to know I was awake. Would I like to join her? she asked.

"No thank you," I said, trying to conceal my combined irritation and bewilderment at this unexpected seizure of piety, and my annoyance that she obviously didn't care whether her clattering around the room at such an early hour disturbed my sleep or not.

"I thought it might be a good thing for both of us."

I didn't know what had come over the loon, and decided I'd be better off not knowing. I'd handle this my way.

"No thank you," I said again, enunciating each syllable very clearly, as if I were talking to a trained lip reader. "I'm Jewish. Those of the Jewish faith observe their Sabbath on Saturday. You go along. I'll wait for you here."

"Okay," she said. Then, "You're not really Jewish, are you?"

"No. Go to church, Jennie Church."

She gave me a look of contained reproach. "What are

you going to do?" she asked, tying a little kerchief around her head.

"Lie in bed and read," I said, opening my eyes a little wider to take in these new antics.

"What will you read?" she asked. It wasn't a bad question, since there was no reading matter to speak of in the room besides the Bible—I didn't want to think about the Bible—and the room-service menu.

I gave the matter careful thought. *"Hiawatha.* Now you just run along."

"Hiawatha?" asked the skeptic.

"There's a copy of the complete works of Longfellow in the bed-table drawer, along with the Bible. You were too drunk to notice the other night."

Her response was to close her suitcase with a gesture nearly violent enough to break it. If she thought I would get her another suitcase if she broke or damaged this one, she had another think coming.

"By the way," I said, "when you get back, ring the room from the lobby before you come up."

"Why, in heaven's name?" she asked.

"I might be with a girl," I answered.

"Jack, are you mad at me for going to church?" She looked and sounded a little penitent.

"Not at all."

"You're not serious about another girl, are you?"

"No. Where would I have found another girl? When? Don't be foolish," I said. It was apparently not wholly reassuring. She stood there, uncertain.

"Do you really want me to ring the room before I come up?"

"It might be thoughtful." It was the only way I could think of to impose my will, as opposed to God's, the latter having enjoyed—if that is the word—a long-standing relationship with my mother. It was natural, in the circumstances, given the lurid quality of the honeymoon to date, that I should be unsettled by my wife's uncharacteristic flight to a House of Worship.

She had begun to cry. "I can't seem to do anything right."

"God will help you, I'm sure."

"Jack, really, I do sometimes go to church. I didn't mean to surprise you or anything."

But I was surprised. And frightened, and hurt. "Nothing would surprise me," I said. "Go ahead now. You don't want to be late."

"Afterwards," she said, "maybe we could go out to the zoo."

"I went yesterday. I think I'll just spend the day reading *Hiawatha*."

"The whole day?"

"If there's any time left before we have to catch our train, I'll dip into *Evangeline*."

She stared at me. "You are mad," she said.

"How do you mean that?"

"Angry." On my part, silence. She said, "Why don't you answer me?"

"God has the answers," I said.

"Jack!"

I looked at her. "You look very fetching. Go on ahead."

She peered at me, cautiously. "You mean it, about ringing you from the lobby?"

"Yes."

"But why?"

"Because I say so."

A pause. Then she said, "I see. See you later." And she left.

I waited until the sound of her tread to the elevator grew fainter, then I picked up the phone and dialed the desk. "Desk," said the desk.

"This is Mr. Church in Room 503," I said. "Mrs. Church has gone to church." I really couldn't resist this; there'd never be another opportunity as good.

"Yes," said the desk impatiently. The impatience took the wind somewhat out of my sails.

"When she comes back, would you have her ring the room before she comes up?"

"Will she collect her key, sir?"

"I think she has it with her."

"Then I doubt she'll approach the desk, though if we see her we'll try to give her your message." He was all crispness. This is a recording.

"Thank you," I said.

"You're most welcome. Have a good day."

Like hell would I have a good day.

I hung up and lay back. I would think. Think this through. But I couldn't think. And so, at last, I wept.

AN HOUR AND A HALF later she keyed her way in. I was still in bed. She came over and sat beside me.

"You didn't ring," I said tonelessly.

"That's right." She sighed.

"Why not?"

"I didn't think you meant it." Her voice was weary, world-weary, as if she'd aged emotionally and was therefore wiser in everything except the experience of pleasure. And pessimistic. But gentle. Her native gentleness. Apparently, nothing could erase it.

She sat still, beside me. We didn't touch.

"How was church?" I asked cautiously.

"Not bad," she said. "I don't think I'll go again for a while."

Silence. So I hadn't lost her to that close acquaintance of my mother's, the Creator.

"We have to check out at one-thirty. We could leave our bags downstairs and go to the zoo," I said with great difficulty. "Would you like that?"

"Not really," she said. "You don't really want to go, do you?"

"No."

"We shouldn't lie to each other," she said.

I began to grow frightened again. "Suits me," I barely managed to say, with my voice not breaking. She touched my hand. I returned the pressure.

"Should we get an early train home?" she asked.

"Okay," I said quietly. "I'll check the train schedule and change the reservations. Could you pack my things too?"

"Yes," she said. It was wifely. I was beginning to feel a little better. Maybe we could rise from the ashes.

DUSK. HONEYMOON'S END. Marriage, uncamouflaged, day one. We went directly to my—our—apartment. "Unpack, why don't you," I said formally. "I'll go out to the deli and pick up some things for supper."

"Oh, I can do that," Jennie said. "It's no big deal, unpacking. I can do it later."

"Unpack both your suitcase and mine. It'll take some time to do that, especially since you don't know exactly where my things go. But check the drawers, you'll see where the socks go, the shirts, and so on. You can manage."

"Yes," she said, looking at me tearfully. She really hadn't expected this assignment; she thought she'd squeeze her belongings into my—our—closet and that would be that. Well, she might as well get used now to the additional responsibilities conferred by her changed status.

"I won't be long," I said more kindly. "Anything special you'd like to eat?"

Her eyes brightened. I decided to dispel any illusions she might harbor before they could form. "You'll be fixing it, so keep that in mind when you place your order, Miss."

"Mrs.," she corrected.

"Right," I said. "So what'll it be?"

"Cold cuts?" she asked me. "Would sandwiches be okay?

Maybe they have some prepared salads you could pick up, too," she ventured.

"I thought I'd pick up ingredients for a fresh salad," I said.

She looked trapped. "You don't think a prepared salad would save us time?"

I relented. "You're hungry, huh?" I said. helping her save face as well as sparing her the hardship and humiliation of having instantly to dive into a second utterly unfamiliar task. The honeymoon was over, but the full torment of marriage could wait a day. "I'll get some coleslaw or macaroni salad or something."

"Thank you," she breathed, as if I'd given her some wonderful present, like her own bed.

"Be back in a few minutes," I said.

"Take your time," she said. A stranger, listening, would think we were being considerate of one another.

When I returned with the sack of groceries, I heard her warbling into the telephone.

"We had a lovely honeymoon," she trilled. "Washington was beautiful. Wait, I think Jack's back. I know he'll want to talk to you."

I didn't want to talk to anyone and made some gesture to that effect as I walked past her into the kitchen and set down the groceries for her to unload. I returned to the living room to face her. "It's Barney," she said, cupping her hand over the mouthpiece, looking panicked. What would I do next?

"What does he want, to come over to borrow a cup of gin?"

"Jack," she pleaded.

I took the phone. "Yeah, Barney. We had a great time." Jennie stayed long enough to hear that, then breathed a sigh of relief before going into the kitchen to face yet another tribulation. "Washington is awesome. Perfect setting for a honeymoon, if that's all you can afford." He got ribald. I laughed. "Glad you called. See you soon. Sure, we'll be doing lots of entertaining."

I hung up. So the lies had not only begun but were indeed growing.

I heard her fumbling in the kitchen and decided my next move would be to go into the bedroom and see how far she had advanced with the unpacking. My suitcase lay empty on the bed, hers still locked and shut in standing position. God, I must have scared her to death. I did a quick check of the premises. My suits were neatly hung in the closet—so neatly, and with just the right amount of space between them to save them from wrinkling—that I didn't see where she could possibly find room for her clothes. My other garments seemed to have been placed in the proper drawers. Why was I so surprised? She was a secretary, after all, and this task was rather like filing. Pleased at this new evidence that in choosing a wife I didn't lack all taste and sense, I went into the kitchen.

"You didn't unpack your things," I said to her, not knowing whether I intended it as an observation or a rebuke.

"Oh," she gasped, faking a laugh, "I'll get to it after supper."

The roast beef, salad, and slices of white turkey meat were being arranged on a large platter. She kept wiping her slightly greasy fingers off on her dress. Her pretty dress.

"You don't need to do that," I said, handing her an apron.

Gratefully, she put it on.

"Do you want to change out of your things?"

She nodded yes.

"Well, why don't you?" I asked. "You're not my prisoner, you know."

Wordlessly, she went into the bedroom. Not knowing what else to do with myself and not being an experienced torturer of women or anybody else, I finished arranging the ready-made components of our supper. The platter looked nice when I'd finished with it—I took care to wipe my fingers on a napkin; what in the world had made her think she had to use her dress as one?—and I spooned the prepared tomato and cucumber salad into my—our—salad bowl. Maybe one of the as yet unopened wedding presents would be a salad bowl. I hoped so. Mine looked distinctly bachelor and tacky. I wanted something more grand and at the same time more fragile, to reflect the womanly nature of the sweet girl I had married. I set the living-room table and put the laden serving dishes in place. I lit a candle and dimmed the lights. What in the world was keeping her?

"Jen," I called.

"Yes." Her voice was ragged.

"Come on in. Supper's ready."

"I'll just be a minute." Her voice sounded strange. I went into the bedroom to see for myself. Her suitcase was open, and she was fumbling through it, clad in her slip, looking vulnerable and quite frightened.

"What are you doing?"

"Looking for something to wear."

"Wear your blue shift," I instructed. "Your things will get wrinkled if you paw through them like that."

"I can press them," she said in an obvious attempt to control mounting hysteria. "Unless I hang them up now? Is there time?"

"Well, it's a cold supper," I said reassuringly. "Why not? Hang them up. I just thought you were hungry."

"I never said I was," she said, sweeping up an armful of clothes and stumbling toward the closet.

"Let me help you," I said gently. She handed me a few things. Her hands were trembling.

"I don't see any hangers," she said.

"Easy does it," I said, reaching for five or six that I had cleverly hidden from myself some time back, before marriage was even a gleam in my eye.

"Get dressed," I said. "I'll hang them up."

"Stop giving me orders," she said, finally, her control dissolving.

"I thought you wanted to get dressed," I said deliberately, pretending not to understand what she was talking about.

"Jack, you're not being yourself," she said, confronting me physically, confronting me ethically.

"What a presumptuous thing to say," I said vapidly. Then I said, "Jen, I didn't mean to hurt you." And I laid her clothes gently on the bed and walked out into the living room. I took my place at the table and waited for her. Everything Rita had ever said about me, and everything my mother had thought and refrained from saying, was true. Maybe I should consult a shrink. Maybe my brutishness was her only problem. She was so truthful, so incapable of guile, that the grossness at the core of my nature, under her unwitting influence, had risen to the surface.

She came into the living room wearing her spotless and fresh and only slightly wrinkled blue shift. To her eye, she told me later, I appeared crestfallen. Thus, truer to my own nature. Apparently she had resolved neither to pick nor to pick up on a quarrel. She was again in possession of herself. Later, much later, I told her we would have been better off quarreling, going the distance with our anger, then and there. But she thought that the true word in such a situation had no function, and that the courteous deed did. That's what Jennie had figured out for herself anyway, that first evening of marriage, half camouflaged again, while it was growing dark outside.

Later, we lay side by side in bed, not touching.

"How do you feel?" I asked her tentatively. She had to go to work in the morning. She had washed the dishes and finished unpacking her own suitcase. While she unpacked, I dried the dishes, to have something to do, to show her I was somewhat repentant and that I would carry my share of domestic chores and burdens, even though reduced, and rightfully so, by virtue of my new status as husband. Normally, I'd leave the dishes in the rack for at least a week. Now they were all placed in their cupboards. The kitchen looked abnormally uncluttered.

She was silent. I inquired again after her health, emotional or physical.

"It doesn't itch any more," she said in a flat voice.

That alerted me and triggered my next inevitable series of questions.

"When did it stop?"

"The night I got sick in Washington." As if I could forget what happened, let alone where. Let alone why.

Cautiously, I asked: "What did the doctor say?"

"I've been trying to think," she said. This was about as romantic as an algebra lesson. "I think he said two weeks."

"How long has it been?" I asked. This was interesting foreplay.

"That's what I'm trying to figure," she said. "I think I got it—" She remembered when she'd gotten it.

"So it's been two weeks," I said without emotion, going to the head of the class.

"Yes," she whispered.

I got out of bed and fumbled around in the night-table drawer.

"What are you doing?" she asked.

"I'm going to put on a rubber," I told her, adding gallantly, "just to be on the safe side."

"That's a good idea," she said gamely.

"Do you want to put it on me?" I asked. I'm sure she must have been immensely flattered by this entire performance.

"I don't know how to," she said. Good Christ, didn't she know how to do anything?

"I'll show you," I said, guiding her hand.

Next thing, I was inside her. "Okay?" I asked.

"Yes," she breathed. Did I imagine it, or did she also flinch?

"That hurt?" I asked thoughtfully, in lieu of the customary endearments.

"A little," she admitted.

I shifted position. "Better?"

"Yes."

It did not occur to me that it hurt not because of our two-week enforced abstinence, or because her recently inflamed flesh might still be tender, but because, as the marriage manuals I had once studied so assiduously would have put it, she was not ready.

She was not ready.

Nonetheless, I was. We, or I, went ahead with it. We would, for the remaining days of this first lap of the young marriage, have just this kind of metronomic and monotonous sex twice a week. Her body held no further secrets for me, I thought. Except one. And that I'd ask about, also metronomically. It didn't occur to me that the conditions for her coming—my caring, its expression in caresses—no longer obtained. I'd numbed myself, gotten—I told myself—in this young marriage, too old to care. I asked her anyway: Did she come? Sometimes, my voice enlivened by my curiosity—my curiosity seemed to flourish as everything else wilted and died—sometimes I'd say: "Jennie, darling, did you come?" Did she come? She never told me. I knew the answer, but I forgot that I knew it. And I never ceased to ask.

SHE WOULD COME HOME from work tired and, in those first few days at least, assemble cold-cuts, purchased at the deli on her way home, for our evening meal. She would vary the salad: cucumbers and tomatoes, macaroni, coleslaw, then fruit salad. Yes, fruit salad. Toward the end of the week it was—a surprise—chopped herring. I put my foot down. And my fork.

"No," I said.

"I thought you'd like it."

"Jennie, didn't your mother teach you anything?"

She blinked. "I didn't want to learn anything from my mother."

"Then learn from me. With cold cuts, no chopped herring."

"What will I do?" she asked.

"Buy a cookbook," I said, adding, "I'll help you."

But I didn't help her. She bought *The Joy of Cooking.* That proved to be too complicated for her. Another cookbook, designed to appeal to those who detested the activity, was, Jennie complained, not properly indexed. She finally lucked into something she could use. The menus were accessible, the recipes easy to follow. She was happy. I shared her relief, not knowing what lay in store.

What lay in store was Happy Time Surprise Salad. It was served up as the main course. She had prepared it on Sunday, while I watched television in the living room, gratified to have her occupied with a cookbook that served both as a guide and a needed source of support. I was tired of being supportive of her culinary atrocities, and assignments were coming my way rather frequently at that time, so when I was not reading the paper or watching television to keep abreast for professional purposes of popular cultural trends, I was out interviewing or at home typing.

At the table, I tried not to choke. One had to be polite. I decided not to ask her what the ingredients were. Maybe the other recipes would be better. The next day, the thing appeared not as the main course but as a salad. The main course was spaghetti. Funny, I hadn't smelled it cooking, and it had taken an abnormally short time to prepare. Also, it was unusually gluey. Then it dawned on me.

"Is this from a can?"

"Why yes," she said. She was wearing a new apron, purchased, she had told me, with some inexplicable anxiety to please, that day at Bloomingdale's on her lunch hour. "It's nice," I'd said absently.

Now, I repeated: "From a can?"

"Jack," she said, "I work all day. I don't see what's so terrible about canned spaghetti."

"I work all day too," I said shortly.

"But I'm at an office," she protested.

"Bully for you." I knew that was ungracious, but I was

filled to the brim with a sense of my own virtue, by virtue of continuing to eat the goddamned stuff.

"What's the matter with you?" she asked, putting her fork down.

"Nothing's the matter with me at the moment. We'll know more later," I went on savagely, "when I've finished it."

"You don't have to finish it," she said, getting up and snatching away my plate. "You're nicer than that to your sister, and you don't like her cooking either."

"I don't live with my sister. I'm not forced to eat her cooking every day," I shouted at her. She had gone into the kitchen. I heard scraping sounds. Good, she was throwing the whole mess away.

I was wrong. When she returned, the spaghetti was indeed gone, but Happy Times Surprise Salad remained on the plate. "Thank you," I said as my wife set the plate before me. I took a bite of the salad. Maybe we could eat all of it tonight, and not have to face it again for a while. "How much of this stuff did you make?" I asked.

"What stuff?"

"This fruit-Jello-y stuff," I said.

"Wait a minute," she said, getting up.

"Where are you going?"

She didn't answer, so I tilted my chair back to get a view of what she was doing in the kitchen. She was examining the cookbook. She returned to take her place at the table. "It serves eight to ten," she told me.

I was horrified. "You made it all?"

"Yes. The book says it's a versatile dish, and I agree with the book. It can be a salad, the main course, or dessert," she said self-righteously.

"Were you planning," I asked, "to serve it tomorrow as dessert?"

"I hadn't thought. Why do you ask?"

"Because on successive nights I have been subjected to

it, first, as the main course, and as a salad, second. I just want to know what to expect tomorrow."

"You don't like it?" she asked.

"Do you?" I asked carefully.

"I don't know," she said honestly. "But then they say that you lose a taste for what you've cooked yourself. I think it's okay."

"Cooking?" I exploded. "You call this cooking?"

"Yes," she said defiantly. "It took a lot of time to prepare."

She rose to get the cookbook, then sat down again, opening the book to the proper page. She read the ingredients to me. I felt, as her soft voice chanted this dreadful litany, that I was a young boy again, trapped in a horror movie my parents had warned me against, about vampires.

"Instant vanilla pudding." She looked up at me. "Whipped cream. Canned fruit cocktail. Twenty-four maraschino cherries. Four bananas. One package of miniature marshmallows. Shredded cheddar cheese."

"I see," I said.

"What do you think?"

"I think I'd like a TV dinner."

"You would?" she asked joyfully. "Why didn't you say so?"

I grabbed both her plate and mine, and piling one on top of the other, headed for the kitchen. She followed me, arriving in time to see me scraping Happy Times into the garbage.

"Why are you doing that?"

I spun around and opened the refrigerator. It was virtually empty. The food she'd planned to inflict on me for still another night was visible and accessible on the second shelf. I removed it with an urgency born of rage. Now she was crying. "Will you throw this away, or shall I?"

"You throw it away," she shrieked.

"Fucking shrew," I said. "You made it. You throw it away." I thrust it into her hands.

"I won't," she said.

"You'd better," I said.

"Are you threatening me?" she asked.

"Just don't ask so many questions. Throw that away."

"Or what? You'll beat me?"

"Don't test me," I warned her.

She went toward the garbage pail with Happy Times Surprise Salad and deposited it into the receptacle. She stood there, bent over the garbage pail, weeping. Weeping as quietly as she could.

I remembered. My mother had done this to me as a child. The humiliation. There had been no rescue. Davey was too young and scared. My father early on refused to interfere with my mother's disciplinary inventions. And Rita was taking a positive joy in my suffering at my mother's hands.

I couldn't rescue Jennie. To go to her would be to admit that what I had done was unacceptable.

I went into the living room. That was the kindest thing I could think of to do. Leave her alone. Let her even break the dish if she wanted to. I waited. No sound, no sign at all from the kitchen.

I went back into the kitchen. She had put the serving dish into the sink. "What are you doing?"

"I'm going to wash the dishes." Her voice was very strained.

"Jennie, why don't you break that dish?"

"What?"

"Break it over my head."

"What are you doing to me?" she pleaded. "I couldn't do that. That's not me."

"I think what I just did wasn't me either," I said.

She began to weep again.

I said, "I'm trying to apologize."

"Really?" she asked, disbelieving.

"I'm sorry," I said. She said nothing. I tried again: "Will you forgive me?"

"Yes. No. I don't know."

"What do you mean?" I was really quite frightened now.

"I don't understand how you could be so cruel. You knew I couldn't cook when you married me."

"It isn't that you don't know how," I said, seizing any point of reference, "it's that you're so damned scared. That's what I don't understand. It paralyzes your judgment. Anyone with an ounce of sense would read those ingredients and throw up."

"I guess I don't have sense, then. I didn't throw up. I thought you'd like it."

"Did you think you'd like it?"

"I don't know. I didn't think I'd mind it. I didn't care."

"You lack sensual intelligence," I said to her, inspired, glad I had found this new tack, trying to be helpful to her, to me, to both of us. "You're sensually ignorant."

"What's that supposed to mean?"

"It means you haven't educated your sensual nature. You haven't learned to cook, you don't really enjoy sex—"

"I do," she shot back. "I love it."

"Well, it doesn't feel like you love it, and the more we do it, with your not loving it, the more bored I get."

"Well, we don't have to sleep together then," she said, hiding her hurt.

"There's only one bed in this apartment, and you've given up your place," I said, turning practical.

"You began this conversation with an apology," she reminded me. "You didn't mean it, did you? You don't want to sleep with me."

"The argument was about food, not sex," I said, bewildered.

"But you linked the two. You don't want to sleep with me. Well, you don't have to. We can lie in the same bed and not have sex."

"Are you refusing to sleep with me? I have rights, you know. I could divorce you."

"I could divorce you too."

"You've got no grounds."

"Mental cruelty."

"I'm sorry," I said. "Look, Jen, I don't think either of us can afford a divorce."

"I could afford it just fine."

"I mean neither of us has the money."

"I could borrow the money."

"From whom?"

"From Audrey. She'd give it to me."

"I don't want a divorce." My teeth were chattering. "Do you?"

"No. But you're like a stranger to me."

"I feel like a stranger to myself."

"So let's forget sex," she said bravely. "If it bores you, it bores me."

"Bitch," I said, and stormed into the bedroom. I flung off my clothes. I ignored her when she came in. She got undressed and into her nightgown. Her nightgown was slightly stained. With what? Why wasn't she cleaner? What was I thinking? Jennie was the cleanest person I knew. Cleanest in every sense. If only she were dirtier. I'd have something to reproach her with.

I pulled my bathrobe from its hook, put it on, and returned to the living room. I went to my desk and examined the half-finished piece that lay beside the typewriter. I would finish it. If she was so dead tired, this noise wouldn't bother her. But maybe it would.

I returned to the bedroom. She was lying there in the dark, eyes wide open. She looked attractive; yes, she would perhaps be desirable to a stranger. The scars I had inflicted were too visible to me for me to want her. Ever again. But I couldn't tell her that. "I don't think I could have sex now, Jack," she pleaded.

"I know," I said. I took her hand. She tried to pull it away. "I've never been married before," I said. "But they say the first year is the hardest."

She was silent. I suppose it was sinking in. Maybe it was reassuring. At length, she said, "Do you want to sleep with me?"

"No. Not now."

She looked hurt. She bit her lip. "Are you still attracted to me?" she asked, uncharacteristically. The uncharacteristic quality of it, as well as the question itself, took me aback. What could I say? I didn't know.

"Yes," I said heavily, releasing her hand. "Go to sleep." She nodded, and I left the room, closing the door quietly behind me.

IN THE MORNING, I looked at her dozing beside me. She shifted, flinging an arm toward me with its elbow pointed in the direction of my eye. I put my hand on her, gently. She opened her eyes briefly, shut them, yawned, and shuddered. I hovered over her now, sitting nearly upright, wondering whether when she awoke fully she would feel better. Feel my protection. I decided not to let her think a thought. So I woke her, by circling her face and neck with tender kisses. By the time I was finished, her eyes were wide open. And expressionless. "Good morning," I said. "Hi," she answered. She almost never said "Good morning." She explained to me that her mother had said it and that she therefore eschewed it. "But most people say it," I argued. "Most people mean it."

"Do that again," she said sleepily.

"Do what?"

"What you were doing when I woke up."

I kissed her neck.

"More," she said.

"It's time to get up," I said.

"What day is it?" she asked, wrinkling her face like a baby.

"Friday."

"Ohhh." She buried her face in the pillow. I kissed her hair.

"You're going to be late."

"I'm going to call in sick." She said this often, but never did it.

"You really don't want to go in?"

"Really." She was awakening, slowly but surely. Seemed not to want to get out of bed. Nor to want me to get out of bed.

"Are you sure your boss won't be annoyed?" I asked, trying to be casual so as not to betray my intense awareness of our dependency on her income.

"He likes me," she yawned. "He'll understand."

"Why don't you just be late? That would be better."

"I don't know what's better for me any more," she said pathetically, sitting down on the bed with the nightgown bunched around her slender thighs.

"I'm better for you," I said commandingly, believing it. "I am," I said, burying my face in her hair, to erase any lingering doubts. "Here," I said, pulling her back down onto the bed.

"Take off my nightgown," she said.

"Why?" I asked, leaping to the task. "It's a beautiful article of clothing. A love of a nightgown." By this time I'd gotten it off her and gotten her giggling. "Wear it often," I said, tossing it on the floor. "It turns me into a raving beast. I lie awake all night wondering how I can get it off you. Forever."

"It was a birthday present from Laraine," she explained.

"Figures. How many years ago? Twelve?"

"About." She giggled again.

"God, I love you."

"Take off your pajamas," she said, with what sounded like urgency. Was she faking? Never mind. Maybe faking would help her get the hang of it.

Twenty minutes later, I relaxed in her arms and disengaged, letting her out of my embrace entirely. I felt a gentle hand stroking the back of my neck, and then I fell promptly asleep.

I woke up to find myself alone, naked, under the covers. I looked at the clock. Ten, probably morning. Where was my wife? Oh, yes, at work.

She came tiptoeing toward the bed. "Where were you?" I asked sleepily, reaching for her.

"In the closet, getting dressed," she whispered. "I didn't want to wake you."

"That's very sweet. Come back to bed."

"No, Jack. I'm all dressed. I'm going to work."

"Is this an unshakable resolve?"

"Yes." She leaned down to kiss me. "Don't muss my hair," she murmured as I mussed it. She sat up. "Do I have to comb it again?"

I peered at her. "Yes," I said. This was the neat early sixties.

She slipped into the bathroom to redo her hair.

"Did you take your pill?" I called out.

"Oh, no. Where's my purse?"

I squinted around the room. "On my bureau," I said. "Use my water glass," I said, indicating it on the bed table.

She swallowed. And then she sighed.

"I'll never understand you," I said.

"Yes you will," she promised me. "Someday."

And she was gone.

*

I LAY THERE. This, for a change, was a promising day. So far, the happiest of my marriage. Maybe. The phone rang. All I could think of was, Oh, Christ, let it not be my mother.

Resolutely, I picked up the phone.

"You okay?" asked Davey.

"Sure," I said with a conviction I wouldn't have been able to muster yesterday. "Perfect, with your call."

"No newlywed blues?"

"Some, but I think we've put it all behind us, Dave."

"I'm coming to New York in a couple of weeks."

"Stay with us," I said, flooded with joy.

"No. Business trip. I'll stay at—" He named a midtown hotel. "I want to see you, but you need your privacy."

"Great," I said, a little absently.

I sat by the phone for a few minutes, so as not to break the spell. The day seemed charmed.

"WE'RE GOING UP in smoke," I told her bleakly the night before Davey's arrival, looking at the charred and tough cut of something that she had put before me. She gave me the look of a frightened rabbit. Designed to make me feel guilty, once again like an ape. Very well, I would leave her. I wanted to say this, but the words stuck in my throat. Did I mean them? Why did she look at me like that? What was she waiting for?

Finally, she said despairingly, "Jack, you know the first year is hard. Barney said Myra used to burn the food."

"It's not just the food," I said. I was not trying to be mean. I couldn't help it.

"What is it?" she pleaded.

"I'm not happy," I said simply. There was no reply. Finally, I said, "Are you?"

"No," she whispered. "I mean I'm glad we're married and I love you, but I don't think one is supposed to be happy all the time."

"I'm not happy any of the time."

She flinched. "Oh, Jack. You can't mean that."

"I wish I didn't. But it's true."

"Even if it's true—" She hesitated.

"What?" I might as well hear it all.

"Maybe you shouldn't say it. Maybe some things should never be said."

"Then our lawyers can say them to each other."

"Jack, you can't mean this. Why?"

"I don't know."

"I make you happy in bed," she ventured.

"No," I said.

She was too frightened for tears. "Why?" she whispered.

"It's a bad emotional atmosphere. That's why."

She shuddered.

"I don't want to hurt you," I said.

"You're hurting me."

"Jen. Only because you hurt me too."

"How?"

"I don't know." Which was true. My thoughts were shrouded and indistinct. I felt I was dangerous to her. I should leave her for her sake.

"We haven't been married all that long," she appealed to me. "You're not giving it a chance."

"That's true," I said tonelessly. I could mount no arguments. I could rely only on my own chaos.

"Davey's coming tomorrow," she reminded me, as if this had some bearing on our interchange.

"Yes."

"Maybe that will cheer you up."

"I don't need cheering up," I said. I needed out. Escape. I couldn't tell her.

"We can talk to him," she said. "Maybe he'll be able to put things in perspective."

"I don't want him to know," I said.

"Why? You trust Davey more than anyone."

"I have to live with this failure, if that's what it is. It's ours. I don't want to burden my brother." The truth was, I was bitterly ashamed. I had evidently chosen the wrong girl, and my error had victimized us both. I didn't want to add my brother to the list of victims.

"Finish your dinner," she begged. "You'll feel better."

"I'm not hungry," I said. I got up and walked into the bedroom. I lay down.

She followed me. "Jack, it's just a mood. Can't you try to think of it that way? Maybe it'll go away."

"Please go into the other room, Jennie," I said.

"Why?"

"I need to be alone. Please."

"Okay," she said quietly.

"I might feel better if I just lie here alone. For a little while." I felt I owed that much to her.

"Okay," she said in acknowledgment. I listened to her retreating footsteps.

The light streamed in through the open door. Intrusive. I knew she liked the light. I couldn't ask her to close the door, adding that hurt to the other hurts I had inflicted, nor could I summon the will to get up and close it myself. I shut my eyes. I heard the sound of water running, of plates being scraped. She was doing the dishes. Good thing we hadn't unpacked the dishes her mother had given us for our wedding. We were still using my familiar plain white plates. Could this be happening? There was a stranger in my kitchen. I tried to think of the Jennie I had fallen in love with. A slight girl, poised, contained, totally clothed. Shy of sex. How appealing that had been. How much I'd wanted her. Maybe I'd changed. No, I wasn't meant to be married. Marriage changed people for the better. Even if it didn't effect such change immediately, one could bear it. I couldn't bear this. Jennie, it seemed, could. How could I face my brother? I thought of Helen. She had my number. Only a crazy man could have gotten entangled with a woman like Helen. Sex, money, a child one couldn't claim as one's own. I wasn't meant to be a father. Not a real father. And if not a father, not a husband. Jennie would find someone else. Perhaps.

She stood in the doorway. "Darling," she said softly, "can I come in?" I couldn't say no. I lay there in terror, but it was her room as much as mine. In fact, her salary paid most of the rent. A property settlement. A financial settlement. Good thing we had little property and fewer finances. "Can I come in?" she asked again.

"Sure," I said.

She stood beside the bed. "Can I lie down next to you?"

"Why?"

"I just want to hold you."

I began to tremble. She stretched out beside me. "I don't think," she said, "that it's as bad as it seems now. This is just a moment. A mood. It'll pass." She was trying to still my trembling. At length, I stopped. I felt more willing to turn myself over to someone else. More able.

"You don't think," I said, trying to keep my voice from breaking, "that it's hopeless?"

"No. I think we'll feel better tomorrow. It's just the end of the week, and we're tired."

I was. Dead tired, with no reason to be.

Later, she got up from the bed and wandered about the room. Careful not to bump into one another, we prepared for bed.

Later, tearless, drained, we lay side by side in my dark. She pressed my hand. Unthinking and quickly, I got on top of her.

Afterwards, almost too weary to breathe, let alone speak, I mumbled: "Don't forget to take your pill in the morning."

Silence.

"Did you hear me?"

Then, in a dead, expressionless voice, she said: "I won't forget."

Sleep.

*

IN THE MORNING, I stumbled out of bed, waking her as I did so. I didn't want to hear her voice. It might make me feel something for her, and I wanted to be numb. "I'm going to ring Davey's hotel," I said. She nodded silently.

He was registered. But there was no answer in the room. I got frightened and clutched the phone, listening to the dead static between rings. Then, the rustle of Jennie's nightclothes. "He doesn't answer?" she said.

"No."

"He's probably gone out for breakfast." She stood waiting with me for a moment while I kept the telephone pressed to my ear. "You could leave a message," she suggested.

"He should have called me before he went out," I said hoarsely.

She left me then and went around the living room raising the window shades.

"Darling," she said when that chore was accomplished, "ring the hotel back and leave a message."

"The damned operator should get back to me," I choked. "Well?" I said to Jennie, "shouldn't she?"

"Yes," she said quietly.

I slammed down the phone and redialed. The operator came on the line.

"I want to leave a message for Room 503."

"Name, please?"

"David Church," I said, exasperated.

"Just a moment," said the bland voice. I was left to myself for some seconds. "Mr. Church is in 607," I was informed.

"That's impossible!" I said. "You, or one of your minions, just told me he was in 503."

The voice said, "607. I'll ring again."

"No," I shouted, "I want to leave a message." But I was too late. The monotonous buzzing had begun again, and the operator had deserted the post. I held on. "Dammit," I muttered, "she's not even ringing the right room."

Jennie said, "503?"

"Yeah."

"That was our room number at the Dupont Plaza."

I turned to her. "Are you sure?"

"Yes," she said. "Wait, I'll check my diary. I wrote it down."

I didn't even know she'd kept a diary. Of our honeymoon, no less. There'd been a time when I might have been curious to see it. Not now. Not any more. But when she returned with the diary, so innocent and apparently pleased to have produced some tangible information, I was ashamed of the melodrama of my thoughts. "Look," she said, pointing to the page. Actually, her diary was a calendar on which she recorded appointments to be kept, chores to be done, as well as abbreviated records of activities engaged in. I hung up the phone and took the book from her hand.

"First day honeymoon, Room 503," she'd scribbled. On the next page, "Itch better, I hope. Smithsonian later."

I closed the book.

"You're not even curious," she said in a flat voice as I handed it back to her.

"It's touching," I said. But it was true. I wasn't curious. The reason: Probably I no longer loved her.

I redialed the hotel, asked for the message desk, and left a message for Davey in Room 607, where he was indeed registered. When I put the phone down, my wife—it was still proper to call her that, at least until the proceedings were begun—had vanished from the immediate vicinity, but had managed to leave her diary on the dining table. Sneaky. Probably in lieu of food. Food for thought, anyway, I decided as I picked it up. I was, if you want the honest truth, more curious about its contents in her absence than when she stood hovering over me, watching my facial expressions change or not, as I scanned her scribbles. No harm to indulge this curiosity now that I didn't love her and the connection between us would soon be broken. Where the hell was she? I heard the sound of water pounding. Of course. The shower. Cleanliness was next to godliness. Despite her pert and initially winning exterior, Jennie probably was quite a kindred spirit to my God-minded mother. I picked up the diary and turned first, inevitably, to the honeymoon section. "Slept on my darling's shoulder all the way down." I blinked back unexpected tears and turned rapidly to another page. "Too much champagne last night. I grouchy in A.M., but he *so* understanding." I tried to remember when I had been understanding. Oh, yes, day two. I was beginning again, through her somewhat childish jottings, to find her endearing, though imperceptive. She seemed to think—or did she only hope?— that I was considerate, that my love for her was durable as rock, that I was not moody. Next page: "Sex disastrous last night. Too bad, because lovely yesterday." I scanned the page. In very tiny letters, at the bottom, she'd written: "Slept this whole honeymoon day away. So ashamed. But he understands." He does? Did she lie to herself knowingly? I turned to the next page. "Went to church and prayed. Jack sarcastic, but I guess I deserve it." I did another double-take. She couldn't believe that either. She was always taking me to task for my sarcasm, as she called it. I flipped back some months and scrambled for a particular page. I'd flipped too far; the entry read: "Don't forget Audrey's party next week." I found the party page: "Julian took me to A's party, but I went home with another man! First time. Kissed me at door! Really seems to like me." How frustrating. What I wanted to know was whether she'd liked me, but she was no more communicative on paper than she was to me in person. Maybe what she felt didn't matter to her. That was certainly peculiar. I cared about my feelings, when I had them. Which wasn't now. I turned a few pages. The next entry I read took my breath away: "I think Jack wants to sleep with me. Can't wait." So she'd been eager! I then reread the entry: "Can't wait." Ambiguous. Maybe it meant I couldn't wait. Why had she so carelessly and inconsiderately omitted pronouns? My hand holding the diary trembled. I wondered if I should forge ahead into the bathroom, corner her in the shower, and give her one final chance to explain herself. I decided to read on. "He explained to me about sex last night. Feel so much better." He did? She did? And she scrawled along: "He wouldn't unless he cared." Wouldn't what? Oh, God. I couldn't carry the burden of her any longer. Jennie's first corsage. The wallflower at the prom, finding Prince Charming, also known as Jack, and blossoming then into happiness which, clearly, was not in her case synonymous with womanhood. At one time I would have felt flattered. Now it made me want to gag. Rather, it simply embarrassed me. Must try not to let my reactions to her become physical, or I would fall ill. Possibly die. I read on, unable to stop myself. A later entry? "Must keep my temper. Am so lucky to have him." Dumb? Or trying to talk herself into something? To my way of thinking, we were born extremely unlucky. Then: "Dinner last night another disaster." A few pages later: "Mother not the help I'd hoped she'd be. But smiled and said she was glad when told her I'm on pill. Good." The stupidity or self-deceit in these pages was astonishing.

The sound of the shower stopped. Instantly, I knew I didn't want to be caught leafing through her diary. Were I Jennie, I'd die rather than expose myself like this. Unless she'd deliberately set it as a trap—catch me in the act of spying on her and subsequently use it against me. Was she natively cagey? These pages revealed her to be stupid, but women had instincts they followed. I tiptoed over to the dining room table and replaced the thing approximately where she had left it.

I stood for a moment or two, wondering whether to dial Davey again, experienced a dizzy spell, and stumbled toward the bathroom. Yes, I knew she was there, but this was my apartment, and I needed to splash cold water on my face. I flung open the door and found her there, wrapped demurely in a towel, studying her face in the mirror.

"Move over, Narcissa," I said. "I need to get to those faucets."

Wordless, she stood aside. Curious what a familiar presence she seemed, even though, minute by minute, I was confronting the fact that we were strangers to each other.

When I backed away from the basin, face dripping, she handed me a clean hand towel. "Thanks," I said.

"You're welcome." A slight pause. Then: "Jack, I know we're married and all, but I wish you'd knock when I'm in the bathroom."

"You could lock the door," I said shortly. I would not make things easy for her. With me or without me, she had to grow up. Proof of this was not long in coming. Your Honor, I cite as evidence the following:

Jennie, in a girlish burble: "I guess this is going to sound silly."

Me: "I'm sure it will. But please go on."

Jennie: "I'm always afraid I'll get locked in. So I never lock the bathroom door."

Me: "I see."

Jennie: "So would you mind knocking?"

Me: "Yes, I would."

I'm sure you see what I mean, Your Honor.

The telephone rang. As I moved to answer it, I heard the bathroom door slam behind me. With that slam, maybe she wouldn't be able to open it again lock or no lock. I hoped.

It was Davey. "Did I wake you?" he asked. "You sound funny."

"No, Davey. I'm wide awake. And," I said grimly, "I don't feel funny."

"What's up?"

"My marriage is washed up," I blurted. "Do you want to come for lunch?" Two sentences, both given equal weight, because both merited it.

A silence. Jesus Christ, he was supposed to be a grown-up. Couldn't anybody around here take anything in stride? "Say something," I said. "If you're coming for lunch, I'll have to run down to the deli and get some food. The bitch I'm married to doesn't see to those things."

"Jack, I'm shocked."

"I'm sorry," I said. "I should have let on to you about her sooner. Her so-called marketing and cooking are the least of it," I said darkly.

Davey broke in, "No, I'm not talking about that—specifics—I mean I'm shocked about the marriage. We had no idea."

What was this we business?

"I shouldn't have broken it to you like that," I said, "but I've had it. Very specifically. With this marriage. Just tell me about lunch so I can get things started."

"I don't like the way you sound," Davey said. "I think you and I had better meet alone and talk."

Talk. I was sick of talk. A divorce lawyer would take action. "Okay," I said wearily, as if I were bestowing a great favor. "So we won't expect you for lunch."

"I think it would be awkward, don't you? When did this happen?"

"Probably the day I met her. I haven't told her yet," I added.

"Jack."

"What?"

"Why don't you come down here for lunch?"

"I'd be delighted to. My present hope is that she's locked herself in the bathroom."

"Jack, you sound crazy."

"I'm not. By the way, how are you?"

"Good," Davey said.

"I know you're good. But are you well?"

"Well."

As I stood there, knowing that I was now as vulnerable to the pain Jennie could cause as to the pleasure evoked by my brother, Pain walked into my living room.

Timidly, "Jack?" said Pain.

"Yes," I said warily.

"I think I was being petty before," Pain said. "I take back what I said about knocking."

"Give some thought to what I said about locking," I told her.

"Where are you going?" She saw that I was putting on my coat.

"To have lunch with David."

"Oh," she said. "I thought he'd come here to lunch. Did he call?"

"I want to be alone with him, which is one of several reasons why he isn't coming here to lunch, and two, yes, he called."

"Why are you so mean?" whined Pain.

"Why are you such a baby?"

"Jack," she said. I looked at her. Pain certainly looked pathetic.

"Jennie," I said, summoning what patience I had left, "read a psychology book or something. Or get yourself on the waiting list at some clinic. You need help, and I can't help you."

"I don't need help," she said in a quiet frightened voice. "I need you."

"I don't want to get into this now," I said warningly.

"What did you tell Davey?"

"What I said to my brother is between me and my brother."

"I'm your wife."

"I wouldn't rub that in if I were you."

"Jack, don't do this to me." I looked at her. Her face was contorted, she looked utterly defenseless against the hurt she felt. So I had become Pain. We'd exchanged roles. Not nice, but I liked it better that way. I knew I was in some way still responsible for her, but I could bear no further suffering myself.

So I said, trying to be kind: "Jennie, we're no good for each other."

"Jack, this is just a mood."

"Don't beg, Jen. I don't want you to do that to yourself."

"Will you bring Davey back for dinner?" she asked, as if that were somehow the key to a solution.

"Maybe. That means I don't know. Live with it." I wrenched my sleeve from her surprisingly strong grip and made it to the door.

I SAT HUDDLED with Davey in the cocktail lounge–restaurant of his hotel. Made to order for me, dimly lit.

"I don't know what to say," Davey said. "Betty was a good cook from day one of our marriage."

"Count your blessings."

He looked bewildered. Or was it contemplative? I'd certainly prefer the latter.

"What do you think?" I persisted.

"I can't make enough sense of it," Davey said.

"She's immature."

"Well," said Davey neutrally, "she sounds dependent."

"She's selfish and aggressive in bed," I snapped. "That's what's wrong." In the silence that followed I wondered how I could have told such a lie. Or was it true? Was this what I wasn't facing about Jennie and what was at the bottom of it all? The myth that I was the pursuer, the near-rapist, and she the violated maiden? Whereas, actually, she had, especially recently, wanted sex many times. Even when she obviously got little if any pleasure from those exertions. Probably I pleasured her ego. Or, rather, her vanity.

After some seconds, Dave said softly, "Don't cry, Jack."

Finally, I said: "I'm not strong."

"I think you still love her."

"What makes you think that?" I was afraid to hear the answer.

"Because the idea of leaving her gives you such pain."

"The pain comes from not loving her," I protested.

"Don't be emotionally rash, Jack."

"Don't be rash," I snarled. "You knocked up your wife."

He looked stabbed. Then he said: "You this rough on her?"

"Yes, she brings it out in me. I wasn't like this before."

"No, you weren't," said Davey, and signaled the waiter for the check. "Let's take a walk," he said. "I could use some air."

WE WALKED. In the sunlight I looked at him.

"Well, how do you like the mustache?" he asked me easily, having endured my prolonged stare.

"I don't know," I said. "It makes you look older."

"That was the idea," said Davey. "I'm the head of the household, and now the director of the lab, too. Gotta look the part."

Something else was different. I was glad to hear he was a pillar of the community, the better to lean on, but I was nonetheless bothered. A block and a half later, I hit on it. "You don't need glasses any more?" I asked.

"Got contact lenses. What do you think?"

"Makes you look younger," I muttered. What was he doing to himself? I took a closer look at him. "You're too thin," I said. "You've lost weight."

"Wanted to," he said cheerfully.

"Put on a few pounds," I told him. "You look skeletal."

"Thank you," he said.

He bore my scrutiny but he didn't laugh. Humorless. I'd better get out of my marriage fast, before the same thing happened to me.

"Why all the changes?" I asked.

"Not so many. I just thought I'd see what life would be like if I varied things a little."

"Sun's in my eyes. Let's get indoors. Come on home."

"I think," he said quietly, "that you should phone Jennie and tell her we're coming."

"I'm not a three-year-old," I said. "Of course I'll phone her."

"I'm going to mail you some vitamins when I get back to the lab," said Davey. "I've never seen you so strung out."

"I've always been high-strung," I said indignantly. "I don't think this is unusual."

"I do," he rejoined evenly. Then, just as we hit the phone booth and I was fumbling for a dime, he said, "Do you think she wants sex? Or do you think she really just wants a baby?"

I stared at him. He handed me that dime. I made the call.

IN RESPONSE TO my curt announcement that I was, after all, bringing Davey home, Jennie had worked herself into a fine happy fuss. She had dolled herself up in a cheerful floral-print dress, sleeveless, and buttoned up to the neck. She looked like an eager, first-year graduate student, not unattractive, but I regarded her with detachment, as if I were seeing her, in a crowd, for the first time. What was she doing in my apartment?

Davey, on the other hand, greeted her like a close and beloved relative. His kiss upon her cheek was graceful and tender, and she melted before it in gratitude.

"It's so good to see you," she said, her eyes sparkling. Happiness? Recently shed tears? Yes, indeed. Swollen. Good that she'd made a recovery. I certainly didn't want a messy scene in front of my brother. I looked at my watch. Four P.M. Too early for drinks or dinner. We would serve tea. Had she thought to go out for some croissants or scones to welcome our out-of-town guest? I didn't ask but watched dispassionately, too jaded to hope, as she vanished into the kitchen and returned with a platter full of crumbly cookies she had purchased at one of New York's chain bakeries, known the length and breadth of the city for its mediocrity.

"I thought we'd have tea," she said breathlessly. And stood there.

"Sit down," I said. "I'll set things up in the kitchen."

I went into the kitchen and hunted up tea bags. I decided not to let myself experience the chagrin of any comparisons Davey might make between these makeshift crumbs of hospitality and the sort his own, capable wife provided. Jennie and I were put together with Scotch tape. At best. Nothing stronger.

"Jack's been so edgy. I think you're the best medicine for him," I could hear her say. My hair stood on end. Clutching three tea bags, I strode into the living room.

"You might bear in mind," I said, "that voices carry. If you're going to discuss me, Jennie, why don't you at least have the common decency to wait till I'm out of the house. Which I might be soon. There's no tea worth serving here, and these cookies are garbage."

"Common decency," Davey mused at length. Davey knew I loathed clichés. Was I becoming one?

I turned to Jennie. Perhaps an apology, however brief, was in order. But she was not going to make it easy. Tears were streaming down her face. Christ. Already, and the tea had not yet been poured.

"Stop crying," I said. "This isn't the time to have a scene."

But she couldn't stop. Davey reached for her hand, and she fled into the bedroom. I stood there. My fist unclenched, and I let the tea bags drop to the floor.

"Very theatrical," Davey said dryly, as he got up to pick up the tea bags. "I'll fix tea— No, don't follow me, I can find my way around your kitchen. Go in there." He pointed to the bedroom.

"Is this supposed to be my fault?" I asked him.

"I'm not handing down judgments today. I just think it'd be nice if you went in there. Be nice. Go on," he said, more gently. "You'll do fine."

"Okay," I said. "You can throw those tea bags away, incidentally. We've got a lifetime supply of Lipton's in there."

He smiled at me and disappeared into my kitchen. In a moment, the sounds issuing from it were the sounds of someone quite competent, who knew his way around. The sounds issuing from the bedroom, on the other hand, were uncontained, disorderly.

Kind. Nice. I had been those things once, and probably would be again, but why did Davey think this little provocateur warranted my sympathy? I needed sympathy. I couldn't ladle it out all the time, I'd have nothing left. I hadn't been all that brusque. After all, Davey was close family, and one could let down one's hair in front of him. That is, I could. Not she. She was slipping out of family orbit. She might still be family legally, but that was all. I walked into the bedroom, saw her shaking on the bed, and felt a chill. How many scenes had been played out in this bedroom? I sat down beside her, trying not to shiver. "I'm sorry, Jen," I said.

"I can't do anything right," she sobbed, sounding frighteningly like her diary. "I've failed you."

"There, there," I said, my hand on her shoulder. Instantly, she reached to embrace me. I shrank back. "Let's just take it easy now," I said, trying not to drown.

"I try so hard," she wept.

"I know you do," I said. I knew no such thing.

"Where's Davey?"

"He's fixing tea. Those are nice cookies you bought," I said, remembering to be nice and kind.

"Then why did you call them garbage?" It seemed to be a question, not a reproach.

"Because I'm a sonofabitch, Jen. I'm not a particularly nice guy. My brother is. You got stuck"—but only temporarily, I thought, consoling myself with the prospect of freedom—"with the wrong brother."

"I don't feel that way."

"That's good," I said as noncommittally as possible. "You're a nice kid. Now dry your eyes, and let's go back into the living room."

She sat up and tried to lean into my arms, which remained unresponsively at my sides. I kissed her cheek.

"That's a kind of brotherly kiss," she said to me, looking frightened.

"Jen," I said, "I haven't got much of anything left in me. It's all I can do to hold myself together. Will you please try to do the same?"

"Hold you together?" she asked in deliberate misunderstanding, her teeth virtually chattering.

"Hold yourself together. Pull yourself together," I added commandingly. That felt much more comfortable, safer.

I left the bedroom. She could tend to the repair of her makeup and her self-esteem. Or whatever it was. I'd tried to help. Maybe I had, a little. How long would it stick?

I shuffled into the kitchen. "I found some real tea," said Davey. "It's brewing."

"Real tea," I said. "No kidding. What'd you do, conduct an archaeological dig?" I looked at the box sitting on the kitchen counter. "Oh, that's from before I was married." (No "we" business for me.) "Premarital tea," I joked, and waited for Davey's laugh.

"How is she?" Davey asked.

"Who?" I inquired blandly.

"Jack," he said carefully, "pull yourself together." He gave me an unflinching look of combined concern and severity. I dropped my eyes before it. So what if it made me look shifty? I didn't care.

"I think, thanks to my ministrations, that she's stopped whimpering," I said.

Davey frowned. "I've also uncovered some camomile," he said. "Would you like that?"

"No," I said. "But I'd like you to move in as soon as she moves out. You're very wifely."

"She's not moving out," Davey said. "And you'd better get hold of yourself. You're turning . . ." He paused.

"What?" I didn't know what I was asking.

"Vicious," he said.

"Davey," I said, "don't do that to me, or I'll get sick. Do I seem sick?"

"Overstrained," he said cryptically, with his back to me.

I reeled with hypochrondria, with terror for my life. "Is my color bad?"

"You seem overstrained, and you keep threatening to collapse," he said patiently.

"There's nothing wrong with me," I protested. "Except the marriage."

"It's not 'the' marriage," he said. "It's your marriage."

"It's Jennie's marriage," I replied.

I carried the tray into the living room.

We had been sipping our tea for some moments in silence when Jennie appeared, composed but pale against the bright colors of her dress.

"Sit here," said Davey, pointing to the place on the sofa beside him. I was ostentatiously slouching in my favorite oversized armchair, with the fraying but comfortably familiar upholstery. I liked it that way. All by myself amid the tatters.

She managed to pick up her cup and take a noisy swallow. I had never before seriously questioned her table manners, but now that would have to be looked into. Did the whole block have to hear her gulp?

"The cookies are good," Davey said, indicating them and helping himself to another. My spouse nodded, and then after a decent interval reached over and delicately partook. Crunch, crunch. God, what a racket.

Davey got up with the platter and brought it over to me. "Thanks," I said, taking something with pink frosting and depositing it on my plate. I loved my brother. Jennie was the problem.

"Do you have any pictures of Libba?" Jennie asked shyly.

With a delighted smile, Davey produced them.

"Oh, she's darling," said Jennie, her voice catching with tenderness.

I couldn't stand my beleaguered posture any longer. I rose from my chair and crossed over to the two people who—once—I had loved best in the world. Only one was left, but I'd temporarily table that. I rested my hand gently on her shoulder and bent down. I felt her quiver.

"Look," Davey said carefully, "I've got a business dinner."

"Oh," said Jennie, disappointed, "I thought you'd have dinner with us."

"Can I have a raincheck?" Davey asked.

"I'll see you to the elevator," I said, and got up instantly, before someone or something else could interfere with my plans.

I followed him into the vestibule. I clutched at his sleeve frantically before he could press the elevator button. "Do you really have a business dinner?" I asked him.

"I have some business things," he said, "and I also think you and Jennie have to talk things out. You may think the marriage is over, but she clearly doesn't know a thing about it."

"We've talked about it. If she had an ounce of sense she'd know we're finished."

"Ounce of sense," he repeated. "She's got more than an ounce of sense."

I calculated: sixteen ounces to the pound. Then I realized this was irrelevant, Davey wasn't testing my arithmetic, he was noting that something seemed to have happened to my sense of language. "I used a cliché," I said, overwhelmed with shame. What was this slippage? I remembered, on the highway, the driver of the motorcycle after he hit me lost control of his speech, became ungrammatical. Terror did it. Terror and guilt. Was the same thing happening to me?

"Jack," said Davey, "I don't give a damn about your verbal tap-dancing, I want you to get connected to your life. Your wife."

"I'm connected to her," I said dully. "That's the trouble."

"You treat her abominably," he said then.

"You're taken in by her," I said carefully, "because she loves Libba. The fact is I don't know why she'd want to stay in the marriage any more than I do," I mumbled.

Davey looked at me. "Children."

"Huh?"

"I think she wants children."

"I don't want any more children," I blurted.

I became aware of what I had said. Davey looked at me, his face expressionless. No, kind. Waiting.

"I knocked someone up too," I said. "I owe you this," I added. "For what I said about you and Betty."

"You don't owe me anything," said Davey, leaning against the wall. We heard the elevator creaking. Neither of us had pressed the button.

"Penance," I said.

"No," he said gently. I waited for the next question. I felt sick. "You don't have to say anything," he said to me softly.

"I want to," I said. "Nobody else knows. Except the mother."

He nodded. "I see."

I told him who the mother was. I told him the child was Morrie. A boy. That I had seen him.

"Jennie doesn't know?" Davey asked.

"No," I said. "It'd kill her. You're the only one who knows. I never told anybody."

"Oh, God, kid," Davey said to me, his voice breaking, "don't see him again. It'll break your heart."

He hugged me and was gone.

ESCAPE ONE. After she went to work the following Monday, I reserved a room for myself from Friday on at the Paris Hotel. I would not be living in luxury, quite the contrary, so there would be no bonuses for me attached to my leaving her. Abandoning her—as some might put it. But they'd be wrong. I tried to prepare her by saying as little as possible to her in the evenings when she came home from work. She said little too. Perhaps the decision was mutual. We were polite to each other, we slept in the same bed. Politely. She took to getting undressed in the bathroom and emerging in the blue or white flannel nightgowns that we had established were left over from her teens. (A passage from her diary: "Book says don't be aggressive sexually. With all my heart, don't want to frighten Jack.") As we put the finishing touches on becoming enigmas to one another, I took the blue or white flannel to mean that she too was saying good-bye to the marriage. Sometimes I sensed she was crying into her pillow. Once or twice my own tears welled. We would cry and turn away from each other. Warm-ups for crying alone. I tried not to think about her but sometimes my heart caught with pity. Not when she cried—that frightened me, and I had to put all my resources into the service of pretending to be asleep—but when she slept. She would sigh in her sleep, and toss and turn shyly, circumspectly, as if she knew she could not give way excessively to her troubled dreams. I too tried to discipline myself, my movement, awake and asleep, so as not to disturb her, not to involve her.

On the evening of the fifth day, Friday, I spent the day steeling myself to tell her when she came home from work. I lived the day in fear, unable to divert myself. Though I felt sure I was right. Human beings were not meant to suffer so. Neither she nor I deserved this suffering, and I would die of it unless I rescued myself from it. Later, when my energies returned, when I'd regained some peace, I'd tried to help her. Any decent man would do that for the woman he was once married to, however briefly. But I could not help her now. Not the way things were. I'd do her in, as I was being done in—by her?—I thought yes, but was too numb really to question or to consider it. We'd, neither of us, survive unless we parted. That was clear. What was going on in her mind? Would she be able to take it? Surely, by now, she too wanted it. I sat there in the twilight, in the ragged armchair, waiting for her return. Would we touch when I told her? Would I pack this evening or leave the next day? The hotel reservation was for tonight. I couldn't bring myself to pack. I'd throw some overnight things in a suitcase after I told her, and return later on for the rest. It would be too painful to tell her and pack in the same evening.

I heard her key turn in the door, and I looked at the girl who walked in, in navy tailored suit and spotless white blouse. Her dark curls had escaped from one of their barrettes and were drifting over her cheek. She replaced her keys in her purse, and while she wasn't looking I gazed at her face. She was unusually pale. Chalky. So she too knew. And had braced herself for this. One couldn't be sure.

"Hi, darling," she said.

"Hi," I said softly. "There are cold cuts in the refrigerator," I told her. I'd laid in a week's supply of food so that that chore would be off her shoulders for the next few, cruelest, days. After that, it would be easier. I hoped.

"You shopped?" she said. I nodded mutely. "That was sweet." She set her things down and went into the bedroom. "I'll be out in a minute," she told me.

No need to account to me, Jen, or thank me, I thought. She was so sweet. Or could be. If only she weren't a child, if only I were stronger, as strong as my brother, I could have helped us. Or could I? Maybe if we had both been stronger, we would have, because of our essential incompatibility, destroyed each other. This way we were getting out in time. It would hurt. But just briefly. And we could remake our lives. Jennie would remarry, in a year or two—without the draining of her salary into the marriage, she would eventually be able to afford Dr. Selfridge's therapy—and I would resume life as a bachelor. I would take Davey's advice and not attempt to see Morrie again. I would lavish all that love on Libba. There was family enough for me to love in the family I was born into. I would not think, for the present, of any other family.

She came out of the bedroom. She'd taken off her jacket. She looked so small: the somber skirt, the stark white of the blouse. No frills. Very tailored. She smiled at me. "I'll just put on an apron," she said breathlessly, "and get things on the table."

I got up. "I'll help you," I said.

We got supper arranged on the table, and as she sat down she reclasped her straying hair in its barrette. I watched, as if fixated. "You're looking at me," she said. "Is something wrong?"

"I thought I'd like some milk," I said, hoping I was evading her question. Neither of us was ready for what was coming, yet.

"Oh," she gasped. "I'll get it."

"Sit still," I said, not knowing that my voice was gentle—knowing only that I was being very, very careful. "I'll get it."

We finished supper. "Leave the dishes," I said.

"Why? Shouldn't we get them out of the way?"

"They'll keep," I said. Then, bracing myself, I said: "We need to talk." We. One of the few times I'd been able to manage that.

"I'll just clear the table, then," she said. I had no idea of what she felt, whether she was as frightened as I.

I looked around the living room, trying to take in the apartment. Soon it would be hers. Hers. Maybe I'd help with the rent. I'd try. The dishes stopped rattling in the kitchen—Jennie, undomestic as she was, never broke a dish, never broke anything breakable—and she came back into the living room.

"Take off your apron, honey," I said. "It makes you look more wan than you are."

"I feel okay," she said, undoing the apron. She turned to go back into the kitchen to hang it on its proper hook.

"Just leave it on the sofa," I said. "Just sit down."

She sat on the sofa. "I guess I do feel tired," she said. And then, trying to smile: "But not too. It's just"—she shrugged—Friday."

"Jen," I began, "we're no good for each other."

"You've said that before," she said. "I just can't go through it again, Jack. Please don't."

"It has to be faced sooner or later, Jen." I was beginning to feel relief. I'd begun it.

I saw her slump. So she hadn't known. This would surprise her. On some level. Possibly shock her. I went to the sofa and sat down beside her. I could risk that now because

I had control. Of myself. The tension went out of her body as she felt me next to her. I put my arm around her. She nestled against my shoulder. We sat there for a moment. I would miss this marriage one day, but not now. It was almost over.

I let go of her and moved an inch or two away. She sat up straight, watching me. Probably frightened. I was numbed, fortunately. That gave me an advantage I now vowed I would not exploit. I would be as gentle as possible. How to begin? Well, factually.

"I've made a reservation at a hotel," I said quietly. "The Paris Hotel. Uptown. I'll leave you the number so you can reach me any time, but I think we should both try to discipline ourselves and not talk to each other for the first week or so. Unless it's absolutely necessary. Good God, what's the matter?" She was trembling violently and had begun to gasp—as if for breath—in a way that frightened me. I stood up.

"Where are you going?" she managed to say. So she was capable of speech. I'd thought she was having a convulsion.

"I'm going to get you a glass of water. Or a shot of Scotch. Which would you prefer?"

"I don't want anything," she said. "Please sit by me."

"Okay," I said. "Jennie," I said, burying my head in my hands, "please don't take it so hard."

"I love you," she said. She still had not cried. "We love each other, Jack." It was a plea. Then I realized that it was also a question. She was waiting for me to reply.

"I don't know," I said. "If we do, then love's not enough." She began to tremble again. "Jen," I said, torn with pity, "you'll find someone else."

"I love you," she said. "I've trusted you."

"I'm sorry," I said. "Jen, I'm not good enough for you." Would a lawyer, if I'd engaged one, allow me to show this remorse? It didn't matter. There was no lawyer. Yet. "Darling, please," I said, "I never wanted to hurt you."

"Is there someone else?" she asked, as if she were able to bear pain.

"No," I said, thankful that it was true. "I shouldn't have married at all, probably. I've wronged you." The nonexistent lawyer stood over my shoulder, telling me to shut up. Admit nothing. But it was true. I shouldn't have married her.

"No," she said. "We're right for each other. We can work this out."

"No," I said.

"It's been less than a year," she implored, trying to bargain.

"I know. But it would hurt more if we waited longer. Please believe me, Jennie."

"Why are you so sure?"

"I can't bear it any longer. I don't know why. It doesn't matter why. It's not your fault."

"My cooking," she whispered. "That bothered you."

I nodded. It had. But there were things that must have bothered her too. I said that.

"We can work it out," she said.

"Jennie," I begged, "think of the things that bothered you. That'll help you. You don't like sex all that well, do you?"

"You told me," she whispered, "that it would take time. You've been so patient. Why are you giving up now?"

"That what would take time?" A pinprick of curiosity had interrupted the free flow of words that followed from my resolve. My resolve to leave her. And now this curiosity. "What would take time?" I repeated. Would I be able to bear the answer?

She must have sensed my remoteness, and some primitive self-preserving instinct guided the evasion that followed: "I love sleeping with you," she said.

"But what would take time? What did you mean?"

"For it to get even better," she said desperately.

A charade. This was a charade. The marriage was a charade. Wait thirty seconds and you'd get a clear reminder, in case you forgot. She was lying. But I didn't want to call her on it. That would hurt. Her. My curiosity faded, taking away also my pain. I looked down at my knees. "We've given it enough time," I muttered.

"You can't just leave," she said.

"Sometimes a clean break is best," I said. Words of wisdom. The truth was, there was no good way to do this. Lucky there weren't children. Just Jen and me. No one else would be hurt. Significantly hurt. I tried not to think about the people who cared about me. Who cared about Jennie? Did anyone, really? Besides me? I thought of Audrey with some relief.

She was whispering something. "I can't hear you," I said. There was a thudding in my eardrums. Like the pressure of descent in an elevator or plane.

"Why didn't you warn me?"

"I tried to, Jen."

"But I thought it was just a mood."

"You hoped it was. So did I."

"Maybe—" She broke off.

"What, dear?"

"Maybe we should see a marriage counselor."

I felt dizzy, nauseated. "No," I said. I looked across at her. There was blood on her white blouse.

"What is it?" I asked. "What's wrong?"

"I think it's a nosebleed," she said. "It's nothing." Another drop of blood spilled.

"You're hemorrhaging," I said.

"No. I get these sometimes." She sat there, then fumbled in her purse for a kleenex. Why did she always keep her purse with her? I must ask her that sometime, when we were friends again. I looked at my watch. Seven-thirty. The hotel would hold the room for me, but I was getting very, very tired. We'd have to cut short this conversation soon. Maybe meet in a neutral place tomorrow, and talk. Maybe a cold-turkey withdrawal wouldn't do. For either of us. I looked at her. The blood on the kleenex frightened me. Ice, I thought.

"Lean your head back," I said to her. "I'll be right back."

I wrapped some ice cubes in a clean kitchen towel and came back into the living room. "I think this is what you're supposed to do," I said, applying the compress, then lifting her hand so that she could administer the pressure herself. I touched her shoulder. "Take it easy," I said.

She started to cry. With tears. Liquidity. Her body couldn't take this. Poor Jen. I hadn't meant to shock her so. "I'll be all right," she told me. And still cried.

Why was this so hard? She must have known. How could one know and still hope?

"Has the bleeding stopped?" I asked, leaning toward her.

"I don't know."

"Let me look." I removed the compress and tried to consider what to do next. "It's better," I said softly. At that, she leaned forward to hug me. "No," I said sharply. "We can't." I knew she hadn't staged her nosebleed, but there were limits to how much I could permit my body to be involved with hers. Better for both of us that we not touch. Or touch as little as possible and still remain human. I found myself counting, trying to figure how many thousands added up to one million. If I lived thirty more years, how old would I be and how much longer would I have to live? What would Jennie be like as she aged?

"Why can't I touch you?" she whispered. "You're my husband."

"For the same reason I can't touch you now," I said. "It would be rape."

"I don't feel that way."

"You will. You're in shock now, darling. I didn't want to shock you, and I feel so sorry—" My voice broke, but I caught myself and went on, "So sorry that I have, but later, when you think about it, you'll know you don't want me any more than I want you."

"You don't want me," she said dully. Why was she listening so selectively? I had told her she didn't want me either. Maybe later, surely later, that would sink in.

"I said we don't want each other," I said tiredly. "Has the bleeding stopped?"

"I guess so. I'm so sorry." She looked so scared.

"Don't be sorry. Keep the compress on for a little while. Just to be sure." Maybe her body needed this minimal attention from me, to ease her shock.

"I guess nosebleeds happen," she said.

"I guess."

Suddenly I panicked. We could not fall into this kind of ordinary exchange, the sort of exchange that augured continuity of some sort. What boring couples talked about well into senility. It had its lure, it could seduce one, but I had guarded against it, caught it—I hoped—in time, and would guard against it now. I couldn't allow either of us to be entrapped by it.

"Nosebleeds happen."

"I guess."

"Guess who?"

"Not me."

(What was this? Some routinized interchange, triggering a memory from childhood? "Knock, knock."

"Who's there?"

"Not me.")

"Jack," she said, a little more bravely, "have you confided in anyone?"

"No," I said emphatically, believing that to be the answer she wanted, and therefore forgetting in the moment that I'd told Davey.

"Can't we wait?" she begged me. "You should at least tell Barney." Oh. So she thought turning to a confidant would change my mind.

"I've told David.

Her eyes widened. "Oh. Was he on my side?"

"There are no sides to this, Jennie," I said, washed out—

how had I permitted myself to reach the point of this exhaustion?—"It's both our faults and it's neither of our faults."

"Tell me what Davey said."

"He said he was sorry."

"Was that all he said?"

"I guess there was more. I told him how I felt, how I didn't think we were right for each other." I was giving her facts. I knew she would not be comforted by them. She wanted more. "What is it?" I asked. She'd been drifting, drifting into her own thoughts, I could tell.

She swallowed. "I was thinking about my father. He would have liked you so much."

I doubted it. I must have sighed, for she came at me again with hope.

"Davey likes me," she said protestingly. "I know he does."

"So do I. I like you."

"I don't want you to like me," she whispered. "I want you to love me."

"Jennie. Don't do this to us. It doesn't matter whether we love each other or not."

"It's the only thing that matters," she said.

"That can't be. We're suffering too much."

"I'm not. But if you leave me, I won't be able to bear it. I can bear anything else," she said.

"Jen, you're stronger than that," I said hollowly, no longer knowing what I was talking about. Maybe she was too frail to leave. But, in the words of the song, she-got-along-without-me-before-she-met-me—she-could-get-along-without-me-now. I began to pray wordlessly.

"Davey likes me," she said again, insistently. "I can't believe that he didn't take my side."

"He likes you very much," I said, remembering for almost the first time that Davey had urged me to marry her, wondering why he had not brought that up when he talked, reminding myself to ask him as soon as I could. "But he said, finally, he couldn't counsel me about the divorce."

"What does that mean?" she asked, panicked.

"I guess it means that he left it to me. It's my decision. And, Jen, even though you don't see this now, it's your decision too. You'll be glad of it, eventually. I know you don't feel this way now, but I think you'll feel later that it was the right thing."

"You can't be that sure," she said.

"Yes, I can."

"No."

"It's over, Jen." I stood up, took the now lukewarm compress from her hand, went back into the kitchen, and came back with some fresh ice cubes. I looked at her. There were spots of blood on her blouse, and it was damp with ice water. I gave her the compress.

"Why are you taking care of me?" she whispered. "You must care about me."

"I do," I said. "One thing has nothing to do with the other."

"I don't understand."

"Don't try to." I didn't know which of us wasn't making any sense. Maybe no sense could be made of it, yet. Maybe I'd never understand it. I just knew I was right about it. There it was.

"I trusted you. Remember the time you just—just stroked me to sleep?"

Which time? I asked her.

She told me. The morning I got the telegram and called my mother. That morning Jennie couldn't or wouldn't make pancakes. She was so scared she shook. I led her into the bedroom. This was before we were married. Something I'd done without knowing why. A ballet, slow, of caresses, the object being to soothe, to lull, not to excite or frighten. And afterward, like a child, she'd fallen asleep. "You wouldn't have done that if you didn't love me. I never trusted anyone like that. You can't leave me. I trust you so."

I was silent.

"Didn't it mean anything to you?"

"Of course it did."

"Then you can't do this to us."

"Maybe it was wrong, Jennie," I said slowly, steeling myself not to recall the moment in its texture and detail, as she had—it would hurt me too much. "If it was wrong, if I've betrayed a trust—" I was beginning to choke up.

"Yes?" She was prompting me, but there was such terror in her voice, her eyes.

"I apologize. If it was wrong," I went on, becoming briefly more sure of myself, "I apologize. I don't remember why I did it."

"You loved me."

"Maybe," I said. "Then can't you just treasure it as a moment? There'll be other moments, with other men."

"I'll never trust anyone the way I trusted you. There won't be any other men." I flinched. Then she asked, falteringly, "Didn't it mean anything to you? Don't you treasure it?"

"Jen, I don't know," I said in torment. I ached with fatigue. I stood up. "I'll know later. Maybe. Now I've got to pack."

"Oh no!" She flung herself at me. I stood there. Seconds passed. She lay on the floor, sobbing, grasping my trouser cuffs, hugging my legs.

"Jennie," I said. "Darling, let go." Somehow, I got her to let go of me. I knelt down and held her.

"Stay the night," she pleaded. "Just don't go now."

"We'll have to face it sometime," I said. Would it be better to delay?

"Not now," she gasped. "I'll die if you go now."

"Not literally, honey," I said, holding her, holding us. "You won't literally die."

"Please don't go. Not now."

"I'll stay one more night," I said to her then. I tried to help her up. She was grasping strands of carpet. "Come on, honey. Nothing's worth this."

"Promise me you'll stay tonight."

"I promise." I would leave in the morning. Maybe that would be better for me too. Maybe I needed more time than I realized.

"Will you sleep in the same bed with me?"

"Yes. Yes. We'll sleep. That's what we'll do." I guided her into the bedroom. "You get into bed now. You need the rest. I'll do the dishes." I was going to phone the hotel too, to notify them to expect me tomorrow and to ask them to hold the room, but I decided I didn't need to tell her that. Maybe she'd overhear me. I hoped she would.

"If I fall asleep?" she asked.

"What?"

"You won't leave if I fall asleep?"

"No, I won't," I said. It was necessary, for both our sakes, that Jennie get a good night's sleep. This scene could not be repeated. And she'd need her sleep to give her strength to face it, and carry it quietly, with a fortitude I prayed was in her, when the time came for me to leave tomorrow.

But I think that she lay awake all night. I awoke, disoriented, my head fogged, my throat dry. Within moments, I remembered that I had planned this morning to wake up in the privacy and safety of the hotel. But the plan had gone awry, and the hurdle I'd planned to clear once and for all now loomed before me on what was to have been the first free morning, the Escape. Instinctively, I shrank from any contact with her. I held my arms close to my sides and lay there, unmoving, hearing only my own breath. She wasn't there. The shade was up, the light was streaming in. She had done that without waking me. I flung an arm across the hollow of the bed beside me where she'd been lying. Lying. A pun. I smiled mirthlessly. The sheet, next to me, still bore the heat of her body. And the damned sun, pouring in, hurt my eyes. Where was she? Had she done anything to herself? As I lay there, the memory of her fierce despair of the night before returned to me. Well, I hadn't enjoyed myself too much either. How could she permit herself this instantaneous onset of what could only end in serious emotional debility?

Didn't she realize that in crisis one had to husband one's resources? Husband. Angrily, I kicked the tangled sheets and blankets away from me. Flinging herself on the floor. Why did she act as if she were an insect I could step on? One had to maintain whatever one could of one's dignity. Self-respect. Where was she? I supposed it was my responsibility to go and look. Probably she was in the kitchen, playing hard to get.

When I found her there, her face no longer white but yellowish, green, as if she were ill, dark circles under her eyes, her eyes staring—vacant?—my heart began to pound. "What are you doing up so early?" I asked, by way of monitoring her vital signs.

She shrugged.

"Didn't you sleep?"

No answer.

I tried again. "Good morning," I said gently.

"Hi." She was barely audible.

"Are you okay?" I asked cautiously. The thing was to negotiate this passage without further wounding her. I had so hoped that by the morning she'd have taken it in, that we'd, both of us, be stronger. I didn't know about myself, my own strength—or the lack of it—but she looked unwell. Should I call someone, her sister perhaps, or, if need be, Audrey, to stay with her? I didn't relish what viperish I-told-you-so remarks would be forthcoming from Audrey, but Jennie's health obviously came first. And her welfare.

"Should I get someone to stay with you?"

She shook her head no. I looked at her terrified eyes. Dry. Beyond tears? Had she cried at all yet today? She kept looking at me. What was she looking for? Was it there? Or was I a mirage? It didn't matter. My survival mattered, and it was linked to hers, and both were linked to the necessity of our separation. Suddenly her eyes closed, and she passed her hand over her forehead.

"You feverish?" I asked. These questions could not go on forever. I could not, whatever happened to her, continue to

---

2 1 3

be involved with her, her body. She had lined up a retinue of competent professionals for her spectrum of ills: Smidler, Selfridge, her gynecologist, or was it Smidler who took care of that as well as other things? Her insides. I looked at her. Her pallor, that tinge of unhealthy color, frightened me. Maybe I should call her mother. She got up unsteadily. I knew I should move toward her and touch her, but what the hell was going on and what would that accomplish? What was all this mystification accompanied by looking ill? What was this illness that didn't have a name?

"Excuse me," she said, as if she could hardly get the words out, her voice was trembling, and she passed by me. Our bathrobes brushed against each other briefly. Then I heard her footsteps quicken. Then her retching in the bathroom. She, who so valued her bodily privacy, had not troubled to close the door. Probably didn't have the time. God, I wished emotions didn't hit the body, Jennie's body, so hard. I couldn't, I told myself I shouldn't, go in and help her. I was frightened. I didn't want to kill her. Resolutely, trying to figure what I could appropriately, ethically, do and not do, I sat at the kitchen table. She'd return. I got up to put up some tea. Sweet tea. That would help her nausea. In a few moments she returned.

"Do you feel better?" I asked.

Her eyes filled with tears. "Yes."

"I've put up some tea. Settles the stomach. Jen. Jen. Please don't cry."

Now she was shaking from head to foot with silent sobs.

"The tea will be ready in a minute. Don't cry. Or tell me what it is, at least."

Sounds. She couldn't get the words out.

"I can't understand you," I said reasonably. "Pull yourself together for a moment and try and tell me."

"Please hold me," she said.

She didn't know it, but she was giving me ammunition. I didn't want this power over her, to inflict pain, to arouse—

occasionally—pleasure, to soothe. I hadn't bargained for it. "You can't ask me," I enunciated carefully, in the accents of a college lecturer, "to do something with my body that I don't want to do."

Something indistinguishable.

"What? Jennie. For God's sakes, talk. Here's the tea," I said, setting it in front of her. "Put plenty of sugar in it, darling." The endearment brought a fresh set of tears. And she began to shake again. I spooned sugar into her tea. I don't know how I went through these motions. I was anesthetized. Her pain dwarfed mine. Or choked it off. Gave it no room to breathe. Even in agony we couldn't coexist. She came first. Ladies first. Don't be a smartass, I then told myself. I was in better shape than she, now. There'd be time for me later.

She took a sip, unaided by me, I was grateful to note.

"Sip some more. Feel better?"

She stared at me. I don't remember when I'd seen her look so unwell. I hoped, through the stages of our separation, our divorce, she'd recover her looks. That look of innocence and health. I wanted her to be well.

She said, "I don't understand how you can be so cold-blooded."

Oh, Christ. Accusations. "Everything I'm doing," I said in a trembling voice, beginning to feel sick myself, "I'm doing for you. Right now. I'm not cold-blooded at all." I wasn't.

"What you said about your body," she said, still in a near-whisper, her voice shaking with her agony—or her rage?

"What about it?"

"I only asked you to touch me."

"You asked me to hold you. I can't hold you now. Look, Jen, if you're going to fall apart over this I'll get someone to stay with you." God, here I was, getting in deeper than I'd planned to again. Why did I overextend? Like the loan to Helen. And the weight from that, that I could carry for the rest of my life. Why didn't I tell Jen to call someone herself, decide on the person, call him or her—preferably her—and get her over here. Girlfriends needed girlfriends. I was the source of her pain, therefore could not heal or assuage or diminish it.

"You won't hold me?"

"No. Don't cry," I said more sharply than I'd intended. "Drink your tea."

We sat in silence for some moments. I wanted to ask if she felt better—specifically, if she was still experiencing the nausea—but that seemed too raw and personal to ask. I felt shy and clumsy. Otherwise, I felt nothing. I was glad of that. I wanted to feel nothing for the rest of my life.

"Do you feel better?" I asked. She muttered something. I couldn't make it out. "What?" I asked her.

"All those plans we had . . ." she was saying.

I dropped my eyes. I suppose we had talked about our future. But there'd be another man. She was biting her lip. "What is it, Jen?"

"You don't care any more about it? About what's going to happen to us?"

"I'm going to get dressed, throw some things into a suitcase and leave here within the hour. The next time we talk about us it'll be on neutral ground. Now I don't think you should be alone, so I'm going to call your sister."

She looked wild. "Don't," she said, swiveling around in her chair. I stood up to steady her. I wasn't about to go through another thing with her flinging herself on the linoleum, then clutching my legs, my ankles, not letting me walk. I put my hand on her shoulder. The most unsensual thing I'd ever done.

"I'm pregnant," she said.

A ringing in my ears. Too much aspirin? I couldn't remember if I'd, in fact, taken aspirin. Recently. "I didn't hear you," I said. I'd heard her perfectly well. And she did not repeat it. I knelt on the floor beside her and put my head on her lap. She didn't touch me. Cautiously, I touched her abdomen. I could, I supposed, if I wanted to, reach under her nightclothes and touch her bare skin. I put my arms around her, around her lower back, and pressed my head against her belly. Was this the way it was meant to be? We couldn't afford it. I'd have to go to work. I couldn't leave her now. Why hadn't she told me sooner? I asked her that. She didn't answer. "How long have you known?" I asked. Then, beginning on some level to absorb it, to take it in as a fact: "Jen?" I said softly. "How many months?"

She sat perfectly still. Long after it was over, I wondered what would have happened if I'd looked at her face, if I hadn't been in this posture of giving myself over to her, to her nature, to the inevitability of her body, to the sense, however briefly experienced, of the concreteness of our future.

"I can't lie," she said.

"What?"

"It isn't true. I'm not pregnant."

"Are you sure?" Slowly, I steeled myself to let go of her.

"I'm sure. I can't lie," she said expressionlessly. But she had.

I stood up and looked at her in anguish. Anguish turning to fury. For the second time—first our marriage, and now this—she'd given me a future and then taken it away. My temples throbbed. I said, "I thought that was why you were sick."

"No," she said, her voice trembling a little. She said, "I got sick because—because of last night. But I've taken my pill. I haven't missed any periods."

"You're not pregnant."

"No," she said quietly. She'd accomplished what she'd wanted. My utter vulnerability. My trusting embrace. How could I be put through anything more?

"Talk about breaking faith," I said.

"What?"

"Breaking faith. Betraying trust," I said. "I seem to recall last night that there was a lot of pious mouthing around on your part about how you trusted me. So shook up I agreed to spend one more night. Now you spring this on me, then socko, before I recover, you spring me another. Now she's pregnant, now she's not. Lady, you are the limit."

"I guess," she said, looking in some curious way deeply relieved, "you have a right to be angry."

"Angry," I echoed. "I don't know if I'm angry or not. I just know I'm getting out of here. I can't live in this sick environment another minute. And I'm not just talking about your throwing up."

"I feel better," she said.

"I don't care."

She reddened. It was nice to see the green supplanted. By the blood of a blush. "What's the matter now?"

"I'm ashamed that I lied."

"Jennie, forget it. The longer I stay, the messier it gets, for both of us. Don't you see that?"

"No. It's your leaving that's making it messy."

"I'm not staying around to argue," I said. I walked out of the kitchen, into the bedroom—first mine, then "ours," whatever that was supposed to mean, soon to be hers exclusively—and looked at the bed we'd shared for what would probably be the last time. From now on, she'd sleep in it alone. I didn't want to think about other men. Would it have made a difference if she were really pregnant? I didn't want to think about that. Libba. Libba. Getting dressed—I'd shower later at the hotel—I said the name more than once, more than twice, to quiet my pounding heart. I could get ill too. Very ill. I wasn't as strong as I thought. Let alone as strong as she thought. She'd find a strong man who'd help her recover from this. She was off to a good running start with that lie. Would he sleep with her in this bed? None of my business, I told myself. I collected my toilet articles in the bathroom. She'd cleaned up after herself. Sprayed the room with perfume. Sick female animals leave no trace. They protect their genitals. They protect their privacy. Damn them. She stood in the bathroom door.

"Watch me if you want to, but it isn't going to change a thing," I said. "Or have you come here to throw up some more?"

She leaned against the doorjamb. "No," she said.

"What do you think it is? Or was?" I asked conversationally, brushing past her into the bedroom. My suitcase was lying open on the bed, her side of it, and I began helterskelter to pack, "A virus?"

"No," she whispered.

"Emotional upset, then?"

"Yes."

"Jennie, call Smidler and make an appointment for a checkup next week. I think you're better, so I'll leave it to you to call Audrey or your sister if you want to be with someone." I added, "Maybe Ezra's still around."

I turned so that I could see the impact of this on her. The blush had, of course, faded. Her skin still bore the tinge of illness, an illness that probably was not physical. Not in its origins. Shock. Emotional upset. "Why did you say that to me?" she whispered. "About Ezra?"

Why the hell had I? I didn't know. There must have been some reason. "Partly," I said, "because I'm nasty, and I want you to remember that so you'll come to your senses and not mourn me. And also," I added gently, glad that I'd thought of it, "to remind you that there are other men in the world who have cared about you, and there will be again. You need more confidence in yourself," I said, snapping shut the suitcase.

"If you feel I need more confidence, why are you leaving? That hurts my confidence," she said. Like a schoolchild.

"Because I am not an emotional pharmacy or supermarket. You can't just reach into me for something you need and throw it into your psychological shopping cart," I said, taking a considerable incidental pride in my metaphor. Then she began to sob again. Christ, I thought. I shouldn't have been a wiseass. This is rough. She's feeling it now; with any failure of luck I'd feel it—or something, probably something painful or bad—later.

"Jennie," I said helplessly, "you'll make yourself sick."

"I am sick. I was sick," she corrected herself. And then:

"And you did that to me. I didn't make myself sick. You made me sick."

"Tell me," I said. "There must have been something about me you didn't like." She frowned. She'd thought of something. Good. Let her say it, and then I'd get out. "Out with it," I barked. She hesitated. Damn it. Another delaying tactic. Didn't she see she was torturing us both? Suitcase in hand, I strode into the living room, nearly made it to the door. She followed me. "Wait," she said.

I put the suitcase down, intending this pause to be brief. She stood there, weeping. "Darling, don't," I said. I literally could not move. I could not leave her like this. She was shivering. "Shall I get you some brandy?" I asked. She looked bewildered. I went into the kitchen and poured a shot and brought it out to her.

"No," she said. She looked at her watch. "It's morning."

Probably it was too early for brandy. On a virtually empty stomach. A morning like this. "I'll leave the bottle on the kitchen counter," I said, walking back into the kitchen with the shot glass.

When I returned, she seemed to have composed herself. Good. That took care of one of us. One to go, and once in the hotel I could attend to that. Must remember to get some booze into the room, in case I couldn't sleep at night. Then she said, "I thought of something. Something I didn't like. I didn't like your not working."

It was spoken in a whisper I could barely hear. But I didn't ask her to repeat it. I knew I'd heard it right. If I could just hold on till I got out of here. I picked up the suitcase. Instantly, she positioned herself in front of the door. Christ, if it were anybody but Jen I wouldn't believe this. What melodrama. And they called it love.

"Move aside, Jen," I said. Forcefully, so that she would listen, I said: "Jen, pull yourself together." I wanted to tell her again that she should not do this to herself, but then she'd cling to that and try, as she'd been trying since this heartache began last night, to cling to me, to prolong each moment, so that each moment would produce myriad other moments. And there would be no escape. "Please don't stand in front of the door," I said with all the control I could muster, and with the vestiges of the thing people called courtesy.

She moved aside. "Thank you," I said.

"You're welcome," she said.

How nice that we both still had good manners.

"It's the Paris Hotel," I began. "The number's—"

"Don't," she said. Panicked? Okay. She'd find the number. I'd scribbled it on our—our?—telephone pad.

Funny, I couldn't bring myself to just open the door and go out. Where was ceremony? There was no right ceremony for this.

"I want you to take care of yourself," I said. Then I added, "We'll be in touch."

Silence. "Do you understand?"

I thought I saw her poised to leap at me again, like a jungle cat. Swiftly, I opened the door. Nobody in the corridor waiting for the elevator. Good. I said what I had to say: "Good-bye."

Apparently that word was not in her lexicon any more than "Good morning." It had gotten scrubbed somewhere along the line.

So I ventured on to another path of finality: "I'm leaving. For good, Jen."

We looked at each other. I remember thinking she looked something like Mr. Rochester's first wife. I wondered if I should josh her, say something sweet and kidding.

"For good," she repeated after me.

"Yes," I said, exhaling with relief.

"I know," she said. "I've always known."

She shuddered.

I walked out. I closed the door.

I got into the narrow elevator and leaned against its wall. I felt like a corpse.

PART 3

E

SCAPE, DAY ONE. Afternoon.

I checked in.

They didn't give me Davey's old room, nor did the room they gave me have a similar layout. But the smell was the same. That was comforting. The chlorine had seeped into the walls. It would rid the system of poisons. I tipped the elderly bellhop, who looked grudgingly at the three quarters in his palm and said something mean about the ventilating system. I wanted him out. Immediately. I'd figure out how to ventilate the place later. I inspected the linen. The sheets looked fresh, clean, though they'd been torn and somehow mended—were those patches?—and the blanket had a neutral, bleached smell. Okay. I unlocked my suitcase and hung up my clothes. Not enough hangers. Damn them. I didn't want to have to ring for more. I let my sports things and other clothes that could withstand wrinkling remain in the suitcase. I got out my pajamas and bathrobe—why had I brought my bathrobe? I wasn't expecting company—and flung them across the bed. Looked at my watch. It was one-thirty. Had I eaten? Did it matter? Should I take a shower? Suddenly, the thought of a shower frightened me. I'd rather be unclean. The pounding of my heart frightened me; I didn't yet want to die. Maybe a hot tub. That's the sort of thing Davey would prescribe. I decided not to bathe immediately. I was afraid of the water. That immersion of my body would strip me of the events of that morning. And I was not ready. What I must do, I decided, was tell the people who needed to know. My brother. I dialed the lab, then into the first ring realized that Davey must be home; it was, after all, Satur-day. Quickly, I dialed again. Betty answered.

"It's Jack," I said cheerfully. "How are you?"

"Just fine," she chirped. "How are you?"

"All right," I said in a steady voice, though I was feeling anything but steady. I was wondering how I could politely, tactfully, get her off the phone and get my brother on in-stead.

Not wanting to offend her by making this request pre-maturely or too direct, I asked: "How is Libba?"

"Adorable. She's getting bigger all the time. She's all over the place, so we just got a playpen so we won't have to worry that she'll play with matches or fool with the wiring." Betty laughed. "She'll just have to be confined."

"You don't keep her in the playpen all the time, do you?" I asked, alarmed. "She's going to need more space if she's going to really learn to walk."

"She is walking and I'm quite aware of that," said Betty. She sounded testy. "A playpen is hardly a prison," she went on.

"Oh, I know. You're doing a beautiful job with her."

"Thank you," said Betty modestly. "Davey helps."

"Uh huh." I was so frantic to speak to him, it was all I could do to control myself, to stay on top of my despair and the urgency of my need. But it became immediately apparent that she took my terseness as a sign of some offensive brotherly indifference to him. He had not been best man at my wedding, and she'd never forgotten. She was saying, "He was at Dr. Frame's this morning with your mother, and now he's on his way to the lab. He's running himself ragged. He'll be back in the late afternoon, and then I want him to take a nap." Was this gibbering a true reflection of her concern, or was she trying to make me feel guilty? How could I tell her I loved my brother? Why did I have to? Why didn't Davey make it clear to her?

"Could he call me back?" I asked.

She sighed. "I suppose so. Later this evening."

"Couldn't he call sooner?"

She said laconically, "You might reach him at the lab."

"I tried him there."

"Just a minute," said Betty, "the baby's crying." She put the receiver down heavily on what must have been a wood surface. My head began to hurt. I didn't hear the sound of any baby's cries, but perhaps mothers were alert to such things. They hear the cry while it is still a whisper in the throat. Except for my mother.

Betty returned to the phone. "Jack, I've got to go. Any message for Davey?"

"I'll try him at the lab," I said, miserably.

"Is it anything special?" She sounded curious.

"Jennie and I have split up," I blurted out.

"Jack!" She sounded shocked.

"I'm sorry," I said numbly.

"It's kind of taken my breath away," she said.

Lady, people do it all the time, and where in the hell is your husband?

"Davey didn't say anything to you?"

"No." She was really dumbstruck. For a change. "Where are you calling from?"

"A hotel. Davey knows it." I gave her the name and number.

"I remember," she breathed. Thinking of her own marriage, its origins. "How's Jennie?"

"Oh, just wonderful. We're both shaky, but I think she's gonna be okay."

"Where is she?"

"In my apartment."

"Yours?"

"Well, I'm turning it over to her."

"That's very fair," Betty said.

"I want to be fair."

"I don't know what to say. I had no idea anything was wrong. Davey and I usually tell each other everything." They did? I felt a pang of envy. Betty said, "I feel I shouldn't pry."

"Pry," I said. She was family, in a way. She had a right to know.

"What happened?" Oh, right off a global question. Wouldn't you know.

"It's a long story."

"Did you meet another girl?" Betty asked delicately.

"No," I said. Silence on the other end. Disbelief? "We just didn't get along, and it came to a head this morning." Last night, actually, but why go into all the gory details.

Still silence. "Betty? You there?"

"Yes. I was just thinking how sad it is for Jennie. I hope I'm not saying anything out of line, but I got the impression she wanted children."

Damn her. I felt stung. What was I supposed to do about that? Why was that all she and Davey harped on? Was it my responsibility to go around impregnating all the young women with maternal longings from coast to coast? Was I just a stud? I decided to deal with this, not let it get by.

"We tried," I said shortly. "I suspect Jennie has trouble getting pregnant." A fine lie. It made me, briefly, less miserable.

"Oh," said Betty, sounding embarrassed, "I didn't know."

"She's young," I went on, taking care to keep my statements broadly worded. "She'll be all right."

"Gosh," said Betty. "I hope so. Are you all right?"

"No," I choked, astonished at my own quick welling of emotion. Why had I lied? Because of Jennie's short-lived but nonetheless hurtful lie this morning, that's why. It had pained me more than I knew. So I'd gotten even with her. Now the question was, since Betty had asked me how I was, would she come through? Would she, for instance, volunteer to take the baby, drive down toward the lab, and look for Davey? Then I remembered it was a one-car household, and Davey probably had taken the car. But I suspected that Betty, even if she had the wherewithal, wouldn't have done it.

"I know Davey will want to talk to you," she floundered.

"I'll try him at the lab," I said heavily. I wasn't going to get any more from her in the way of sympathy.

"The family will be so upset," she said. Fuck the family. "We'll have to break it to your mother gently." Chatter chatter. I had to feel mean, even if I didn't act mean, so that I could once again feel numb.

"Yeah," I said.

"I'd better go and change Libba," Betty said. "I'll have Davey call you later on if you can't reach him at the lab."

Later on wouldn't do. It had to be now. Soon. Didn't she understand? Suddenly, I realized that she was truly very frightened. She was Jennie's age, and Jennie's plight was somehow close to home. "Okay, Betty. Thanks. Try not to take it hard." I was only half-sincere. I knew some part of me bitterly wanted the whole world to suffer as I was suffering.

"I'll try," she said with a quite inappropriate obedience. Didn't anybody know how to talk?

"Well, good-bye," she said shakily.

Click.

Babies. What would my limp prick do for entertainment from now on.

The futility of sex. The tragedy of it. The emptiness of all human interchange. Or most of it. The burden of my news probably sat more heavily on Betty's shoulders than on mine.

Maybe I shouldn't tell anybody else. This news had a life of its own, meant something different to each hearer, frightened or pained each in a way that I could not control. Everyone I broke it to would suffer, as Jennie—to whom I had broken it first—had. And I was numb, so I suffered least of all. I always knew, somehow, that my life would be as bleak as this room. That's why this room comforted me. I was in my future.

I don't remember how long I sat there. I got up once to pull down the shades. That was all. I was motionless, waiting for nothing, in the chair. Trying to expect nothing. Really nothing.

It was growing comfortably dark in the room, while I pondered whether to go out and buy some Scotch to put myself out with later. I was safely emptied of pleasure and pain—anesthetized—but sleep might be a problem. I might suffer nightmares that I was sleeping beside Jennie. That I would hurt her. Physically. Or do her some other kind of harm. Emotional harm. What was she feeling or doing now? I hoped that the realization of her good fortune in being free of me would come soon. Today, perhaps even tomorrow might be too early for that awareness to dawn. But I prayed it would come soon. I didn't want her on my conscience. I was okay. Sitting here, in the soothing near-dark, was healing. Maybe soon I'd have the courage to get up and take a bath. Or should I go out for the Scotch. Maybe there was a liquor store in the neighborhood that would deliver. Surely the hotel would know. Soon I'd feel strong enough to ring the desk, ask them. But not now. The sound of another human voice, a strange one, might rock my boat. No life raft. That's what I'd given her when I'd left. Hadn't I? Life was really quite simple, when you thought about it, allowed yourself to experience the simplicity in a small, nearly bare room. Not bare enough, but it would do until I had the strength to make things simpler.

The phone rang. Davey. Or Jen. I hoped she wasn't cruel or foolish enough to try and reach me now. Let it be Davey.

It was. But why was he sounding so worried?

"I'm fine," I answered him calmly. "What's that noise in the background?"

He said, "You sound awful. Damn it, I didn't think you'd do anything this quickly."

"Well, I told you I would," I said reasonably. "So I don't see why you're upset. Did Betty say I was upset? If she did, then I'm afraid I have to tell you she was exaggerating."

"She was crying when she called me," Davey said.

"Well, I'm sorry about that, but I didn't say anything to make her cry."

"Jack, what you do and say affects other people. Can't you get that through your head?"

"Why are you so angry?" I asked him. Then, before he could reply, I repeated my earlier inquiry, which he'd dodged: "What's that noise in the background? Are you at the lab?"

"I'm home now. Betty called and asked me to come home."

"Jesus."

Silence.

Then I said, "There was no need for that."

"She's very shaken."

"I'm sorry to hear that," I said carefully, "because I feel wonderful. Jennie and I are going to be good friends. It was an amicable parting."

"This morning?" he interrupted me.

"Yes. She told me she'd go to Bonwit's this afternoon and take advantage of a lingerie sale they're having."

"Are you serious?" Davey asked me.

"Why shouldn't I be?" I said. "I'm sure neither Jennie nor I is as upset as Betty. Or you," I added meanly. Why hadn't he been home earlier, before I'd worked myself with great difficulty into this precarious peace of mind. Anything could disturb it. That probably was why I was telling these white lies. I had meant to be merely ironic, but had gotten carried away. Now I was married to these lies. Which were, after all, a kindness to my brother. He and his wife apparently were not taking this news in stride. Betty's hysteria—for that was what I assumed it was—didn't surprise me, but my brother's agitation did. How immature. That's what the complacency of marriage probably did to one. Wrecked the imagination, so that any departure from what the married person took to be the norm proved very threatening. Led the married person to draw wild inferences.

"Look, Jack, why don't you come out here for a while?" Davey asked.

"Why should I? I'm comfortable where I am."

"You sound damned uncomfortable, and don't lie to me. I know you too well. You're lying about yourself, and I don't believe for one minute that Jennie is spending the afternoon at Bonwit's. Have you been drinking?"

"No." Suddenly I was cold sober. I had gotten drunk on misery and on my wish to hurt.

"You do realize that your news is not exactly a birthday party?"

"Yes."

"Okay. Now we're getting somewhere. I'm not asking you to worry about Betty and me, which I gather you have no intention of doing anyway—"

"I don't want to hurt you or worry you," I broke in to say.

"Betty and I will be okay when we understand what's going on."

I guessed that there was no way of divorcing him from Betty. They went together like a horse and carriage. I knew in my bones there was no love in that marriage, which was why it would endure, and which was why he kept invoking her name with every breath. I couldn't say: I don't care about Betty, I only care about you.

"What's that noise in the background?"

"There's no noise in the background. Either there's a poor connection on your end or you're having auditory hallucinations."

I said, "You sonofabitch."

Davey said immediately, "I'm sorry. I don't mean to be rough on you, Jack. I'm worried about you."

"You told me to marry Jennie."

"You're a big boy. You didn't have to listen to me. You wanted to marry her."

"Yes, and I wanted to leave her, and now I've done it. What's your beef?"

Davey said, "Only that you sound as if you're going to get even with everybody by going bananas"—beef and bananas: I found myself amused—"and it's not clear to me that you've acted responsibly toward Jennie."

"There's no way to be kind in a situation like this," I told him. "Maybe that's hard for you to imagine, since you've never been in such a situation."

"I'm not talking about that kind, I'm talking about responsible," he said.

"In fact," I said, "it's a kindness to be unkind."

"Which is what I've gathered you've been."

"I had to, Dave. Believe me, I had no choice. Besides, she's no angel herself."

"No kidding. She's human. I'll be damned." But the testiness had gone from his voice, and the background noise had faded too. I'd worry later about whether I had imagined it "Tell me how you left her," Davey said.

Dumbass question. "I packed a suitcase, opened the door, said farewell forever, and left."

"Did you discuss the divorce or whatever this is with her this week?"

"She's not in a condition to discuss anything. She's not rational. She keeps saying she loves me."

"That is irrational," he said gently. He was trying to josh me back on to his wavelength.

"Look, Dave, I gave her my apartment, we weren't married that long, it'd hurt more if we dragged it out, this way there are no children to worry about—"

"Betty said you told her Jennie and you were trying for a baby. Why in hell were you trying if you were also thinking of divorce?"

"I wasn't thinking," I said miserably, probably the truest thing I had said all day. "I'm still not."

"So I gather. Which is why I'm worried. And if you don't come out here, I'll fly in to see you."

"Threat?"

"What are you, paranoid?"

"Maybe," I said.

"I see," sighed Davey. He sounded very near the end of his rope. The contented father and husband had a margin that could be exceeded after all. Why did I envy Davey in this moment? He had what I didn't want. I decided I'd probably scrambled communication beyond repair by lying, and decided to experiment with doling out bits and pieces of truth.

"What shall I do?" I asked him in despair.

"Do you want me to come?"

"I think I can get by okay. Can we talk, maybe every day, for the next couple of days, though?"

"Sure. Do you want me to call her?"

"No," I said.

"Why not?"

"I don't know."

"Okay. Let's table that for now," Davey said. "How do you feel?"

"Better," I said. "I'm really in awful shape, Dave."

"Well, you'll live. Do what you can to relax. Let me think about some next steps for you and her—"

"Just me," I said. "Not her."

"You and her," he repeated. "I'm doing the thinking because you're lousy at it today. I'll send you those vitamins, and I'll call you tomorrow."

"Does Betty disapprove of me?"

"She just got scared," he said, to my astonishment. "She thought I might leave her."

"What about the rest of the family?" I asked, hoping he'd let me off the hook on that one.

He did. "I'm not going to tell them anything yet. I take it Jennie won't be prompted to call?"

"I didn't think of that," I said. "If she calls anyone, it'd be you. I don't think she cottons to the rest of them."

"Dutiful wife," he said shortly. "Shares all your likes and prejudices."

I sighed.

"Okay," he said, in acknowledgment of what he knew to be my limits. "We'll talk tomorrow."

If only I didn't think about Jennie, I'd be okay.

I took the hot bath. And, naked, crawled under the sheets. Lay there. Dozed. I was—maybe ill was not the right word. Convalescent. Convalescent from the marriage.

I LOOKED OUT of the dirty hotel window. It was dark outside. I went to a diner on the corner, ate a sandwich. Tasteless, or my taste buds were numb. All of me was numb. It was less sad to be so, since I'd spoken with Davey. He seemed to know what the psyche and the body together could stand, and never pressed me. I should have been his younger brother. I could count, as they say, on the fingers of one hand the number of times I'd come through for him. One was his marriage, of course. How easily Betty could be scared. A scaredy-cat, behind all that matronly hustle, bustle, that officiousness. How could she imagine that Davey would abandon her? Leave her, ever? I walked another block and purchased a quart bottle of cheap Scotch—I must budget now, in case Jennie wanted some token alimony; I couldn't imagine her being greedy for more—and walked back to the hotel with it. Mustn't think about Jennie, I reminded myself. I steeled myself to ring room service—didn't they give themselves airs, helluva room, and service was barely serviceable—for ice. It came. In a paper bucket. I tried not to be reminded of my honeymoon. I tipped the grizzled bellhop, the one who had earlier shown me to the room, and he looked at the dollar surlily; he also threw a curdled glance at my booze. Damn him. I wasn't going to offer him a drink. That bottle was mine.

I took deep full gulps till I felt myself relaxing. I could face this divorce. I had done the right thing. Davey was backstopping me, but soon I'd be so strong, I wouldn't need him. Mustn't rush it, but at least now that seemed possible, whereas earlier any envisioning of the future beyond the sentence I was serving in this room seemed unendurable. In fact, couldn't be done. I was gratified to note that the booze was making me drowsy, not melancholy. I was in better shape than I thought. At ten, a decent hour, I went to bed. Instantly to sleep.

I GROPED FOR my wristwatch, with its luminous dial, before I became aware fully that the phone by my bed was ringing and had been for some time. Two A.M. An emergency. Bewildered, not knowing quite where I was, I grabbed the receiver. In the hotel, that's where I was. "Hello," I said, fearfully, into the phone. No answer. You don't get crank calls from strangers in hotels. I knew who this was. "Hello," I said more firmly. Fiercely. "Jen." I paused. "I know it's you. Jen?" Click. That was nice. A nice way to treat a guy. Why the hell hadn't she gone home to her mother, if she was in this kind of state? I pondered whether to get dressed and go over there, which was probably what she wanted. No. Worst thing for both of us. Yet, I cared. My wife. Had I acted responsibly? Davey had asked. I sat up, then went into the bathroom to rinse my mouth. Then I fished my address book out of my suit pocket and flipped through it. Yes, it was late, but Audrey was trained to deal with emergencies.

"You're babbling," Audrey said, about three minutes into my considered recital of the facts.

"I am?" Now I was worried about myself.

"Shut up," she said. "It's two-fifteen in the morning. You're in the Paris Hotel, and you've just had a call from someone who didn't say anything. You think it's Jennie. Are you in your right mind?"

"Yes. I left her this morning."

"Left her where?"

"In the apartment. We've separated. Do I have to tell you why?"

"No, not now," she said impatiently. "I just don't understand why you're calling at this hour."

"I'm worried about her," I said defensively.

"Then why not call me at two P.M.," said Audrey. "Why wait till the middle of the night? You scared me to death. I thought it was one of my patients."

"I wasn't worried at two P.M.," I explained responsibly. "I think she just called me and didn't say anything, and hung up the phone. I think somebody better check on her, and I think I'm the wrong person to do it. Do you follow?"

"I follow," she said instantly. "Is she suicidal?" she asked, too brightly.

"No," I stammered. "She's not like that."

"How would you know?" said Audrey. "You're only her husband. Poor Jennie."

"Yes," I said. "What are we going to do? If you like, I'll pick you up and we can go over together. I'll wait downstairs. I don't think she should see me."

"Who are you to decide whom she should see and not see?" Audrey said. "She's not a mental patient."

"Well, I know what kind of state she was in this morning. I upset her."

"What you're saying," the trained clinician explained to me, "is that you don't want to see her and that she upsets you. All you're thinking about is yourself. That's the trouble with you."

"I'm willing to buy it, but not right now," I said. "Can we decide what to do about Jen? What's that noise?"

"The telephone fell," Audrey said. "I'm trying to get dressed. I'm going over there."

"I'll grab a cab and pick you up," I said.

"And wait for me in the street? Go fuck yourself," she said.

"You don't want me to?" I asked, relieved.

"That's right."

"You won't need me?"

"Right again."

"Will you let me know?"

"If I have time," Audrey said. "If you are worried about her suiciding, you must have been unspeakable to her. Have you got a lawyer?"

"No," I said, frightened. "Maybe I should call a doctor."

"So long," she said. "I'm leaving. I'll call a doctor if it's necessary." She hung up.

Instantly, I phoned her back. "Hello?" she said.

"Audrey—" I began.

"Fuck off," she said. Click. I felt better. I deserved that. I wondered where my responsibility lay now. To disregard Audrey's instructions and taxi over there anyway? To wait in the street? Or to go upstairs? Jen was probably okay and only needed to talk to someone. She could lean on Audrey. Audrey would probably get her a lawyer. That meant I'd better get one too. That's why Audrey had asked me if I had one. To get information for Jen. A trained interviewer's trick question. But, still, I was glad Jen had someone to look out for her, since I couldn't. I was beginning to think perhaps no man could. She was a little unstable. More than a little. How odd, that refusal to cook. Did she think babies—which she wanted to have—lived on mother's milk and prepared baby foods forever? My mind was racing in a way that frightened me. I poured myself a drink. And tried to calm down. And think.

In the end, I decided to go over there. I got dressed, in fact put my clothes on over my pajamas. Action was better than waiting, not knowing. I took another swallow, quickly, directly from the neck of the bottle, then went to the door. Phone rang. I grabbed it. It was Audrey, speaking in a sepulchral voice.

"Jack," she said, "I'm home now—"

"I can hardly hear you—"

"Jen's in the other room. I've lowered my voice," she explained. I realized she'd been crying.

"Is Jen okay?" I asked, wild with fear.

"Oh, yes. I just thought I'd bring her home with me. She shouldn't be alone."

"I agree," I said fervently. "I'm glad she's with you, Audrey. Did she make that call?"

"Yes," she said. Her tone was flat and brittle.

"How long is she going to be staying with you?" I pressed.

"Good-bye," said Audrey. And hung up.

I SAT UP for the rest of the night. I knew I wouldn't sleep, so no point in trying. I didn't want to think of the apartment, empty, without Jen in it. Audrey could have extended herself just a little to tell me how long it would be empty, without Jen. I didn't like to think of her in Audrey's apartment, though I knew she'd be safe there. What did I mean by safe? That's what Betty prayed for, Davey had said. Safety. Pusserette would meow around. Pusserette. Jennie's first night in my apartment. The apartment. Would she make it hers? Maybe she'd move in with Audrey or into a hotel for young women, where she could get her meals prepared and be surrounded by other women who might be supportive and set some sort of example for Jen on how to behave with men. Other divorcees could probably tell her how they'd failed and she'd profit from hearing their experience.

Her first night in my bed. Now she was sleeping alone. So would I. If I ever allowed myself to sleep, to sleep peacefully, again. My eyelids felt grainy. But I wouldn't sleep. Not tonight. I owed something, I didn't know what, my wakefulness. This vigil.

239

ESCAPE, DAY TWO. Morning. I strolled out for Sunday brunch. Not the diner, this time, too tawdry, and I owed myself the treat of a decent decor and ersatz-continental West Side food—it looked pretty, even if the sauces were piped from a central underground kitchen—after the night's wakefulness. I found a nice place with wood paneling and dim lights. Bloody Marys with the Eggs Benedict. It was nice not having to share this. Kids could pretend to romance, to intimacy, in such a setting, but I knew better. Let them bend their heads toward one another, their torsos encased in shirts and tight blue jeans, while they sipped at their Screwdrivers or Bloody Marys and coffee, pretending to the world that they were indifferent to what they had done to one another the night before. In my dignified solitude, I ordered, then looked around imperturbably at the denizens of—what was the place called? In astonishment I looked at the match cover, and there it was: The Cheap Date. Somewhat more furtively, I inspected the premises and the occupants again. I had evidently wandered into a singles hangout. That was silly. I was a little old for this, though in the right sociological category. Single. I liked the sound of it. It sounded like money. I didn't know how much, but a nice sound, so probably a nice denomination. My food was served. I sipped at my drink. Screwdriver seemed childish; I should have followed my first impulse to order a Bloody Mary. The bar was becoming crowded. A long-legged girl, no, a woman—too bad I couldn't see her face more clearly; did I need glasses for distance vision?—was perched on one of the stools at the corner of the bar nearest my table. She seemed to be unescorted. Probably was waiting for someone. It then dawned on me, as she appeared to flash me a smile, that she was not waiting for someone in particular. She was waiting for anyone. Anyone: maybe me. I smiled back, then lit a cigarette with trembling hands. I began to wish I had shaved. I ordered another Screwdriver. Her head was bobbing around, her breasts, her ass, nicely displayed by the fashionable denim rags she was wearing as she swiveled with a faked but nicely practiced restlessness in her chair. Satisfy me, her body said. Neither a dare nor an invitation. That was nice. Just a neutral imperative, which could keep things from getting messy. Youngsters seemed to know how to do this. Good, let them set an example for the older generation. It was probably too late to save Jennie—I brushed aside an unexpected pang—she was too conditioned by her upbringing and the climate of the times, but these young folks might be able to give me a good time. I decided to go to the men's room, which involved passing by her, to get a closer look. Her smile was unmistakable. "Keep an eye on my jacket and newspaper, would you?" I commanded en route, and she smiled and nodded. When I emerged from the rather messily kept john— some graffiti marred its walls, which somehow offended me— she had joined my table.

"You asked me to keep an eye on things," she said. "I thought I could do a better job from here." In the old days they called them hookers. Now she was just a nice kid—maybe no more than twenty—on the present, culturally sanctioned prowl.

"How old are you?" I asked bluntly, noting with some regret that the Hollandaise on my plate had congealed too soon.

"Twenty-five," replied the liar coolly. "Why didn't you shave this morning?"

"I've just left my wife. It's a mark of the seriousness of our mutual suffering." I decisively speared the white of the egg. She looked respectful. I had impressed her. Good. The sarcasm, to which Jennie had, with an abundance of whimpers, objected, was in this girl's bones, at the center of her soul. It had led her to her temporary proper mate. I hoped we could go to her apartment. I didn't relish the notion of having her squirm on the mattress, which I imagined to be stained as well as lumpy, of my bed at the Paris Hotel. "Would you like a cup of coffee?" I asked her, deciding I'd better take it slow. She might be too fast for me.

"I'd like a drink," she said. My heart jumped. The girl might have been imitating the young Joan Bennett or a blonde Lauren Bacall—someone she'd squinted at on television, once a heroine of the silver screen. But it didn't matter that it was an imitation. It was effective. It was doing something to me. And, clearly, I was doing something to her.

"What's your name?" I asked her, resolving to give her a hard time. I'd order her a drink, but she'd have to tell me her name first. This thing had to be properly established at the outset as a transaction.

"Babs. I want a vodka martini on the rocks. With an olive."

"Sorry, Babs." Babs? "What you get is a Bloody Mary or a Screwdriver. This is brunch, not dinner. What'll it be?"

"Screwdriver," she said evenly. Something in her tone

made me feel oddly out of my depth. Was I going to get taken?

I signaled the waiter, who, ignoring me, allowed Babs to order her own Screwdriver.

"Is your name really Babs?" I asked, with what I hoped was just a touch of derision.

"Short for Barbara," she said. Then she smiled at me. The relief I felt at this smile astonished me. How had she so easily managed to establish her control? She was, after all, a cliché. Babs, for Barbara.

She sipped at her drink.

"You picking me up?" I asked her. It was important to get some things straight. Maybe she was a hooker, and I didn't want to get a disease.

"No," she said. "You picked me up. Actually, I'm waiting for my boyfriend."

"I see," I said casually, successfully keeping my emotional turmoil at bay. "Is he standing you up?"

She shrugged. "He doesn't care about things like punctuality," she said. I decided she was not a hooker. Hookers didn't use words like punctuality. An undergraduate. Or dropout. No more than twenty. "He's Negro," she volunteered. Oh, Christ, I might get a disease after all.

"What does he do?" I asked cautiously.

"What's your name?" she countered.

"Jack."

"Are you going to take me to dinner, Jack?"

"Why the hell should I?"

"You mentioned dinner," she said. "And I want that martini."

"I see." Silence. "What does your boyfriend do?"

"Dinner okay?"

"Sure." I was out of my depth and needed to get back to the hotel to think this over.

"Tonight?"

By tonight I'd have it figured, and I deserved some good

sex. I could control this precocious pubescent skin-and-bones with the superior mastery of the world conferred by my age, experience, and general intelligence.

"Tonight's okay," I said indifferently.

"How old are you?" she asked me.

"What does your boyfriend do?" I tried not to appear anxious as I glanced around the room looking for a Negro face. Damn it, it was an irritant. I wondered if Babs was Jewish. I must remember to get her last name. Then I thought of Jennie. All I needed. Thinking of her could render me impotent on tonight's sheets. I'd practice not thinking of her all afternoon. I would turn my mind into hardcore pornography. I'd read *Lady Chatterley's Lover* if I could find it on a drugstore rack, once I got out of here.

"How old are you?" Babs repeated, draining the last of her drink.

"Thirty-five," I said. I could lie too.

She looked at me. "You're in good shape for thirty-five," she said.

"Thanks." I was pleased. But had better put a stop to that. I was trying at once to be indifferent and to have the upper hand. And letting her please me would give her power over me.

"You Jewish?" I asked.

"His name is Jeffrey," she said with a true coldness. Or was it merely indifference? Was her indifference in any significant relation to my numbness? If it was, we'd really hit it off.

"What's your last name?"

"He doesn't work for money," she said. Smug? Arrogant? "He and I both do sit-ins. Civil rights."

"I know what sit-ins are," I said.

"We travel. Together."

"That's nice," I said. "What's your last name?"

"Mississippi," she said. She got up and said: "Thanks."

"What time tonight?" I asked.

"Rattner," she said.

"What?"

"That's my last name. My father was Jewish." Was? What had happened? Did I want to know?

"Seven o'clock," she said. "Here."

"What's your telephone number?" I asked. "In case something comes up?"

She shrugged. "I'll take my chances."

"Like with Jeffrey? Suppose I don't show?"

"You'll show," she said. "And Jeffrey'll turn up sooner or later. If you see a Negro guy, big, come in here, tell him I've gone home to finish Gide. Okay?"

Gide? "I'm leaving myself," I said angrily, getting up, fumbling and waving at the waiter wildly to bring me the bill. Gide?

"Take your time," she said. "See you later." And was gone.

Who'd won that round? I sat back down again heavily. Might as well relax over another cup of coffee. The broad had tried to push me around. Well, it was probably a draw. The waiter brought me another cup of coffee. I drank it slowly and looked for the Negro she'd described. He never came. Probably didn't exist.

Mississippi. Gide. Rattner. I was going home, not to my father, who art—not. To the Paris. My temporary home.

BARNEY PHONED. "How'd you get this number?" I barked.

"Jennie gave it to me."

"You talked to her?" I was agitated. I hadn't expected this. I wanted—needed—the whole afternoon to get ready for my date.

"Briefly. She said I ought to know. She said I should check on you."

"Check on me? I'm fine," I said. "She's out of her gourd."

"Forgive me for intruding," said Barney. "I thought I was a friend of the family."

"You're a friend. There is no family. I need my privacy. You mind, Barney?"

"I had a lot of hope staked on you two kids," he reproached me.

"I'm no kid," I snapped, thinking of the kid I'd just lucked into and needed to prepare for, Babs Rattner, a true kid. "This was a considered decision. Mutual. Got to ring off, Barney," I said, and hung up.

I was sick of everybody. Why didn't they leave me alone?

Later, soaking in a hot tub, seeking a modicum of comfort, I began to feel somewhat more charitable. The dissolution of a marriage took some time, apparently, for the community of one's friends and family to absorb, to understand. It was not as simple for them, curiously, paradoxically, as it was for the principals, Jennie and me. Marriage, one of us had said once, was a publication of one's feelings. Barney, to whom words meant everything—probably he drank because it let him experience the words without suffering their meaning—probably found it particularly hard to bear. Now, nearly all precincts had been heard from. All that remained, for me at least, was the rest of my family. In Indianapolis.

By the end of my fourth day on freeside, Babs turned on the spigots: "I hadn't counted on a one-night stand," she sniffled.

"I don't know what you're crying about," I said, sick of women's tears. "We've had more than a night."

"You know what I mean," she flung at me.

"I don't," I said, not knowing whether I was speaking to her or Jennie. It was true. I had no idea what she meant.

"Three nights," was her plaint. "And you won't tell me when I'll see you again. We've had a three-night one-night stand." Right. Sunday, Monday, and Tuesday. Like my honeymoon.

"So?" I said. "You know I've just separated from my wife. I need a breather."

"You're an emotional fascist," she spat at me.

"Well, you don't want to hang around with fascists when freedom riders are ripe for the plucking. So get out."

"You've forgotten something," she hissed.

"What?"

"We're in my apartment."

Right. So I got out.

I DIDN'T CALL Babs till Monday afternoon, from a phone booth.

"You sound funny," said Babs.

"Yeah, well you sound wheezy too."

"I waited all weekend for your call," she said flatly.

"Isn't it uncool of you to tell me?" I was both taken aback and pleased at this admission of need. Jennie would have been far more sly—strategic—but didn't at all have the hardness of this girl. This girl was a winner. How flattering to be told one had kept a winner waiting.

"Yes. But I'm turned on," she said. "When I get turned on, I can't wait."

Neither could I. For a moment I forgot everything, and took a quick prospective and retrospective look at Babs in the sack.

"Can you wait an hour?"

"I'll be out tonight. I gave it to Jeffrey."

"Gave what to Jeffrey?" I asked, bewildered.

"The night. When you didn't call, I figured the hell with it."

So I hadn't got her figured. She wasn't flattering me, she was slapping me down. Very well then, I would beg. I needed her and didn't care what it took to secure her for the evening. "Break your date with Jeffrey," I ordered her—the form of begging that would appeal to her because she wouldn't immediately identify it as such—"I'll be there in thirty minutes."

"Okay," she said. A game, that's all it was. Trouble with Jennie was, she didn't know how to play. Teased a guy into thinking it was the real thing; worse still, duped herself.

"I'll grab a cab."

"Okay," she said.

"I'm a little hungry," I told her. "See if you can't find a scrap of something to feed me." A pause. "Before." I rang off, rather pleased with my performance. Let her wait for it some more, and meanwhile she might feed me a decent meal.

I WAS LATE to Babs's. "The pizza's cold," she said. She sounded pretty cold herself.

"Pizza?" I said, bemused. "You ordered pizza?"

"What did you expect?" she asked. "It was that or Chinese. You owe me two bucks." Wordlessly, I handed her two bucks.

"I expected," I said, "that you might scramble some eggs."

"I don't keep much food in the house."

"Can you cook?" I asked.

"You're shopping for a wife," she said indifferently. "What difference does it make whether I can cook or not."

"I'm curious," I said.

"Sure I can cook, when I want to," she said. "Come for dinner sometime."

"I thought I was doing that. Tonight."

"You invited yourself. I cook dinner, I do the inviting. Courtesy is timeless," breathed this horsey person, attired in a black sweater and blue jeans, as she took her place at the table.

"Sorry," I said. "Thank you for telling me the house rules."

"Welcome," she said graciously. Why did she have me off tilt all the time? The thing was not to pause to think, just keep on moving. I moved toward the pizza. She had set the table rather nicely.

"You get rid of Jeffrey?" I asked. I had just burned my palate on hot mozzarella. She'd reheated the pizza in the oven. Hadn't even told me. Considerate without making a production of it. Second nature, like everything else was, to her. I began to feel better.

"For a while," she said, in answer to my question about Jeffrey.

"I'll meet you in the bedroom in five minutes," I said.

She walked, as instructed, into the bedroom. I liked a woman, as cool as she, who could still take and follow orders.

We were in the middle of energetic rapture when her telephone rang. "Don't answer it," I commanded. Apparently under the impression that I was not her superior, she reached for it. There ensued a scene out of a sixties as distinguished from a forties movie. It was Jeffrey. She let me know this by uttering his name into the mouthpiece with stereotypical languor. Then—as a way of letting him know something—wedged herself into some variant of an erotic connection with me that was particularly compatible with speaking on the telephone. As I thought back on it later, I became aware that I didn't like the intrigue. At the time, I simply didn't like the interruption.

"Hmmm," she said to Jeffrey. "No, you didn't exactly wake me up. I'm busy. I'm studying. I guess I may have fallen asleep over this book. Umm," she said, caressing me—her words were profoundly irritating, but her touch was a joy, so I let the one compensate me for the other. "Still Gide." At that, I pushed her away. With some ferocity, she maneuvered herself back to where she had been. Her conversation with Jeffrey seemed to be expertly coordinated with what she was doing to me: she continued to do both, without skipping a beat. I surrender, dear. "I'll call you tomorrow," she said. "I just don't feel like talking now. I love you too. Knock it off," she giggled. Was she lying, or did she really love him? If she loved him, she shouldn't be doing this with me. Jennie would never do that. Of course, sexually, Jennie never got to first base. When I was a kid I liked sports. Baseball. Maybe a revival of that interest would give me pleasure, would divert me now from all my troubles. Why didn't this shallow kid get off the phone? I yanked at the cord. She looked at me coldly. " 'kay, baby," she crooned into the mouthpiece. "Talk to you tomorrow." She hung up.

Two-timer, I thought. But if I said it, it might strike her as corny. "Do you do this often?" I asked.

"Do what often?"

"Cheat on your boyfriend."

"You're cheating on your wife."

"We're separated," I spluttered.

"Legally?"

"No. But we will be."

"If you're not legally separated, it doesn't count." She forestalled my reply with something that was as distracting as my briefly entertained thoughts about baseball.

In the middle of a heavy embrace, she gasped: "You like me, don't you?"

"Christ," I said. "How can you ask?" (A neat way of not answering, she told me the next night.) I kept at it, she was pleasurable as hell, and every time we paused, I thought of my misery and grabbed her again. Working off my grief. Best way. Briefly, I wondered why she had asked that whiny, unnecessary question. It would be a long time before I realized it was because she really wanted to know the answer.

(Mid-showdown, two nights later, I asked her in astonishment: "How can you talk about commitment? You got laid. Isn't that what you wanted?"

"No," she said. "That was what you wanted."

"Go fuck yourself," I said to her. "You wanted it as much as I did."

"My shrink was right," she said to my further astonishment. "Don't sleep with a guy on your first date."

"Your shrink? You have a shrink?"

"Yeah."

"What's her name?"

"It's a guy, and his name is none of your business."

"You don't see Dr. Selfridge?"

"Dr. Selfridge? You have me mixed up with someone else. How much sleeping around do you do?" she snarled.

"I've just left my wife. I've done none until now, but I intend to do a lot more," I shouted at her. Why had I assumed her shrink was Dr. Selfridge? I'd get off that hook by interrogating her some more:

"Who pays for your shrink?"

"None of your business."

"Who?" I said menacingly.

"My father." Terrific. I'd lucked into a square. A nice Jewish middle-class girl. Which suburb was she from? I asked her. Specifically.

"The Oranges?" she said in bewilderment. "No. I'm not from New Jersey. What made you think I was from New Jersey? How many girls have you got, anyway? I'm not into promiscuity."

I had hundreds of girls, all named Jennie.

"I hope not," I said to her. "I don't want to get a disease."

"You are a disease," she told me.)

Back to loving embraces: I couldn't help it. I knew she was set to come, but I was wilting, nature's way of telling you to slow down, and I fell asleep. On top of her. As she later reported to me.

Asleep, I dreamed of Barney. Kentucky Bourbon, but cheap. My father, Kentucky born. No, I protested in the dream, how can one's father die twice? He's not dead, he just passed out for a little while. What do you mean he won't wake up? He passed out, he'll wake up. My father died once. I can't remember when. Why must I remember? Does Davey's life depend on my remembering? I'm not dependable. I'll tell you in a minute. Just a minute.

Babs shook me awake. "You've got to get out," she said inhospitably—all women were, one way or another, I was discovering, inhospitable. "I'm going to class."

It didn't seem sufficient reason to throw a guy out, after he'd done his best for you the night before. God, it was good to know women were as needy as men. Still, she ought to be more gracious, even if our relationship was—so I thought—grounded in nothing more than barter.

"I'll see you tonight," I said, kissing her good-bye at the door. Once again, she didn't give me breakfast. You couldn't ask for everything. She was in ways that maybe counted most a very warm and generous and loving girl. I told her so. A guy ought to let a girl know that she was a lot of fun. She seemed pleased by the compliment. A nice little self-respecting nod. I felt expansive. Accordingly I said, "You won't be able to reach me today. I'll be out. But I'll be by later."

"What time?"

"Does it matter? Can't we leave things a little loose?"

"Sure," she said with a shrug. I was relieved. I wanted us to be casual. I didn't want to be pinned down. For both our sakes. She made me feel good about myself, I reflected, as I descended her five flights of stairs. God, how had I climbed them the night before? And the night before that? A guy could have a heart attack. Babs's Hellespont, her brightly lit stairs.

I needed some rest. She should understand. She could give Jeffrey a call. Even though I was the beneficiary of her attentions, I didn't like her cheating on another man. Still, it proved that she was casual. I frowned. If one thought about it, her behavior toward him was rather indecent. But I didn't want to think about it. I needed a decent night's sleep.

I got it. The sleep, and the next night more scorned-woman's wrath. Unbelievable. I couldn't believe this chit was throwing me out twice. For good. You really had to be careful in singles joints and of the company you kept let alone picked up. Appearances were deceiving. All women were sisters under the skin. A stitch in time saves nine. Still, I missed her. I didn't understand that. I had begun to explore, to mine a vein I hadn't mined before, and she'd thrown me down the side of the mountain. You had to respct the strength of a girl who could do that. I missed her. I missed her strength. Jennie was weak. But why had Babs hurt me so? Why did people hit a guy when he was down?

AGGRIEVED, I put the question to Audrey some days later. Or a form of it. She invited me for coffee, after I phoned to inquire after Jennie—she was all right, Audrey said stiffly, she had gone back to her place (her place?).

"Am I glad to see you," I said, slumping into her big chair. "I've had a helluva week." (Did I expect sympathy, I wondered.)

She glowered, I smiled placatingly.

"I'll get the coffee," she said while I sat there, muscles relaxed, waiting for compassion. After all, she and I were old friends. I heard her moving about in the kitchen. It was nice to know a woman who knew her own kitchen. "How are things in your neck of the woods?" I yelled. No answer. As a matter of reflex, I stood up and went in, nearly bumping into her as she came out bearing a tray with a solitary steaming cup of coffee.

"You take it black," she said, staring at me. I stared back at her.

"How do you know?"

"Jennie told me."

"She tell you anything else? Intimate and personal stuff like that?"

"Go sit down," said Audrey after a heavy sigh. I did, and playing waitress—or, if you like, hostess—she put before me the tray. I removed the coffee. I was being put through some paces. Why? Apart from the obvious reasons, which I could guess at: I was on probation with Audrey.

"I'm glad Jennie has a confidante," I said heartily.

"Don't use me, Jack," she said at length.

"I don't know what you're talking about," I said, feigning perplexity. I knew damned well what she meant. I wanted her sympathetic ear. I wanted to find out the extent to which

Jennie had unburdened herself and given her distorted accounts of our life together. For a moment her face was obscured by sunlight streaming through the window behind her, and I thought I saw my Jennie. The cup clattered in its saucer, as my hand shook. Mustn't think of Jennie. Audrey wasn't her surrogate.

"Light bothering you?" Audrey asked. I realized that I had lifted my hand to shade my eyes.

"Somewhat," I said. "I don't like light."

"So I've heard," she said.

"Jennie mention it?"

"Yes." Audrey pulled down a couple of shades, and now we were seated facing each other in the quality and degree of gloom in which I was normally at ease.

"Let's not talk about Jennie," I said.

"How are you?" Audrey asked.

"I'm near collapse, actually." I was. My body was trembling again. I wanted Audrey to soothe me, as I had once—many times—soothed Jennie. I was owed something. Jennie Owen. Now—or soon—she would have her own self back.

"Take it easy," Audrey said softly.

"We're friends, aren't we?" I asked her.

After a moment, she said: "I don't know what the word means right now. I care about you, or you wouldn't be here."

"Aren't you having coffee?" I asked.

"No," she said. "I've got to get to bed early and caffeine keeps me awake." Was she propositioning me? Was I having a breakdown?

"Audrey," I said, "am I having a breakdown?"

"I see no clinical signs of it," she said. "If you're concerned, I can refer you to a psychiatrist."

I laughed. She did not. Then I asked: "Is Jennie seeing that Selfridge woman?"

Silence. Uneasily, I said: "I forgot. We weren't going to talk about Jennie. That's really best, you know."

Still, she didn't speak. I said uneasily, trying to keep this light and sociable, "Don't you want coffee?"

"No," she said, and retreated into a silence that seemed impenetrable.

I was never more happy to see Pusserette. The animal had crept silently into the room, then leapt upon my lap and nestled against me. Did she smell Jennie? Some lingering fragrance from her skin, her clothes next to which mine had hung in our—now her—closet? I decided not to ask Audrey. Instead, I'd continue to keep things pleasant with light chit-chat and passing observations.

"Look," I said. "Pusserette likes me."

What the hell was the matter with Audrey? I was a visitor, not a patient. Why wouldn't the woman make normal conversation? "Doesn't Pusserette like me?" I nagged.

"I wouldn't know," said Audrey. "She doesn't confide in me."

"Cat got her tongue," I said, and laughed. "Maybe she needs to be sent to the catalyst." It was good to know my sense of humor hadn't deserted me. But why did Audrey merely snicker? Swiftly, I deposited Pusserette on the carpet. The cat reminded me of a kittenish girl I had been married to. But I wouldn't think about Jennie. Certainly not talk about her. I drained the last of my coffee. I ached from my wounds. I had left Babs with the word fascist ringing in my ears. She had hurt me, even though I had quickly picked up on her cool style and gratified her unsentimental sexual needs. I'd just barely escaped with my life, and gone home to sleep a near-comatose sleep in my hotel. Davey had called, interrupting this dreamless respite, once—or was it twice? I'd told him I was fine, that I'd broken up with my new girl— and then asked him, crankily, if he'd sent the vitamins yet. He would, he said; the baby had been sick. I understood, I told him, then fell asleep again.

I decided to explain all or some of this to Audrey. I got as far as Babs, and she said tartly: "What?"

"A girl I've been involved with. It was very sudden, and it ended badly. What are you doing?"

"Pouring myself some bourbon," she said.

"Better be careful with that stuff," I said and laughed.

"It's not funny," she snapped.

"Are you expecting company?" I asked.

"No," she said. "But I'm getting sick and tired of you."

I swallowed. I ached with a need to know about Jennie. I told Audrey this. It seemed to make her soften.

"This display," she said quietly. "You think that you're having a breakdown from missing her. You think what you feel is sorrow for Jennie, but it's something else, it's sorrow for yourself. Self-pity."

Bury me not on the Lone Prairie, I hummed. *As I walked down the streets of Laredo* . . . "Self-pity," I mused. Why, self-pity—that bastard child of the emotions, that neglected child of the emotions—was the motif of ballads, from Elizabethan England to the Lone Prairie. "Bury me not," I said aloud. Bastard, I thought, Morrie was a bastard.

"What?" asked Audrey sharply, penetrating my reverie.

"Self-pity," I said. "It's such a convenient tag to put someone down with. But haven't you ever thought, Audrey, that self-pity is a legitimate thing to feel? Even a necessary thing to feel? Who will pity us if not ourselves?" I went on about Scottish and Elizabethan ballads.

"Very interesting. I'm sure that scandal paper you work for would print that rot if you couldn't find a home for it in the *Sewanee Review*." How did Audrey know about the *Sewanee Review*? Had I underestimated her? She went on, however, interrupting my reassessment of her intellectual resources and credentials: "Grief is legitimate. And you have no right to feel it for Jen. It's not as if she were dead, Jack. You left her. She is bereft."

"She is?" I asked hopefully. Bereft? Bereaved?

"Wipe that dumbassed smile off your face," said Miss Sewanee Review. "Your selfishness and self-importance have always sickened me. All that quixotic shit about your leaving the magazine because Barney got canned. I never bought all that. You were too lazy to work, so you married a nice young girl who trusted you and whose salary would bring home the bacon."

"She may have brought home the bacon," I said, "but that isn't why I married her, and besides I had to fry the bacon."

"You poor slob."

"Where'd you learn the word quixotic, anyway?"

"At the Fulton Fish Market," she said, looking me straight in the eye. Still and all, a girl with this much anger at me might have compassion on the flip side of anger's coin. I'd try it.

"Could I have another cup of coffee?"

"Yes." She picked up the cup and vanished into the kitchen. The cat approached me then, rubbed its body against my legs. That sick rubbing. To calm myself, I thought of Babs, convulsed with a pleasure I had never been able to give Jennie. Babs gasping. Jennie so frightened and tiny, with her cat's claws, suffering her foreshortened pleasure. Yet, there was Babs throwing me out of her apartment. I had not wronged her. Why did she do that? I began to tremble.

Audrey stood over me. "Okay?" she said.

I nodded yes. "Thanks, Aud," I mumbled. "I don't know what's the matter."

"Go out and get a job," Audrey advised. "That way you won't have so much time to think about it."

"Is Jennie suicidal?"

"No."

"She's really too considerate for that," I said, and began to choke.

"Put the coffee down," Audrey directed. "Have you got a handkerchief?"

I withdrew a dirty handkerchief from my pocket and blew my nose noisily into it. "Been a helluva week," I murmured apologetically.

"For all of us, brother," she remarked quietly.

"You too?"

"It's scarcely a pleasure to see a friend wrecked by a bad marriage and to try to get"—she paused—"the friend safely away from the center of the wreckage."

"I don't think it's the marriage so much," I said. "I've seen the marriage coming to an end for a long time. It's really this girl Babs." I asked her if she wanted to hear about it, and when she didn't reply I told her as much as I could of the whole story, leaving out the clinical details. Maybe that was an important omission. Audrey should perhaps be told, one way or another, that I badly needed good sex. It would tell her, one way or another, something she might want to know about her friend Jennie. I told her, using delicate language, that in Babs I had found a good lay. But that she put out for her boyfriend, too, and therefore betrayed two men. And accused one of them. Me. Unfairly.

Audrey, listening to this recital, said acidly: "Infidelity is infidelity. You were unfaithful to Babs too."

"That's a pretty fine point, Audrey. I don't think it withstands scrutiny."

"Neither does your behavior."

"Babs was unfaithful to her Negro boyfriend. Did I tell you he was Negro?"

Audrey looked sick. "No."

I said: "Well, he was. Is. And as far as being unfaithful is concerned, how do we know Jennie isn't knocking off a piece?"

Audrey said in a strange voice: "Would you go?"

"What?"

"Would you get out?"

"I haven't finished my coffee."

"There's a Nedick's on the corner. I'd like you to go."

"Okay," I said. "I guess I shouldn't have told you about Babs. But it helps me to get it off my chest. I'm sorry you think I treated her unfairly," I said, trying to muster some dignity. I felt myself swaying.

"Would you please leave?"

Babs had thrown me out too. Women were inhospitable.

Not nurturing, really. Babies, like Jennie, or phony mothers, like Audrey, or phony babies, like Babs.

"Inhospitable."

"What?"

"I'm discovering," I said evenly, "that women are basically inhospitable. You keep throwing me out. All of you."

"Take your dirty handkerchief with you."

She opened the door and stood there.

"Can we keep in touch?"

"I don't know," she said. "I don't think I can be in the middle."

So. Some of it had to do with her own failing. Or feeling. I'd forgotten which was which. Audrey slammed the door behind me. I was a prisoner—the doors of homes were barred to me.

PRISON, Paris Hotel. I slept the days away, turned into a person with no body-clock. Twilight would come and I would awaken, sometimes eat, sometimes not—Jennie's ignorant cooking had nourished me more than I now nourshed myself—and I would sleep again. I would come awake in the hours after midnight, jolted out of sleep by some interior violence. And to subdue the violence, which threatened to overload my system, displace itself upon the walls of my cell, I would dress and go down into the street. And I would walk aimlessly along the Drive, silently daring anyone to mug me. When I felt I had invited fully the quota of danger I deserved, I would trudge east to Broadway, which was brightly lit and where I could spot the hazards and, if I chose, avoid them. I rarely kept track of how long I walked; indeed, of when I left the hotel and what time I returned. I would turn, bleary and unshaven, to the unmade bed—I kept a DO NOT DISTURB sign on my door virtually around the clock—and flop again on the used linens. I would draw the ragged blanket about my shoulders, and in all this squalor, have the wit to thank Nature—that was what I believed in—that I was alone. Without the burden of a wife. A wife would not understand these erratic late-at-night prowls; she would resent them and take them personally. Or she would worry. For me, but more really for herself. No woman wanted to be a widow. Now, if the divorce were set in motion, Jennie would not be a widow if anything happened to me. She would be a divorcee, and that had a certain cachet; it marked her as a woman of the world.

Babs. Babs had been temporary. Babs had thrown me out. Jennie had let me go. Not without theatrics, but still I opened that door myself and walked through it. Freeing us. Babs, by expelling me, had imprisoned me.

And so, one night, earlier than usual—midnight, perhaps—I found that my freewheeling and aimless prowls had brought me to the street of Jennie's apartment building. There, I was able to say it. Her place. A prowl car had parked there. Had anything happened? I asked the two boys in blue, and they replied no, they were just resting up from the last family quarrel they had been called to investigate. They looked me up and down for a moment. I explained that my sister lived in the building. One of them—Irish—grunted, thereby letting me off the hook, and the other, stationed at the wheel, took his cue from his companion, and drove away. Probably a Wasp, I thought; he had that upwardly mobile look. Once he was done with applying the interesting training he'd gotten at the Police Academy, he'd probably go on to law school.

To make my behavior consistent with the harmless lies I'd told the police, I entered the vestibule of the building and stood there examining the name plates. J. Church, it said. How convenient that we had the same initials. It augured well for the property settlement. Since we shared initials, it was entirely likely that there would be no ruckus about who got what. Since we were both essentially fair people, the sense of deprivation would be mutual and the overseeing of proper distribution of goods would also be mutually undertaken. Even though we should have as little to do with each other as possible.

The door to the lobby opened, and a young woman, a scarf covering the huge rollers which were unbecomingly pinioned in her hair, advanced into the vestibule. She was holding a leash, to which there was attached a dog. Funny looking little mutt. Suddenly, I realized I knew him. "Hector," I said cordially. To Hector's mistress, I said in greeting: "Long time no see." She lived on our—I mean Jennie's—floor, and we had had the usual minimal neighborly interchange, but Hector was not easy to forget. He had a particularly pesky and erratic barking pattern.

"Right," said the girl. What the hell was her name?

"I'm sorry," I said. "I don't remember your name."

"Ella," she said. "Have you been away on business or something?" she asked.

She'd noticed my absence. How flattering. "My wife and I have separated, and I gave her my apartment," I said.

She glared at me.

"It's very amicable," I said.

"I understand," she said, somewhat more softly, giving me an appraising glance. "Is the divorce final?"

"No," I stammered. "We haven't actually begun the proceedings. But we're going to."

"I see," she said.

"Tell me," I went on, "is she dating?"

Ella shrank from me. "I don't know," she said. "I can't say. I don't want to get involved in anything legal."

Neither had I. Beginning with the rotten wedding.

"You going up to see her?" Ella asked.

"No. Look—I'm at the Paris Hotel. Call me if you feel it's necessary."

"Good night," said Ella. At that Hector went into some

kind of humanoid paroxysm, and it took considerable yank-
ing of his leash on Ella's part to get him to behave like a dog
again. Since she was staring at me, and the staring made me
uncomfortable, I left the vestibule and, taking an opposite
direction from Ella's, prowled another street.

At dawn, I went home—to the hotel—to sleep. And in
the dream she searched for me, she hunted me, she dogged
my midnight footsteps. No, said Audrey in the dream, she's
not hounding you, she doesn't want you, you want her. You're
a liar, I said to Audrey, she's snapping at my heels. Jennie's
not like that, Audrey said. My feet are bare, I tried to say to
Audrey, and no sound came forth. Put on your shoes, stupid,
said Rita. But when I tried to, I could find only one; it was
being worried by Hector, who held it in his jaws, puncturing
the fine leather with his teeth, cutting all the way through
the leather to my flesh. Get on your feet, kid, said Davey.
Stand up, Jack. In my sleep, I pressed my heels hard against
the mattress, trying to stand. My flesh, exposed to Hector's
teeth. Fierce cramp in my instep. I awoke and the room was
empty. Hector hadn't bitten me. Hector had vanished with
my dream. I was alone in the room with my pain. I lay there,
flexing the foot. No one had said, Stand up, Jack, get on your
feet, kid. Five in the morning, said my watch. On watch,
alone, in this dinginess and silence. On watch: What was I
watching for? Or waiting.

THE PRISONER SAT in the chair by the window, overlooking
the courtyard. Wristwatch said: seven-thirty.

What do I have?

I have my brother.

And he had me. When the phone rang an hour later I
was there for him.

"I've been trying you for days," said Davey. "Didn't you
get my messages?"

"I haven't picked up my messages," I said. Must remember to do that. Other people might have called, and here I'd

been thinking I had no friends. "Have you been calling a lot?" I asked eagerly.

"You okay?"

"Sure," I said. "Why've you been calling?"

"I said I would." Davey's answer. He always kept his word. Except about the vitamins. Must remember to ask him about that.

"How's the family?" I asked.

"I told them."

"What did Mother and Rita say?"

"They were sad." His words were measured.

"C'mon. What'd they say? I'm curious."

"Curious," Davey repeated. "Such an impersonal word."

"I'm not feeling very personal. My life has become impersonal. I live in an impersonal hotel. I am not a personal person. Maybe I'm not a person at all. Will you send me the vitamins?"

"This week," he promised. "I don't like the way you sound. Come out here and stay with us."

"No," I said. "I don't want to be a burden."

"I'm going to fly in then. I want to see you."

"Davey," I said, "I'm drowning."

"Do you have a doctor you could check in with?"

"No. I know a woman social worker. She's taken Jennie's side. Davey, there's no one."

"There's gotta be."

"There isn't," I said flatly. "Do you really think you could come?"

"I'll try. I'll get back to you in a day or so."

"I love you, Dave," I whispered.

I don't think he heard me, or he would have replied.

THE HOURS PASSED. I had no strength to dress and go down to eat. The nearest place—other than the diner, which had a dinginess I could not stomach—was The Cheap Date. I was certain I would find Babs there, lying in wait for me, stalking me, and even though their food was good I did not trust myself not to fall into Babs's trap. The trap of fucking. So I would nearly starve, then go out to the corner deli and sneak a sandwich. And at twilight, I would have a drink. I looked gratefully at the bottle on my night table. I was drinking in moderation, to save money as well as wear and tear. Somewhere toward noon, I crawled into bed and, clutching the pillow to me, took deep breaths to quiet my heart's thudding. The irregular hours I was keeping were at fault. Emotionally, given the crises I had been through, I was doing as well as could be expected. I fell asleep and dreamed of my beautiful Babs. How gentle and forgiving she was in the dream. How pale. I didn't dream of Jennie with the light brown hair. Because she wasn't pale, she was dark. Dark brown hair. Ringlets left on hotel bathroom sink, and in various places around my apartment. What a nuisance. Like having a pet. After a certain point you had to decide which meant more to you, the pet with the shedding hair or your possessions. In my case, since I'd given Jennie everything, my sole and in any event most valued possession was myself.

My phone—I mean the hotel phone, I no longer had even a phone—rang. "Yes," I said sleepily, hoping it was Davey.

"Jack," rasped a voice, familiar, out of my childhood. My father?

"Who's this?" I said, not wanting to wake up and lose my father.

"Dr. Frame here," he said heartily.

I sat up, alarmed. "What's wrong?"

"Everything's all right here," came the reassuring voice. "David asked me to call you."

"He should have told me he was going to do that," I said dully.

Dr. Frame was giving me a telephone number. Numbly, I jotted it down on the edge of the pad. "Now, will you call him?" Dr. Frame asked. "He's a good man."

"Who is he?" I asked.

"Dr. Farmer," Frame replied. "I just told you." He had?

Dr. Farmer. I laughed. "What are you laughing at?" Frame wanted to know.

"You have a good sense of humor, Doc," I said magnanimously. I had never in my life called him Doc. Why had I done so now? Did one call a lawyer "Law"? Or a dentist "Den"? I laughed again.

"Jack, call Dr. Farmer right away, will you?"

"What kind of doctor is he?"

"He's a psychiatrist. I told you." He had?

"I don't understand," I said carefully.

"You might need medication," Frame said gently. "Antidepressants. Something to make you feel better. Unless you want to come out here."

Suddenly the thought of facing my family, anyone but Davey, filled me with horror. They'd kill me, they'd shame me if I came there. I'd be coming in defeat, alone, not with a wife, and they'd shame me.

"I won't go to Indianapolis," I said, "under any circumstances. They'd have to drug me and put me in a straitjacket—or a stretcher—or whatever—before they'd get me to go home. I'd go to Kentucky, I'd even go to New Jersey, which has got to be the worst state in the union, next to Alabama, before I'd go home to Indianapolis. New York is my home for good. Don't I sound fine to you?"

"A little overexcited, Jack."

"Okay," I said. "I'll try and call you back." I hung up, bewildered.

Something was happening. Something was going to happen to me. Hadn't Jennie sensed that emotional turmoil had caused her vaginal infection? The principle must apply to me too: my emotional turmoil may have caused a sexual disease. An inflammation. I must abjure sex, and not even examine myself for symptoms, until I stabilized, emotionally. I could risk The Cheap Date, then, because I'd know enough to stay away from Babs. She might think me a heel, but I wasn't heel enough to give a woman a disease and wasn't about to begin now, no matter how enticing her manner. I decided to dial Dr. Farmer. A colored woman answered and put me on hold.

When she came back on the line again, she asked me to give my name and state my symptoms. "I think you need to see a urologist," she said firmly. "Dr. Farmer doesn't deal with that."

"My referral is from Dr. Frame," I said emphatically. "He insisted that Dr. Farmer reach me today."

"How do you spell that?"

I'd teach the hussy a thing or two. "Today is spelled t-o-d-a-y. Y as in yes or yelp."

"I'll have the doctor call you," she said. "Give me your number." Which I promptly did, then hung up, bathed minimally, got dressed, and went over to The Cheap Date to eat.

Babs wasn't there. Lucky for her. I ordered corned-beef hash with a fried egg, broccoli, and a baked potato with sour cream. It was three o'clock in the afternoon. I packed away lunch, then ordered crème caramel and a brandy. That felt good. I paid the check with my American Express card. "I know it's about to expire," I snarled impatiently to the waiter to hurry him up, and left the restaurant feeling replete. I returned to the hotel and threw up. Violently. I decided to go to the hospital if Farmer didn't call. I sat by the phone—the nausea had not left me, but I didn't want to throw up again—and waited. An hour passed. The sonofabitch. Then it rang. I grabbed for it. "This is the Desk. You gotta message here from Dr. Framer."

"Farmer," I corrected.

"Says Framer here," said the Desk. "I didn't take it." Nobody took responsibility for anything these days. And here I was, sick.

Desk said, "The doctor's number is—"

"I know the number," I said, and slammed down the phone. And called the number, reached a delicatessen, and hung up. Wearily, I recited the number to the switchboard and reached Farmer's answering service.

"He's off call now," said Service. Did you call earlier?"

"Yes," I said. "And he returned my call, but I was out. I had a late lunch." I had a bitter taste in my mouth.

"What seems to be the trouble?"

"I don't know," I said, miserably, "I can't think."

"Can't think," she repeated automatically. "And you're referred by a doctor in Indianapolis, and you're calling from New York."

"Yes. I'll wait by the phone for his call," I promised. "I won't go out again. That was dumb of me."

"All right," said the voice, puzzled, noncommittal.

"Will he call me?" I pleaded.

"I can't say. I'll try and reach him. I have other calls to take, Mr. Crutch."

"Church," I said, panicking again. Couldn't they get my name straight? Did they in all the messages they took transpose letters? So now I was Crutch. I waited by the phone. Once I got up to try to vomit, but got scared, didn't want to lose any kind of control and retreated to the big chair and waited for sundown. At sundown, the phone still silent, I turned to the bottle, which had bided its time, and began to drink.

I must have at some point stumbled from the chair to the bed. Where I slept. No rest for the self-indulgent, however, for as I lay in a condition of boozy slumber, the fucking phone rang again. If it was Desk again, I would smash him to splinters. I don't know what my voice sounded like. "Hello," I said, and waited for dear life.

"This is Dr. Farmer." Neutral tone.

"Dr. Farmer. You in collusion with Dr. Frame?"

"Dr. Arnold Frame?" Toneless, like my mother, even when seeking information.

"In Indianapolis. Yes."

"Yes," said the Farmer.

"He wanted me to get in touch with you."

"Yes."

"I'm not sure why."

"I'm not sure I can do anything about that on the phone.

Are you having any symptoms?" I decided not to mention the possibility of a sexual disease, it sounded too gamey and even to my ears now a little far-fetched. Something about this man's utter expressionlessness was bracing.

"I've been under a lot of strain, my wife and I just separated, and a girl I got deeply involved with walked out on me. I suppose I don't sound as if I'm in the pink, and my brother, who's been calling me long-distance, got concerned and called old Doc Frame." There was that Doc again. Now you say it, now you don't.

"How deeply involved were you with this girl?"

"I think two or three nights."

"When did you and your wife separate?"

"I've lost track of time," I complained. "Maybe two weeks ago, maybe a little less. I gave her my apartment."

"Are you able to function on your job?"

"I free-lance," I said haughtily, "so I don't have to report to an office regularly. I guess you can say that in most important respects I function. Except that I threw up a little while ago."

"When did you last have a checkup?"

"I don't know exactly. I can't think."

He sounded amused: "Is that what you told my service? They told me that was the symptom you reported."

"They can't get anything straight, if you'll excuse me for blowing the whistle on them, sir."

"This episode of vomiting," he said. "You have any idea of what caused it?"

I thought of lunch and immediately thought I would have to excuse myself and race to the bathroom, but then it passed. I decided it was no more suitable to tell a strange doctor what I'd eaten for lunch than to tell him about my sexual disease. Unease. No, disease. "I can't think what caused it. Strain, possibly," I said.

"You taking any medication?"

"Only liquor." I laughed. Why didn't he register some amusement at that?

"Would you like to come and see me?"

"Yes," I said, with relief. He had been sent, through Frame by Davey, and yes, I would see him. I wanted to, I wanted the peace he could give me. The rusticity of his name. Well chosen. Maybe not even changed from something else.

We made an appointment for sometime the next day. Eight A.M. The only time he had. I scribbled down his Park Avenue address. "Oh, wait a minute," I said. "About the medication."

"Yes?"

"I don't take any, but my brother is going to send me some vitamins."

"Fine," he said, as if he didn't mean it or didn't know why I was telling him. "See you tomorrow then."

"Yes," I mumbled. I hung up and rang the desk. Told them to ring me at seven in the morning. I needed a wake-up call at that hour, and no kidding around.

Then I undressed, crawled under the tangled covers, and tried to sleep.

As it happened, the wake-up call was on time, but I was late to Farmer's office. "We only have fifteen minutes," he told me as he ushered me into his office, filled with a bust of Freud and reproductions of Etruscan art.

"That doesn't seem fair," I protested. "We can't get at the root of whatever it is in fifteen minutes."

"Are you on any medication?"

"You asked me that yesterday. No for yesterday, and no again for today."

Pen poised in midair, he said to me mildly, "You're pretty belligerent. Any idea why?"

"Yes, but fifteen minutes doesn't give me enough time to go into it."

"World treating you badly?"

"Yes. What are you writing down?"

"Feel rested?"

"No." My voice broke. "Do you think I have a chip on my shoulder?"

"I wouldn't put it that way," Farmer said gently. All of a sudden I looked at him. Middle-aged, well dressed, but no standout in a crowd or even face to face.

"What are we going to do?"

"I'm writing you a prescription for some medication. I want to see you again this week. Friday at eight?"

"I'll try," I said. Friday was the day after tomorrow.

"Good," he said. "Phone me if you and the medication don't seem to get along."

"I get along with everybody. Most of the time," I said morosely.

"My fee is forty dollars," he said, leaning back in his chair.

Forty dollars. More than Selfridge. He must be crazy. "I was only here fifteen minutes," I stammered.

"You were late," he reminded me. "Get the prescription filled, and I'll see you on Friday."

I thought I heard him say good-bye. I said nothing.

I hung around a fancy pharmacy I discovered two blocks south on Park Avenue, waiting for the proprietor to arrive so I could get the fucking prescription filled. I probably needed sedation—I assumed this was what the medication was—but I hoped it wouldn't cloud my head. Maybe after this was over I'd visit Helen and tell her about the divorce, try and hit her for the five hundred, charge her five dollars interest, and take a look at my sole remaining New York relative, Morrie.

The pharmacist whistled through his teeth when he finally examined my prescription.

"What is it?"

"Low dosage Thorazine," he told me.

"Thorazine!" I exploded. "That's for crazy people."

"Not always," said the druggist cautiously. He disappeared into his sanctum.

"How long do I have to take it?" I asked.

"He's given you two days' worth. You take it through Friday morning."

Foxy Farmer. He'd only given me enough to bring me to the next appointment, begging for more goofballs and forking over forty dollars.

The pharmacy bill was outrageous too. I paid it, complaining bitterly. Then, depleted, I took a taxi back to the Paris, sat in my room on the bed, swallowing the allotted dosage with the glass (from which I had rinsed the traces of Scotch), and pondered whether to call Helen.

I would call Davey, I decided. He had seen to it that I be helped, brought to this chemical peace. I looked at the time, midmorning here, a little earlier in Indianapolis. I rang the lab. He wasn't there. I called his home. Betty answered. "Isn't he at the lab?" she asked.

"No. Should he be?"

"Well, yes. He didn't say anything about anything else. How are you?"

"I feel better," I said. "It's a rough time, but I think we'll weather it." The "we" was a nice touch, had just slipped in there—had it meant I was thinking too of Jennie? "I'll never be able to thank Davey enough."

Betty laughed. So she was not without warmth or spirit. "Of course you will," she said. "It's so nice to see brothers who care about each other the way you and Davey do. It makes me think we'll be cheating Libba if we don't give her a little brother or sister soon."

I laughed. "Is this a reality or still a gleam in Davey's eye?"

She gave what seemed to be a little yip of delight. I imagined this was as ribald as I would ever get with her. "Just a gleam," she said cheerfully. "I'll tell Davey to call you."

The conversation concluded, I wondered at the peace that suffused me. Betty had never seemed more kind or more agreeable. Had I been uncharitable to her thus far? Maybe I would have a second chance in life.

I waited for what must have been an hour, and still Davey did not return my call. I decided then to let him get in touch with me when he could.

I waited, I think—though time gets telescoped here—till midafternoon. For Davey's call. Waiting without anxiety. How agreeable. Was it the drug, or some arbitrary and mysterious restoration of the self? Did the drug itself make possible the restoration? Perhaps I had suppressed myself so as to make leaving Jennie less painful. Now, a new birth of freedom. Davey's help—he was behind it all. I remembered Jennie and me standing before the shrine, the Lincoln Memorial, on our honeymoon—which day? It didn't matter now. Why hadn't our feelings for each other and for the world remained that pure? We had stood there in awe.

Why hadn't the innocence of our love lasted? And that spell of grandeur that had overtaken us and enveloped our newborn marriage, while we stood in the shadow of the memorial. Almost a century later, and one still mourned.

Marble and stone. Why did people live in the prison of unpredictable bodies? We—Jennie and I—had invaded and corrupted each other's bodily separateness. We frightened each other, we were irritants to each other. And finally we were repellent to each other. At first, the psyche served to shield the lover from the horror of the other's nakedness. But then, the psyche too gave way, broken by the lover's pain. My own pain had been transmuted into a numbness. Perhaps that had been a perceptual distortion that the drug was now correcting. But the drug also conferred an insulation from pain. With this insulation, this remedy, one could look back upon the pain and feel regret. But the regret differed distinctly from the raw suffering that had preceded it. The regret carried with it a certain comfort, as if the self were being told that it was mending. Perhaps it had not even been that badly broken. In any case, I had permission now not to suffer. I lay down to rest, slept briefly, awoke refreshed. The drug did make one drowsy, but that was good—it meant that sleeplessness was perhaps a thing of the past.

I got up, stretched, yawned, My smallest gesture, even my reflexes, gave me pleasure. To know that I was alive. What a luxury life was, the freed body was. How grateful I was to Davey, who had set the chain of my recovery in motion. The pain for Babs had receded. The girl was in shadows, scarcely visible in that cliché, the mind's eye. Mind and body. How could I forget that there was such a thing as the perspective natural to adults, now that this perspective had returned to me. I resolved not to think of Jennie now. I knew that if I did I would hurt, and that the shattering of our love—however inevitable it may have been—warranted my grief. But I could not afford to grieve now. I was recovering my strength but not yet in full possession of it. I was convalescent. I glanced at my watch. In Indianapolis it was now about four. Davey's lunch had probably taken him more time than he'd figured. And the work must have piled up in the meantime at the lab. He'd probably wait till he got home to call me. After he had played with Libba and eaten the supper Betty had prepared. I probably would not remarry. But Davey and his family would be mine, and I would lavish all the fatherly love I had on Libba. I had, with Frame, my new doctor here, and Davey's family a solid network of supports. Jennie would remarry. When I was altogether well again, I'd try in some way to make reparations to Jennie. I didn't know just how, but I had the sense that I must have failed her as a husband just as much as she had failed me as a wife. Meanwhile, from afar, I could wish for her a support system as strong and reliable as mine.

Funny how the drug made one lightheaded, at the same time that it stripped the body of its lethargy and lifted the mind's depression. I could move, slowly, as if I were walking through vast amounts of water, water of great density, but I was grateful even for this, for it made me aware not only of the luxury but of the miracle of the body. It felt almost newborn. A new clarity of mind, an intimation of happiness.

I felt hungry but that was good too, even if uncomfortable, a sign of life and the knowledge that my body could obey me, that I had power over it. But I had promised to wait by the phone for Davey's call. I had probably alarmed him more than he'd let on, and he was owed this vigil. He loved me. My brother. My hunger would keep. I lay down. I'd rest some more. Sleep was curative. I'd been reprieved.

In the dream, I was cradling Jennie in my arms. Where were we? Why was she even tinier than in life? Elusive. Like a toy one lost among the sofa's cushions. The sofa with the familiar floral print that smelled of camphor. Take away the camphor, I said to the woman who was hovering there. Her presence was a fearful rebuke. Belle. No, my mother. She had won something. What was it? Had she hurt my father? Why didn't she leave me alone to find my toy? I don't like her, Jennie wept. You promised we'd never come here again. Where are we? Where are you? I asked. She'd vanished once more. Indianapolis, answered Belle. My mother cackled and hugged Belle. Take your hand away from there, my mother said, as I searched for Jennie amid the crevices between the sofa cushions. I know what you're doing. My mother was triumphant, she had caught me out, I had chosen a wife too small for me, one you could lose. And the sound of her laughter was vicious and wild, unlike any sound my mother had ever made. Where's Dad? I asked. Isn't he home? Had she killed my father? You're not in Indianapolis, don't you know I'd never let you come home, said my mother. But I want to come home, Mother, I said. Never, she said, feebly. Suddenly she was old and ill. Guilt-stricken, I said, Mother, I must come home. I'm ashamed to tell you this, but I need to urinate. You'll have to wait, she said in her long-suffering voice. You left us, and there are other bathrooms. I can't wait, I said, let me come home. You made your bed, she said, lie in it. I have to go, I said. In a faint voice she said: Pray.

I awoke and the need to piss was urgent, but the phone was ringing, and it would be Davey, and there was no question of what came first, the ridiculous message of my body or the fidelity I owed my brother. My priorities were set. Behave like a grown-up, I instructed my bladder with some amusement, then shivered with a premonition, not having shaken the dream, and picked up the phone.

"Yes, Dave," I said.

"Jack, come home," said my mother.

"Mother?"

She was saying something, it was incoherent. I stood up, an effort to take charge of myself or some situation.

"There was a package in his hand. Carl said they had to pry the package from his hand."

Then I knew, but I wouldn't yet let myself know.

"Mother? Mother, what time is it?"

"Oh, I don't know," she keened. Ghostly. I groped for my watch. Eight P.M. here, so seven in Indianapolis. Outside it was dark.

"He was on his way to the post office," she said. Then she said something else. She was unintelligible. "Damn," I muttered, unable either to let go of the phone or to reach the light switch. I was cursing the dark.

"What?" she said. "What?"

"Mother, just tell me. Just say it. What's happened?"

"Davey's gone."

"Dead?" I was numb from heat to foot. I felt the moisture on my pants, I was urinating. I would never be the same again. "Mother, tell me, Mother, I love you, tell me what happened." I had said I loved her; there was a shattering.

"They found him on the ground. He was holding a parcel. His fingers were stiff. It's addressed to you, Jack."

My voice went on without my body. "Where is it now?" I would have that, at least. Shock was rescuing me. I could— I would be able to—think clearly. Do what had to be done. My trousers were soaked. I would throw away these clothes.

"The parcel," I said.

"I don't know," she mourned. "I think they brought it home to Betty."

"Where is he?"

"In the funeral home." Her voice was fading.

"Mother," I said, trying to breathe life into her, "Mother, I love you. Tell me, when did it happen?"

"Maybe lunchtime. I don't know if he got to eat lunch."

I didn't understand. "Mother," I said, the room was starting to sway, I had nausea, and a ringing in my ears, "how did it happen?"

"I don't know. God's will."

"Mother, I love you," said the person I had become.

"Will you come home?"

"Yes, tonight." My hands were shaking. I would have to think quickly, but I could think, thank God I could think. "Is anybody with you?"

"Carl's coming over. And Dr. Frame."

"Betty?" I asked.

"Rita's gone to be with Betty. Jack, I can't talk."

"Is Rita there now?"

"No. People will be coming soon. I want to tidy up. There'll be visitors. What will we do? My baby, my favorite."

"Yes, Mother," I said, "I love you. I'll be there with you tonight."

I hung up the phone. I looked down. There was a stain spreading on the carpet. I walked into the bathroom, discarded my trousers and undershorts, threw them in a heap to the side of the toilet, and urinated. A ceaseless stream. These things, these most primitive things, that Davey would never do again. Davey will never piss again. Finally I stopped. I took a towel, soaked it in water, and sponged myself off. My wet thighs, my legs. What did I feel? No time to think of that. My hands were shaking, must get my body under control.

I needed to make some calls. I needed to know more. Rita. I wanted my sister. I put a call through to her home, no answer, then with the beginnings of an agony that would soon supersede the shock—I'd have to wait till I had done everything that had to be done—I called Betty. I prayed that

Rita would take the call. Not Betty. Betty should have sedation. How had it happened? Libba. Libba would not know her father, except through what others would tell her about him. Davey would never hold her again. Davey would never have sex again. He would never have another child. He had barely known the child he had. Libba would grow up without him, would become a woman without him. Libba. Davey, her father.

A strange woman took the call. When I explained, in answer to her question, who I was, she summoned Rita to the phone. "Is she all right?" I asked the woman.

"As well as could be expected," the woman said. It would become a refrain. How did I know so much about death? My father had died so long ago. Yet I knew the things that had to be done. Had I always known about death? Foreknowledge?

Rita came on the line. "Jack? Oh, Jack." She began to cry.

"Hold on, Reet," I said gently. "Reet, I'm taking the first plane I can get. I'll be there tonight, just hang on." Davey's words. To me.

"Jack, I love you," she wept.

"I know. Reet, take it easy."

"I never meant all those digs I used to make. It's just that you were my kid brother, and I was a big pest. I wanted to play with you and Davey, being shut out made me feel so big and ugly, I wasn't fair to you." I had a sudden memory of Davey as a kid, snickering with me at Reet, then sheepishly chiding us both for our lack of compassion. "Jack, forgive me," Rita was saying. "Please forgive me."

"Reet, you've done nothing." I absolved her. Why this guilt? The guilt was mine. I was the brother who should have known better than to torment my sister, my big sister. And why hadn't I been there for Davey? He'd had only hours, days, left to live when we'd last talked, and we didn't know it and we—he—took care of me. Always, Davey had been the wisest. I said to her, "Hang on. Listen, I don't know what exactly happened. Mother told me he was found a few hours after it happened."

"Yes. He'd taken a shortcut to the post office, through a vacant lot—it didn't use to be there, but they've torn down buildings—and he collapsed. And just lay there. Oh, my God."

"But Reet. What happened? I mean, I don't know what happened."

"I know. You want to know what he—he—" She began to gasp, she was making choking sounds, she could not get her breath.

I said quietly, "I want to know what he died of." I'd said it.

She was trying very courageously to compose herself. Valor and grace, she was exhibiting now. Worthy of Davey. Who would live on in all of us. I would try to the end of my days to supply what he took with him on that unfinished errand. "Tell me what it was, Reet. Reet, I love you." There. I'd said it again. I had changed. My life had broken. Mind separated from body. Davey's soul stripped from the body.

Shattering.

Reet was saying, "A heart attack. That's what they think, anyway. We don't know if Betty will give permission for an autopsy, and we don't want to ask her just now. But they think he died—he died"—her voice again became stran-gled—"instantly." Instantly. And apparently alone. A vacant lot. On the ground, my mother had said. Amid grass? Amid weeds? Greenery? Desolation? How long had he remained there alone?

I asked, "Who found him?"

"One of the postmen. Mr. Cromwell's son. Remember, he used to be our postman before he died? Before Daddy died? His son works for the post office now. Red Cromwell. He found him and called the police and Dr. Frame. They think it was a massive heart attack, and nothing could have been done to save him. We must try to believe that, to hang on to that, Jack." Hang on. Davey's words were part of Rita now too. Davey. So vivid to me in what shall I call it—the exaltation?—of grief. What I know about death now is how vivid the person remains to those of us who survive him, in the days that follow upon the death. Davey. Remains.

Dead. Davey was not thirty. Suddenly I was not believing it. Was it Davey trying to protect me? Hovering close by, before an ascent? I did not believe in my mother's god.

I said, "I'm going to call the airline now, Reet. I'll be there tonight."

"I'm so glad," she sobbed, "he was found by someone we know."

"Yes," I said. Dimly I remembered Red Cromwell as a kid, when we were kids. Freckles and that thatch of orange hair. A father who'd gotten ill—a stroke—so young. We'd all grown up together. Davey would never be old.

"Reet, I'll get in late. I'll take a cab from the airport."

"I'll wait up," she said. "Drop by here if you can. And stay at our place. I think we'll take Mother there, and you and Carl can be with her and I'll stay with Betty."

I couldn't focus on the logistics of this except that I thought I should—no, wanted to—be with my mother. I wanted my mother. I said, "How's Betty?"

"Dr. Frame gave her a shot. She's up in her room. She doesn't sleep, the shot didn't work, and several of us are here. We take turns being with her."

"I guess she's in no condition to talk, huh?" I said softly. (Vaguely, I remembered I'd want at some point to ask about—to see—the parcel for me Davey'd died holding.)

"No. She doesn't talk." And Rita wept.

"The baby?"

"In her crib. She wants her mother, and she's sucking her thumb."

"Don't cry, Reet," I said tenderly. Foolishly. Of course she should cry. So should I. But I couldn't. Yet. I had responsibilities to meet. And I would meet them.

"Reet," I said, my voice catching, "I'll say good-bye now, and I'll see you tonight."

"You haven't called me Reet in so long," she said, as if she'd come home at last.

I said, "I love you. I always have. Always will. I'll be there with you as soon as I can. I'm with you."

"I love you, Davey," she said, and hung up before she could correct her slip. I never knew, never asked her if she knew that she'd called me by his name. Davey. I was, I would be, Davey now.

AIRBORNE, I took an aisle seat, so that I could get water to swallow my pill without disturbing my fellow passengers. I could not look at them. I closed my eyes so that I could not see them. The man in me had died with Davey. The woman in me had died with Jennie. Jen wasn't dead, merely divorced. I had killed her. Betty was alone now. But I would, for the rest of my life, stand in as best I could for Davey, be surrogate husband and father to his wife and child. "I don't want any gum," I whispered to the stewardess.

It would be self-pity to hurt for the loss of Jennie. I had dissolved the marriage, and I had no right to hurt for what I myself had done.

I stood outside in the dark, under a light, bleak Midwestern drizzle. A taxi pulled up.

"RITA," I said, and hugged her.

"I can't stand this," she whispered to me.

"Neither can I."

We held on to each other.

"Davey told us a little about you and Jennie. Was it awful?"

"Yes." I buried my face for a moment in her shoulder. She was nearly as tall as I. Big and ugly, she had thought herself as a girl. Poor Reet. Not true.

"Oh, Jack." She began to cry. Whether for my shattered marriage or Davey, neither of us knew. We would have cried if a cup had broken, if we'd spotted a stain on the rug.

"Where's Mother?" I asked.

"At our place," she said. "Dr. Frame's there too," she added.

Good, I thought. I can pick up a prescription from him if I catch him there, which I hoped I would. Or I could get it from Carl. "How is Mother?" I whispered.

"I can't tell," Rita mourned. I tried awkwardly to dry her tears with my handkerchief. But she was so tall, my arms were heavy, dead weight.

"Are you okay?" Rita asked.

"Dandy," I said and smiled at her. "I'm sedated. Don't worry. The junk I'm taking doesn't disable me. It just keeps me from collapsing." It was making me efficient. I tried to tell her that. She seemed reassured.

"Can I see Betty?"

She lay on their bed. She stretched out her hand to me. "Poor Jack," she said. "Your hands are so cold."

I whispered her name. "Davey," she replied.

"I know," I said.

"What will we do?" she implored.

"Betty," I began, "are your folks coming?"

"I don't want them," she said. It was the first defiance

of mores I had heard her utter. Ever. Then I remembered an earlier defiance: the untimely pregnancy.

"Betty," I said softly, "I can call them. Now or in the morning."

"Would you?" she asked, looking at me gratefully. "Maybe call them now," she said, her voice trembling. "The funeral's on Saturday."

At the sound of the word funeral I was awash with horror. How could the word have passed her lips so casually? Better keep hold of myself, I said to myself—did I have a self?—hold on.

"Could you ask my parents to call Jerry?"

Jerry. Who was Jerry? I'd ask her later. Did she have a brother? I thought of my brother, and I backed out of the room, and I wept.

I got off the phone and reached for one of my few remaining Thorazines and managed to swallow it without water. Why did the mechanisms of the throat work? The rest of my body was numb, nearly paralyzed. I staggered back to Betty.

"I've told them," I said to her gently. "They'll be here tomorrow."

"You're being wonderful, Jack," Rita said, following me out of the room.

"Will there be an autopsy?"

"Do you think we should have one?"

I tried to think. My mind, again, was clear. "I think yes. Because of Libba. They might find out something that would at some point bear on Libba's health."

"You're right," Rita said. "I'll tell that to Betty."

"I want to see Davey."

"Yes," she said. "The casket's open. Tyler's funeral home."

Old man Tyler, the mortician. "His son in the business now?" I asked.

"No," Rita said. "His son went to medical school. He's a doctor in town now. Maybe," she said with a giggle, "he routes all terminal cases over to his father after they've passed on."

"Sort of like first refusal rights," I said. She laughed but stopped instantly as she saw my face distort with a tic.

"Jack," she said, holding on to me, "don't go to the funeral parlor. You've got to get some sleep. What's happening to your face?"

"Like Spencer Tracy," I tried to joke, "in *Jekyll and Hyde*."

I showed her the nearly empty vial of capsules. "I think it's a side effect of Thorazine," she said. "Shall I call Carl?"

"No," I said, taking deep breaths, "it'll wake Mother."

"I think there's an antidote for this."

"I'll go to the funeral home," I said. "Maybe we can run down young Doc Tyler."

We stood there. I took deep breaths, the tic seemed to go away. We argued, but then she saw she couldn't keep me from seeing Davey.

And so I went. In a cab. Alone.

I LOOKED AT the face of the dead man. Thin. So thin. Even thinner than he'd been when I last saw him. Eyes closed, of course. Contact lenses probably removed. Or had he reverted to glasses? Yellow hair. The strange mustache. A look of strain, even in death. Some hint of struggle, even in this repose. No evidence that there had been, ever, any contentment.

Davey had died of pain.

WITHOUT MY BROTHER, alone with the parcel, I tried to undo the twine. My hands were trembling. Maybe Carl was right. Something was wrong with my motor coordination. I bit through the twine in frustration. My teeth were strong. Teeth were invaluable in the identification of bodies in plane crashes, other disasters. Teeth endured. How nice for dentists and coroners. I unwrapped the package with my unsteady hands. So much wadding in it. What had Davey been trying to protect with these layers of wadding, laid on with so much care?

I knew of course. I came finally to the small containers of vitamins and minerals, this one for stress, that one for the restoration of strength, another for possible deficiency of calcium, another for possible deficiency of iron. A neat note from Davey, Scotch-taped to another carefully wrapped packet of something, urging me to get a complete checkup. He was hoping, he scrawled—even this scrawl had a kind of beauty—that I would also enjoy looking at the "mystery package," to which this note was taped. Love, he said, Davey. Then, for some reason, he had crossed out the y of his name. "Love," it read, "Dave." Why had my vision suddenly cleared, why had my hands stopped trembling? He was here, he had written this note, he was still alive. I opened Davey's package. Snapshots fell into my hand. I leaned back on the pillow to get my breath.

I was breathing, but my mind and body both—disobedient—veered from some fixed standard.

I closed my eyes and waited until I could summon the image of Davey not as he was when I last saw him, wearing his frailty with bravado and a determination to change, for better or worse, until death do us part. But the original, younger Davey at my wedding. And the time before that. And earlier even than that. And.

I opened my eyes and picked up the first of the snapshots. There he was, the old Davey, with glasses, heavier, no falsely jaunty mustache. Smiling carelessly into the camera. I reached for the next. Davey with the baby in his arms. Hard to make her out—somehow a shadow had fallen across her face and little pinafore. Who had taken the photo? Betty, probably. She probably hadn't noticed the shadow; she wouldn't have wanted one of her two dearest people to upstage the other. Then I thought, Libba would live. She would, from now on, more and more upstage Davey's memory, merely by being alive and by perpetuating the qualities she had inherited from him. Heredity versus environment. Since we would all in some measure become Davey now, Libba would have her father within her and outside of her. Sort of like a double lock. I would lock this child in my heart. And the next photo I saw was of Libba with her mother, her small face smiling, exuberant, mischievous. She was trying to wriggle out of Betty's arms into the photographer's embrace, the photographer being Davey. Little mischief, childishly, innocently, playing one parent off against the other. What a responsibility to have a child. Davey, the photographer. Davey: Just a memory and a photograph now. I began to cry. I hadn't expected him to die.

I WAS AWAKENED not so much by light as by the day. I groped for my watch.

"Six-thirty," Carl said gently. I had lost an hour someplace, in the flight home, not to Kentucky where my father had gone when he died, but home. To Indiana.

"Do you know," I asked, struggling into a bathrobe, "if Davey left a will? Life insurance?"

"The family lawyer says there is some kind of will," Carl said. "He and the insurance agent will come later."

"I'll go up to Mother now," I said.

In my mother's room I saw a shrunken child, propped up against her pillows. When she saw me, she began to cry. I went to her, sat on the bed, and hugged her. What was she saying, cradled against my shoulder? I listened. "You're not Davey," she said.

DAY TWO, without Davey. Daniel Morrissey was our first caller of the day. He had not come to condole but to explain to us Davey's rather complicated insurance situation.

"I'm very unhappy to be here," he said to me. For that, I liked him. "I knew your brother," he went on, not letting go of my hand. "We were at State together."

"I thought so," I said. "I recognized your name."

"I have his medical policies here—" By this time we were seated. "And there's no indication that he had heart trouble."

"Dan—" I said—curious how grief made everyone everyone else's immediate buddy—"did Davey have life insurance?"

"Yes." He handed me some papers, documents. I couldn't focus on them. "It's a policy for ten thousand dollars."

"Oh, my God," I said, "is that all? He had a family. That won't see them through much more than a year."

"I guess," Morrissey said sadly, "he was planning to augment it as time went by. He couldn't afford higher premiums than this when he bought the policy."

"Didn't the company pay?" I asked.

"Only part of the premium. If you'll forgive my saying so, it's not a very enlightened company about these matters."

"I don't mind your saying so at all," I exclaimed. "I agree with you one hundred percent."

"Unfortunately," said Morrissey, getting to his feet, "there's nothing we can do about it. The company likes to haggle about such things, but I'll handle that with a flat no, and if they don't like it, they can stuff it."

I walked him to the door. "Tell me, Dan," I said, as I helped him into his coat, "what would you have wanted to be if you hadn't gone into the insurance business?"

He looked at me, dazed. "A writer," he said.

We shook hands, and he was gone.

ONE TO GO. Kevin O'Dare the lawyer arrived about an hour later. "Still raining," he said, handing me a soaking coat.

He reached into his briefcase and produced an envelope, which he handed to me. "I don't normally do business this late in the afternoon, but under the circumstances—" I brushed aside his explanations. "This is a copy of your brother's will."

I held it. I couldn't open it. Finally, I whispered, "What were Davey's assets?"

O'Dare looked pained, in a formal sort of way, as if it were a function of his office. "Well, he had some money left that he'd inherited from your father."

"I see," I said. I too had inherited money from my father. I'd drawn on it in these last months and was planning to apply some of it to cover the costs of my divorce. Why did money make one think of money?

"You can open it," O'Dare said encouragingly, looking at the envelope. "Betty has the original, and your sister has seen it."

I looked at the document, reading rapidly till I came to my name. Two thousand dollars for my brother, Jack Church, and two thousand dollars for my sister, Rita Koenig. Two thousand dollars. My God. A fortune for Davey. Why had he done this? Extravagant.

O'Dare seemed to think I was disappointed. "I'm sure he would have added to it if he'd lived."

"I don't know," I said dully. "I really don't care about that. I'm going to turn the money over to Betty, of course."

"I believe your sister intends to do the same thing," said O'Dare.

"How come," I asked, "there's nothing for my mother? Did you draw this up for him?"

"Yes. About a year ago. Naturally he assumed that she would predecease him."

O'Dare went on about probating the will, getting into Davey's safe-deposit box, transferring the money from a joint account to a single account for Betty.

"Do you handle divorces?" I asked.

O'Dare said in somewhat hushed tones: "I happen to be a Catholic. And I'm not really a divorce lawyer. However, I could refer you to a colleague. But aren't you from New York?"

I nodded yes. "But I'm not sure where I'm going to live, after all this . . ." I trailed off.

"I understand," said O'Dare. "Perhaps this is not the time to be thinking of it."

"I guess not. The mind does funny things when it's in shock," I said, wanting to make a good impression, to show him that I had not been trying to kill two birds with one stone, that I was not crass. I wondered what it would be like, now, if Jennie and I were still together, if our marriage had survived its miseries, and if she'd accompanied me here. Now. Did I miss her? The truth is, I could barely remember her, I could scarcely bring the memory of her face to mind. Heart-shaped, it was. Or wasn't it? What color were her eyes?

"About the bill—" said O'Dare. Suddenly I knew what I'd do with my bequest. Pay his fucking bill, and Rita would take care of Mother. Maybe we'd devise some lie, explaining that the money was from the two of us. And there'd be money enough left from my inheritance from Dad to give two thousand dollars to Betty too. I hoped.

"Send me the bill," I said shortly. I gave him Jennie's address. "I'll be in New York, for a while anyway. My wife will forward mail. There's no bitterness between us." I showed him the door.

RED CROMWELL, who found the body, was next. I borrowed Carl's car when he returned from the airport with Betty's parents, and drove over to a diner near Red's post office. He was seated when I got there. The place was diner, U.S.A., no different from the place near Elmira where I'd left Jennie on our memorable first date. Booths. And formica everywhere.

"Hi, Red," I said, slipping into the seat opposite him.

"Jack?" he said.

I smiled. "Yeah, we've grown up. It's me."

He tried to smile, his mouth twitched, and he looked back down at his coffee.

"I wish to God," he blurted out, "it hadn't been me."

I ordered a cup of tea and asked him to tell me. He pieced out a jagged story. I asked him question after question: the look of the lot—sandy, he said. Whether he knew immediately that it was Davey—yes, he said. The position of the body—he'd lain flat on his back, Red said. The expression on Davey's face—at that, Red began to cry, and I felt shame for my question. "Forget it," I said softly. "Forget that I asked it."

Red gazed at me. "I don't know, exactly," he said, not letting me take him off this hook. "I think he looked surprised."

I nodded. "A look of struggle?"

"They say the dead don't look like that," Red whispered. "They say when you die you find peace."

Maybe that's what they said in the books he read—inspirational? or what?—but I'd seen dead men, I'd been a reporter, most recently for a newspaper that dealt in death and profited from it, so I knew better.

The dead die according to their natures, their deaths are as individuated as their lives, and the expressions on their faces tell one something about their deepest side, the secrets that they had reconciled or not. I knew my brother. I had always known. Harmonious, except— Content, except— At peace, except—

Red shook his head in disbelief. "Jesus," he said.

LATE AFTERNOON of the second day without my brother, in Carl's car with Mr. and Mrs. Ernest Gobisch.

"You'd think she'd want her mother," Mrs. Gobisch complained.

"I'm sure she does," I replied, trying not to think ill of the living.

She wants to see us, Wanda," said Mr. Gobisch. "No doubt about it."

"When is Jerry coming?"

"Tomorrow. He'll be at the funeral."

The car veered, and I was reminded of Davey's curiously unsteady driving when he was taking Jennie and me to the airport. I applied some drastic discipline to my mind and got the car back in control.

We got there. The Gobisches piled out of the car, and I was left slumped over the wheel. I sat there, probably for longer than I knew. At some point, in the dusk, in the steady drizzle, Rita came out of the house and slipped into the car.

I smiled at her. "Don't fasten your seat belt," I told her. "We're not going nowhere."

"You okay?"

"Nope. You?"

She shook her head no and leaned against my shoulder. "Rest your weary head," I murmured.

"A quote?" she asked.

"I don't know." I looked at her. "If you weren't a girl, I'd think you were Davey, come back to haunt and comfort us." She was Davey, for moments, on and off, in the days to come. The Church kids, how they seemed to read each other's thoughts. Cluck, cluck, said the neighborhood matrons, as Rita staggered into adolescence. So much taller than her brothers, and her gym teacher told me she menstruates now. The boys seem to be embarrassed around her, and they hang out with each other more. No, it's that Rita's embarrassed by them. After all, she's maturing now, and doesn't want her kid brothers around her. Her mother says she wants to shave her legs. Alma says she told her, shave your legs and I'll cut my throat. No, Alma said she'd tan her hide. Oh really? I thought she said cut her throat. I don't think a girl should shave her legs until she really has to. I don't think so either. What does Edith think? Edith? Her legs are pretty hairy. There was no denying that, so Alma—my mother—pouted in her middle-aged way, and gave in. But the ensuing stubble along Rita's calves was the subject of whispered idle talk among the matrons who were my mother's bosom buddies for months after she went ahead with the razor. And then it all changed. She matured, as they said, she dated, she married, she became a Koenig, a mother, and a stranger. But in these brief moments, beside me in the car, Rita was the girl with her back to the wall, locked in combat with my mother, with the controversial razor waiting at the sink. I glanced down. Long legs, muscular, not unshapely. She sighed. I put my arm around her. "Oh, Davey," she wept. "Jack, help me please."

"I'm here, Reet," I said. "Cry. You're a girl."

"Stop it," she said, grinning through her tears. "You're not supposed to joke, you'll make me laugh."

"Do you think," I asked her, "that Davey lost his sense of humor toward the end?"

"I don't know," she said, puzzled. "I never thought about it."

She wouldn't have, of course. She'd given her own up, probably together with her virginity, when she married Carl and life got serious.

I said finally: "What's with the Gobisches? I can't figure out whether Mrs. Gobisch is too salty or too sour."

"I wouldn't worry. Come on in the house. You must be hungry."

"In a minute. Reet, don't be edgy. I don't have to be fed on schedule. Just sit a minute."

She sat there quietly, breathing in, breathing out.

DAY THREE, without him. Rita and I sat on either side of our mother, each of us holding on to her. Betty's parents surrounded a very pale and composed Betty. I'd lost track of who'd gotten sedated on which day. Dr. Frame was in the row behind me and pressed my shoulder from time to time as the minister eulogized Davey briefly in his flat Midwestern twang. There were interludes of ritual, citation from scripture, music Davey had liked. Who was this minister? I thought of the other Reverend I hadn't liked—Turbot, at my wedding.

"The Lord is my shepherd, I shall not want. . . ." Spoken by a hushed chorus of voices around me. But I shall, I said. "Ashes to ashes"—I'd seen or heard this in some movie, what were we, Methodists?—"dust to dust."

Then someone handed me a spade, and I saw Rita nod, and I took it. A spadeful of earth into the grave. The coffin had been lowered. Frame had ordered it closed before the funeral. Funeral. I must remember to ask him whether that decision had anything to do with the autopsy. The instruments they had used. What was I to do, now that I had helped to cover my brother's coffin with the damp impurity of earth? My mother shrank from me as I turned to look at her, and covered her eyes with her hand. Rita held her. She wasn't turning from me, I told myself, but from this ritual. Frame came forward and took the shovel from me. "I'm not family," he muttered to me, "but may I?"

"Yes," I said fiercely. And so Frame threw the dirt into the grave. That's what it was. Dirt. And Frame knew it. Never mind the prettiness of ashes to ashes, and dust to dust. Death was dirt.

YOU MADE YOUR BED, I could read in Wanda Gobisch's face, now lie in it. Libba had been the subject of the morning's flare-up of argument, the first since Davey's death. Should or should not his child be carried to the service, then to the cemetery? Frame made the decision: No, he said. We arranged for a neighbor to stay with Libba. Now, out of the corner of my eye, I saw Betty disengage from her mother's clutching and move toward the stranger at the crowd's edge. Good-looking guy. Gary Cooper, at high noon, at the wrong time and in the wrong place. They looked at each other for a moment. Betty saw me watching them and signaled me to come over.

"You made it honey," I said to her. "We made it." Gratefully, she nodded, and I hugged her. I was surprised by the strength of her responsiveness. The emotional strength, the physical self-possession, the knowing of how to give one's self over, unafraid. After this loss, though, what could Betty fear? We drew apart, in tandem. "I'll never forget all you've done, Jack. You've been noble."

Her eyes were bright. There was a certain exaltation in this moment. Our glances were locked.

Gary Cooper entered the moment, and the magic extended to him. "You know each other," she said.

"No," I said softly.

"Jerry," she said.

THE DRIVE TO THE AIRPORT, Carl at the wheel, had been through dense fog.

"Drowsy?" Carl asked me, not taking his eyes off the road in front of him.

"Beat," I murmured.

"It must be the medication," Carl said. It must also be my grief, I thought, but what the hell, he meant well.

I TRUDGED THROUGH the familiar lobby of the Paris.

"There's mail for ya," the desk clerk grumbled, and then just stood there.

"Any messages?" I asked.

He walked at a snail's pace toward my box. There was an envelope addressed to me in a hand I knew well—I gripped it hard, for dear life—and an illiterate scrawl on a message pad.

I picked up my suitcase and these precious pieces of paper and walked to the elevator.

The maids obviously had been in my room, making a clean sweep of things in my absence. Fresh towels, fresh linens, same blankets and bedcover.

I sat on the edge of the bed and opened the envelope of Jennie's letter.

It was not a letter, strictly speaking. In her handwriting, full of effort, she had copied for me the entire Stephen Spender poem.

It was dated Friday, the second of the days without Davey.

It began: "For Jack, on Davey's death, our poem—"

THE TRULY GREAT

I think continually of those who were truly great.
Who, from the womb, remembered the soul's history
Through corridors of light where the hours are
    suns,
Endless and singing. Whose lovely ambition
Was that their lips, still touched with fire,
Should tell of the Spirit, clothed from head to foot
    in song.
And who hoarded from the Spring branches
The desires falling across their bodies like blossoms.

What is precious, is never to forget
The essential delight of the blood drawn from
    ageless springs
Breaking through rocks in worlds before our earth.
Never to deny its pleasure in the morning simple
    light
Nor its grave evening demand for love.
Never to allow gradually the traffic to smother
With noise and fog, the flowering of the Spirit.

Near the snow, near the sun, in the highest fields,
See how these names are fêted by the waving grass
And by the streamers of white cloud
And whispers of wind in the listening sky.
The names of those who in their lives fought for
    life,
Who wore at their hearts the fire's centre.

296

*Born of the sun, they travelled a short while toward
    the sun
And left the vivid air signed with their honour.*
                                by Stephen Spender
                                from
                                    Jennie

I reached for the telephone.

"Jen," I said, "what a dear thing to do."

"Jack, I—" Her voice faltered.

"I can't talk very well now," I managed to choke out.

"Are you in New York?" she asked.

"Yes." She had not said home. "I'll call you later, Jen."

"G'bye," she said softly as I hung up.

I lay down. The room was dark. I held the piece of paper against my chest. "Born of the sun, they travelled a short while toward the sun . . . And left the vivid air signed with their honour."

For the first time since Davey's death, I knew I was alone.

Two hours passed. I did not sleep. I got up mechanically, on schedule, to take my Thorazine, which I washed down with water. I looked at the Scotch and wondered if I should pour it down the sink. There seemed to be less of it than I had left. The maids tippled. Good for them.

I placed a call to Dr. Farmer. Tomorrow morning at eight. I would be on time, I told him. From now on, I would do everything right.

I got undressed and into bed. Clean sheets. But I could not sleep. Sleeping on the plane may have killed my sleep for the night. But around three or four, I began, on and off, to doze. And was awake at six. I had forgotten to request a wake-up call from the desk, but it had apparently not been necessary. My instincts were serving me.

"I THINK," Farmer said carefully, "that you're being too stoic."

"No," I said.

"You're in a place," he said, "where you can give way to your pain. It's safe here."

"No," I said.

"Have you cried?"

"Yes, on and off." He seemed pleased by my answer. My report card was being prepared. I wondered how the score would tally, and whether we'd all be pleased by the results. I slumped forward. "Oh, my God," I said.

"Now," he said, "let's see. You're separated from your wife. Have you been in touch with her since—this happened?"

"Yes." I pushed the Spender poem across the table. He read it, gave it back to me. He seemed moved. "I talked with her briefly last night," I said. "To thank her. But I couldn't really talk. I was afraid I'd break down."

"What would have been wrong with that?" he asked.

"I can't afford to. But I'm more in control today. Maybe I'll try her later on."

"Can you come in tomorrow?"

"I'm not sure I can afford this."

"We'll worry about that later. I think I should see you tomorrow."

"Okay." Let Farmer do the secular steering, and trust that Davey was seeing to the other-worldly kind. And then I cried. Broke down.

"I'll see you tomorrow," Farmer said. Time was up. So it wasn't a safe place to cry. If one let go, broke down, the hands on the clock were still immutable. Before I'd left, he'd said: "Are you sure you should get in touch with your wife today?"

"She won't mind," I muttered. "Dr. Farmer, can't you

give me a few minutes more? I can't leave now, in this shape."

"I'm sorry," he said. "Our time is up. Call me if you need me, and if I can, I'll of course return the call."

"Of course," I said. "Thank you."

He ushered me out. Out. I stood in the lobby of his building, then stumbled out into the bright sunlight. Blinding.

I went home. Back to the hotel.

I LAY DOWN. Breakfast should have been eaten while I'd been out. I didn't want to go to the deli, or to The Cheap Date. I was in no condition to evaluate whether the date I'd picked up had been cheap or expensive. Time would tell. Time. They said time would heal also. What did they know? "And time has left us now," the song went. I slept. "Upon a journey without ending . . . Uncharted waters beneath our bow . . . The green familiar shore is fading into time. . . ." I woke up, thinking of Davey's grave. I had no recollection of what I'd dreamed, but it was a dream, it must have been a dream, in which free rein had been given to grief's ache. I awoke in pain. Things to do: Eat, sleep, stay in some contact with people had been Dr. Farmer's litany; call me, and of course, if I can, I will of course. Off course. I was off course.

But I must try to follow the rules. The rules were rational. Farmer had questioned me about the wisdom of being in touch with Jennie. What had he meant? Was I strong enough? Jennie and I knew the worst about each other, Jennie would understand that in my loss I would be weaker.

Not permanently, but temporarily, of course. Time would heal. Maybe this loss would bring Jennie and me back together. What an odd thought. Did I want that? I suspected that Davey had wanted it. He would have, when he'd come to New York, probably told me to see Jennie. Encouraged her to see me. Stand between us in order to bring us back together. Be a buffer. Till we felt safe with each other again.

I sat up. I thought sitting up would help me to think more clearly. There was no point in thinking about the future now. There was just today, and I had told Jennie I would call her again.

"JENNIE," I begged, "just for a little while. What could I do that would harm you?"

She was weeping. "Jack, I know it's so selfish of me to cry, to think of myself now, but my doctor says I mustn't see you."

"But Jennie, why?"

I heard her intake of breath. "She feels I was hurt too badly and that I'm not recovered yet. That I haven't understood what happened between you and me. She thinks I shouldn't see you till I'm ready."

"And you're not ready?" I asked softly.

"I guess not," she said.

"Jen, is this Dr. Selfridge?"

"Yes." She began to cry again.

"Does she know about Davey?"

Jennie sobbed: "Yes."

"Jen, darling, I don't want to hurt you." I bit my lip. Why was I so dangerous to Jennie? Should I stay away from her? What had I done? I needed her. But if you loved someone, shouldn't their need come first? No, that was a denial of the self. I had no self. But I didn't want to hurt her further. "But Jennie, Jennie," I said, "you were so sweet to send that poem."

"She didn't want me to send it. She didn't want me to talk to you. The only reason I can talk to you is because Laraine's out."

"What happened?"

"I just got very upset. When you left. I'm going to be okay, but we mustn't see each other now. Jack, when you get a lawyer, please let me know. My lawyer will be in touch with him."

"I see," I said. These words were so cruel. How could Jennie be saying them? Why didn't I understand? Something was missing.

"Will you let me know about the lawyer?" she asked.

"Yes," I said.

"You still want the divorce."

I supposed that was a question. "Yes," I said softly. I had begun something for a reason, and in my pain, my need for solace, I must not forget that I had, in the beginning, reasons. "Do you," I asked her, "want the divorce?"

Irrationally, I hoped she would say no.

"Yes," she said. I thought I'd faint. I remembered the airplane. Yes, she'd said. A long time ago. Yes, to marriage. Now yes, to the other.

"Okay," I said, sitting down. I'd gotten dizzy and knew I must watch it, or I'd be no good to anyone. "Jen, I understand." I didn't, but then I didn't understand anything. "I'll let you know about a lawyer. When I get one."

"I'm so sorry about Davey," she said, still crying.

"Don't. Jen."

THE NEXT MORNING, again on the dot of eight, I sat across from him and earnestly told him my reasons for going home. "I'm not needed in New York," I said. "My wife's therapist thinks she should not see me, and I think she must be right." He said nothing. Uneasily, I asked: "Do you think it would be bad for me to see her?"

"You don't need that right now, let's put it that way."

"We're going to go ahead with a divorce, so I guess there's no point in pouring salt into my wounds by trying to see her," I said.

"It's good that you understand that," he said.

"I'm angry at her for sending the poem," I blurted out.

"You feel teased?" he asked sympathetically.

"Yes," I said.

"It's good that you recognize that," he said. A kind man. Supportive.

"I have an illegitimate son," I said.

"Are you in contact with him or his mother?"

"Not really," I said.

"Is any of this germane to the immediate issue of your decision to go home?"

"Not really. Only you and my brother know about the kid."

"Your brother knew?"

"Yes, I told him last time he was here. I never told my wife."

"Why don't you," said Dr. Farmer, "put it out of your mind for now." I was glad he thought I had a mind. "Now when do you want to go home?"

Today is Tuesday. In two days it will be a week without my brother. Dave. I'd fly back on the one-week anniversary of his death. I decided not to share this private resolve with Dr. Farmer.

"I think that I'll be ready to go before the end of the week," I said carefully to Dr. Farmer. I paused. "I think," I said, weighing each word, "I'll try to wrap things up so that I can fly back Thursday."

"I'd like to see you before you go," said Farmer. Good, I thought, he wasn't going to try and stop me.

"How do you think I'm coping?"

"Adequately, I'd say."

"Admirably?" I asked, briefly elated.

"Adequately," he repeated in a more unmistakably firm tone, to avoid any repetition of my misperception. "Everything considered, you're doing well," he added.

I sat there, silent with gratitude, and he sat with me. The room was still. The clock ticked. I did not look at it. At length, he stood. "Jack," he said, "we've gone over the hour ten minutes."

"Ten minutes," I said numbly.

He put his hand on my shoulder. "No charge," he said.

IN THE MORNING, I made arrangements with American Airlines and Rita for my return. I went to the bank, with a stamped, addressed envelope ready to be sealed. I withdrew two thousand dollars from my savings account, and mailed it off to Betty, along with a short, loving note. I was efficient again. Good. I went to Dr. Farmer and handled the hour with him efficiently too. I did not break down or cry. I asked him not to invite me to, that I couldn't afford that now. I was needed.

"I understand," he said. He looked concerned. Well, why not? Catastrophes don't happen every day.

Conscious of the limits on Dr. Farmer's own time, I arose on the stroke of the forty-five-minute "hour" and accepted his warm grasp of my hand. "Stay steady now," he said, and "Keep in touch."

"I shouldn't call my wife again, should I?" I asked.

He said, "You really have to judge for yourself."

It was really easy to judge, because when I got back to the hotel there was a message that a Mr. Grandison had called. I returned the call. He was Jennie's lawyer. I stood for a moment, drawing a few deep breaths. The lawyer was nasty. He said something about desertion and mental cruelty. He was threatening. "Did Jennie really say all this to you?" I asked, astonished.

"That sums it up nicely, I think," he said.

"I'll have my lawyer get in touch with you, Mr. Grandison," I said, omitting to mention that I didn't have one and didn't know when I would. God, she was acting fast. "Is she going to take me to the cleaners?"

"You don't have a legal leg to stand on," he said pleasantly.

A shyster lawyer she'd gotten. God. The former Miss Owen. I wanted to tear up her laboriously copied-out edition of the Spender poem, decided against it, then wondered why her words couldn't have been her own. Easy to copy out a poem, and then cry, touchingly, and say you're under doctor's orders not to see Boris Karloff.

"My lawyer will get in touch," I said, and hung up.

I stared at the phone. Fuck Grandison. I began to pack, that is, to remove from the dusty bureau drawers the gray underwear. I assembled them on the bed. Their next stopping-off point would be my suitcase. I left a message with Dr. Selfridge's answering service to have the doctor tell her patient to forward all my mail to Indianapolis. I spelled out the street names and the digits and had a rough go with her over the zip code. She seemed to have some form of verbal dyslexia. All told, I thought my doctor's answering service was nicer than Jennie's doctor's answering service.

I was getting things done. Tomorrow I would be on the plane.

WESTBOUND ON AMERICAN. I slumped in my aisle seat, with relief. Now I could relax. I'd extricated myself from New York, where I'd once belonged, and now had the sense to know where I did belong. Home in Indiana. Mustn't get too corny, I cautioned myself, and turned—in the interests of avoiding excessive self-involvement and brooding—to look at my seat mate. "Smoke bother you?" the man in the middle asked me.

"No," I said. "I don't mind at all."

RITA AND MANDY met me at the airport. "Did you have a good flight?" Rita asked me. She seemed somewhat breathless and out of sorts.

"It was okay," I began.

"Mandy, stop that!" said Mandy's mother. I felt deflated and decided to wait before chatting. "Let's get to baggage claim," said Rita. What had brought her to this point of closeness to the last straw? I looked at Mandy. She was assiduously biting her nails.

"Mother's still with us," Rita said, "so we'll put you in the sun porch."

"I could stay at Mother's. That'd make things easier on you."

"It would and it wouldn't," said Rita. "I could do without feeding extra houseguests. On the other hand, I might need you to drive while Carl's at the hospital, and to look after Mother when I'm out. If I ever get out again," she said grimly.

"Reet," I said, "you're exhausted. What's been happening?"

"What's been happening?" she nearly shrieked. "You know perfectly well what's been happening! I need to get our lives back to normal." Why did Rita suddenly look so old? Too old to be called Reet. Maybe I'd never call her that again.

Mandy spoke up. "Mama's been doing the cooking and cleaning for three whole families," she said, sounding quite impressed by what she had reported.

"She means," said Rita tiredly, "that I've been bringing food over to Betty's when I can, and cooking for everybody who's moved into my house, and going over to Mother's in my spare time, trying to sort things and straighten and go over her floors with a wet mop."

Wet mop. "Jesus, Rita, can't you just let Mother's place go for the time being?"

"The longer I let it go the more impossible it will be for me get it back into any semblance of order. And I'm not sure she should go back at all. For a while, anyway." Her speech was driving. I imagined her wet-mopping was driving too. A new furious energy, a desperation to survive. And not suffer?

"Maybe I could at least help you at Mother's," I said.

"Nobody can help me," she said. "You'd just be in the way."

"I want to help. I know how tired you must be," I said to my sister, reaching across Mandy to touch her shoulder. Muscle, cartilage, bone. And responsive to my touch. Yet I knew it wasn't personal. Something irreversible had happened to Rita. Something final: She would never again be responsive to certain kinds of appeal, or touch. Was there more to know? I felt suddenly tense, a knot in my stomach.

"You're still on medication?" she asked. I nodded yes, told her still Thorazine. For a moment her guard dropped, and the look on her face said: I am entirely helpless and alone. I looked at her in anguish. I'm here, Rita, I wanted to say. What if she knew, with this misery overtaking her previously stony features, that the dosage had been, in Farmer's words, stepped up. Finally, I said: "Rita, don't worry about me." She sighed. Relief. Okay, understandable. Who needed more trouble? And with this stuff in my system, we had insurance that there wouldn't be any.

I brought up the question of turning a portion of our bequests from Davey over to Mother.

"I think," said Rita, making a ferocious turn into her driveway—we'd come such a long distance in such a short time—"that the last thing Mother is thinking about is money."

"Is what?" I honestly thought I hadn't heard her.

"Money," she said.

BETTY GREETED ME at the door. Wan. She felt slight, perhaps brittle, in my brotherly arms. "Come on in," she said. I followed her shakily into my brother's home.

I asked for water so I could swallow another Thorazine. Betty looked at me, puzzled. "What is that, Jack?"

"For some boring ailment. Nothing serious, but my internist back in New York thinks I should stay on this until my system stabilizes itself again."

"Please be well, Jack," she said.

"I am well, dear," I said. She looked uneasy. What was it? Wasn't it okay to call her "dear"? "Can I see Libba?" I asked.

Betty hesitated. "She's sleeping. She knows something's wrong." Her voice broke. "She cries for her father. Sometimes. It might upset her or confuse her to see another man."

I said quietly: "Maybe it would help her."

Betty said: "Jack, you have to trust me to be the judge of what's best for my child."

I flinched. I was the child's uncle. Betty seemed to notice my discomfort. Quickly picking up on it, she said: "Jack, the check you sent. So generous."

"I just want to help in every way I can," I said. "I wish I could do more."

Betty's lip trembled. "I just want to check on Libba." It was understandable, I supposed. A fear that lightning would strike twice.

"Can I go with you?" I asked.

"I don't think that would be a good idea right now," Betty said with some of her old acerbity.

"Betty, I want to see her."

"Well, you will," Betty said tartly, as if the matter were of little moment. And she left the room. Was I overreacting? Was she trying to reassure me and at the same time normalize her life? How could I best help? By not pressuring her, or anybody, I decided.

I heard, from above, sounds of whimpering, sounds of crooning, and became anxious. Don't be unreasonable, I told myself. Libba is an infant still, infants have schedules, they have their own body clocks as well as the schedules imposed upon them by adults, and her mother, now taking charge, understood quite correctly that she was the best judge of Libba's needs. I must learn patience. I took another pill.

Betty was long in coming down. The phone had rung, and she had left her child to take the call. Minutes passed. Betty came down and back into the living room. She sat down, looking as if she had misplaced something. "Do you want me to pour you some sherry?" I asked.

I couldn't just sit there. I had to do something. I was on the verge of volunteering to write her another check, say for a hundred, when she said, "Okay, fine," adding absently, "thank you."

"Do people drop in a lot?" I asked, pouring the sherry, as the awkwardness between us appeared to thicken.

"Yes," she said. "A little less than before, but that's only to be expected." What would Davey have expected of me?

"Are you doing okay? Tell me really, Betty," I asked softly.

She answered, "Yes. Now that things have died down." Died down. My God. Well, let her say things her way. If I interfered with her style of language and coping, she might let down her guard. And then there would be no end to her crying. If I let down my guard, I knew there would be no end to mine. I looked at her. No widow's weeds. Blue slacks and a pink blouse. Pretty. Gallant of her, and probably intelligent, not to indulge the trappings of mourning. She was too young.

"How about you? How are things going for you?" she asked me.

"Okay," I said, clearing my throat. "I want you to know I'm here for you."

"I know," she said, frowning. Didn't she want me? My doubts were immediately dispelled by her next words: "Why don't you stay for dinner?"

I hesitated. "Wouldn't it be trouble?"

"No," she said, eying me warily. "I'm having a guest anyway. We'll just set an extra place at the table." Extra place? There'd be one empty—Davey—and I didn't know if I could bear it.

"Who's the other guest?" I asked.

"My old friend who came for the funeral. He's staying on here at a motel." She named it. I felt a fierce cramp in my belly. We were partners in the instability of grief.

I thought I knew whom she meant. "Jerry?" I asked softly.

"Yes," she said, as if awakening from a dream. A nightmare. Whose nightmare?

"What's his last name?" I asked sharply, reporter's fangs

and claws extended, a surviving brother's claws and fangs extended.

"Jeremy Rich." She crooned each syllable. Swine, I thought. The man she loved before my brother. Swinburne: "Thou hast conquered O pale Galilean." Jeremy Rich. I looked down at the rug. Swine. "Thy dead shall go down to thee dead." Rich. Well, she, Betty, always did want to come up in the world.

"Maybe I should stay for dinner," I said.

"Jack, please take a raincheck," she said urgently. "Rita needs you more."

"Sure," I said, "but I'm sort of back to stay, Betty. I want to help." I felt chilled sweat streaming over my unpredictable body.

"I'll take you up on it, Jack," she said. Meaning to be reassuring. "I know you want to help." Who was she? Did I ever know her at all? "I'll phone a taxi," she said, rising.

I watched her down the rest of her sherry. I suppressed the impulse to beg her to let me see Libba. I did not understand why she was denying me.

In the Midwestern dusk, I went like a zombie out of Betty's house to get my taxi. Betty had gingerly kissed my frozen cheek. Why the numbness, the chill?

AT FIRST THEY WOULDN'T believe me. Carl's first words to me were: "You're feverish."

"No, I'm not," I said angrily. "I'm shivering."

Rita came out of the kitchen, bedecked in a gingham apron, whose pocket was torn at the seam. Mother had always stressed the importance of the seam; a tear there, so easy to mend. Otherwise, God alone knew. "Why are you cold?" Rita accused me. "It's fifty-nine degrees, I just heard it on the radio."

"The radio never lies," I said.

"What's wrong with you?" Rita repeated. Mandy came out to watch.

"I don't feel well, and I think I've learned something rather unpleasant about Betty."

"Jack," said Rita, as if she were giving me one last chance, "the last thing we need now is a family quarrel. Did you go over there and stir up trouble?"

"I didn't have to," I said. "Trouble is there."

Carl frowned. I smiled. Then they all stared at me, Rita, Mandy, Carl, in Koenig unison.

Rita took charge. "Go into the parlor and lie down. You're probably tired."

"If I lie down," I said, "I want to lie down upstairs, where I can get some peace and quiet. But I think you should all know what I've found out about Betty."

"When did you take your last Thorazine?" Carl inquired gravely.

"I took two, about twenty minutes apart, at Betty's," I said righteously.

"You're not supposed to do that," Carl rebuked. "Let me see your prescription."

"On the condition," I said, "that you'll give it back to me. Will you?" I asked. I felt like a character in some Western movie, but then the Old West had been a serious place. People got hanged. Ballads got sung. Self-pity.

"I'll watch it," I promised. "I guess that was foolish, which is why I may be chilled or feverish, but I did get upset at Betty's."

Rita scowled. "So? What did you expect? It's a heartache to be there. I can't afford to wallow in it. He was my brother too."

"I'm not wallowing," I protested. "There's something you don't know."

"What?" Mandy asked.

"Mandy," said Rita, "scat!" Mandy exited, stage right, and sullenly too. Scat—wasn't that something one said to animals?

"Well?" said Rita, sounding none too interested. Or was she merely hiding her interest? "What is it?"

"Betty has a lover," I said.

I saw tears in Rita's eyes as she looked at me. "Jack, please go and rest. Please. You're tired."

"You don't believe me," I said evenly, summoning from the past my most professionally authoritative tone. I was a superb, accomplished, and experienced gatherer of news. And they were not going to get away with forcing me to live with this information alone.

"Don't shout," Carl advised. Had I been shouting? "Your mother might hear you."

That'll be the day, I thought. When did she ever see or hear me?

The three of us stood there, silent. "I need a drink," Rita said. Carl dutifully went to the bar and began rummaging around. Her drink, apparently, was vermouth. "Mandy," shouted Rita, going to the sofa with her glass, "keep an eye on the stove, will you?"

"Okay," shrieked the obedient child from the kitchen.

"She's probably helping herself to ice cream," Rita sighed.

"Probably," said Carl. "But what can we do?" They looked at me, then exchanged significant glances.

"Whatever you have to say," Rita said, "say it. And then for God's sake take a nap."

So. I was in the way. "I know this is hard to bear," I said shakily, "but I really can't carry it alone. She has a lover. That man Jerry."

"Oh, for God's sake," said Rita. "He's an old friend from her home town who's stayed on to help with chores. She and the baby are rattling around in that big old house. I don't know why Davey ever bought it. The mortgage. My God."

"I don't see why," I said carefully, "an old girlfriend couldn't have performed the same services."

"I don't think Betty has many women friends," said Rita, looking as if she was wondering when this interrogation would be over. Jennie used to look like that, I thought. Then it suddenly occurred to me that Rita might not care that Betty had a lover. So soon. If Betty had a man to take care of her, that would take Betty off her hands. Our hands. Was that what Rita was thinking? I asked her. She slumped on the sofa. Brocade, I noted, resentfully. These people had, in another incarnation, been loathsomely pretentious.

"First," said Rita, "I don't believe Jerry is her lover. Second, if he is, it's none of our business. Third, you come back and make trouble. Every single time. Why can't you just mind your own business and look after yourself and lend a hand here and there?"

I said my intention had been to do exactly that.

"But you don't mind your own business," said Rita. "It's always something with you. Now it's Betty has a lover."

"I do not think this man is her lover," said Carl. "He is simply a help to her."

"Well," I said grimly, "he's staying in a motel." That shut them up. They looked at me bemused. I felt triumphant. I'd proved my point. I said so.

"It proves nothing," said Carl.

"Would you feel better if they were living under one roof?" Rita asked. "Of course he's staying at a motel. He and Betty both have a sense of propriety. You just have a dirty imagination."

"It's not my imagination," I protested. "It's true."

Rita said, "Jack, if you don't stop this, I might just have a nervous breakdown. Or are you planning to have one?" I was stunned. She added: "I suppose, knowing you, you'd like to take the rest of us down with you."

I thought of Jennie. I'd nearly taken Jennie down with me. But I wasn't down now. I was there to help. Why wouldn't they help me, let us help each other, deal with this new disturbing piece of information? Betty was Davey's widow.

"Carl," I said, "don't you believe me?"

"I don't know what to believe. You haven't caught them

in flagrante," Carl said with Teutonic delicacy. "I think what you are obsessing about doesn't matter for the moment. This, what you tell, if it is true, is none of our business."

"Yes, it is," I insisted. "It would be so bad for Libba."

"Damn you," Rita said. "You're not thinking of Libba or Betty or us. You're thinking only of yourself. As usual."

"How can you say that?" I spluttered.

Mandy called from the kitchen: "Mama, dinner's burning." She sounded entirely delighted, and indeed, an acrid odor wafted into the living room. Tiredly, Rita got up to go.

"Wait a second Sis," I said. I had never called her Sis. She paused and waited. "Don't you see? Don't you understand? This man is fucking Davey's widow."

I DON'T REMEMBER EXACTLY what happened next. I believe I was sent to bed without supper. Also, in an apparent conviction that I belonged in solitary confinement in an institution for the criminally insane, I was given a bed in an upstairs room. I knew enough to know this was Mandy's room. Well, let the little precious sleep in the fancy-schmancy parlor so that her uncle could continue to serve as the Rock of Gibraltar, which he was, whether his idiot relatives knew it or not. All he needed, I thought, was a little rest. The goddamned flight, the ride in the car with my disagreeable sister, and the lurid visit to Betty's. God alone knew why she wouldn't let me see Libba. Could she be trusted with the child? Would Libba end up as a battered or neglected child in the custody of her mother, of whom the best that could be said was that she was crazed with grief? "Go away," I muttered as Carl drove a hypodermic needle into the vulnerable flesh of my arm. Bruises to the bruised. Couldn't he have tried my other arm? "What are you shooting into me?" I asked.

"A sedative," he said calmly.

"I want it in my left arm," I mumbled. "The other one hurts."

"Jack," said a ragged voice, "Carl's giving you the injection in your left arm." The speaker was a giantess, a female Goliath, my sister. Squinting, I could make her out despite my rapidly blurring vision. Rita, my harridan.

"It's good of Carl," I said with difficulty; my tongue had suddenly enlarged. "Good of Carl to hit my left arm." Goddamn them, they were taking away my power to speak, my control of words. "What are you giving me?"

"He's going to sleep," said Carl, as if I were not there. These people were uncivil.

"I'm hungry," I said, feeling woozy, drugged.

"If you wake up after we've gone to bed, help yourself to whatever's in the refrigerator," said Rita.

"Rita," said Carl warningly.

"I'm not yet ready to assume he's crazy," she said, if I heard her right. Could she be crying? She did always, even as a child, have a very special whine. To me she said: "I think you'll sleep till morning."

Exit Carl and Rita. Clatter, clatter down the stairs. Wasn't love wonderful. Libba, alone with Betty. Survivors. I used to interview survivors. The little girl who fell down the well.

In my dream, they were touching, the man and woman, whose faces I could not see. Naked, they were, touching each other, not with lust, but with the familiarity of regained love. He and Betty. Jerry and she. They were repossessing each other, she with her hand on my inner thigh, a kiss upon my knee. Jerry-Jack. Then Betty went down on me, God it was gorgeous, slower, sweetheart, I said, I don't want to come just yet, Jennie darling, wait, Oh my god, darling, you came back to me, did you come too? We're going to be so rich, she said swallowing. I can't have children, said Rita, so don't look to me for children. But Jennie, how did you learn to do that? No pregnancy fears now, you can't get pregnant through your mouth, you can just let me nourish you. The naked bodies were entwined then with an ugly lust, I was dismissed from the coupling, and as a bystander I watched Betty and her Jeremy-swine, clutch and gasp. Jen, just a moment ago your touch was tender, don't scratch me and bite me, my arm is still sore, I'm not a stranger, who've you been with, for God's sake? Lovers? No, she said. Before I could thrill to this, Jerry's prick went into Betty, whose hips moved furiously. I loved the way she moved, the slut. Jennie, then, in his, no—my—arms. I came, Jack, she said to me as I grew hard inside her. Did I make you come? I asked. Look, she said, pointing. We were surrounded by coins, by stacks of bills. She took one and gently, using it as a band-aid, placed it over the sore spot on my aching arm. How did you know to do that? I asked gratefully, awed. It's simple, she said, moving her body away from me. Tenderly, she said: it has adhesive. But then Jennie slid out of reach and all I could see was Betty's nakedness. Put something on, dear, I said gently, reaching for my trousers, didn't she know that I shouldn't be allowed to view her breasts, even if I was family, that she should cover her body and seal its openings in memory of him? Davey. Betty, you're naked, dear, cover it, don't show it to me. I hurt, we shouldn't, you shouldn't. I shouldn't have, I'm so ashamed. This is indecent.

I awoke in shame to feel the wet, sticky sheets adhering to my body. Adhesive. Wet dream. Polluted dream? What to do now with the fucking sheets? What time was it? I tried to move, my limbs were heavy from whatever strength of the drug Carl had shot into me. Jesus, what had I said or done to warrant this: Alone, half-dressed, in my seven-year-old niece's room, the sheets and my body and my undershorts covered with—come. That was nice. Hadn't happened in about twelve-and-a-half years. My mind was functioning, I noted, maybe the result of Carl's remorseless injection. But what had I done? Was it the fault of the drug that in my sleep I had been overpowered in some orgiastic fashion by the bodies of my living and estranged family, that I had permitted myself to dream the sexual intrusion of Betty's lover? Was he her lover? Jennie, a dissembler in life, in my dream had told me truthfully she'd come. Forget her. How dare I dream that I forced my way into her mouth? What had I done, how had I come to this place—in Mandy's bedroom, in the bitterly shameful aftermath of my wet dream and something that I couldn't remember, that had preceded it, that had led to Carl's shot. Needle.

Rita stood in the doorway. I saw that she was in robe and nightgown.

"I heard you moaning," she said expressionlessly. "Are you all right?"

"Yes," I said. "What time is it?"

"Midnight. Are you hungry?"

"No, not particularly. Listen, I don't remember what happened."

"You became hysterical," she notified me. "And you began to threaten."

"Threaten what?" I asked, frightened.

"To kill yourself."

"Oh," I said, relieved. "That's good."

"What's good about it?" she asked, approaching the bed, her face an engraving of misery.

"I wouldn't want to harm anyone else." I let my mind go. I knew I'd need my body sometime. Maybe. But to keep it, I'd have to forfeit my mind.

"Isn't there anyone in New York who can take care of you?" Rita asked.

Under the sheets, my hand brushed the wet, stained fabric of my crotch. Rita would see the stains. Oh, my God, how did one deal with this? Had Rita ever been ashamed of menstruating? What did she do with the evidence of her blood?

"What's Jerry's last name?" I asked. "Is it Blood?"

"Are you serious? It's Rich." Rich. Looking out for herself.

"I really forgot, honest, Rita. No, there's no one in New York, and Carl's shot has done the trick. I'm here to help. Maybe I'm wrong about Jerry. Jesus, I didn't mean to make a scene."

"Are you really feeling better? You sound better."

"I am," I said emphatically. What should I do, just let the sheets dry? Leave mysterious stains on the mattress of a child's bed? "Go back to bed, Rita. I'm okay. Honest."

"We'd better have you check in with Dr. Frame in the morning," she said.

"Yes," I said. "And I have a doctor in New York. I can call him too." I was not a pauper, I had resources. The only thing I didn't have was my brother. Rita saw the tears on my cheeks.

"It doesn't do any good to cry," she said.

Maybe it does you no good, I thought, but I can't help it. I loved him more, I loved him most.

Rita said, "You were crying out in your sleep."

A reproach? An expression of concern? Or merely an explanation. So: I'd cried in my sleep. Cried out. I'd done something else in my sleep too. If she'd go, I could unobtrusively remove the traces. Some memories of my adolescent ingenuity were flooding back. "Get some sleep, Sis. I'm okay. Honest. I love you, Rita. I'm here to help." I tried to say it and I succeeded.

"I think you mean well," she answered me, "but I don't think you're making it."

"I'll be okay. See? I'm okay now." I found myself shivering and praying.

"Get some sleep," she said.

IN THE MORNING, I found that my suitcase had been dragged, probably by my overwrought sister, into Mandy's room. I unlocked it, changed underwear, and dressed. The logistics

of taking a shower here, with my elderly mother and a brat-
tish child running around loose upstairs, were too boring to
warrant any serious attempt on my part to cope. I inspected
Mandy's mattress. Still a little damp. God, if you are still
watching over us, could you please prevent Mandy from yap-
ping something to the effect that her grown uncle might have
wet the bed? I descended the stairs.

"Good morning," I said. Carl nodded approvingly. I had
cleared, then, the morning's first hurdle. What next? I hoped
Rita would make French toast or pancakes for breakfast.
Then I should probably go in and give Mother a peck on the
cheek.

She was in the dining room with Dr. Frame. He was
holding her in his arms and patting her shoulder until she
had finished her weeping. It had the look of a ritual: Maybe
it had been going on daily for a week. A week and a day,
beginning today, without Davey. Frame looked at me over
the shoulder of my mother. Gently, he released her. "Jack,"
he said, coming to me, "come upstairs, I want to talk to you."

"Is this," I asked tremulously, "a social or professional
call?"

"A little of both."

"Please don't humor me," I whispered.

Now we were at the top of the stairs. So early in the
day—a week and a day without him—and how many times
had I climbed them?

"For God's sakes, don't look so scared," said Dr. Frame.

"But I am," I said as we sat down. "They think I'm crazy
or that it's not important, but I know that Betty has a lover.
That man at the funeral, Jerry, he's her lover." I looked at
him beseechingly.

"Look," said Frame, "it may or may not be true. If it is
true, she must live her own life, and at some point the family
must bow out."

"But she's all that's left of Davey," I said.

"No," he said. "She and Libba. I don't think you'll lose
them."

Lose. The word terrified me, and I began to tremble.

"Don't you think it would be okay for me to go over there?" I asked.

"Wait till your medication has taken effect, an hour or so, and then go. I'd give you a lift, but I haven't got the time to wait."

SHOWERED, SHAVEN, and fortified by the medication, I taxied over to Betty's. I would either have to rent or buy a car, I speculated. As we passed through the familiar streets, I felt a stab of grief. My mother had pressed a trinket into my hand, a present for the baby.

"That will be a dollar thirty-five, sir," the driver said.

"What?"

"We're here," he said.

"Thank you," I said courteously.

The cab drove off, leaving me on the sidewalk in front of Davey's house, and looking at the pathway to the front door, I suddenly felt weak. I felt ninety. I dragged myself to the front door and rang the bell. I didn't have to wait long. Betty answered it.

She hugged me and buried her face in my shoulder. Was she crying? I felt a shudder in her body, and the vision of it—naked and urgent in last night's dream—came fleetingly to mind, but I dismissed it. She drew me into the living room, and together we sat down on their sofa, and we sat back, my hand clasped in hers.

"I'm so glad you're here," she said, gently withdrawing her hand. "I was sorry after you left that you didn't stay for dinner. It's so hard to make decisions. I can't decide what to wear. What to eat. I lose things," she went on. "I couldn't find my checkbook last night, and I got hysterical. Little things and I go to pieces."

"It's the little things that throw us," I said gently.

"Yes," she said. "That's what Jerry said. He found it for me. The checkbook, I mean." Again, that short, nervous laugh.

"What'd you need it for?" I asked.

"Oh, I needed to pay the funeral home," she said. "So many bills. They just mount up. I don't know what I'll do."

I was about to say: You have me, but then I remembered that I mustn't make commitments until I'd become certain that I had myself a steady source of income, as well as a place to stay. "I'll try and stand by," I said instead.

"You've done so much already," she breathed. "This must be hard on you," she said. "First Jennie, and now this."

"One has nothing to do with the other," I said. "Sometimes life deals you cards like that."

"What a swindle," she said bitterly.

And Jerry came into the room. Automatically, I stood up, and we shook hands.

"I hear you've been sick," he said to me. "I hope you're okay now."

What was he talking about? "What'd you hear?"

"Betty mentioned that you were taking pills for something."

To underscore even to myself that I was truly stable, I got up and crossed to a rocker, and sat there and rocked furiously.

"Better watch that chair," Jerry said with what seemed good humor. "It may not be all that sturdy."

"The President rocks," Betty said, smiling.

"If he does, I guess I can," I said, forcing a smile, too agitated to go easier on the chair. The cradle will rock, the cradle will fall.

"Darling," I said, turning to her—she blushed—"do you have any photographs of Davey?"

"Oh, yes," she said, as if relieved. "And his clothes. I'll give you his clothes."

"I don't want his clothes," I said in a panic. "I don't think they'd fit me." Not Davey's clothes. Jesus, Betty would have to go through those closets, and she mustn't be allowed to do it alone. I'd help when I could; I hoped she'd wait about a week. In a week, I'd be strong enough to face that.

322

"We'll give the clothes to Goodwill," said Jerry. "It's tax-deductible."

Jesus Christ, Davey's clothes on a stranger's dirty back? "No," I said.

"She can't live in this house with all those reminders," Jerry said.

"If you all can wait a week," I said, "I can go through the closets with Betty, and we can give the clothes to Davey's friends."

"He didn't have that many friends," said Betty.

"Then we can give them to Red Cromwell—"

"That man who found him?" Betty cried out. "Never."

"He was really hurting, Betty, when I talked to him."

"I can't bear the thought of that stranger leaning over him in that dirty uniform."

"It wasn't dirty," I said helplessly.

"Yes, it was," she insisted. "You'd think he'd have the decency to wash before he came over here."

I was confused. "I didn't know he'd come here at all," I said, close once again to stammering. Had I forgotten?

"Yes, just for a minute, after he left your mother. He just wanted to shake my hand, he said. So I shook it, and then my hand was covered with dust."

"Betty," I said, "he'd come from the sandy lot where he found Davey." She screamed, but Jerry steadied her and she stopped. "Betty," I said, "he's a decent man."

"I suppose," she said, still shaking, still being steadied by Jerry. "I just can't bear the thought of his having Davey's clothes." She shook her head.

No point in arguing, she was entitled to her widow's prerogatives even if they seemed, to me, incomprehensible. What did I know? Was grief rational? At least she was grieving, more than my own sister had the decency to do—all she did was wet-mop, patronize me, and complain—and grief had to be respected and taken on its own terms. Taken on faith. I abandoned the rocker for an armchair, to everyone's relief—if they noticed—and my own.

"Well, then," I said softly, "we could give the clothes to Daniel Morrissey."

"Who is Daniel Morrissey?" Betty asked. "I suppose," she said wildly, "that you'll want to give some of his things to the mortician too."

I thought I would vomit. I went to the window, opened it, and took a few deep breaths. Davey's body. What had they done to it? What did it look like now? A vision of its decomposition was overtaking my brain, and I would die if someone didn't help me and help me quickly.

Help came. Betty was there at my elbow, and she said: "I'm sorry. I didn't mean to upset you."

"It's not you, dear," I managed to say. The nausea receded. I must have looked chalky, for she backed away a little and in a frightened voice asked if I wanted a glass of water. "Please," I said.

"I'll get it," said Jerry, sounding exasperated. Betty and I looked at each other and almost simultaneously smiled. Peace. Jerry came back with the water, no ice, for Christ's sake. I thanked him.

"Let's sit down," he directed. We obeyed. "Look," he said, "I don't see what all the fuss is about. David's clothes can and should be given to charity. It is a tax deduction."

I decided not to remind him he'd already said that. "I know," I said, "things must be so tight. It's good you have your cooking column."

"My cooking column?" she said as if I had made some favorable reference to the practice of infanticide. "Do you have any idea of how little that pays?"

"No," I said earnestly, swallowing the tepid water. "Tell me." She told me. Half of what I got from *Earful*. "That's not much," I said.

I heard her hard self-pitying sigh. Well, I knew about self-pity and was one of the few who could normally be counted on to view it with favor, but something in me now felt shut out. If you pitied yourself, did that mean others couldn't enter your circle and give you their own pity? I became aware that Betty and Jerry were waiting for me to say something. There was something about the peculiarly glassy and expectant focus of their eyes.

"He was so proud of you," I said. Silence. Apparently I'd made a gaffe. "You're right. The clothes should go to charity," I said softly. "I think he'd want that."

"I want it," said Betty. "I think it's best, all things considered." She dabbed at tears.

As Betty's tears subsided, I asked Jerry quietly, "What do you do?" As Betty's friend, he should be reassured about Davey's family and the solidity of their support.

"I'm a contractor," he said.

"Oh," I said, trying to be interested, "buildings and that."

"Yes," he said.

"Betty, darling, could I see the baby?" I paused, unable to plead my case further, to explain. Surely her instincts would guide her, as would her thoughts of Davey. She looked to Jerry; he nodded. What was that all about? Then I remembered that beneath her surface composure and competence had always been a frightened girl. "Just a kid," Davey had said—hadn't he?—when I told him that Jennie and I would divorce. "A scared kid," Davey'd said. Betty had gotten frightened for herself. No wonder she needed a man around, someone she'd known a long time, to help her steer. Till she could heal. Did one ever heal? Never, I told myself, and then became aware that Betty had left the room, and I was alone with Jerry.

"You're a writer," he said, eying me skeptically.

"Yes. And an editor. I've done both," I said.

"Who do you write for?" he asked.

"I'm free-lance now," I said.

His brows knit, and he appeared to be about to frame a question when Betty entered the room, with Libba in her arms, clad in a golden yellow.

"Here she is," Betty said, a little breathlessly. "She's wearing her newest dress."

Libba clambered out of her mother's embrace and positioned herself a little uncertainly on the floor. She was bare-foot and looked sleepy, but seemed pleased with her lacy, frilly dress; she tugged at its hems and fingered its frills. "There's your Uncle Jack," her mother whispered softly. She toddled toward me; what trust. And then I bent and picked her up. For moments, she clung to me, that live bundle, grown but still so delicate, who had been her father's greatest joy. "Lib, Lib," I crooned. It occurred to me that perhaps her head should be supported, didn't one have to do that with infants?—and I frantically searched for, what was it called, the fontanel?—Jennie would know—on Libba's head.

"What is it?" Betty asked.

I explained what I was looking for. Betty looked astonished. Jerry said: "Only infants have that. This child's going on sixteen months." She was? How did he know? The guy was a contractor, not a pediatrician. I abandoned my feverish exploration of Libba's head and hugged her hard, then held her at arm's length. I smiled, she was irresistible, and she smiled back. Then she said: "Da-da." A word. For a second my arms grew slack, and I feared I might drop her. "Da-da," she repeated. My grip on the baby tightened, my embrace. She wanted to put her cheek against mine. I heard someone say: "She liked her father's scratchy beard." Betty? Libba rubbed her face against mine, and suddenly I knew I couldn't stand it, I would mishandle this if I didn't do something immediately, and I tossed her playfully high into the air, and caught her as she landed, howling, in my outstretched arms.

The sobs were loud and unbearable to the ear. Inexplicable. I held her and tried to soothe her. Then she was taken from me. Jerry took her and carried her to the sofa, and sat down, and there they were, a tableau, she and he, he who hardly knew her, knowing how to comfort her, as he bounced her on his knee and settled and soothed her on his lap.

"Why?" Betty was saying. "Why did you roughhouse with her now of all times?"

"She seems okay," I said, abashed.

"Why make her cry? She's fifteen months old and she's lost her father," Betty exploded.

"But she thought I was her father," I said, bewildered. What had happened?

"He never, never threw her into the air," Betty shouted. "You could scar a child for life with something like that."

"I meant no harm," I said, miserably. "Babies cry."

"She thought you were her Daddy," Betty said, accusingly. "And you threw her into the air. You're not even in any shape to catch her." Betty began to cry. "She might have fallen to the floor."

"Betty, she's okay. I knew I could catch her."

"You frightened her," sobbed the mother. Libba began to sob too. "Mama," she cried. I felt a pang, stronger than any I had ever felt. What had happened?

Jerry took Libba away, spirited her upstairs ("Upstairs," Betty nearly shrieked as I begged her to tell me where Jerry was going with the child), and I was left alone with my overwrought sister-in-law, her mother, who in last night's dream had perhaps revealed to me her true self. Maybe the dream was precognitive, and I was a sensitive. I looked at her. Why did she shudder now, as she had shuddered an hour earlier in my arms when I'd arrived in this place, the house of my brother. Were lust and grief flip sides of the same coin? I looked at this woman now and felt sexually dead. I had failed. I did not know why or even whether my failure was serious enough to warrant this passionate and bitter rebuke which shamed me so deeply. I had failed with the child; it could have been a trivial incident, but then my strength had failed me briefly, something had drained from me when she had uttered the stutter of Davey's name: Da-da. I could not rise to this need. Funeral, funeral, funeral, my disobedient mind heckled, as I stood silent and trembling before Betty. She had, through the medium of Jerry, reclaimed her child. I was dead, sexually. And the seconds passed. Small time, small town time. Just seconds.

"Betty," I began, having no idea what I would say next. "Betty, please. Say something."

"If it weren't for you," she said, "I wouldn't be a widow now."

"Why did you say that?" I whispered.

"If I hadn't married Davey, I wouldn't be a widow. You made us marry."

"You chose each other," I said.

"I was pregnant," she cried.

"But he loved you."

"Jack, how blind can you be? Didn't you know your brother? I'm not going to pretend this isn't a tragedy, but that marriage was a charade."

"Did Davey think that?" I asked her, not believing I was standing in my brother's house hearing this.

"I don't know what Davey thought," she said to me. Shock. Knowledge. Was there any difference? Davey had died of a wife who didn't want him. Would Jennie die?

"We tried, but we were just going through the motions." It seemed to relieve her to say it. But why to me?

I can't listen to this, I thought. Yet I said: "What are you going to do?"

"Leave," she said, "as soon as I can." She was weeping. Damn her and her tears. Those tears spilled out of a fundamental self-misunderstanding. Or did she really understand herself, and I was insane?

"I don't see how you can do that," I said.

There was a silence. We seemed to be at eye level with each other, and I asked her, "Are you going to leave with Jerry?"

"Yes," she said.

"I don't mean to pry," I mumbled.

"Yes you do," she said.

"Do you love Jerry?" I asked.

"He loves me."

"Do you love him?"

"It's not your business, Jack."

"I don't mean to pry."

"You said that."

"Will you marry Jerry?"

"Yes."

"Then you love him."

"Yes." With an overpowering bitterness, she said, "I want to be happy. He loves me."

But Davey had, hadn't he?

I forced the next question: "Was he the man before Davey?"

"Yes."

In terror, I asked: "Is Libba Davey's child?"

Her voice was thick. What could she possibly be feeling? She said harshly, "Libba was Davey's child." She sounded sick. Should I care? What did I have left?

Will Jerry adopt Libba?"

"I hope so."

"When will you go?" I asked.

"I don't know." Her voice was trembling. I realized that my eyes were closed. When had I shut them? Who had shut Davey's eyes?

I opened them. Mine. Jerry was in the room.

"So," I said, "you've returned."

"Yes."

"Contractor."

"What?"

"You're a contractor. That means you contract. You shrink. And you also stink. Get it?"

Jerry moved protectively toward a woman named Betty. He positioned himself, in fact, in front of her. Good. Let them try it that way, the pair of them, animals.

"I will want," I said, "occasionally, more than occasionally in fact, to see Libba."

"I don't see," Betty said, "how that's possible. With things as they are."

"Speak up," I told her. "I can't hear you way back there in back of him."

"You're sick, Jack," Betty said. "Jerry, please take him out of here."

"Don't touch me," I said warningly. And then I looked at him. He looked—frightened? Alarmed? Puzzled? How in the hell did a man look who had only one or two expressions and talked about charity, tax deductions, and fontanels in the same scum-covered, slimy voice? "Don't be scared," I told him patronizingly. "I wouldn't hurt you or anybody. You Jerry-built jackass. Contractor." I dug my fist into my pocket and touched the gift my mother had asked me this morning to give to Libba. I had forgotten about it. How could I forget? I removed it from my pocket. Jerry and Betty stood rooted to the floor. How nice for them, for all people who had natural roots. A string of small, shining beads. "For Libba," I said, and began to cry. Betty came forward and took them. "They're from my mother," I said.

"Thank you, Jack," she said. "Thank her for me."

I looked around vacantly. I understood everything. Except Davey's secret, which was beyond the reach of my curiosity now.

I saw an ashtray on the side table. Handsome, transparent but thick glass, maybe crystal. Must have been a wedding present. Had I given them one? Had I ever given Libba a present? These beads were from my mother. Give not, get not. Get not, give less. Blindly, I reached for the ashtray, fingered it for a moment, then moved back from the carpet and hurled it to the floor with all the might that had once gone into my effort to love, my capacity to fuck, my now nearly sapped rage, at Betty's betrayal, and at the betrayal that inhered in the death of my brother and the secret he took with him. His death gave the lie to any notion I might have harbored that the world had the answers. Let him go. He'd left me, let me leave too.

Breakable, it shattered, and there were splinters of glass glistening on the floor. "I'm not sorry," I said quietly. "I had to do that. Do you understand?" Jennie would understand. Or would have. Once upon a time.

"Yes," someone said.

"Good," I said. "It's good that we understand each other."

Someone went to the telephone. A neighbor came and held Betty in a barricading embrace, while someone—Jerry, I guess; who else?—dialed. Upstairs, someone's baby cried. I didn't try to make out any betraying syllables. And Carl arrived with Frame, and the two of them drove me away.

DID I DREAM or imagine it, or did I really in that brief interval speak to Barney? Long distance? "If you play your cards right, maybe you can get to see the kid once in a while." "Once in a while?" I gasped. Did he then amend it and say, soothingly, "Now and then." If he said it, I wasn't soothed. It could have happened, a remnant, a shred of my capacity for total recall. But, as they tell me, I wasn't lucid in that interval and in the interval after that. Lucid. I had always hated the light.

I DON'T REMEMBER the drive home. I mean to Rita's. But I do remember that when I entered my sister's house, Carl at my right and Frame at my left, I immediately crossed the room to my mother, seated expectantly on the maroon sofa. Had she been waiting for me? I was alive with pain, and I knelt on the floor and tried to rest my head on her knees. For balm. The balm was bony. The lady didn't budge. Nor did she stroke my hair. She did not try to hold me. Her angularity refused me. Goddamn her, I had come out of this woman's body. Fuck her. Damn her to hell for shrinking from my need, the rotten little shy flower. You'd think she was a virgin. "You're frightening her," Rita said to me.

"She's a rotten coward," I said cheerfully, crawling away. Once safely out of the vicinity of Ma, I said, "Never could take care of her children. Look how she let one of them die."

Since her knees had given the message to take my head and lay it elsewhere—the guillotine, her eyes seemed to say, would do nicely—I got up. And stood there.

I said distinctly, "Out of the cradle, endlessly rocking. Walt Whitman, Mother." I felt dizzy, but suddenly dead to pain.

"Please take him away," begged Alma Church.

"Out of the cradle, endlessly sucking," I snarled in reply. I had amended the poem nicely.

"I can't turn this house into a hospital," Rita said.

"Try not to break down," said her husband, sounding annoyed.

"We never should have let him go to Betty's," Rita moaned.

"How is Betty?" I inquired conversationally.

"I meant well," said Frame.

"Goddamn it, everyone means well," Rita said, and left the room.

What was going on? I would die of my bewilderment. Why couldn't my body rescue me? To throw up now would be a pleasure. Better still to faint. I didn't feel the least bit faint. I had never felt more alert, more physically well. I just stood rooted to this floor.

I thought I'd try talking. If I could talk, I could prevent them from putting me in an iron lung. Which they could do, in their ignorance.

"You," I said, turning to Carl, "are a truly authoritarian personality."

Mandy and Rita entered the room. "Mama says you're off your rocker," announced my niece. There followed the sound of a slap. I was startled. I looked at Rita. She had slapped her own daughter.

"Go to your room," said Rita.

"But Uncle Jack's moved into my room," said Mandy.

"No, he hasn't. Get out of here!"

Mandy fled upstairs.

"Why are you so rough on her, Rita?" I asked gently.

She looked at me in amazement. "I'm only trying to spare your feelings."

"I have no feelings," I said. "Please tell Mandy that." Poor Jennie.

"Mother," Carl said, turning to my mother, "go upstairs and rest. We'll inform you of our decision."

"I want to stay here," she said feebly. "He's my son."

"It's gracious of you to acknowledge me," I said, turning to her, and then to no one in particular: "She rebuffed me when I tried to put my head on her lap." I was trembling.

Carl took hold of me and led me into the sun porch.

"Swallow this," said Frame.

"No," I said. "It's not abnormal to want to rest your head on your own mother's lap, is it?"

"No," said Frame softly, "it's not abnormal."

"It's best," said Carl, apparently to Frame, "that he know where reality begins and ends." To me he said, "A grown son does not normally put his head on his mother's lap. The answer to your question is yes, it's abnormal."

Had I ever put my head on Jennie's lap? Rested there? Between her knees?

"I won't swallow anything," I said.

Rita stood in the doorway. "We can move him to Mother's," she said. "He can go in the upstairs bedroom. One or the other of us will stay with him, or we'll hire someone till they have a bed, and we'll worry about the money later."

Money. Something was on my mind having to do with money. What was it?

"No," I said. "Mother doesn't want me. Not a hospital."

"Don't be scared," Dr. Frame said. "It won't be for long."

I heard Carl: "Don't lie to him. We don't know how long."

"Close your eyes, Rita," I said, "or you might see something you shouldn't see."

"I've seen everything," she said. "Everything."

"Don't, dearest," Carl said—dearest, for Christ's sake, didn't he know he sounded ridiculous? "You have thought things out very well."

"She's efficient," I said, hoping to gain the approval of this strange assemblage of relatives gathered in the sun porch, home in Indiana.

"So maybe don't knock him out till we get him to Mother's," Rita was saying.

Frame was bending over me: "I don't know, Rita. I'm out of my depth."

And so they put me, as I piece it together now, into a deep sleep.

IN THE DREAM, I said to Jennie, "Is Libba Davey's daughter?"

"I know," she said, smiling, "what it reminds you of. I'm reminded too."

"Am I my brother's keeper?" I murmured in the dream, still numb to pain.

"Shhh," someone said to me. "Sleep."

"I am asleep," I said, "so you are redundant."

"Words are redundant," said someone. "Not people."

"I'm a word," I said, giving in to what someone I still trusted, Frame, seemed to think was best for me, sleep. Would I ever come out of it? And what would I be if I did? A word: Sleep.

THREE DAYS LATER, my American Express card expired.

BUT FIRST, there was the lovely stay at Mom's. Mom, of course, was not there. They put me to bed in an upstairs bedroom, not the one I had occupied as a child. Was it Rita's old room? It certainly was old. The pillow on which my head rested was too soft, its feathers pliant and decayed, even though clean. Everything in my mother's house was clean. I must thank Rita for her wet mop and her wet blanket, too. But I couldn't rise to any occasion. I lay there, numb, the overused pillow yielding to my dead weight. I was a nice heap of bones, without my brother. I must remember to thank him, too. I lay in this upstairs bedroom of my mother's house and listened to the sound of crickets, the hum of someone's lawn mower, and I felt I might as well be in some flea-ridden flophouse on Skid Row. I was a city boy, anyway, and if I was going to go out, why did it have to be in the sticks? Hicks. I closed my eyes and saw a broken windowpane, a shade flapping weakly against it (gallant try, shut out the light), asking me to come here . . . come here . . .

I thought I heard someone mumble, "Uncle Jack . . ." I opened my eyes, and there was Carl, shooing Mandy out of the room.

"What's the matter?" I asked thickly. "Am I for adults only?"

"Rita's about to drive home, and Mandy must go with her," said Carl, sounding at the end of his wits.

"Well," I said, "if she must, she must."

I raised my head a little and saw Rita, Mandy's mother, who had sneaked up the hallway and was now framed in the door. I looked at her framed in the door—all rectangles were coffins—and I turned away in horror. Tried to bury my face in the pillow, but something was the matter with my neck, my neck muscles were paralyzed, and the pillow had changed too. It was rough and fought me, clearly now following someone else's orders. "Rita," I called out. She was my sister, after all, and maybe she'd help me. I needed an explanation.

"You can do no good now," Carl was saying. "Go home."

"You don't mind staying with him?" she whimpered. God, what an awful marriage. She had to ask permission for every little thing. Except she had slapped Mandy on her own initiative. What a creature. One day, if I lived, I'd do a feature story on her. If there were no market for a story on Rita Church Koenig, I'd create one. That's what I'd do. If I lived.

"Rita," I said again, "maybe we could begin the interview now."

"What?" She was standing over me. "What is it?"

"What is it who? You left something out."

"What are you talking about?"

What was *I* talking about? Didn't she know she wasn't making sense? I'd have to help her. "You left out my name."

She looked bewildered. "Just say my name," I told her, "and everything will be okay."

"Jack," she said, and fled sobbing to the door. Since I couldn't bear to see her framed in the doorway, I closed my eyes. No great loss. Hardly a vision of loveliness, old Reet.

"Now," said Dr. Carl Koenig to his frau, rhymes with cow, was I being fair? I did at all costs want to be fair, "Will you go home? You upset him."

"No, she doesn't," I said, sensing something had gone awry. Carl hadn't, in the past, exactly been my best friend and staunchest defender, and if he was going to play some kooky game, playing me off against my sister, I would not be a party to it. "Rita's okay. Stick around, Sis."

"You're right," she said in a resigned voice to her husband. "I'm going home."

Jesus, this was a mess. Well, I was sick and sleepy, let the healthy and wide-awake ones straighten it out. Gobble-dygook was all I got out of their yatter. When I opened my eyes again, Rita was gone. I could open my right eye before my left, that was interesting, maybe I'd join the circus if I lived and make some money. My brother-in-law was dancing attendance. The waltzing bear.

"Carl," I said, "I've been meaning to ask you a personal question."

"Yes?" he said, as if I were a patient.

"Why did you change your name from Charles to Carl? Why the hell did you do a crazy thing like that? Most krauts would want to keep their names Anglicized." I lay back to see how he'd handle it.

"I was named," he said formally, "for an American uncle, Charles. He, however, died very young"—here, we had to pause for the speaker's gigantic sigh—"and after that, I thought it would be best if I didn't keep his name."

"Huh?" I wasn't hanging on the explanation's outcome, only waiting to see if it would make any sense.

"It pained my mother, who was my uncle's sister, to be reminded so poignantly of her brother. So, I was an adolescent then, or maybe it was after I graduated from medical school"—he meandered on dreamily—"I took the name Carl. Why should my mother suffer," he inquired rhetorically, shrugging, "over such a simple thing?"

"I'm sure I don't know," I said, "except that from now on, I think, out of respect for your uncle's memory, I'm going to call you Uncle Carl."

I looked at Carl. He looked haggard. "It's time for you to sleep again," he said. What was he going to do? To sleep—they put dogs "to sleep."

"No," I said as he came closer, "I'll do it myself."

"Do not be foolish," he said.

"I'm not foolish," I said, "I'm frightened."

"Jack," he said hollowly, "don't you know that after all this time you can trust me?"

"Trust you?" I said incredulously. "How can I trust you? You're going to put me to sleep, and you have that needle in your hand."

"It won't hurt."

"Where's Dr. Frame?" I asked. The needle had penetrated my skin, the contents of the hypodermic, whatever they were, would enter my system.

"Try to relax," he said, "and keep your arm still."

"Is Dr. Frame dead?" I asked, knowing that the answer would be yes.

"No," he said.

"You're lying to me."

"No," Carl said, withdrawing the needle.

"Where is he? I want him."

"He's at his office," said Carl heavily. "He has other concerns besides you," he said.

IN THE FINAL DREAM, I was confronted with a vast topographical map of an unknown country. Explore it, they said, and I passed my hands along its various ridges, along its inclines and orifices, and then, dutifully, up and down over its mountainous bumps. I don't know what it is, I muttered to my inquisitors. My hands trembled, and the beads of sweat danced out along my forehead. I don't know where I am, I told them, but I swear to God this looks like a—gland. It's not a gland, they said. Try some other organ, they told me. Oh, sweet Jesus, why didn't I listen to my mother—I would have if she'd had anything to say—why didn't I study for this course, why did I forget I was enrolled in this course? For a moment, I was with Davey at State, but then he went in to take his exam. And the door closed behind him. He took the exam, I tried to tell them, so why did you flunk him? He left of his own accord, said some kraut. What about you? Identify this. Africa, I tried, that being a suitably dark and swollen continent. No, came the voice, in the same Teutonic accents of this instructor. England, Norway, Asia, I went on in a rush, nostrils. You're getting close, said the voice with a tincture of contempt. My hands closed over it, and I prayed for revelation. That's the human brain, they told me then. And I woke, knowing this was a topographical map of the human brain. "That's the human brain?" I had asked them. "It looks so strange," "That's what it is," they told me. When I went to peer closer, they said, "Now you know." Curiosity killed the cat.

"Feeling better?" Carl, the author of this preposterous question, was stationed at the foot of the bed.

"I feel like a baked worm," I croaked. "What did you put into your syringe?"

"A drug to make you sleep." Alma Church had always been particularly anxious that her children get a good night's sleep; sixteen hours would do nicely for small boys between the ages of three and fifteen and a half. As a concession to my adulthood, Carl told me what the drug was. A tripartite chemical compound which was not only sedative, he said in the tones of someone trying to believe, but which had in some instances restorative powers as well.

"You are a crafty devil, in cahoots with my mother," I told him to prove I wasn't stupid. "There are other things to do in this world besides sleep. What is this, the Swiss sleep cure?"

"I told you," said Carl, "the drug also, if it is effective, restores mental faculties."

"Am I brain-damaged?" I asked in a panic.

"No," he said sadly. "But you are not mentally well."

"Carl," I said, struggling to get a grip on my mind, which I knew I would have to forfeit if I didn't want to die, "will I recover?"

"Sometimes," he said pensively, "you seem almost recovered. But we medicate you so much."

"Why?" I asked.

"Because when you are not medicated, you are irrational. You broke a valuable piece of crystal at Betty's. You say inappropriate things in front of your mother and my daughter. Who knows what you will do next?"

"Are you afraid I'll be violent?"

"Perhaps," he said. His eyes were melancholy. Well, to hell with his melancholy.

"Do you know," I asked cheerfully, "that Betty is sex-crazy? If that's not inappropriate, with her husband scarcely in his grave, I'd like to know what is. Give me some water."

"You are dehydrated from the medication," he said, not unkindly, pouring me some ice water from a pitcher, which had been thoughtfully set up on the bed table. Goddamn, if they hadn't turned Mother's place into a hospital. Davey boy, look what they've done.

I handed the glass back to Carl. "You want some more?" he asked.

"No," I said, "but that was good. Thanks. Especially the ice."

Now there was something he ought to know about Rita. Should I tell him? Might as well, this giddiness might never happen to me again. "Carl," I said—my tone elicited a look of true alarm, it was nice to have impact, especially when helpless in a strange bed—"Rita used to be what my mother called boy-crazy. Did you know that?"

"I don't know what you mean." He made a great straight man.

"I mean she dated a lot. But I don't think she did any serious fooling around. I'm sure she was a virgin when she married, you would know better than I, and I just know, knowing Rita, that she's faithful."

Carl looked stupefied. Maybe I'd hurt his feelings. Well, since there was no telling what one might do from one minute to the next, one must ration one's apologies. I lay back, satisfied. Let someone else apologize. Some other time.

"I forgive you," said Carl trickily. How come he'd seen through me? "I do not think you mean to hurt me."

"Am I physically well?" I asked.

"Arnold says yes," said Carl. So Frame was alive. Good. And I was well.

Rita appeared in the room again. "How is he?" she asked sepulchrally.

"The same," Carl said, shrugging. What the hell was that shrug supposed to indicate, medically speaking?

"You sure sound gloomy," I observed.

"How are we supposed to feel?" said Rita. "I can't believe it's Davey's dying that's hit you so hard." Right, I thought, I am taking it well, so what could it be?

"It's coming home, isn't it?" said Rita, looming up toward my bed. God she was big for a woman, poor soul, now what was she saying? From the sound of it, she had victory in her jaws. Chomp, chomp. "After all this time, stalling and waiting and putting it off, waiting until you're in trouble, so that you can come home again like this."

"What's this epiphany now? I don't get what you're saying, Sis."

"What I'm saying is that for years you've been dying to collapse, and collapse here on our doorstep," she said flatly.

"Nope, I'm a city boy. I didn't want to collapse here. I like the city," I said, getting thirsty again. "Maybe it's Davey's death," I said, trip-skipping over the words, they were only words, sticks and stones were the things that could kill you, "but I don't think it's only that. I think it's Betty."

"You hardly know Betty," Rita exploded.

"It's Libba, then," I said as a last resort.

"Libba," exclaimed Rita. "She's a baby. You hardly know her."

"But she's Davey's," I said, and tears began streaming down my cheeks. "And now I'll never see her again."

"You don't know that," said Carl.

Rita said, "I don't want to talk about Davey any more."

"Not ever?" I said.

"Oh, be quiet," said Rita. She seemed to be crying.

I was getting sad. These people were getting to me. I felt I owed them an explanation. What kind? After I gave it, I'd reward myself with water. Carl would pour it for me. He had that much compassion. "Rita," I said, entranced, seeing the light, "I have no one."

"No one? You've mobilized the whole family, paralyzed us. We do nothing but hover around you, you big baby!"

"You're pretty big yourself," I told her. "And besides, I can't both paralyze and mobilize."

"Don't try to have a conversation with him," Carl warned her irrelevantly.

"Oh, let her," I said airily. "She doesn't often get the chance to talk with a sophisticated person like me, and she is bright, or used to be. What'd you come here for, anyway?" I asked. "You could have married into some other family."

"I love him," said Rita. She meant Carl, of course. Sickening. But I wouldn't let on.

"Bless you both," I said magnanimously.

I opened my eyes. Dr. Koenig was embracing his wife. A charming tableau. "Ugh," I said, rather loudly, averting my eyes. But how long could they stay averted? My neck was getting stiff. "Wouldn't you kids," I asked them, "like to go somewhere and be alone?"

"How is he?" someone asked.

"Dr. Frame?" I said excitedly. "Please come here, I want to talk to you."

Frame approached the bed, but I couldn't look him in the eye, his eyes would be knowing and full of pain.

"He's impossible," said Rita.

"He can't help it," said Carl stolidly.

"I believe he can," said Frame. "Jack, boy, give it a try."

"I don't know. I think I'd rather go to that hospital, after I wind up some business matters here."

"The hospital's expensive," said Frame in a low voice. "And it might foul up your future to have that kind of thing on your record."

"I don't care," I said grandly. "I'll take responsibility for it."

Why the hell was Frame acting like such a scaredy-cat? Not like him. My "record." The army would never get me again, and I had a way with words, which meant—or used to mean—earning power, and maybe I'd stay in the hospital for the rest of my life, anyway. I didn't want to be sad. I'd had enough pain. Even the word hurt. I blinked back tears.

"What business affairs?" asked Frame gently.

"Money," I said. "Something having to do with money. I'll think of it in a minute. It'll help pay for the hospital," I said brightly. Even in my diminished condition, I could try to be a useful member of a shrunken society. "Rita," I asked, suddenly worried, "why are you here? Did you leave Mandy alone with Mother?"

"With a baby-sitter," she said.

"What do you have to pay baby-sitters these days? Seventy-five cents an hour?"

"Jack," said Rita, thrusting some paper into my hand, "this came to our place for you."

"What is it?" I asked. How good that I felt nothing.

"It's from a lawyer in New York," said Rita. "Jennie has apparently engaged a lawyer. A Mr. Grandison."

"Oh, yes," I said. "We're getting divorced."

"No," said Rita, "she's divorcing you."

Couldn't we even get divorced together? Why did everything have to be he or she? How many days had passed anyway? The itsy-bitsy former Miss Owen moved with lightning speed. Never should have married someone that small, gave one illusions of grandeur. And I used to be afraid I'd crush her. Look how unhesitatingly she was trying to crush me. "We're divorcing each other," I reiterated to Rita; that'd put her in her place. "Let me see that thing." She handed it back to me. I tried to look at it, but my vision blurred. Maybe the medication. My heart began to pound. I heard my own sobs. Carl took the letter away.

"Give it back to me, you Nazi," I said, actually grateful that he'd taken it away.

"Why do you call me a Nazi?" asked Carl. "You've called me that several times in your sleep, you know."

"Germans are Nazis," I said with a thickened tongue.

"Jack," cried Rita, "how brutally unfair."

"Maybe it is projection," said Carl soothingly; odd how his mumbo-jumbo could soothe, probably because it didn't mean anything, "projection" was one of those words you used to fill the emptiness left when meaning was gone.

"We'll get you a lawyer," said Rita.

"Thanks, Sis," I said, closing my eyes. It would cost money. Everything would. Money.

"Oh, Jack, we're not going to abandon you," said Rita. Was she still crying? "Don't cry, Jack."

"You'll get me a lawyer?" I asked. Law.

Desertion. Mental cruelty. *I think continually of those who were truly great.* I felt a great wave coming from the center of me, not like sex, which traveled in a different direction, this one was headed up, toward my upper body, my . . . I couldn't find the word. But I heard these unearthly sobs. "Easy, easy," Frame was saying. Someone placed a warm cloth across my forehead. So the sobs were my own. I wanted Rita to say again, "Don't cry, Jack," so I could promise her I wouldn't. Vows.

After a long interval, I was quiet. And quietly, someone asked: "How do you feel, Jack?"

"Heartbroken," I said.

AND THEN I ASKED THEM to put me to sleep. And they did. I trusted them. I knew they wouldn't let me die. Even if I wanted to. Maybe I did want to. "Lie still," someone said. "I thought I was doing that," I whispered. If you died, I mean if you made yourself die, first you had to get beyond the reach of all pleasure or pain. To empty out all the things that tell you you're alive. "Am I going to die?" I asked.

"No," said Frame regretfully. He wasn't regretting the fact that I would live but the fact that I was entertaining other possibilities.

Betray, I thought, thinking of Jennie, of Libba whom Davey had let slip from my grasp, of some self-betrayal I didn't yet understand. Suicide?

"But I won't," I said aloud to Frame. I figured I owed him that.

"We won't let you," he said, holding on to me grimly, as the saying goes, for dear life.

IN THE MORNING, I was able to bathe, after a fashion, and under Carl's watchful eye, shave.

"Swallow this," he said.

I swallowed the tablet and waited for something to happen.

"There's good news," said Carl, clearing his throat. "There is a bed free at the hospital. We will drive or fly there tomorrow."

"How long have I been here?"

"Two days," he answered.

"Good," I said. "I want to go to the hospital. I don't want to cause anyone any more trouble."

"There's more good news," he said.

"What?"

"Mr. Roper, your lawyer, has agreed to come and see you here."

"Good," I said enthusiastically.

"Don't get too excited," he said, eying me.

Carl, it doesn't hurt a bit.

So I RECEIVED Mr. Roper. He seemed a nice sort.

"You do want the divorce," Roper said.

I said, "It was my idea in the first place."

"Did you leave her?" Roper asked.

"Yes. I walked through the door, but there are two sides to the story, just as there are two sides to a door. Entrance and Exit."

"What is your side?" he asked.

Exit was my side.

"She wouldn't cook, and she didn't like sleeping with me."

He looked puzzled.

"Relax, Mr. Roper," I said. "I know we don't have much of a case. Mr. Grandison told me I didn't have a legal leg to stand on."

"What did you tell him?"

"I told him that my lawyer would be in touch with him."

Roper smiled. "That's neutral enough. Did you ever force relations upon her? Sexual relations?"

I closed my eyes. I forced it every goddamned time. "Technically, I guess the answer to that is no. She was never overtly unwilling."

Roper made a note, then looked at me. "You don't seem so sick to me."

"I'm probably heavily medicated. What does she want?"

"Money."

"They all want money," I said impatiently. "What does she want it for?"

"To pay for her therapy," Roper said.

"Jesus," I exploded, "I'm going to the bughouse, and she wants money to pay for her therapy."

"Do you have money to pay for her therapy?"

"I doubt it. She knows how few assets I have. Why is she doing this?"

"I would imagine," said Roper, still busy with his note-pad, "she's following Mr. Grandison's advice."

"Mr. Roper," I said, "would you please tell Mr. Grandison to hang himself?"

I FORGET how the interview went after that. Or how it ended.

I asked Rita: "How did my interview with my lawyer go?"

"Don't you remember?" she asked sarcastically.

"Sarcasm is unbecoming in a woman," I said.

"Too bad," she said. "It runs in the family."

"Jennie didn't like it," I said.

"Then, if you wanted to stay married, you should have adjusted. I adjust."

"Fuck you."

"Frankly," said Rita, "I can't wait till you get to the hospital."

"Frankly, I want to get the hell out of here too. Any loony bin, anywhere, is preferable to the one you're running here without a license," I said, gnashing my teeth.

"Swallow this," said Rita, handing me a pill.

"I don't think it would do for me to immediately swallow it," I said. "Rita," I asked in the pained silence, "what was wrong with what I just said?"

"I think what you would consider wrong with it is that you split an infinitive."

*

We left the next day. We were to fly. Carl would accompany me, and he had with him a piece of paper signed by Frame, and by me. I had agreed to commit myself. Why did all those signatures matter, then? Well, it was nice to have them as souvenirs, to carry with me as we went west. Mother came as I was dressed and packed, ready to go. She got out of the car which Carl would drive to the airport. Mandy was beside her.

She hugged me. "I'm sorry about the divorce," she whispered.

"It's okay," I said. "Take care of yourself, Mom. I mean it, Mom." I knelt down and gave Mandy a hug. My remaining niece. Oh, well, beggars can't be choosers.

"How are you getting home?" I asked suddenly, just before I got into the car. Mandy, my mother, and Rita were standing in front of my mother's house, stranded.

"We're going to call a taxi," said Rita. She trembled. She had not hugged me. I went to her and kissed her cheek. Briefly, she rested her head on my shoulder, then withdrew decisively, and holding her daughter and our mother by the hand, one on each side, she went into the house. The door closed on my family.

I slept through the flight.

I dozed on the taxi ride to the hospital. "Are we in a different time zone?" I asked Carl.

"Yes," he said.

He and I filled out forms. This is necessary, I told myself. I'm good for nothing, so I might as well be it in a place where I was not unique. How nice to know one is not alone in one's worthlessness. "Perhaps you have to pity yourself," said Frame just before I left. "Perhaps it's necessary to your survival."

"It's not fashionable, you know, to say or even think that," I said, and smiled with not too much effort.

"Then," he said, "it will remain our little secret."

Standing at the doorway to the exit, which would lead Carl back on to the hospital grounds to another taxi, I said to him: "I'm going to need a new American Express card." I'd surrendered all my credit cards inside at the desk, and now the orderly was waiting for me, tapping his foot. Impatient? We had all the time in the world. Time. "Carl, my old one expired today."

"We'll get a new one for you," he said.

I watched him drive away. Would he be important only in this strange passage of dead time?

I turned and followed the orderly, whose name was Seth. I asked him if he was related to Rabbi Seth Jacobs of Indianapolis. He said he wasn't Jewish, and went on to tell me the story of Jacob and Esau, which I already knew. I offered, in turn, to fill him in on Cain and Abel, but we'd reached the door to a landing, and someone else took over, a nurse, who showed me to my "semiprivate" room. Some semiprivate. Living with one's invasive though minuscule wife was recollected bliss compared to this assemblage of eight, count 'em, crazies, all of the same sex. But there was no time to count or brood. Count or contemplate. Especially not the latter. I was accommodating at first, and then, having been told I was not different from the others, became difficult. Very. As you've gathered, haven't you? Difficult means different, and since that was the only option they appeared to be offering me, I exercised it. I only know that what I was doing was forced upon me by the remnants, the shreds of my self. I had to get it back from those two, who'd turned their backs on me: Jen and my brother. Between the two of them, somehow, they'd lost me.

I GOT BETTER in the bughouse. You get better in such places, if you recover at all. Because you have only two choices: Stay or leave. His or hers. Befogged by their drugs, you become a synthetic. And I didn't want that. I wanted to be real, to be flesh and blood, to be mortal. Women liked that better. Jen.

Disease is to cure as death is to life. Was Davey's death the price of my life? It didn't matter. I would mourn him always. But if you are going to live at all, you retrieve your brain from the custody of others who mean well or ill—it's your brain, after all. So, one day, divorced from her, I left. It had been a year. But I knew I had to oversee the balance of my recovery myself, and so I uprooted myself from that state west of Indiana, and went, on my own steam, to San Francisco, to heal. To regain my equilibrium, standing, walking on nearly vertical streets that dared you to fall. I regained it. Equilibrium means sanity.

PART 4

FISHERMAN'S WHARF. Unsteadily, I made my way there. I don't know what I had in mind. I stood on the dock. The Pacific was turquoise, and the sun was bright. I shivered a little and went over to sit on a bench in the sun's path. The girl whose privacy on the bench I'd interrupted smiled at me, then looked away. "I'm trying to get warm," I said to her.

"Oh, that's perfectly all right," she said. Gracious. Well bred. A far cry from Babs Rattner. In the hospital, I refused to go to the dances, and when I sat on the lawn, I sat by myself. I wrote my ex-wife once, acknowledging that I was in receipt of our divorce papers and wishing her well. I'd drafted my letter three times, and then when the words seemed right, rewritten it in my longhand three times. I wanted it to look steady and upbeat. She didn't answer. I wondered if she'd found a new friend.

Again, I shivered and looked to the girl for some explanation. It was summer, after all. "It's chilly here in August," she said. "Are you from around here?"

"No," I said. "I'm from New York."

"Our August is like your October," she ventured. Time.

"I see." That didn't make a lot of sense. I frowned.

"What I mean," she said, "is that it's usually best to take along a sweater." She indicated her own. Cashmere. Flesh-colored. Nice. I looked at my own bare arms. Goose bumps. She was right.

"Thank you," I said. "I'll know better next time."

"You're just visiting?" she asked.

"Yes. I took the bus." I named that state from which I'd taken it.

"That's a long bus ride," she said gently.

"It was," I said, and sighed, and closed my eyes against the sun.

"Perhaps you should get some sunglasses too."

"Yes," I said. "I guess if I'm going to stay I'll get all that." I felt shy. Then as the silence lengthened, I began to feel sick with my shyness. Bashful, my mother had once explained, nodding her head in my direction, to the lady at the lending library. I was about ten, and she could have inflicted no worse humiliation. She wrote me regularly, however, when I was in the hospital. "Dear Son," she would begin.

I opened my eyes. The girl was reading a book. I craned my neck to see the title. She looked and smiled at me. "I'm sorry," I muttered, "I don't mean to intrude."

"You're not intruding," she said, and held the book up for me to see. Willa Cather. *My Antonia*.

"My God," I said.

She looked puzzled.

"I'm sorry," I said. Where had my words gone? Was I going to spend the rest of my life in search of the lost, the right, the appropriate word. "I'm sorry," I said. I wished I were a deaf mute. I closed my eyes.

"I'm taking an English-lit course," the girl was saying. "I'm not reading this for pleasure." She sounded apologetic.

Maybe everyone was shy.

I opened my eyes. "It's a good book," I said softly.

"I'm enjoying some of it," she admitted.

I smiled. She said, "I'm waiting for my husband," and, simultaneously, I noticed the small gleaming ring. The ring.

"That's nice," I said. I looked at her, trying to tell her: I understand. I didn't misinterpret your kindness. I don't want any more than you've given.

She blushed and looked back down at her book. I looked directly into the sun.

Then a man loomed into view. I listened to them murmur to each other. Why did I just sit there?

The girl stood up. "This is my husband," she said.

I stood up, and her husband and I shook hands. "I'm Jack Church," I said.

His name was Earl Waltham. Her name was Jane. "Would you like to join us for lunch?" Earl Waltham asked me.

"No thanks," I said. "I've got to get hold of some sunglasses. But thanks for asking me."

"It's been nice talking to you," said Jane Waltham. Her smile and her voice were pleasant. "Watch out for the glare."

"I will," I promised. Vows.

They walked away from me, arm in arm, along the pier. I watched Jane, in beige slacks and sweater, strolling with her husband, Willa Cather tucked against the curve of her hip.

There were vendors along the wharf. I thought I'd browse among them. The sunglasses could wait. Goods of various sorts. Edibles. Soft ice cream, seafood.

A crowd of kids had clustered around one of the stands. I ventured closer. Live turtles, small ones, were being retrieved by the attendant vendor from a tank, and placed in small boxes. Their backs were painted, some red, some green. They wriggled their miniature heads, neither in fear nor in hope. No animal instinct of the one or the other in evidence here. No sign even of resignation. I drew back a little and squinted at them from a distance. From a distance, they looked like toys. Toys. People were buying them as jokes for their childish adult friends, or as remembrances for their children. "It'll make a nice souvenir for Joey," a man my age, more or less, was saying to his wife. How old was Joey? I was, I thought, thirty-one. A long passage.

I elbowed my way closer to the turtles, still eavesdropping. Joey, it developed, was eight. My age, and they already had an eight-year-old.

I selected a turtle on the small side. For Jennie.

"It goes," the man was saying, "to Master Joey Klein."

"Master?" the wife inquired.

"It's correct usage," her husband told her. He gave the vendor an address in Brooklyn. I closed my eyes and imagined I was in a taxi. With Marcella. Going to Brooklyn.

"Where's yours going?" asked the vendor. I opened my eyes, and the wind, the salt-air breezes, were bracing. I gave him Jennie's address. "Two New Yorkers," the vendor said cheerfully.

The couple walked away, and the vendor packaged my live gift. He marked it HANDLE WITH CARE, and I asked if I could add FRAGILE and also PERISHABLE.

"We'll take care of mailing him," the vendor said.

"The turtle is a him?"

"Yes," said the turtle's custodian emphatically, getting a little impatient. There were other customers. I shelled out the five bucks plus tax, thanked him, and walked away in search of sunglasses.

But the day turned cloudy, as it does unpredictably in San Francisco, and I made my way back to my hotel. It was a nice hotel. Rita was paying for it. I would repay her someday.

I liked the lobby of the St. Francis. Plush. Red-carpeted. An interior that glowed with color, yet shut out the light. I took the elevator up to my room, the third floor, not the nicest room but a good, affordable room. Then I remembered that I hadn't stopped at the desk for my messages.

I phoned the desk. There was a message from Amanda Koenig, age eight. I smiled and returned the call. "Hi, honey," I said to her. She had become less of a brat, more of a little lady.

"Are you having a good time, Uncle Jack?" Yes, dear. "What time is it there?"

"I think we're two hours behind you," I said, glancing at my watch. The band was frayed. They had held it for me in the hospital vault for a long time, but the crystal was intact and the thing still ticked. "So," I went on, "it's four o'clock here and six o'clock there."

"That's right," she said breathlessly. "Uncle Jack, we're so glad you're having a good time." Was I?

"Honey," I said, "tell your mother that I said it's okay for you to be ill-mannered once in a while."

"Okay," said Mandy. "I'll tell her. Do you want to talk to her?" she asked.

"Not yet," I said. "It's good to be here." The words were coming in a rush, so what I was saying must be true. "I bought a pet turtle." Instantly I regretted what I'd said.

"For me?" she asked delightedly.

"No," I improvised, "for a friend's child. I wanted to find out first if you'd like one."

"Yes," she said firmly. "Um . . ." She hesitated.

"Their shells," I said gently, "are painted. Some red, some green. Which would you prefer?"

"I'd like to be surprised."

"Okay," I said, for the moment unable to remember the color of the one I'd sent Jennie, then it came to me: red, like the hotel carpeting, red, like flowers, red, like blood. Innocent and cleansing. I'd get Mandy a green one. Kids did like the color red, but green was the color of money.

"Mandy," I said, "there's the most super thing in this hotel. There's a machine that washes money."

She giggled but took it in stride. "How does it do that, Uncle Jack?"

"I don't know, but I'm going to find out and let you know next time we talk. Absolutely," I said. "And Mandy, why don't you just call me Jack? My friends call me Jack. 'Uncle' sounds a little formal, and I'm a slapdash sort of a person."

"Yes, you are," she agreed. Too readily.

"I'll talk to your mother now."

A brief silence. Then that family financier Rita said: "Let's not talk long. Betty moved today. I've just come from there."

"To say good-bye?" I asked softly. Why this dread? The worst had already happened, and I was cured.

"Yes," she said. "We helped her load some of the last-minute things into the car."

Libba was—how old? Two? Two and a half?

"They haven't gotten married?" I asked.

Rita said heavily, "Betty wanted to wait a year."

How is the baby?

"But they will get married," I said quietly.

"Yes. Next month. She wants us at the wedding, but it's too long a trip. I'll send a present."

"I hope she'll be happy," I whispered. How conventional. I felt self-conscious.

"Different things make different people happy," she volunteered.

"Sounds like something you embroider on a sampler, Reet."

"That doesn't make it less true." She sounded old and discouraged.

"This call is getting expensive," I said.

"Yes," she said. "We'd better ring off. Take care of yourself."

*

358

Seconds passed. I raised the shades and let the clouded day-light in. I looked at the ticking watch. Time. What time was it in New York? Seven-thirty, maybe.

I gave the desk my room number, and then I gave them Jennie's number. If she still lived there. Hadn't even considered that possibility. She might have moved, and some stranger would receive the turtle, the package would be marked addressee unknown, and the turtle, in its wrappings, would lie in the dead-letter office till it died.

I moved into slow time. On the fifth ring, she picked it up and said: "Just a minute."

Then she came back to the phone. "Are you there?" I asked. No answer. I went on: "Thou foster child of silence and slow time." Silence. I said, "It's a quote, Jen." My voice shook. If your own words don't work, borrow some. As she did when he died.

"I know," she said distinctly. "Keats."

"Yes."

" 'Grecian Urn,' " she went on tonelessly.

I could go on quoting, or I could say something else. Instead I stood there with the receiver pressed against my ear.

"Where are you?" she asked. The conversation was getting sensible. That was good.

"San Francisco," I managed.

"They've let you out of the hospital," she breathed.

"Yes," I said, rather unhappy that she seemed to regard me as a released prisoner. They've let you out. What was I, an ex-con? Mustn't be defensive. Once in the bughouse, always in the bughouse, one way or another.

"How long have you been out?" she persisted.

"Two weeks," I said.

"I see."

"Am I interrupting your dinner or something?" I asked,

knowing what I meant by something—another man. I wanted her undivided attention.

"No, I'm not eating," she said listlessly. It seemed less a comment than an explanation. Of what?

"Are you glad I called?"

"I don't know why you called."

"To forewarn you, I guess."

"What?" she asked. "Is it something about the apartment? I think the lease is in my name now, and I'm paying the rent."

"I've sent you a turtle," I said. "A gift from Fisherman's Wharf."

"I don't think I want a pet."

"You don't have to keep it," I said, crestfallen. "When do you think it'll arrive?"

"Not sure. Maybe a couple of days. I don't think it would live much longer than that in the mails. Is Eddie still the super?"

"Yes, but he's married now."

What did that have to do with anything?

"Well, he's less available than he used to be," she said, measuring each syllable, as if each vowel, each consonant, took grave effort, was life or death. "I don't understand why you sent me a present."

"I don't understand why I did, either. Jen, I'd like to see you."

"Well, I'd like to see you too. Sometime." She started to cry.

"Good night, Jennie," I whispered.

"Good night, Jack."

GOOD NIGHT, MOON. A child's story.

I was, once again, in a hotel room, with plans to make, a plane to catch. I was going to cross the country. All of it.

In the lobby, I stopped by the money machine and found out how it worked. At Fisherman's Wharf, I bought a green-painted turtle and sent it off to Mandy. I searched the hotel room high and low and couldn't find my keys. I might have to rely on Eddie.

I packed.

> *It's the thirty-third of August and I'm fin'lly touchin'*
> *down.*
> *Eight days from Sunday finds me Saturday bound.*

The thirty-third of August. It became emblematic of the day I took that flight back to New York. It became a stand-in for all other dates. In and out of time.

"Chewing gum, sir?" the stewardess asked.

"Christ, no," I said with my old, accustomed charm.

I saw the light of the city. Dusk here. Cocktail hour. My city. Lights. I'm finally touching down.

"SOME OF MY THINGS might have spilled out of this suitcase," I said, accusingly, pointing to the gaping tear.

"Well, look through it and if there's anything missing, put it on the form," said the clerk.

"You mean look through it here and now?" I snarled. "I've flown clear across the country, it must be ninety degrees in here—"

"Ninety-eight," he broke in pleasantly.

I zipped my suitcase shut and elbowed my way through the thicket of complainers to the clerk. "You can put on your form," I told him, "that my house keys are missing."

"Your house keys?" said the clerk, coming to life. "Pretty stupid to put your house keys in your suitcase."

"Those are the facts. Just note them down. My house keys are missing. Got it?"

"Got it," he said, bored. With some satisfaction, I watched him write it down. Then, with a certain glee, I went out into the hot New York night and hailed a cab. What fun to lie.

I scanned the bellplate. There it was: J. Church. Her voice, accompanied by static, issued from the intercom. "Yes?" she said.

"No," I replied, and waited for her to buzz me in.

In the elevator, my heart began to pound. I'd left my bravado at the airport, in the taxi, somewhere. This was real life, and I was scared. We creaked up to her floor. I walked to the door of the apartment, stood before it a moment, and then, suitcase still in hand, I tiptoed to the incinerator closet and opened the door. A spray can. Hair spray. I hoped it wasn't hers. When I emerged from the closet, I saw her in the doorway.

"What were you doing in the incinerator closet?" she asked me, standing in the half-dark.

"Nothing much," I said.

She stood aside, and I brushed past her into the apartment. I set the suitcase down, inhaled deeply, and waited for my heart to stop thudding. I was afraid to face her. What to do now?

It stopped thudding, and still not having looked at her, I embraced her. Small. Smaller than ever. What had happened? I switched on the light.

"I don't particularly like the way I look," she said.

Thin. Alone. Not eating. The payoff.

"It doesn't make any difference to me," I said.

"That's hard for me to believe," she said.

I saw my own shadow on the wall, oversized, and thought of myself. Trade-off.

"I'm glad you were home," I notified her. "I never did find my keys."

"I'm glad too," she said politely.

"In fact," I said, "I lied to baggage claim. They destroyed this suitcase, so I reported that my house keys were missing."

"Oh, Jack," she said. Which meant: What am I going to do with you?

"A harmless lie," I said. "And it made me feel better."

She looked at me. "There's anger," she said, "even in the tenderness of men."

"I'm not angry."

"Yes, you are."

She went into the kitchen and put up coffee, and brought me back a cheese sandwich. She had one too.

"Are Eddie and his bride happy?" I asked with my mouth full.

"I would have melted the cheese," she said, "but I thought that might take too much time." What did she mean? Didn't we have time?

"I really mean it, are they happy?" I asked.

"I don't know if they're happy. They seem happy. Are you going back to work?"

I didn't answer.

"Jack, I don't want a turtle now. I want a baby now," she whispered.

"Now is the only time any of us has got," I said.

"Who said that? Did Davey?"

"I don't remember. I don't think so. Davey made plans."

I went over to the sofa and reclaimed her, held her. She let herself be held. Then she began to move, to touch me, to repossess me. The dream. Virginal. Should we have been virginal at the beginning? Should we have pretended, and by pretending let it come true?

We were in her bedroom. Whose bedroom? To hell with pronouns. Still clothed. We would be clothed with each other for some time. But in each other's arms, now frail, now cradling. Which was which?

Into the night, in each other's arms.

I had bartered my sick soul for the ticket back.